To Thomas,

Thank you so much for your support, my friend.

May the odor of this book make for fine memories down the road...

Feb. '23

THE AELFRAVER TRILOGY

BOOK I

THE RAVE

J. R. TRAAS

For more about *The Aelfraver Trilogy* and other works by the author

visit www.blankbooklibrary.com

This is a work of fiction. Any resemblance to actual events, situations, and individuals (living or dead) is purely coincidental.

Cover illustration © 2020 Ömer Tunç

Cover and book design by J.R. Traas

Editing by A.M. Sanders

ISBN: 9798761768246

to Isabella

Acknowledgements

The fact that this book exists is a testament to the kindness and helpfulness of several wonderful people, so:

Thank you to my beta readers, Val, Matt, and Jemma.

Thank you to Kaytlan, an avid YA reader who provided encouragement, direction, and criticism.

Thank you to my mother for her proofreading eye.

Thank you to Dan, who helped finally bring the beginning to an end.

Thank you to Silas for the many long phone conversations spent hashing out the details, and for calmly, steadily believing in me. Also, we've written over a dozen books together, so that's pretty swell, too.

Thank you to my partner-in-destiny, Erin, whose persistent support continues to push me uphill.

And, thank you to Buzz for the invaluable inspiration; for being a tireless, valiant patron of the arts; for the countless late-night hours spent guiding me, stumbling with me, fighting for me, as together we traverse the perilous mires of independent publishing.

CONTENTS

Aelf /Aylph/ (n.): Monsters of alien origin; neither beasts nor men. An umbrella term denoting any group or individual, the word "Aelf" falsely suggests to many that these creatures are of a single race. However, there are hundreds if not thousands of varieties. Some thereof are animal like and possess only the barest ruthless cunning, a simple survival instinct like that constantly displayed in the natural world; rarer are those endowed with a certain sentience akin to that of Man. Of uncertain origin, their relationship with humanity ever contentious at best, the Aelf are humanity's primary rival for the title of apex predator. The two species grapple with one another atop the food chain, each variously teetering over the brink.

Aelfraver /Aylph-ray-vur/ (n.): One who kills Aelf.

Gildmaster Ragkal Ulfd'nai

From his seminal publication,
The Lightless Path:
A Raver's Field Manual
Volume I, Chapter 1, pg. 1

1

THEIR FINGERS LIKE FISHHOOKS, the pair of boys trawled the depths of the dumpster outside the Silver Spoon pawnshop in the City of Truct, Nation of El. They were alone on the streets of their midnight playground, up to their elbows in orange rinds and plastic bottles. Then the older of the two—twelve as of last week—held aloft his prize, a scuffed and discolored r0b0-d0gz Hassle-Free Companion mark four. "Nice! From before they added holograms."

"What, so it always looks the same? That's dumb," said the younger boy, ten.

"You don't want it? Guess it's mine then." Even if it was too busted to be his toy pet, he might be able to sell it for scrap at the junkyard.

"There's no way that battery still works."

"Shut it. Is that the remote? Give it here, Pawal, I wanna see."

"It's mine, Tomik. I found it."

"What are you going to do with a dead remote, eh?" Tomik's quick hand latched onto the plastic controller.

All the windows overlooking that street corner were dark and bolted shut. So, the boys' antics—as far as they knew—went unnoticed, though their grunts echoed up and down the way as they wrestled over ownership of the item. A rat scurried out of their path, hiding beneath one of the many nearby rusting, bald-tired cars.

Pawal stopped struggling.

Tomik frowned at him. "I knew you'd surrender."

"I saw something, just now," said Pawal. He pointed. "In the window. There."

Suspecting a trick, Tomik clutched close his new possession as he traced his friend's grubby-fingered gesture to the front door of the Silver Spoon.

"Something moved, fast. Like it dived away when it caught me looking at it," said Pawal, and he grinned. "Maybe it's a ghost."

Tomik stared at him. The broken r0b0-d0gz model fell onto the sidewalk between them with a *clack-clack*.

Pawal said, "You wanna go find out?"

"Who, me? You're the one who saw whatever it was."

"What, you scared, Tomik?"

"Not on your life. I—"

The door to the pawnshop creaked, gliding open.

Tomik tensed. Pawal chuckled and slapped his friend's arm. "This is amazing. We *have* to go in."

Tomik took a step back. "I don't know about this."

"Come on. Tell me this isn't the most interesting thing that's happened in forever. Let's just take a quick peek. In and out."

The shop's ratty awning flapped lazily with a sudden gust of autumn wind. The little bell hanging from the door handle tinkled.

"You first," said Tomik.

"It was my *idea*. Do I have to do everything myself?"

Pressing his clammy palms and nose against the window, Tomik's breath fogged the glass. He couldn't see anything inside. Total darkness. "Fine. We'll go together. Fair?"

"Fair."

They spat into each other's hands and shook on it.

Voices cracking, they counted down: "One, two, *three*!" And they dashed forward, across the threshold, and into the dark of the shop.

For a few moments, the only sounds the boys could hear were their own shallow breaths. The faint bit of streetlamp light that entered the building only extended as far as their toes; in front of their noses, the shadows were heavy, the air as thick as a sheet of obsidian.

Finding the place completely empty, they looked at each other, ready to laugh in triumph over their fears, laugh in relief that there'd been nothing to fear in the first place.

The door slammed shut behind them.

"Hey! That's not funny!"

"I didn't do that. *You* did!"

A creaking of floorboards made them turn on their heels, and they watched, knees locked, jaws clenched, and eyes wide, as a tall man-shaped shadow sloughed off the wall and lurched toward them.

Its arms extended, bent at an unnatural angle, the figure jerked and spun its snapping limbs as it approached. Its feet never once touched the ground, nor could its face be seen in the gloom.

It stood over the boys, now, and the only details they could make out were the whites of its eyes and the blood on its teeth.

They opened their mouths to scream.

Responding to a call about a noise complaint, deputies Saskow and Zej sped toward the scene of the disturbance. Their squad car's built-in Virtual Intelligence continuously flashed the codes for vandalism and breaking and entering, noting that the suspects had been described as "delinquent teens" by the witness who'd made the call some fifteen minutes prior.

"Here we go again: some teenagers break a window, and another busybody is woken from her much-needed beauty sleep," said Zej through a yawn. "Oh, no. Call the mayor. Schedule an emergency meeting with the Viceroy."

A particularly juicy bug splatted against the windshield.

Saskow shook his head and gripped the steering column a little more tightly, trying to wake up both his hands and himself. He could have easily flipped on the autopilot switch, but he didn't want to drift off before he got there. He needed to focus, stay alert. One more misstep on the job and he could kiss his credentials goodbye.

"I'm sure this isn't a burglary. Just kids being kids," he said. "I'd be willing to slap a ten down on it."

"Oh, sure. I mean, what else *is* there for our energetic youth to do in this town—besides break a bunch of stuff that isn't theirs? It's not like I don't have any sympathy for them, but all I'd wish is that they'd occasionally take a week off." Zej rolled his shoulders. His neck cracked loudly. "You're probably right, Sas, but I'll take that bet anyway. Maybe add a sliver of excitement to this shift. At least, if I get popped by some trigger-glad *misckie*, I'll earn ten gelders for my pains."

"Don't think you have to worry about that, what with Urra and their gang getting picked up by Central two days ago."

"Really? First I'm hearing of it. So, Urra finally became someone else's problem? It's shaping up to be a good night."

"Here's hoping it stays quiet." Saskow cracked his knuckles. A minute or two later, he said, "There it is." Pulling the car alongside the curb, leaving the violet emergency lights flashing, he popped open his door and got out. He poked his head back in for one more swig of lukewarm coffee from his thermos, and then gestured for Zej to take point. The other deputy drew his service weapon, and the two approached the front door of the Silver Spoon.

The beam of his flashlight showing him nothing but empty shop, Saskow rapped the window with the back of his hand. "Truct Sheriff's Department. We know you're in there, you little sneaks."

"Come out, kiddos," said Zej, "and the worst you can expect is a slap on the wrist."

"Don't make us come in there."

They waited. No answer.

Zej grumbled, "How shocking."

Saskow reached for the handle, but the door opened, swinging inward, well before he touched it.

There were no motion sensors that Zej could see. "Okay, that's cute," he said, gripping his pistol more tightly. "You've had your fun. Get out here. Now."

Silence.

Zej entered first, his partner following closely behind, their flashlight beams sweeping the room. He nodded toward something on the ground. A boot. They got a little closer, and noted that it was attached to a man, a very large and still one.

When they caught sight of the man's face, they recoiled; the flesh had sagged inward to the point of looking like melted wax.

No sign of anyone or anything else.

Swallowing, Zej said, "I'll be collecting on our bet later, partner. Is this—"

"Doyen. The owner. Yeah," Saskow whispered. "Can't tell if he's breathing." He checked for a pulse, pinching the unmoving man's wrist, and immediately jerked his hand back.

"What?"

"His bones." Saskow was trembling now. "They're—well, see for yourself."

Zej shook his head, grabbing Doyen's meaty arm. He dropped it straight away. When the arm struck the floor, it sounded like a bag filled with shards of glass. "They've been—they've—"

The deputies' attentions turned once more to Doyen, whose expression was strained, and whose eyes had been closed—should have been closed. Now, the lids opened, and the eyes flicked to the right, locking with Zej's.

The deputy screamed, springing to his feet, leaping toward the door

It slammed shut before him. From behind, Saskow shouted, "Holy Plutonia, what is—"

And they watched as Doyen bolted upright, his head jiggling awkwardly, his every movement putting to mind a marionette on strings. He lifted off the ground, and each of his twists and spasms sounded like the bunching up of huge wads of printer paper.

"Zej!" Saskow yelled.

Clutching his pistol in a death-grip, the other deputy grabbed the door's handle with his sweat-slick free hand. It wouldn't turn—locked.

Zej kicked the door as the corpse of Doyen drifted closer and closer.

"Out of the way." Forehead drenched, Saskow aimed his weapon at the locking mechanism and fired three plasma rounds, punching three small, irregularly shaped, orange-rimmed holes in the metal. He shouldered the door open, the force of his leap sending him rolling onto the sidewalk beyond.

Zej vaulted after him, and, within seconds, they were back inside the squad car. As Saskow jammed his thumb onto the communicator's switch, Zej grabbed his elbow and pointed at the Silver Spoon.

The front door was again shut and appeared entirely undamaged.

The two deputies hurried through every gesture and sign they knew to ward off evil.

Tremors running from his elbow to his jaw, Saskow put the speaker microphone to his lips. "Get the Sheriff down here."

Gaze fixed on the pawnshop's entrance, Zej barely registered Saskow's growl. "You had best wake him up then, Wita. We have a, uh—There's a—just get Lowing involved. Now."

In the driver's seat, Zej started the car and, slamming his foot down, backed the vehicle up. Its tires squealed; its engine backfired.

After a few moments, within the shops and apartments surrounding them, lights switched on. Curious and worried faces watched Zej park the car on the opposite side of the street, get out, dash over to the trunk, and retrieve a rifle. Leaning on the hood, his sights remained fixed on the front door of the Silver Spoon.

He didn't dare blink.

The electric streetlights, set on tall, rusted poles, finally flickered out as the early morning washed with inky gray light the narrow, two-story brick and concrete shops and townhomes. Somewhere nearby, growling hungrily, a dog could be heard knocking over a metal trashcan.

Two hours, four deputies, and a dozen cups of coffee later, and the Silver Spoon had been thoroughly cordoned off. The deputies busily walked the perimeter, warning away the bolder of the onlookers who had, by now, formed a small crowd on the sidewalk across the street from the pawnshop.

Sheriff Lowing leaned through the open driver's side window of his vehicle and over the receiver, listening. When City Councilman Kulch had finished screaming at him, he took the opportunity to interject. "Yes, sir. I understand." The round face surrounding his mustache flushed. More colorful interruptions followed, peppered with a few explanations and several threats. "Cameras? Now? How much time—No, I have no idea how they found out about—Sir, all due respect, my men know better than to blab to the media. I—Yes, sir. Well—Frankly, we're not equipped to contend with *whatever this is.* It's like something straight outta one of the old stories, and—Hello? Hello?" He stared at the speaker for a few seconds. "Hung up on me. That sonova…" To Deputy Saskow, who stood at attention, he said, "Listen, I've just been informed that news's got its nose all in this. We've got maybe half an hour before the eyes of the whole Nation are on us. It's about to get *political.*"

"Sir, I hope you know that Zej and I would never—"

Lowing looked at him from over his purpled, drooping eyelids. "What? 'Course. I know full well you kept a lid on it. It's those Triple-I rats we have to thank. They must have been listening in on our chatter. Or they hacked our comms. Either way, don't much matter: the chuckleheads from their Puur HQ are inbound. If we're gonna avoid being made fools of, *live* on the midday news, we need this wrapped up as of five minutes ago." The sheriff faced the steadily growing crowd of gawkers, raising his voice. "Alright, everyone, I'm gonna need you all to take another good few healthy steps *back.*"

Someone in the crowd challenged him: "People heard gunshots a while ago. From inside the building. Have you arrested anyone?"

"Is this a manhunt?" demanded someone else.

"Why won't you just tell us what's happening?"

Lowing rubbed his temples with thumb and middle finger. "The noises you heard must have been bursting pipes. What we're dealing with here is nothing more interesting than a gas leak. But that's why you've got to move back. There's a risk the whole building will go up."

"What about the children?"

Glaring at the cluster of faces, searching for the one who'd spoken, Lowing said, "Children?"

"Yes, sheriff, my mother's the one who called your office. She said she saw two kids break into the building. Where are they?"

The back of his neck, his chest, his armpits, nearly every bit of him growing increasingly saturated with sweat, Lowing said, "There *may* or may *not* be two minors inside the building. We are doing everything we can, I assure you."

"Everything you can?" a woman said. "My son's been missing for hours. No one has a clue where he's gone, and you haven't done anything to find him. For all I know, *he's* in there right now, and you're sitting here on your thumbs, you useless—"

"Ma'am, please. We have the best and brightest out there looking for your child. We take our job of protecting and serving this community with the utmost gravity, I swear." Dabbing at his forehead with his pocket kerchief, he added, "We've called in a specialist. They'll be here any minute now." He stared hopefully down the length of the street toward the point where it curved into a tunnel. "I know this is particularly difficult for you, ma'am. Just, let's give it another few minutes."

Finally, a taxi cab trundled up to the curb and jittered, with one last backfire, to a standstill. The front passenger door opened, and out stepped a lanky young woman in a frayed duster.

With a bandage-covered arm, she waved the cabby off. Her thumb flicked across the screen of her phone, a bright blue bubble expanding from between her lips. Four more chews, and she spat her gum onto a little piece of paper, neatly folding and tucking it into her inner jacket pocket. This action revealed a bandolier strapped to her chest, its loops holding glass containers, like soda bottles, each of which was filled with a different vibrantly colored liquid. Though her hair had begun to gray, her face revealed that she couldn't have been older than nineteen, and was probably even younger than that.

Her long ponytail swished against the back of her duster as she walked right up to the Silver Spoon's front door. There, she paused, fingers lingering above the handle for just a beat too long. She cast a glance over her shoulder at the milling public, the deputies, and the sheriff.

Lowing shook his head. "See, there's our specialist now. Right on time."

Murmurs exploded through the crowd as the young woman opened the door and stepped into the darkness.

Alone inside the Silver Spoon, Alina K'vich drew a long, halting breath. Dust dancing along its edges, a single gray shaft of sunlight was all that held the shadows at bay. Shadows that pressed against her like sweaty bodies in a packed subway car.

During the entire cab ride from her home to this place, she had puzzled over a troublesome thought: unlicensed and unproven as Alina was, Sheriff Lowing must have been truly desperate to have called on her.

Now, she understood why. Even outside the building, she had felt it—a shapeless terror—seeping through the door. Inside, the feeling became overwhelming. Like static-charged air. Like the buzz of battery acid on the tongue. There waited for her, inside the pawnshop, something old. And cunning.

No sign of the kids. There'd never been much hope for them; there was less now.

Phone in hand, she "borrowed" the wireless Aetherthread signal from a nearby unprotected network named "GET UR OWN CONNECTION PIETRE." She checked her Phys-i and Niima bars—real-time displays of her own vital and magical energies—and found both to be full. (She didn't need an app to tell her how healthy she was feeling or how deep her magical reserves ran, but seeing the small-font "100%" status displays was reassuring. And jailbreaking her phone to be able to show those stats had taken a lot of effort, so checking the bars often made that whole ordeal feel like less of a waste of time.)

Once connected to the web, she pulled an Auggie bottle from her bandolier and chugged the glowing amber potion, scowling as the bitter viscous liquid went down. Pocketing the empty container in her pouch (*waste not*), she burped a fiery breath.

Her focus exploded. And then there were two realities: the physical world and another one parallel to it. The second of the two was usually private, unseen by others. But, today, she needed to open that secret door, fling it wide, reveal what lay inside.

Called by many names—mind-world, dream-world, etherium—by many different peoples, this place (or non-place) existed within every sentient being. It almost always remained locked away behind the impenetrable vault doors that separated the individual from their own unconscious.

Magic, however, could access it because Niima—magical energy—derived from the life's energy within every living thing. The potion she'd just taken acted as an amplifier of these energies, broadcasting the ebbs and flows of this inner sphere of her existence.

The process did not have to be unpleasant, but it never failed to be intense. She steadied herself against an antique armoire, her thoughts scattering, recombining. After a few tumultuous moments which made her feel as though she'd just dived over the edge of a waterfall, she was able to sculpt the needed images in her head with perfect control. She saw with her mind's eye a slideshow of her fiercest thoughts and feelings. Thanks to the potion, she could now flip through these pictures and video clips at will.

Casting aside the mind-stuff she didn't want, she weaved the rainbow bursts of her mental movies, focusing on the sights, sounds, tastes, scents—what she needed to feel in this moment.

What she needed to feel in order to lure *it* out.

Snagging Mracis's stuffed lion and running off as he cried.

Spending her grandfather's money on a box of firecrackers, when he'd asked her to go buy eggs and milk.

Standing in front of the window display and praying for the pair of shiny water-walking sneakers on the mannequin's feet.

She caught hold of the thread she'd been looking for.

It sounded heady and thick. It smelled red.

Hopefully she would be proven right about the nature of the creature, that it would be attracted to her desire for riches. If she turned out to be wrong, well…

For her plan to have any chance of succeeding, she would have to heighten the intensity of her desire, make it drunk off her fantasies. Make it careless.

She thought of the drag races in Tinniby, of betting every penny to her name. She thought of what she'd do with all that money, all the scores she'd settle, all the expensive dinners she'd buy. The luxury.

Sooner than expected, she found that she wasn't in the pawn shop anymore, but outside it. She had been transported to the country, near the highway. A long, straight road. The place where the races were held each month. She knew it well. There, many times, she'd slapped down her hard-earned money. Hoping for a chance at a better life. She had yet to win.

Good news: the plan was working so far. Already, the creature attempted to rope her in with its illusions.

Crouched in the middle of papery, brittle brush and nettle bushes, she focused on refining the shape of her desire.

She imagined it—the rush of air as the cars screamed past, the press of other cheering spectators against her, the jingle of coins in their pockets, the rustle of bills. She thought of how many times that moment of hope had soured; she remembered losing all her cash, and how she'd conjured dreams of stealing, cheating, begging, all so she could throw down just a few more gelders. To squander everything on the thinnest of chances, to walk the blade's edge, thinking only of herself. Her own gain, at the cost of everyone else's.

There it was. She could feel *it.* Watching her.

Eye-less sight in shadow-less dark. And hunger. So much hunger. Like it had never once been satisfied, though it stuffed itself to bursting.

Every target has its weakness. Her grandfather's words, strands woven into the fabric of her thoughts. *Knowing your prey is both the first step and the last.*

Well, the creature she now hunted certainly knew how to weave a powerful illusion. This was no ordinary demon. It had spun her web of fantasies into a vision so real-looking that she couldn't tell the difference between it and the pawn shop in which she must still be standing. This place certainly *felt, looked, and sounded* real, even though it was all in her head. The Silver Spoon had faded like a dream touched by morning sunlight.

Whatever lay in wait for her would be the most dangerous enemy she'd ever faced. She'd have to remain on her guard at all times. Or risk her soul.

Fueled by her artificially enhanced and broadcast desires, something *leaned in*, a shadowy presence, unseen, but clawing and sucking at the very air around her. A starved thing, it pawed and gulped, and Alina got the distinct impression of claws. Tentacles, too. Teeth.

When she licked her lips, her tongue lapped up dewdrops. As the moments wore away, eroded by the silent storm of desire swirling from her and around her, it took every effort to remember that she wasn't *really* in that place she'd fixed in her imagination.

Her one advantage, for now, was her prey's unawareness of her purpose. She concentrated, straining to not reveal her true motives, and threw back the hood of her tattered old coat.

Well, she'd set a *really* solid trap. Now, to find out who it was for—her target or herself.

Her breath fogged in front of her on that field of gray morning. She rose, took a step, the blue grass crunching under the heels of her knee-high hiking boots.

"Delicious," said the voice then, caressing the syllables of her language like someone tasting a delicacy for the first time. "Such craving."

Hands at her hips, she cocked her head. She waited.

A wisp of mist encircled her, wafted past her, joining with another. Then another. After a few seconds, a figure began to take shape within the moisture. A lopsided grin, a quirked eyebrow, a thin nose, slit-like nostrils. The thousands of dew droplets hovered there, revealing the ghostly outline of a man's body. Next, color flooded the figure—porcelain-white skin, gray three-piece suit, golden eyes.

It adjusted its red tie with ring-heavy fingers, the platinum glowing palely, blending with tentacles of soft luminous mist.

"Who—" it cleared its throat. The word had come out sharp, like a rusty nail jabbed into the ear canal. The creature had the decency to look embarrassed. Tugging at the knot of its tie again, it said, in a more human-sounding voice, "Why, who are you, my beauty, with your skin the hue of hazel fay and eyes like purest olivine?"

"I've been looking for you," said Alina. She mustn't let it know anything about her. Not even her name. "Who I am is not important. We're here to talk about you."

"Oh?" said the man. No—not a man, she reminded herself. An almost-man, and barely even that.

The apparition's features took a turn for the strange, elongating, warping. Its shadow no longer bore the same shape as it did. "You won't tell me your name, then?"

"You first," she said, watching tentacles erupt from the shadow, then fade.

"Tut-tut." The creature waggled a platinum-ringed finger. "Nice try. I see your games now. It seems you have me at somewhat of a disadvantage."

She nodded. The less she said aloud, the better.

"And yet, by your caution, you unmask yourself, girl. You are an Aelfraver."

Damn it. She glared at it.

"The truth is revealed." A swirling, wriggling mass, its shadow stretched out. Rearing up behind her. "It has been some several decades since I've tasted one of your kind. Tell me, how many of my people have you destroyed in your short career, young hunter?"

Though she tried, she couldn't let that provocation go. "None," she grunted.

"None?" It took a step forward.

She, a step back. "I don't kill."

It chuckled wetly. "Foolish."

From the Sheriff's descriptions, her guesses about this supposed "ghost" had been right on the money, but she didn't yet know how old or cunning her opponent truly was. So, she'd have to play this game of questions a little longer.

Even as she mentally ran through the list of relevant spells and counter-spells, she nudged the conversation in a different direction. "You don't look exactly like Doyen."

An interested smile from the gold-eyed non-man. "Who?"

"The owner of this shop. The one you killed. Your disguise, though—it's hardly perfect."

The creature scoffed, spreading its fingers, pressing a palm to its chest, its expression a parody of innocence. "I didn't kill him. I'm like you. I do no harm. Intentionally."

"Oh, you're telling me he twisted his own bones, till they snapped? And what about those two kids? They asked for it?"

"As you wish." The non-man shrugged. "All I say unto you is this: *I* did not kill them."

"Then what did?"

"Their desires."

"That's ridiculous, and not how *anything* works. You seriously expect me to believe that you made them *want stuff* to death?"

"Sweet girl, this mask of bravado ill fits your inviting face. You misunderstand, besides; I repeat, I did not kill them. I merely partook of their essence, and, perhaps, in the case of the older one, got a mite… carried away in my appetites."

"So, that's it? You're a sloppy eater? Why didn't you drain him slowly, for years? Like the rest of your kind does? Probably, no one would have noticed till he had one foot and two elbows in the grave."

"You genuinely care to know the answer? I was bored. Now, don't you strut about, wearing the mask of concerned mother, chiding me for playing with my food. What fun is life without play? What does it matter if I make a game of the monotony of consumption?" Something rippled across its forehead. Like a worm wriggling beneath the flesh. The non-man dismissed her scowl with a wave of its hand. "A man must eat."

"You're not a man." Alina crossed her arms. "The mayor's wife wears fox fur. Doesn't make her a vixen."

"What a sharp wit." The creature leaned in. Its red tie swayed between them like a lolling tongue, and its smile began to fade. "Goodness, how I do grow weary of your mockery. Best take care, now. You have seen of what I'm capable when left undistracted."

"I'm honestly getting tired of this myself. The children you took, where are they?"

"My, how you focus upon such humdrum. I would rather talk about you some more. What you want—"

"The boys," Alina insisted. "Are they alive? Let them go, and then *maybe* we'll talk."

"Hmm. How badly do you *want* them to be safe and sound, eh? Enough to take their place?"

Her insides burning partly from frustration and partly from fear, Alina slowly nodded. "Let them go. Free them, and I'll stay."

The un-man grinned, its eyes rolling backward. For a split second, she thought she could see a second pair behind them, a pair that blinked sideways. Made her think of bog-dwelling bottom-feeders and serpents inside their damp holes, waking.

"Your terms are agreeable," said the creature.

Half-shrouded by mist, two translucent forms—smaller, and shadowy but humanlike—stood up. They solidified, becoming people again, and Alina recognized them from the pictures Lowing had messaged her earlier—the missing children, Tomik and Pawal.

The boys spun in place for a moment, heads bobbing, expressions advertising their confusion at their surroundings.

She shouted at them, "Run! Run straight forward, as fast as you can, and don't look back. Don't stop until you're with your parents."

Appearing unsure of where the command had come from, looking through her as if she weren't there, the boys took off at a run, and soundlessly passed straight through her.

"As you can see," said the gold-eyed man-like creature. "I have granted your requested boon. Now you simply *must* stay here with me."

The illusion surrounding Alina remained as she watched the boys disappear from view in the direction of the front door of the pawnshop—a door that she could not see, trapped as she was within her dream-web of a world.

Well, she'd done it: she now found herself alone with a voracious predator.

"How do I know that wasn't an illusion, just now? As if I can trust you, that you've really let them out."

"You wound me," it said through its toothy smile. "But you have my word that I did as you asked. In my supreme honesty, I confess to selfish motivations: any *Rel'ia-tuakr* such as I could see you are *far* more interesting than those little brats and their nebulous needs. Perhaps they'll be more flavorful once they… ripen. You, however, are the much better catch." It licked its dry lips. "Now, it is your turn. Tell me more about your wishes, girl. I can make them come true, you know."

"Like you did for Doyen?"

"Doyen was lower than a Liliskur—a worm."

It was her turn to smile. "And what does that make you, goblin?"

"Do not goad me. There will be consequences." The color drained from his face and suit, and he looked much like a moving, centuries-old, sepia-toned photograph. "Do you even know who I am, stripling?"

"A stupid little greed-feeder who can't work up the nerve to take on princes and prophets, so he sticks to shopkeepers and kids in podunk towns." She snorted. "I've seen what you are, and I'm not impressed. You just leave the real hunting to real hunters."

"Insolent." His face grew longer and longer still, until his chin dropped below his waist. His suit spread out behind him, tearing, wrapping around his arms and legs, which split into two or three pieces each. Then his eyeballs fell out, replaced by triangular mouths—rows of razor teeth in each. "Do you see now, child, to whom it is you speak so flippantly?"

"Pfft," said Alina, standing in the shadow of the hulking beast. "Third-rate tricks. Seen better."

She was halfway through her defiant reply when the multi-limbed monster with its mouth-eyes pounced on her. She was pitched backward, her spine slamming against the damp earth of the imagination-twisted world in which they'd trapped each other. Pinned to the ground, she stared at the writhing, pinkish, green-veined, scaly midsection of the demon. Then it lowered its bulky, lopsided head, and opened its *third* and largest mouth, shattered teeth protruding from the waist of the false-man shape it had worn up until moments ago. The red tie was now actually a slobbering fleshy red tongue sliding up the side of Alina's cheek.

The creature said, "Gaze upon my glory."

She choked on the stink of its durian-mixed-with-week-old-cat-crap-breath. "To think," she gasped, "that I'd be put outta my misery by a two-bit, no-name, bottom-of-the-barrel scavenger like you."

"Little mammal," it bellowed in her face, smacking its fat, veiny lips. "You will respect me, for you are in the presence of royalty. I am a prince of my people. It is a terrible honor you receive now, Raver-girl, to be devoured by the great Osesoc-ex'calea!"

That name. Alina mentally cycled through the vast number of Aelf encyclopedias under which her grandfather had buried her childhood. Was it Tinochlese?

The pressure of its talons on her chest and shoulders.

Oronorish?

The stench of its withered maw and flapping, grasping tongue.

No, it was Iorian! And it meant—

A wicked grin on her face, Alina said, "*Ergon'a'tleth al-tilithlin*, spirits of the earth and sky, by their names, I call upon you, Osesoc-ex'calea. And by your name, *'Hubris,'* I bind you."

There was a pause. The monster's mouth-eyes chewed on their eyelid-lips.

Osesoc-ex'calea guffawed, and streams of steaming saliva spilled over Alina's face and arms. Through its laughter, it said, "To think that so feeble an incantation—writ by a doomed and forgotten people—could have given you even the slightest power over me! You simpleton, you dog-brained blusterer. I have had my fill of your childish games. Now, I shall have my fill of you."

The demon's weight crushed her body, squeezing the air from her lungs.

"Ah-ha," said Alina weakly through half-lidded eyes. "That was just a distraction. You've fallen right into my trap." Clutching something in her hand, she thrust her fist forward. "With this talisman, I—"

A flick of one of its tentacles, and the demon snatched the thing from her grip. The object it held—her cellphone—shimmered as the screen lit up. Osesoc-ex-calea inspected the foreign item between its talons. "This?" it said, its right mouth-eye nibbling gingerly on the corner of the phone. "This is your holy weapon? Perhaps I should return to the void, if *such* is the depth to which Aelfravers have sunk. You lot can provide no more sport, I now see." It turned its mouth-eyes to Alina again. "I have had far and away enough of this. Prepare to be consumed by Hubris, and consider it an hon—"

"*Iingrid*," Alina enunciated, "send my drafted message to ThimbleBoy@TownshipMail.mag, subject: 'Osesoc-ex'calea Hubris Demon DO NOT OPEN – K Thanks.'"

The demon looked at her, then the phone, then her. And, though it retained zero human features by this point, it appeared confused.

She finished her command with, "Text body: blank. Send."

Her phone's Integrated Intelligence software sounded a dainty chime. In the voice of an annoyed middle-aged school principal, it said, "Sending message."

The demon's mouth-eyes swallowed—its unique way of blinking, perhaps. "What in the seventy-seven hells was th—?"

From the phone's screen, a flash of blue light speared Osesoc-ex'calea, raking across its spined and thorny flesh. It roared in agony, and then dug its talons into the earth,bracing itself as its face was sucked up against the phone, which now floated ten feet in the air. Its claws tearing up the earth and grass, the demon's face, head, and shoulders were crushed and drawn into the 5.8-inch display.

The demon's distorted, garbled scream was clipped short as the rest of it was pulled into the cellphone. And then Osesoc-ex'calea was gone.

There was no weight on Alina's chest any longer, nothing pinning her down. The drooling evil thing had vanished into thin air.

She chuckled quietly to herself, coughing.

The phone fell to the ground and pinged one more time.

"Message sent."

Alina lay still for a few moments, holding her breath.

Iingrid said, "Message delivered."

Alina let out a heavy sigh. "Thank you, Iingrid."

The dust settled.

She was no longer in the field by the road but back in the Silver Spoon. The dark closed in on her, but that was alright. It was a familiar darkness, a non-threatening one. A darkness specifically lacking in demons.

Her phone had fallen on the ground. She crouched and snatched it up. Her Niimameter—the measure of her remaining magical power—had dropped to 2%. Close call. Alone in the dark, she shook her head.

She flipped on the flashlight. It immediately petered out. Low battery.

Unsteady, knees shaking, she found the front door, but not before slamming her foot into the base of a tarp-covered harpsichord. Limping now, she slipped out of the pawn shop.

The one element that had carried over from the fantasy world was the fog, thick as a blanket and leaking from the shop into the street. She could barely make out the people on the other side.

As she walked over to them. The townsfolk gasped and muttered to one another.

Sheriff Lowing, the curling edges of his frizzy mustache twitching against his doughy pink cheeks, said, "Ya made it. And? You get whatever it was?" Thumbs looped through his belt, one wrinkly pant-leg in front of the other, one of the deputies added, "Was looking dicey there, for a hot minute."

A wad of cash passed from one deputy's hand to the other. Both men looked relieved and embarrassed.

"Where'd the fog come from?" Lowing asked, tensing. "We need to get everyone outta here?"

Alina shook some of the numbness from her brain. "That? No, it's an illusion. Mostly. The stuff's spilling out of the pseudo-reality that was created when my potion-enhanced thoughts met the demon's, uh—what's the word I'm looking for?—*hangriness*. That kind of thing can happen when a powerful Aelf is met head-on with magic."

"You're sure we're okay standing here?"

"I mean, it's magic. There's standard safety guidelines or warning labels, if that's what you're looking for. Niima surges have side-effects sometimes, sheriff." Alina rubbed her neck, feeling the bruises developing. "What about the kids? Did they come out?"

Sheriff Lowing stepped forward. "They're here. Shaken and dirty, but that's about average for them."

Alina followed his gaze, and locked eyes with Tomik and Pawal, who were wrapped in blankets, crying, clinging to their parents, but safe. Shaking, Alina let out a shuddering sigh. "All's well that ends well, except for Mr. Doyen. Guess that means the job's done, though. So." She held her open palm between herself and the sheriff. "The bounty."

"What was it, though?" said Lowing, doing far less reaching for his wallet than Alina would've liked.

"The Aelf? Oh, I had it pegged for a Greed-feeder. I was wrong. Turns out you were dealing with a demon. They behave similarly, but demons are much worse." She shrugged. "Anyway. The big bad is done for, and that's all that matters. Took care of it for you. Won't be bothering you again. Now." She tapped her fingers onto her still open palm. "My payment, if you please."

"You killed it, then. Thank Buthmertha for that." He nervously eyed the skies, watching a Skye-Eye News drone carrier rocket toward the scene of the crime. It was still a fair distance away, but, at its current speed, would arrive within minutes. "They're almost here. C'mon, let's see it then."

"Huh?"

"The trophy, Alina. The head or claw or whatever you pulled off the monster. I need a bone to wave in front of the slobbering press." He pointed a chunky finger at the gleaming carrier bristling with tiny camera drones.

"Trophy? Hang on, we agreed—"

The sheriff's mood made an about-turn, his ruddy complexion darkening on the way to purple. "Am I missin' something? Were you not able to recover *any* part of it after you put it down? Was it a ghost or some such?"

"It wasn't a ghost." Alina pressed her fingers to her forehead, a migraine oncoming. "I just *told* you what—"

"Okay, so, demon, yeah. Still." The sheriff nodded toward the building. "Are you tellin' me I have to stand in front of the eyes of the entire Nation and the Gods and my old mother and tell our countrymen that they'll just have to—what—take my *word* that the situation's been resolved? There's got to be something—some kinda proof the beast is dead."

Alina cleared her throat. "Dead?"

"Am I speaking Tinochlese or something? How are we failin' to understand each other, here?"

Syllable by syllable, Alina explained, "As I told you before, on the phone, when I took on this job: I don't kill. Not the Aelf, not anybody."

The sheriff took a reflexive backward step as if he'd been physically stricken. "You—you—" with thumb and forefinger, he rubbed his eyes for a solid few seconds—"let the monster *go*? Little lady, do you have even the tiniest inkling of what it is you've done?"

Alina glowered at him. "Aside from *saving the hostages*? And all of you? You wanna know all about the incredible, difficult service I just provided? Let's get technical! That was *not* your average Greed-feeder, which any bozo could've handled. It was an ancient demonic *prince*. I had to put myself practically in its *jaws* and play to its arrogance, all so that I could trick it into revealing its name. And that's when I used my modified version of the spell Uindval Drakehammer's Irresistible Command—"

"What? What are you even goin' on about? I don't need to hear—This is terrible. Gods have mercy, I can hardly even look at you right now."

Alina talked over him, "*Basically,* I bound the demon to a cloud-storage account I made, breaking it into a billion fragments of compressed data, and, using a spamming program freely available online, I sent a digimail to my friend's account. A digimail, by the way, that is the only key to unlocking the Aelf from its new forever-home. The key that is forever out of its reach."

She took a breath. "Now, will you be paying with cash or app? I don't have a HivePay implant, but I'll gladly provide you my GelderPass info. Could also do MoneyPlz. Whatever's faster."

The autopiloted camera carrier had arrived, obscuring the sun. Hundreds of circular drones peeled off it, and these zoomed in all different directions, capturing wide-angle, bird's-eye, and three-sixty-degree footage of the scene, the people, and the sheriff's department.

Lowing turned to one of his deputies. "Zej, I need you to get these people in line. Put the kids up front with me. If we play up their rescue, maybe there's still a chance to sidestep this firepit. By Buthmertha."

Lowing turned to Alina again. "The fact that you've left a demon—Mr. Doyen's murderer, the abductor of two innocent children—roaming free… Frankly, I'm disgusted."

"It's not 'roaming free,'" she snapped. "It's trapped in a combination cloud-storage and program loop that—"

"Shut up. Just shut up. You've left me to deal with an unholy mess. And, somehow, you want me to give you four hundred gelders."

"Yeah, *'cause I took care of your 'monster' for you*." She gestured emphatically as she spoke, as if she were chiding a dog for dragging its rump over a new carpet.

"Ms. K'vich," he said, his voice gone cold, "this is just unacceptable. I took a chance on you, girl, and now you've gone and made me look a right fool. Which I must be for having hired you on in the first place."

"What?" she shouted, the fog muffling the echoes of her voice.

"For all I know, you didn't do *anything*. Because you ain't got no proof for me. Maybe you think you can pull one over on old Mr. Lowing, huh? You head into a dusty old building, fabricatin' all sorts of tales about what's goin' on in there. You're probably sittin' inside, twiddling your thumbs, while Doyen's killer is long, long gone. You find the kids hiding under some junk and send them out. Then you hang back for a while because you need everythin' to look above-board. At last, you step outside, babblin' nonsense. Heck, for all I know, you found a fog machine in there and flipped the switch to add to the mystery of this whole situation." He growled at her, "You Aelfravers and your malarkey—honestly. Most of you are the absolute worst, cheating honest folk outta their hard-earned money. I thought we could maybe, maybe trust *you*. Given what stock you come from. But, clearly, your granddaddy was the exception that proved the rule. You're nothing like him, I can see now. *He* was a master of your craft. He knew how to deal with beasts like that one in there." The sheriff jerked a thumb toward the Silver Spoon. "He'd kill 'em and return with proof of the deed, put everyone's mind at ease, 'cause he knew that's what it takes to keep the peace. That's my job, you know, keepin' the peace. And it's why I can't abide this betrayal of my trust. How do I know, without seeing the corpse with my own two eyes, that you actually got him? Maybe you both struck a deal in there and you let him go easy, so you could collect the reward."

"Are you kidding me, Lowing? I was fighting for my life. How dare you treat me like I'm some child playing dress-up? Worse, you're accusing me of—what—entering into a contract with a demon?" She took a breath that caught in her throat. "This is my job. I'm good at it. You'd never talk to my grandfather this way. Know what I think? I think you're looking for a reason to rip me off."

"The fact that you're only worried about your pay tells me everythin' I need to know about your priorities. Dimas K'vich," said the sheriff, drawing himself to his full height (five inches shorter than Alina), "was a true man of action. Why I went and hired a no-name unlicensed pretender, I'll never know. Woulda been better off tackling this problem myself." He sighed."You were one of our own, so maybe I figured I'd give you a fightin' chance. Well, look what good it's done me. That demon's probably out there, plotting its next attack. And you want me to pay you based on what, huh? Your dang word?"

"The word of a K'vich," said Alina.

"I believe I speak for the town at large when I say ain't no K'vich here. From where I'm standin', you've put us all at risk. We're just fortunate those kids turned up safe. And you're lucky I don't put you under investigation, girl. Go back to school, Alina. Get yourself an education and an honest trade. You just aren't ready. The world's too big for—"

"A 'little lady' like me?" Alina glared at all of them, hate in her eyes and bile in her throat. "You're screwing me out of money. Money that I *earned.* That's all this is. You're stiffing me because you know I won't hit you back. Well, that's what you think. That's the real gamble, here." She let slip an acidic laugh, hissing as it passed her lips. "You'll regret this one day. All of you."

"I'm gonna pretend I didn't catch those threats. And you'd best get out of my face, Alina. I may be lettin' you off for now, but, if—after today—I'm still sheriff, there'll be a reckoning."

"Thieves," she barked, and she turned away from all of them.

The townsfolk watched her retreat like a kicked dog. No one stood up for her. She didn't need them to, but the gesture would've been appreciated.

Scumbags. The thanks she'd get for saving them all? Bean milk and old cheese for dinner. Again.

The sheriff called after her, "One day you'll have to decide, Alina. Do you wanna be like your granddaddy and make a fair living actually helping people? Or, are you plannin' to cling to your tall tales and nonsense? You hurt yourself as much as others, actin' as you do, abusing your heritage."

Alina grinded her teeth, pressed her fingernails into her palms. But she didn't look back.

She swatted a shiny, platinum-colored camera drone out of her way. It bounced off the nearest wall and zipped over to the crowd instead. There, already, several people were giving their accounts of what had happened that morning. Or what they'd thought had happened.

The deputies ushered the two moist-eyed children up to Sheriff Lowing, who smoothed his mustache with two hands and cleared his throat. The swarm of cameras circled around him like flies.

Of course, Alina didn't stick around for his speech.

She walked the several miles back to her grandfather's empty school.

She couldn't afford the cab fare.

2

THE CLOUD COVER DARKENED her way home. With hardly a shred of Niima left in her body, she felt woozy. A heaviness on her heart.

It was late afternoon by the time she got back to her place. The two-story, soot-blackened concrete building cast a shadow over her as she noted, once again, the battered sign advertising "…ich Martial Arts." The three characters that had fallen off—the "K," apostrophe, and "v"—had been set aside on the second-floor balcony. At least all the letters were equally discolored. It would take more than a fresh coat or two of paint to restore them to their once bright crimson.

She shuffled toward the front door, which she slammed open, and made her way up the narrow, creaking stairs at the far end of the dark hallway. Wafting from the doorway to her right came smells of freshly baked bread, cinnamon pastries, roasted dates, and chargrilled eggplant, and Alina couldn't recall a time she'd felt hungrier than now.

A flickering blue electric light guided her away from that blend of delicious aromas and into the musty upper floor where she lived.

Her grandfather's school. *The School*—where for four decades he'd trained young people for The Gild entry and licensing exams—sat above *Al'Ques,* a restaurant run by Mr. and Mrs. Qamasque, immigrants from Kadic, far to the south. Alina had no idea why anyone would willingly come to the Torviri Province of El, but here they were. And, forty years ago, Dimas K'vich had come to Mrs. Qamasque (the real brains behind the budding culinary business) with a proposition. Alina's grandfather (or "Tahtoh," as she called him), Dimas K'vich, had been a Master In Good Standing of The Gild and well-respected—even revered—member of the community. The Qamasques, meanwhile, made the greatest curry in the world. A strong partnership. If they promoted one another, they'd each double the size of their clientele. The rest, as they say, was money-making history.

The last decade had been tough on everyone. The layoffs. The famine. The riots. The strikes. The riots—and the riot suppressions. Truct had fallen on hard times, to say the least. And it was not alone. So many of the towns living under the shadow of New El found themselves in a similar state. But what could you do? You just worked, and lived, and carried on… until you couldn't any longer.

The several-year-long economic recession had finally forced the Qamasques to get on Tahtoh's case about the rent with ever-increasing severity. Until Tahtoh couldn't take it anymore.

Then, one day, he'd left Alina alone.

Alina thrust the key into the lock, which was in dire need of oil. The key stuck, as always, and she braced herself against the door, lifting it slightly so the brass key could hit the tumblers just right. After a minute more of gritting her teeth, she gave up and pulled the scuffed-up old key out of the lock.

From her pocket, she fished a length of stainless steel stiffener. She'd pulled the wire out of a wiper blade from an abandoned car about a month ago. She'd since bent the slim length of steel into an "L" shape using a torque wrench and a pair of pliers, and—bingo—home-made lockpick. This she now used to open her own front door. Because the pick wasn't scratched and toothless, unlike the old key the landlord would never bother to replace for her, it actually worked. A few seconds of tinkering with the tumblers and she nudged the door open.

Inside the vacant school-apartment combo, she set down her bag on a pile of dust and torn up cardboard boxes that served as her bed. She'd pawned the real thing for rent money last month. Or had it been two months ago? Unclasping her belt, she ambled over to the bookcase and carefully set the Auggie bottles she'd brought with her to the Silver Spoon—all three of them, the only ones that remained—on the shelves.

She glared at the empty one, whose contents made her nauseous even now. What a waste.

Scanning the dark room, she tugged her jacket collar around her neck and hugged herself, shivering. The grimy floors showed a trail of her footprints leading to the windows on the far side, the ones that overlooked the rotting garden out back. Nothing but withered roots and leafy mulch.

Between her and the windows lay the hearth—cold, empty. Firewood was a luxury. Electric heat was a luxury. Running water? Take a wild guess.

She tugged the rope hanging from the ceiling above her head, drawing open the hatch that led to the attic. The ladder slid down to meet her. She climbed.

There was a hole in the roof, covered with a tarp. Under it, a series of buckets. She dipped her water bottle into one of the half-full buckets, brought it to her chapped lips, took a drink. It was icy. She wanted to gulp it down to soothe her scratchy throat, but her already upset stomach forced her to take it slow.

A knock on the door. (Even with electricity, the doorbell wouldn't have worked. Maintaining it had been the first casualty of the K'viches' necessary neglect of the property. Years ago.) Alina, grumbling all the way, slid down the attic ladder and walked to the door. The knock mutated into persistent banging, impatient, irritated.

She didn't glance through the peephole. She knew what this would be about.

Swinging the door open, she said automatically, "Mrs. Qamasque. What can I do for you?"

"You could pay me the rent you owe. Last month and this month. And the three months before that, half unpaid."

"I did a job today," said Alina, her gaze falling at her landlady's feet. "I'm just waiting to get paid."

"Always same story with you, Lina." Mrs. Qamasque shook her head, wavy black tresses of hair dancing, silver strands glinting in the light emanating from the hallway. "You're like family to me, but I have business to run."

"I understand." Alina sighed. "But I just need a little more time. Please. This place is all I have."

For what it was worth, Mrs. Qamasque's eyes were red and puffy as she said, "Lina, I try to be good and patient of you. But I can't not make the money when the money to be made, you know? I need think about my husband's health, and my little grandson's school fees."

Alina gave a heavy-shouldered shrug. She couldn't meet her landlady's eyes.

Mrs. Qamasque's lips stretched, thin and white. "I give you until beginning next month. That's two weeks and two days. But you need to pay everything."

Alina nodded, risking a smile. "Yes, Mrs. Qamasque. Thank you. I'll figure something out. I will."

"I hope so." The landlady and businesswoman's voice dropped low, and she sounded much as she used to—Little Lina's babysitter on Tahtoh K'vich's busy nights of training: "I don't want kick you out, after everything. My heart breaks for you, child."

Alina bit her tongue to stifle the sob welling up inside her.

Mrs. Qamasque finished with, "But family is everything. And, so, so sorry to say, my family come first."

That night, she peeled the bandages from her arms, doing her very best to ignore her own discolored, scabby skin. Closing her eyes, with a cotton swab dipped in rubbing alcohol, she dabbed at her elbow, down her forearm, and her wrist. It stung. She repeated the process on her other arm. Then, applying fresh dressings, she muttered a prayer to Buthmertha, asking for compassion, strength, and protection against curses.

Despite her best efforts, she had noticed that her flesh had begun to turn gray.

She couldn't tell anyone about this… whatever was happening to her. Even if they didn't brand her a freak, even if they sincerely wanted to help her, no hospital would give her a checkup free of charge. She could only hope that faith and time would cure her.

Later, leaning over the balcony overlooking the garden and wall that separated it from the adjacent apartment building, Alina chowed down on her last bag of peppery potato chips and squinted across the street at the neighbor's Watchbox. No matter how frigidly cold or svelteringly hot it got outside, he always left his big sliding glass door open. He also must have been hearing-impaired, because he had the volume way, way up. Like, irresponsibly, call-the-cops loud. For these two facts, Alina was grateful: with the aid of a pair of binoculars, she could watch the news or cartoons free of charge. Whiling away the night hours when she wasn't working.

The neighbor guy, with his clean-shaven head and crisp white button-up shirt, worked for the Torviri family. Alina had no idea what specifically he did for a living, but she knew that much. He was one of the very few in town who could afford to park himself on a leather recliner, nestled under his electrically heated blankets and sipping his two-hundred-gelder bottle of booze. His high-tech drone-swarm security system kept his belongings safe from would-be thieves. (No, Alina hadn't thought about it. Not for too long, anyway.)

Currently, he had the Watchbox set tuned to El-Vision, The Capital's official news channel. Dumb propaganda and election updates, that's what they were all about. Except tonight.

Alina craned her neck, cupped her ear, strained to listen. She caught quite a bit of what was said by the generic-looking news anchor. His chiseled jaw and bouffant hairstyle both flapped as he proclaimed, "Nothing to be alarmed about… Official task forces… under control…" Alina strained to make out the words. As if in answer of her silent plea, her neighbor increased the volume. Then, the neutrally good-looking man in the box said, "Nevertheless, as an additional precaution, the Viceroys of all provinces of the nation have instructed us to forward the following message, direct from the Twelve Plutocrats. Quote, 'Gildsmen of the Nation of El, you are hereby summoned to The Capital to serve your homeland. Recent attacks on the governors of our financial institutions—the life's blood of our society—have been proven to be the work not of an organized resistance force as previously suspected. New El has been plagued this past fortnight by a bane of unknown nature and origin. Thus, we authorize this Open Contract that this matter might be resolved in as timely a manner as possible. Those qualified individuals interested should report to the Western Precinct Station in The Capital for briefing and details concerning the sizeable reward.'"

Alina's eyes glazed over as she repeated mentally what she'd heard. That had to be a *hefty* reward. Open Contract? In The Capital? The Plutocrats running scared? There's no way they'd put this out for Terries to see unless it was supes chaotic up there by now.

How much were they offering? The Twelve had deep, *deep* pockets. It was no exaggeration to say that most of the money flowed to them—from the banks, the businesses, the surface-dwellers taxed half to death. This was the first she'd heard of the Plutocrats calling for a Rave. As long as it was business as usual, the elite didn't worry themselves too much about the Aelf running amok on the mainland. Guess that had changed now that the elite had been hit where they lived.

(Granted, the news anchor hadn't used the word "Aelf," probably because it would incite a panic. But the coded language was transparent enough. As the broadcast wore on, he tossed out terms like "unknown assailant," "prowling," "multiple murders," "brutality," "dire necessity." The implications were obvious to anyone really paying attention.)

This "bane" represented a potentially catastrophic blow to the reputation of the Plutocrats, The Authority, and the whole bureaucracy. And if *she* were the one to stop this threat, whatever it turned out to be… The money…

It would solve everything. Everything.

How many months' rent would this one bounty be worth? Maybe she could—*gasp*—buy food, pay the utility bills, or—*double gasp*—buy clothes so she could get out of the hand-me-downs from her Tahtoh and his former students.

Mind spinning, she leaned on the balcony railing.

She allowed herself a minute or two more of wild fantasies. Then she forced her responsible side back into her mental driver's seat.

Fact was, she was broke as broke could get. There was no other way out. She was about to be homeless. Mrs. Qamasque was bearing down on her like a hawk about to snatch up a field mouse. She could starve to death next month.

This was it.

Realistically, she had three options.

First, she could fall back on dying, penniless and alone, unloved, and clawing at her empty stomach and parched throat—maybe not ideal.

Second, she could get another barista job. Yeah. All she had to do was find a shop far enough away from the ones she'd already been fired from but that was also somehow within walking distance of her home because she had no hopes of owning a car within the next several years. At best.

Third, she could rise to the occasion, dispatch the monster in New El, receive the no-doubt disgustingly fat reward, and live out her days a wealthy and famous queen of her profession.

She slid onto her bed made of thinning cardboard and newspaper clippings, laying her head onto her equipment bag-turned-pillow.

Option three might have sounded amazing at first glance, but she had no way of knowing what she was up against. Every Raver in the country—and beyond—might end up gunning for that bounty. To say nothing of the Aelf itself, whatever it might be. And she'd be butting heads with the residents of The Capital. That was a problem because, even down here, no one took her seriously. Sheriff Lowing had talked to her as if she were a child playing monster hunter. How could the high and mighty Elementals do anything but look down their noses at her?

By contrast, option two was safe. If she scraped together a pair—maybe a trio—of jobs, really stretched her toilet paper reserves, and only ate off-brand cereal *forever,* she might just be able to pay the rent. As long as she didn't get sick, like, ever. Yeah, with enough gumption, if she kept her head down for the next—oh, forty years or so—she might just be able to crawl her way out of the debt-hole inside which she was currently trapped.

A choice between devils.

On the one hand, the devil who'd kept her company since she was a child, who whispered in her dreams that a minimum wage job was perfectly acceptable, that everything was fine, that this was her lot in life, that she should never want anything better. That nothing should come easily. Hard work was its own reward. It was the nagging voice in the back of her mind that demanded she remain complacent, that only wanted a couch and a Watchbox and a hot shower every day. Simple wants. If she worked herself halfway into her grave, she might even get a few of them.

On the other hand, there was the devil of the unknown. An all-or-nothing quest in the sky whose pursuit required her particular passion and skillset: she'd be using what her Tahtoh had taught her; she could bring to bear all of her Raving skills. She could finally prove to herself that she had what it took to be a Raver. That, after all, she really was Dimas K'vich's granddaughter.

Option two would keep her close to Calthin, the one friend she'd known all her life. Stability had its own appeal. And she wouldn't be risking her neck for the slimmest chance of a reward.

Taking option three would pit her against some of the most dangerous people on the planet. And the astronomical sum the Plutocrats were promising for the successful completion of the job had her considering whether—maybe—this job was just a bump or two above her paygrade.

The money would do her no good if she died trying to get it.

But then she looked at the dusty envelopes piled on the mantelpiece. Bills going back *months*. Some of those debts had been accrued even before Tahtoh had disappeared. Any day now, the repo men would be by to extract what little they could from The School. And then, not soon after, she'd lose The School, too.

Whether by pouring pre-rationed thimbles-full of skim milk into burnt-bean coffee or mounting a hunt in The Capital, she had to put gelders in the bank.

So, why shouldn't she go big?

A memory popped into her head: well into his seventies, for exercise, Tahtoh would strap a harness to himself, stick a bit in his mouth, and pull trucks along the road. Sometimes uphill. In the rain. With his face. Tahtoh hadn't ever favored caution over bold, decisive action. He would have taken whatever chance was in front of him.

She clenched her fist and stared blindly at her neighbor's Watchbox.

Then she rushed to her closet, ripped what few clothes she had left off their hangers, and piled them on her cardboard bed. Next, she found her suitcase in the attic, blowing the dust off it.

Unzipping and flinging open her suitcase, she crammed her stuff inside.

She'd show them all. Sheriff Lowing, Mrs. and Mr. Qamasque, Calthin and his parents, and all the people of Truct. She'd show them what it meant to be a K'vich.

3

SHE'D WOKEN UP AROUND five in the morning. Running off maybe three hours of sleep, her mind buzzed like a glitching computer.

Pin pricks in her fingertips as she tapped the countertop bell in *Amming & Sons*. It was a gorgeous day. Annoyingly gorgeous. Golden sunlight peeking around Mount Morbin's purple face. Like everything was and would remain fine. Like the world was playing up the "gray skies are gonna clear up" attitude that Alina had forced herself to maintain all morning. *Positive thinking*. She'd read about how that was a good thing, once. Read it in a book. About philosophies that historically have driven their practitioners insane.

Too much time to think could be dangerous.

Soaking into her skin, the familiarity of the tailor's shop. A place she'd been inside a million times. Mile-long strands of green and red twine looped their way through hoops drilled into the walls and posts all around the cozy building. Furniture cluttered the narrow hallways leading to the fitting and changing rooms. There were boxes filled with spools of thread—every color, sheen, and thickness imaginable—on top of which lay dozens of half-used rolls of tape, discarded scissors and shears, and pins and needles of various sizes. The ceiling beams emitted the scent of old sunbathed wood, and were coated in the dust of a lived-in home. Ironically, the broom leaning against the wall beside the front door was itself covered in a coating of white dust. It had been there long enough that, if someone made an attempt to move it, the whole place might collapse on itself.

Alina tapped the bell again.

"Gods bear witness, I will *cut* you if I have to," came the voice of Calthin Amming, son of Uther Amming, and heir to Truct's premier (only) tailor shop.

"Wow. Uncalled for," said Alina.

She couldn't yet see him. He remained deeper in the store, in some back room.

"Not you. It's—I'm dealing with a delicate situation at the moment. Hang tight." His voice sounded muffled, like he was yelling through a wet paper bag. Or the sleeve of a sweater.

"You got stuck again, didn't you?"

There was a tellingly long pause.

"No," Calthin answered eventually.

"Come out here." Alina rolled her eyes when he appeared before her; his head and entire forearm were indeed stuffed inside a half-finished sleeve of an intricately patterned turtleneck. "What are you doing?"

"The, uh, the detail work." From somewhere inside that sleeve, he cleared his throat. "Can get tricky. Hafta, um, get in close." His shoulders sagged. Well, his free shoulder did. The stuck one just kind of twitched.

"Do I need to help you out of there? Or are you capable of living a real life?"

"No, no. I've got it. If you tug from your end, the whole—" he swore, spun around a few times—"thing'll unravel."

"Okay. Whatever you say." She watched him fumble, the bumps in the turtleneck sleeve her only indication that his fingers were working away around the inside of their fabric prison. "Look," she said, leaning on the counter, lowering her voice, "I came here to tell you I'll be leaving for—well, for a while. Not too long. Maybe several days. Maybe more. I'm not sure. I just need someone to watch The School while I'm—" She stamped around the counter, grabbed his arm, and glared down the dark insides of the sleeve at him. "Are you getting any of this in there?"

Even from within that shadowed tube of cloth, his eyes were an ethereal green. Like Niima fire from a spell gone bad. He said, "Yeah, 'course I heard you. You're leaving, blah-blah-blah."

She jabbed her fists toward the ground, taking a step back. "I'm serious."

"You've been—" A complicated series of ducking, weaving, and backpedaling motions occurred, and Calthin finally freed himself from his self-made trap—"'serious' before." The lingering static electricity set his strawberry-blond locks on end, like swamp reeds gently nudged by the wind.

"This is different. It's for a job."

He squinted at her, smoothing down his hair. "What kinda job?"

She narrowed her eyes right back. "The paying kind."

With a foppish shrug, he expertly folded his new creation and laid it on the counter between them. As if for reassurance, he pressed his palm onto the turtleneck before saying, "Raving?"

She softened. "Yeah."

He nodded. "Okay. Well, I have something for you."

"I really have to go, though."

"Right this very second? Can you give me, like, one minute, Alina?"

"Okay. *Fine*," she said, stretching the syllable like an elastic waistband past its prime. "But I've got an appointment at the bank, and then—another thing."

He raised an eyebrow at that last statement. With a little puff from his lips, scratching the back of his neck, he said, "It's a gift. I made you something."

"Oh."

"It's nothing much." He held up his hands, and Alina's Raver-trained eyes swept over the callouses on his fingers. Emblem of his trade. "Be right back. Stay. Please." And he dashed around the corner.

Alina called, "Is your dad around, by the way?"

"What?" A rapid succession of crashes and bangs. The sound of toes slamming into a tin bucket. Swearing. "Oh. Dad? No. He's out getting groceries."

"I'd die an old maid waiting for him to get back."

"Yep." Calthin growled as he audibly grappled with something bulky. When he returned, he said, "True that. This one time, it took him literally an hour to pick out one avocado. That being said, best damned guac I ever ate. So fresh."

Alina couldn't help but notice that he'd come back empty-handed. "Trouble finding this gift of yours?"

"What?" Then he understood what she'd meant. "Oh. Oh! No, I wasn't—I was feeding Pigeon."

Pigeon was the Amming family's pet peregrine, a bird of prey with a wingspan to rival a jet plane. No wonder Calthin was so frazzled. That magnificent beast could probably have eaten him in two bites. Bones and all.

"Your gift," said Calthin his game show announcer voice, "is right here behind curtain number one." He stooped behind the counter. Unrolling his lanky body to its usual six feet again, he passed her a brown paper bundle. "Open it. It's not done, just so you know. I'd planned to work on it more, but—ah, just open it."

She accepted the package, unwrapped it. Discarding the paper, she gasped and told him, "It's too much, Calthin."

He waved away the comment. "Supposed to be a birthday thing, but you're going to need it. Now more than ever. What with you headed to the big city and all."

"How did you know?"

"Saw the news last night." He laughed softly, looking away. "I know you."

On accident, their eyes met. They held each other's gaze long enough for things to get a little uncomfortable.

"So?" he said, gesturing toward her present. "Put it on, already. The suspense is killing me."

She took a breath, nodded, slipped one arm into the jacket. Pause. Then the other.

He was talking all the while: "It's fake leather, 'cause I know you don't want anything to do with murder—and I like cows, too, anyway. Um. But it's real warm, with that lining and all. And I put a couple extra pockets on the inside. You can clip them shut. In case you wanted to carry something. One of your bottles or something. I dunno." His excitement wore down until his words grinded to a halt. "Is it dumb? It's dumb, isn't it. Look, you don't have to wear it just 'cause—"

"I love it," she blurted.

Pause.

She zipped herself into the jacket. It was umber-colored with burgundy trim. It had a hood. She pulled the hood over her head. There were pockets everywhere inside. Lots of places to hide useful things.

It was so… thoughtful.

From the depths of her ridiculously warm hood, she muttered, "I totally love it."

He seemed surprised. Or maybe relieved. Both. "You're welcome."

"Let me give you some money," she said quickly.

"You don't owe me anything. That's what 'gift' means."

"Not for this, then." She looked around, for inspiration. "Your dad. For the rent money he fronted me last month."

"You don't owe him either." Calthin's nostrils flared. "We're happy to help you out."

"You don't seem too happy," she joked. But it was too late. She could tell he'd been irritated by something. Something she'd said, or something he'd thought up because of what she'd said, maybe. It hardly mattered which. He'd retreated into his shell.

Why did he *always* twist her words like wire around himself until they were tight enough to choke him?

Since the damage had been done anyway, she added, "Besides, I don't need 'help.'"

"I know that." He blushed. "But we're glad to give it anyway. The Ammings and K'viches have been friends for years. Will always be friends. Friends and allies."

She rolled her eyes at him. "You always get verbose when you're upset."

"That surely is the farthest thing from the truth."

Neither of them breathed for a few seconds. They just held themselves, puffed up like birds squabbling over a sidewalk crumb. Then they deflated, chuckling as they caught each other's expressions.

She said, "You really oughta let me give you some money. Just a little. This might be your last chance to recover the loss for your dad. Because I could *actually* die up there, you know."

"Please. Now who's being dramatic?"

"Oh, shut up."

"You'll be fine."

"Yeah." She clicked her tongue, swung her arms back and forth, rocked on her heels. "Hey, I'd better go."

"Okay."

"Just one more thing, alright?"

"Name it."

"If I die—"

He sighed. "Alina—"

"If I *die*, I want you to promise me…"

"Alright, *what*?"

"Promise me that you'll tell Sheriff Lowing that he couldn't find a horse's ass if it fell on him. He'll know what that means."

"You sure?" He laughed. "Might be too subtle. But you'll tell him yourself. When you get back."

"*Calthin*."

"Alright. Al*right*." He held two fingers over his heart. "I solemnly swear that I will relay to the good sheriff your message in the event that you prematurely depart the mortal plane."

"See? Wordiness. You're nervous."

"Whatever, whatever."

"So…" She inched backward. Toward the door.

Calthin came over to her. He shuffled closer. There was only a hand's span—pinky to thumb—between them. He reached up, hand gliding. His hand stopped. He took a step back. His hand was still hovering there, at waist level.

On reflex, she grabbed and shook it.

"Be careful," he said.

"Always am."

And she threw open the door and speed-walked down the street.

"Alina?"

She skidded to a halt, her cheeks burning.

"How am I getting into The School? To look after it?"

She turned, face-palming. "Right. Yeah, I'm leaving it unlocked. Key is useless and there's nothing valuable left to steal in there anyway, so… Okay, then."

She dashed off.

Over her shoulder, she shouted, "Thanks for the jacket, Calthin. It's awesome. I mean it."

The last she saw of him, he was holding his hand up. A motionless wave.

Five seconds later, she looked back again. He'd gone.

***

At the local branch of Geldwerp Community Bank, Alina was, for a change, one of the least miserably annoyed people in the building. It was four o'clock in the afternoon; everyone else had scrambled in right after work, some having cut an hour or three off their shifts to be certain they'd make it in time. They were here to cash or deposit a measly check, transfer a balance, pay a bill, plead for a loan. A dark sight, these Assets scraping by. Alina, on the other hand, felt content in the knowledge that this would be her last time inside this or any GCB branch. Once she completed this job and got that big fat payoff, she'd buy a bank of her own, call it Alina-Loan Inc., where every Alina would be a VIP. And, when there wasn't space enough to hold her millions and billions of gelders, she'd rent a cannon—damn the cost—and fire the excess into space. Just to make room for ever larger quantities of cash.

She let out a long sigh, settling in for a long wait.

The holo-card the bank greeter had given her proclaimed that her number was W-88, whatever that meant. Out of boredom, she twisted the card this way and that until the symbols floating in the air were no longer visible. Every half-minute, a "Thank You For Your Patience" note would appear, followed by "The Next Available Representative Is Assisting Other Valued Customers And Will Be With You As Soon As Possible." Nowhere, by the way, was there any indication as to what number was *currently* being served.

Both the exterior and interior of the bank were all about function over form. A big, square block of concrete hollowed out to fit as many customers as possible at any given time. Eleven rows of metal folding chairs had been lined up in rows of ten, and there still weren't enough seats for everyone waiting to be helped by the five employees currently servicing accounts.

While waiting in this "lounge area," Alina sat close to the wall, and so was finally able to charge her phone. To stay ahead of the pins and needles in her legs, she kept shifting in her metal seat.

The tellers sat behind physically and magically reinforced glass walls with a built-in speaker. Getting to them would be next to impossible… unless you happened to know that the Maggo who performed the shielding spells every week was a notorious drunk and left way too many gaps. Of course, Alina *hadn't* noticed this information and *definitely* never secretly daydreamed about exploiting it to clean out the vault.

The vault itself was a simple rectangle of metal, many inches thick. It was guarded at all hours by a quartet of round, white automated gun turrets which almost looked like cameras when not in use, buried in the walls as they were. But one wrong move toward the vault door and they'd pop out and turn you into a fishing net in seconds.

The gun turrets weren't the only pieces of smart-gear in the bank. The tellers worked with computer consoles projecting holographic displays of their customers' transaction fees and credit card bills. Their eyes were blurred by the blue, white, and yellow light of the text and jumping graphs reflected in them.

It would take hours for a representative to see Alina; closing an account, especially one as tiny as hers, wasn't exactly a priority. Suited her just fine, though. Gave her all the time in the world to conduct a bit of research.

Thumbs clacking away, she banged out the keywords, "Gild License," and got nothing relevant to what she needed. She tried a blunter approach: "Fake Gild License for sale." She scrolled through the search results, sipping from the cup of slightly stagnant water she'd been offered a few minutes earlier. This time, she found a hit that seemed promising.

She chuckled bleakly to herself when she imagined what Year-Ago Alina would think of her present-day self: using a public net connection—at a government-funded bank—to get the hookup for phony identification cards. But Year-Ago Alina hadn't had nearly as many money-related problems. So, she hadn't needed to know about Virtual Private Networks to hide her Aetherthread searches. Or how to jail-break unregistered phones that had "fallen" off the back of a drone-carried cargo crate.

"Okay, Mr. xxGildzM4st3Rxx, if that even is your real name…" Present-Day Alina mumbled to herself. She narrated her message: "'Need a way into the pig pen. Day before tomorrow. Can you make that happen?'" It wasn't a subtle code, "pig pen," but the Authority's Integrated Intelligences were always trawling the net for specific key-phrases. That one hadn't been compromised. As far as she was aware.

Within one minute, xxGidlzM4st3Rxx responded:

will cost you. but doable.

She wrote,

the damage?

1k

A thousand gelders? A thousand? She could *feel* the sweat gushing from her face. She felt like a phoenix ready to explode in a fiery inferno.

Taking a second to collect her thoughts, she replied,

deal

She didn't have the money, of course. If she had, she wouldn't have been in this position in the first place. But she'd figure something out before it came time to make the exchange.

She texted Calthin.

You got my last digimail I hope??

Fifteen minutes later, he answered with,

'course. I *should* open it, though, rite? I mean it says 'DANGER DANGER DONT OPEN,' but that just means it's an embarrassing picture or something & I should definitely open it.

She wrote,

Ha.

And waited.

watsup?

there's a demon in there

yep. so I gathered from the subject line

the sheriff stiffed me. screwed me outta money that I really really really could use right now

i know, Alina.

The little icon showed that he was still typing.

She waited. Waited some more.

And all she got from him in the end was,

im srry. Really.

so am I

She hit send. Thought a minute. Then:

I could set the demon free

The conversation lagged. She wondered if she'd gone too far. Then he messaged,

you'd kill the whole town outta spite??

She smirked.

that'd teach em.

He answered,

a lesson they'd never 4get.

yeh cuz they'd b dead.

Calthin was typing.

But the bank teller called her number, then, so she quickly wrote,

Gotta go. L8r

Calthin's last message popped onto the screen just as she rose from the metal chair. It read:

little brother misses you btw. Still always blabbing about wanting to be your student. Dunno where the kid gets his crazy ideas. You teaching = scary. ;P

She grumbled to herself, hitting the lock button and slipping her phone into one of the multitude of pockets in her shiny new jacket.

She thought about how good the Amming family had been to her ever since her grandfather had… moved on. Summer barbeques on the back porch, free patching of her clothes, the occasional late-night movie. They'd have had her in the guestroom by now if she hadn't insisted that someone needed to keep an eye on The School, that the old place needed a warm body to keep it company.

For the first couple months, the return of Dimas K'vich had felt like a distinct possibility. As the weeks wore on, however, that hope became less and less justifiable. What irked Alina—maybe more than anything else—was the look on the youngest Amming boy's face: Kinneas had been dead-set on signing up for The School's program next year (seven was the traditional and widely accepted age for beginning Aelfraver training).

The look on his face when he found out the old man was gone…

And it wasn't long before—over ice-cream sandwiches—he started yammering about Alina teaching him. Him and his friends. She'd be so amazing at it, he'd proclaimed. She was the toughest and smartest lady he knew.

But he was just some kid. He didn't know her at all, really.

The teller gestured for Alina to hurry up and get to the window already. On the other side of the glass, the woman set down her nail file, slid a tablet towards her, and proceeded to try to pick up a stylus about thirty times before realizing her pencil-length black nails would not allow it. Brushing aside her straight, black bangs, she sighed and used the knuckle of her pinky finger instead, flicking aside translucent boxes and static glowing projections.

"What can we do for you today, Ms. …?"

"K'vich. Alina. I'm here to close my account."

"Oh, I am sorry to hear that," she said flatly. "May I ask the reason?"

"Business opportunity."

"Starting a company, are we?" She asked, eyes fixed on her fingernails.

"Not exactly."

The teller idly blew on the fresh coat of polish on her nails. "Well, why don't you take out a personal loan? We have some great packages with low, low interest rates starting at just 8% for the first three months. I could call for our Work-n'-Play Finance Facilitator, Illain, and they could lay out your options for you."

"Thanks for the offer, but—"

"It's really no trouble," the teller said, yawning, even as she struggled to pick up the phone. After a moment or two, she cleared her throat and was about to make use of the voice commands, but Alina interrupted her.

"Just the withdrawal. Please."

"Alright, then. Account number?"

"I never remember it. I have my debit chip with me, though."

"Hold it up to the screen."

Alina did so.

The teller's nails illuminated the amber keys of the projected keyboard as she typed, slowly, languidly. When what felt like quite a while had passed, she looked up and said, "You're starting a business with *this* much? That's it?"

Alina shrugged. She might have been offended, but she knew how broke she was. It wasn't a surprise, by any means, and she'd come to terms with that fact. What did worry her: over the next several days, she was set to spend every penny she had left. And it still might not be enough.

As the teller flicked several more commands, Alina started to panic. It wouldn't help in any way, submitting to the terror of not knowing where her meals would come from, how she'd ever land on her feet if she failed, but that's the thing about panic attacks—they don't wait around for their turn. This one barged right in, like all those before it, kicking and screaming, even as the bank representative counted the bills, placed them in the metal sliding drawer, and pushed all of Alina's savings towards her. So she could flush them all down the drain.

But then she had an idea. A way to stretch out her funds just a little more. The panic subsided enough for thoughts to flow freely again.

She'd have to go back to The School one more time before she met up with her cartoonishly shady net contact…

When she was done closing out Alina's account, the teller passed over a form using the metal sliding drawer. "Sign at the dotted line and initial each page. Thank you for banking with GCB, 'Where You're Family,'" she said, clearly regurgitating lines from a script. "We do hope you'll consider coming back to us in the future." Under her breath, she muttered, "You and your handful of pocket change."

Pocketing a few thin rolls of five-gelder bills, she left the Truct branch of the Geldwerp Community Bank. Outside, she pulled out her phone again and reread Calthin's last text. She answered with,

tell Kinneas i'll see him soon. but im no teacher

Five minutes later, as she jaywalked in plain view of Sheriff Lowing's blubbering deputy—giving him the finger—she checked her messages. Calthin had seen hers, for sure. The two little checkmarks never lied.

No reply.

With a little over two hundred gelders in cash and a package underarm, she slinked along the back alleys of Truct as the late afternoon wore down to a nub of sunlight. The faint rays were no match for the bitter winds that only grew stronger as twilight caressed the streets with its vermillion and cerulean fingers.

The sun had set behind the abandoned apartment bloc. As Alina walked in cobalt shadow, she became acutely aware that she was very much alone out here.

Her pace slowing, she considered that this was probably a trap. The man she was meeting thought she'd be carrying *a thousand gelders.* Cash money. A trap sure seemed likelier by the minute.

Then a different part of her brain chimed in, noting that the joke's on him. He was about to be one disappointed thief.

She might have giggled nervously if she wasn't sure that even the faintest sound would carry for what must have been miles and miles of run-down residential byways. Barred or boarded up windows and doors; mangy yellow-eyed cats; so many crows perched on the rooftops and balconies; the occasional stripped-down car. This wasn't a place to come to without backup. And, yet, here she was. Alina K'vich, ready to make a deal with whoever slithered out of the sewer.

On cue, a man whipped around a corner, staring her down: a young man, maybe a handful of years older than Alina herself. His oily, fiery crimson hair hid his right eye. He glowered at her, baring a set of graying crooked teeth.

"Who the hells are you?" he said.

Stunned, for a heartbeat Alina could only stare at him. "Um, I'm the one who messaged you. About the license."

He stabbed his pointer finger into his lips. "Shh! Not so loud."

Alina scanned the area, hands automatically shifting into casting positions. "Are you afraid we're being watched?"

His gargoylish composure broke. Seeming quite timid now, he said, "A man doesn't get to be in my position through carelessness. You think I survived five raids—no less than three flashbangs—by being gullible? Puh-lease. I only play dumb to get girls." As he spoke, his eyes bounced from alley wall to alley wall to floor to sky and back again. "I'll ask one more time. Who are you?"

"You think I'm gonna tell you my name?" Alina said. "Hah! This may be my first face-to-face illegal transaction—"

"For the love of all that is holy, woman! Keep it down."

"—but I'm not a total moron. And I'm gonna keep blabbing until you give me what I came here for."

"No way. I don't know you. And I don't do business with peeps I don't know."

"Gah. Fine." She threw up her hands in defeat. "How about a codename?"

"No good. Only the real deal. Breeds trust. I need to be able to trust you, my lady. But, tell you what, since you're a noob with this stuff, I'll go first. They call me Rooster. 'Cause I crow. I'm the best at it. The cops are always coming after me. 'Cause I know… things, man. They want me to rat. But I. Don't. Rat. Yeah, they come to stuff the Rooster. But, you know, he ain't gonna cry."

As soon as he paused for breath, Alina said, "Call me Stitcher, then."

"Beautiful name. Suits you, m'lady fair. So, uh, confession time. I didn't know you'd be a girl. And hot, at that. Didn't think girls online could even be hot. Especially not as hot as you."

"Hey, thanks for the compliment," Alina said, tensing, resting her weight on the balls of her feet, ready to run. "But I'm in kind of a rush, here. Gotta bust out of town pronto. I'm sure you know how it is."

"I most definitely do, Stitcher. Can I call you Stitcheree? Yeah, I don't mean to brag, but I'm pretty much the record-holder for most arrests. That's in the whole county, though. I'm basically one of the Usual Suspects. Anytime the law comes down from The Capital looking for someone or other, they round up the gang—me, Ginny Split-Lip, Gangrene, Dope Sandwich, *ex setra ex setra.*"

Alina couldn't guess if he'd meant that as a brag. She no longer believed Rooster planned to hurt her, though. She'd dealt with his type once or twice before: compensating for zero self-confidence, bearer of the underarm musk of poor personal hygiene, hopelessly deluded about what flirting is; in short, a Thredder. Conspiracy theorists, Masculinists, authoritarian propogandists, and anarchists—these represented a mere handful of the hundreds of subsets of the virtual found on the Darkthreads. The worst of these people were dangerous due to their delusions of importance, but Rooster seemed to live in the mostly harmless scruffy basement-dweller category. He appeared to be a danger mainly to himself.

Alina found herself feeling sorry for the guy, but no way would she be sticking around any longer than she had to. "You got the license?"

"I got a template." And Rooster preened much like his animal namesake.

"What's that mean?"

"Means I just need a photo of you and the spell I wove—I mean *stitched*—" he said with a wink, "will do the rest."

"*You're* a Maggo?" Alina blinked.

"Third generation, after my ma and grandad." Rooster pushed out his insignificant and bony chest. "This counterfeiter charm isn't my own design, but I modded it. I call it 'Cockadoodle-Duped.'" He paused. For laughter, probably. He added, "Right? 'Cause I'm the Rooster and—"

Alina held up a hand. "I got it, don't worry. I'll just be much gigglier when I have the finished product in my hands."

Rooster grinned. "Well, so what you got for me, Stitchee-o?"

Her heart fluttering, she put all her metaphorical chips on the table, saying, "Rooster, buddy, pal, my co-conspirator… I don't have a thousand gelders."

"Treachery!"

"Hear me out, though. Please. What I do have is this Niima-powered Backup Generator. Easily worth a grand. Easy." And, with that, she pulled the item from her bag and held it in front of Rooster's face. The Niima generator her grandfather had personally recharged ten thousand times. The magic cylinder that, by its spinning, had provided hot baths after training, cool breezes on long summer nights, and cooked food every day for years and years. The obsidian cylinder had chipped in places through loving use, but any Maggo worth her salt could tell that the thing still hummed with power. Old, but quality craftsmanship.

Tahtoh had shaped it himself, his mind the only tool he'd needed.

Rooster whistled. He rubbed a finger along the generator's tiny regularly-spaced ridges. "Huh. It's worn, no doubt. Needs significant repairs. Looks nice, though. Real nice. Silky smooth in all the right places. Slight imperfections. Handmade…" He trailed off, frowning in concentration. "This'd get you most of the way there, for sure. But even this beauty ain't worth a thousy. How much dough you got on you?"

Alina bit her lip. She'd hoped it wouldn't come to this. Giving up one of the last mementos from her Tahtoh and still falling short. She only had two hundred gelders now, and she needed every scrap to fund her jaunt to the city.

"Fifty," she lied. *Still too much to lose.* She tried hitting him with something closer to the truth: "It's all I can spare."

Sucking on his teeth, Rooster's bouncing eyes absorbed the state of the generator. Then he very clearly spent several long seconds checking Alina out. Finally, he clicked his tongue and said, "Deal. But only because we're celebrating our new friendship."

Risking a smile, Alina said, "Thanks. I appreciate it."

"Happy to make you happy, m'lady fair. If you don't mind me asking, though, what you planning on doing with the phony ID? Just curious, of course, of course."

"Where I'm going, I need to pass for a Gildsman."

He whistled again. "That is super-dupes dangerous. You know that, don't you? Do I have to tell you about what happens to people who get snagged doing just that?"

"No, I'm aware."

"It ain't exactly catch-and-release when it comes to Aelfravers. Why in El would you wanna pretend you're one of *them*?"

"I said I'm faking *Gildsman status*." She crossed her arms. "I actually *am* an Aelfraver."

"You?" Rooster gave her another once-over. "Really? You?"

"Yeah," she growled, the air around her crackling, locks of her tangled wavy hair rising as if caught by a sudden breeze. Except there was no breeze. "What of it?"

Rooster raised his hands, waving them quickly. "Nothing, nothing. I was caught off guard. A thousand pardons." He held up his phone. "Now, then, let's nab ourselves a lovely little mug shot of you, shall we?"

"Where should I stand?"

"Doesn't matter. The background is auto-deleted. Nifty, huh?"

"Nifty," she agreed.

"Smile!" said Rooster.

The three-burst flashes swept over her extremely neutral expression. Rooster, however, was unfazed. "Wow! Radiant! A vision from legend." He showed her the trio of pics he'd snapped.

"Yeah, they're decent," she said. "Middle one's the best." They were all identical.

"It is done," he said, swiping his touch screen frantically. He kneeled and set the blank holocard on the ground, dragging something invisible from the camera to the white plastic rectangle. Muttering a few words over it, he punctuated the conclusion of the spell with a snap of his fingers. Triumph smeared across his face, he stood up, handed Alina the card.

She'd seen enough official Gild Raver-X Licenses to know that this was a solid imitation. You'd have to inspect it very closely—and probably with the aid of tools or charms—to spot the differences.

"Okay, I'm impressed."

"I live to impress my lady fair," said Rooster with a theatrical bow. And he laughed, which sounded more than a little like a rooster's crowing. She chuckled along politely. Then he said, "There's just one more thing."

Alina braced herself.

He cupped his chin in his pale hand. "You're headed to The Capital, yes? And your goal is to blend."

"Ideally."

"It's just that—please don't take this as anything but a compliment, but…"

"What?"

"Your hair," he said, pointing. "It's so long and gray and *big*. You're way too beautiful and natural for the crowds of artificial posers in The Capital. They'd pick you out of a lineup from a thousand feet off."

"What are you getting at?"

"You need a new 'do." Rooster combed strands of his stringy hair behind his grimy ear. "Hasta be something in fashion. Something those fake-os in New El wouldn't look twice at. I could—you know—if you want. Cut it for you, I'm saying."

Alina's hand subconsciously glided to the ends of her curls that reached halfway down her back. Her mother had been the last one to cut them. The idea of shearing them off…

Rooster was right, though. It was a good call. Blending in. But she'd be damned if she was going to let some random weirdo put scissors to her neck.

"Rooster, hey, it's been—it's been something *special*. But I gotta get back home."

"It would be quick and painless. The cut. I'm really good at it."

"I bet you are. It's, uh, not you, it's me?" She started to back away. "I'll call you when I get the money to buy that generator back. Don't pawn it off till then."

He blushed. "But will I see you again?"

"Yes, if you hang onto that generator for me."

"I shall guard it with my very life, then."

"Great. Uh, guess that's it then. Thanks for the, uh," she said, holding up the license he'd enchanted, "the card, and, well, happy trails."

She walked away. Quickly.

Fewer than five minutes later, Rooster texted her,

> You have my number! ;) ;) ;) ;) ;) ;) ;) ;)

So. Awkward. She shuddered. But he'd gotten the job done.

And she *would* be getting that generator back, she swore. Just as soon as she could. No matter the cost.

4

IT TOOK A COUPLE of showers to wash off the lingering weirdness of her meeting with Rooster. And by "showers," she meant dunking her face into and scrubbing herself with the rainwater she'd been collecting each day. She rubbed her gray bar of soap down to a nub. It just barely did the trick; she smelled less like sweat and more like lemongrass.

After she got cleaned up, she went to the kitchen drawer and grabbed a pair of old, slightly rusty dressmaker scissors. No point in delaying any longer; she set to the task of cutting her hair.

Ever since she'd been a kid, Alina had, in a general sense, thought of people as pretty much the same as animals and even the Aelf. Humans were creatures of habit and instinct. Some had complicated desires, while others' were simple and obvious for all to see. Some had power. Most were weak. But, ultimately, all people were the same in one way at least: they all wanted to be seen. *How* they preferred to be noticed depended on the individual, but every person was, in the end, a peacock in one way or another. From their clothes to their hair and makeup and little personality quirks, everyone put on a show for *somebody* in *some* way. And if you wanted to learn a whole lot about a particular person, you first should see who they were trying to *wow*.

This concept had been an early discovery of Alina's, and it grew in complexity and depth the more she thought about it. Eventually, she started doing research to back up her claim, studying the human animal as a natural scientist would a rare insect.

A big perk of being a social outcast was that you had a lot of time to think. (Then again, a big *downside* of being a social outcast was that you had a lot of time to think.)

Alina's fascination with observing her fellow humans from the outside had led her to hoard some highly specific types of materials, including video archives of makeup tutorials, books on historical fashion trends, literary magazines put out by independent publishing companies, and more. Her theory was that all that stuff had been created thanks to the same impulse—to show off.

And, now, all those years of collecting discarded style magazines from recycling bins would finally pay off. Or so she hoped.

She blew the dust off each cover before opening. Flipping through page after page of airbrushed sassy, sexy, mysterious, or angelic models, she dog-eared the ones she liked. An hour later, she put the last magazine down.

Fifteen minutes of staring at her tired reflection.

"I don't want to do this," she told her mirrored self.

She picked up the scissors and watched her reflection frown.

The first step was the hardest. A quick series of slices that removed eighty percent or more of her hair. She winced as the scissors scythed through cord after thick cord. The tangles unraveled, clumps falling away by the handful, and she rinsed her hair again to help her more easily gauge length.

She left only enough in the front to frame the right side of her face. Most of the rest she clipped short. With all that weight disappeared, the result was a bouncy lopsided bob.

All that hair, gone.

Dimas used to say that it was from his side of the family that Alina got her thick, wavy hair. Also, the gene that had begun to turn it gray and white exceptionally early… Alina's mother had had hair just like hers. She, too, had worn it in a loose ponytail, long and coarse, like an unraveling hangman's noose. It was one of the few things Alina could remember about her mom.

She shook off the nostalgia. It served no purpose.

The last step—dye. In no way could she have justified dropping gelders for this task. Forget about salon products or those fancy little bottles with pictures of pouty-lipped, icy-eyed women on them; she couldn't even have afforded one of those convenience store generic brands.

No, Alina went about it the only way she could figure how: after wracking her brain for an alternative, she rummaged around under the kitchen sink and pulled out the nearly empty bottle of bleach.

Since she was naturally going white, she might as well lean into it.

She, of course, diluted the bleach significantly with what rainwater she had left.

There was something missing, though. A touch of flair.

Contemplating, she snapped her fingers, following the trail of her thoughts to the alchemical cabinet, where she found a dusty vial of Hyndun venom and a dropper. Just two drops ought to do it. Three, and all her hair might fall out.

Heart rapping a staccato beat against her chest, she carefully dripped two globules of the viscous yellow venom into the bucket-full of watered-down bleach.

A quick prayer to Buthmertha, and then she knelt over the bucket, put on her yellow rubber gloves, and got to work.

A harrowing handful of hours later, wincing in anticipation, she inspected the results in the mirror. The mixture of bleach and venom had done the trick well enough.

The color had come close to platinum. And, thanks to the distilled lethal Hyndun excretions, there was at the front, just above her right eye, a tuft of gas-flame blue.

Tired but too excited to sleep, Alina stared out her window.

It was either very, very late at night or frustratingly early in the morning, depending on how she might decide to think of the dark purple sky, overlaid with a yellowish haze of light pollution.

Using her phone, she purchased her ticket for the earliest bus to Gladjaw Junction. From there, she could get a train ticket to New El.

She had three hours to get to the bus stop. All that was left was to pack.

She returned to her cardboard bed, where she'd laid out the umber jacket Calthin had made for her. She uncrossed the arms and stared at it. It still smelled like the Amming family shop: chemical-cleaned nylon; the metallic tang of zippers and buttons; rubbing alcohol, for when Calthin snagged the pads of his fingers with his shears.

Into the pockets she stuffed some essentials. Rolls of bandages, cobalt lipstick, the last scraps of change she had to her name.

Then, one by one, she unclipped three of the six special clasps Calthin had sewn into the inside of the jacket. She only needed three, for now, given what she would be using them for—storing her Auggies.

The human body could only do so much. There had always been as many limits on its capabilities as there were leaves in a forest. Certain types of training could push back those limitations. There were stories of shamans who could punch through solid walls of ice, of cornered parents summoning unearthly, raging strength in defense of their children… Aelfraver schools tended to focus on power and endurance. An integral part of all serious programs, learning to channel Niima more efficiently, automatically enhanced the natural powers of the body. If you had Niima and could control it as easily as you could your breathing, you would achieve feats of strength and speed *far* beyond what the average human being could hope to match.

It boiled down to the whole "union of body, mind, and soul" deal. Feeding one part of your self over the others created an imbalance, which resulted in suffering and (in combat) defeat. If, however, you cultivated all three facets of our being equally, if you found harmony within your self, your natural human limitations would shrink away. Leaving only *you* and your power.

Most humans could find that balancing point, if they tried hard enough and were diligent in their practice. But even that level of commitment was hardly good enough to be an Aelraver. To survive in that line of work, you had to be *more.*

More significant enhancements could be manifested through the use of magic. There were, for example, spells to increase one's stamina, power, persuasiveness, awareness, and many other abilities. Even magic that could bend or stretch time itself could be mastered, given the right teacher. Magic being "the creation of miracles through force of will" according to arcane scholars working out of The Gild, it of course could propel human mages far beyond their peers.

For some, however, the years of practice and study needed to master any of the spells that could alter a person's body were too much of an inconvenience. They wanted results *now.* In search of shortcuts, they turned to Ability Augmentative Elixirs—"Auggies" or "Licksies" for short.

Dimas had been a master brewer of such concoctions. He'd even invented several of his own. Their creation was one of the many talents that had made him famous.

Alina hadn't yet figured out the trick. To say nothing of lacking the funds for the ingredients.

Luckily, her grandfather had left behind a few, and she'd used them as needed.

She had only three left, which she now laid out on the bed, taking stock.

1. *Chymaeric fortissimio.* "Bull's Blood." Chug the whole vial or nothing happens. Uses up all your body's stored adrenaline, borrowing some from the next several days as needed. Long story short: punch through walls today, sleep for a week starting tonight.

2. *Calchonarine tufelis-scrofa.* "Hogsnout." Smell down to the minutest detail. Can be used to scent the lay of the land, or to track a particular target. We're talking not only the easy stuff, like what deodorant they wear, but also the subtlest traces of powder or food stains on their clothing or what factory the threads originally came from. Particularly strong blends of this Augment could even help the drinker *smell memories and emotions.*

3. *Mafflam Impesignis.* Street-name, "Fyrevein." Exceedingly rare—partly because the main ingredient is Shadowwing ichor—this potion doubles both one's Niima and physical stamina. For a brief three hours. Then, the inevitable and joint-searing crash. This Auggie wasn't named for its intended effects so much as its

hangover—the burning is intense. Like flushing your arteries with boiling water.

Sliding the bottles into the pouches made especially for them, she clicked the metal clasps together, locking the precious potions in place.

With any luck, she wouldn't have to use even one of these. And, when she was filthy rich, rich beyond all reckoning, she'd hire a team of the cleverest alchemists to teach her how to make more on her own.

She put the jacket on, carefully, then flipped the hood up over her head. She took one last look around the place, making sure she hadn't forgotten anything.

She'd been about to wash her face with the bleach water but stopped herself. She poured the smelly stuff down the kitchen sink.

Next, she checked all the doors and windows, the cold fireplace, the empty fridge. Dark, dank, and depressing. All was in order.

Waiting by the front door, backpack dangling from her fingertips, she was stalling again.

Eventually she worked up the nerve to open the door, take one last look around, and sigh.

She snatched her keys off the hanging hook, closed the door behind her, and remembered not to lock it. So Calthin could get in later.

She kissed the little rubber cat's head keychain for luck, and crept downstairs, down the hallway, and over the Qamasques' welcome mat.

5

IT WAS DARK BUT FOR the harsh purple-tinged white glare of the street lamps. The only people out and about at this wretched hour in the morning were the few most dedicated commuters, those who endured day after day of hour-each-ways. And then there was Alina.

As she made her way to the Kipsalis Interchange bus station, she couldn't help but notice the weird looks shot her way by random people on the street. Self-consciously, she ran her fingers through her now much shorter and brighter hair.

She stopped in front of a closed shop, nervously examining her reflection in the smudged display window. Contrasting with her skin, her bleached hair drank the glow of the streetlamp, and the tuft of acidic blue appeared almost neon. Still in Truct, she was drawing the attention of randos on the street, but this *loud* hairdo should actually help her blend once she arrived in the Capital. If her magazines hadn't lied to her, that is. Well, too late to worry about that now.

She winded along Tillicus Road toward Kipsalis. Where she could throw away another huge chunk of her meager savings.

She did her best to ignore the few stares, but, from the back of her mind there still came that nasty little voice that stirred up doubt and fear because it never had anything better to do. It told her, *They're staring because they know you're an imposter. You may have the I'm Somebody hair—a pale imitation of it, anyway—but you're dressed in rags. Everyone down here knows what you really are. And everyone up there will know it, too.*

Alina shrugged off the useless criticism. She'd never before quit anything she'd started in earnest. This time would be no different.

Kipsalis Interchange lay just ahead. It was a run-down, sad commuter station, made all the dumpier by the shabbiness of Truct all around it and the backdrop of the jagged, hooked peak of Mount Morbin. The only reason people came here was to leave as quickly as possible. It was a stepping stone on the road, one covered in unidentifiable filth you'd rather not put your foot in.

The automatic doors caught on a mop handle resting beside a discarded plastic tub of cleaning fluid. Alina squeezed through the narrow opening, her damp feet squeaking on the grungy brown-tiled floor.

The interior of the Kipsalis Interchange was wide and open. At its opposite end, under the malfunctioning digital clock and lists of arrival and departure times, were a series of booths for ticket sellers. Only one of them was occupied.

The nasally voiced, spade-chinned clerk behind the glass informed Alina that a one-way trip to The Capital would cost no fewer than twenty-five gelders. That price included the shuttle to the train and the train ride itself. But there'd be no meal service (not even a bag of tree nuts) or onboard entertainment. And there was a bag checking fee. And a customs fee at the end of it all. Even though she wouldn't be declaring anything on arrival. That's economy class for you.

As she forked over the twenty-five gelders, she mumbled, "Highway robbery."

She turned right and hustled, making for the actual curbside bus stop, behind the building. Throwing open a cracked glass door by its sticky steel handle, she stepped into a long tunnel.

Ahead, a surly custodian with floppy ears and a bulbous, veiny nose shuffled some dirt around with his broom. (The maintenance bots at this lowly outlying transportation node—far away from any major hub—had long since broken down. Here, manual labor was once again performed by humans.) Alina avoided his eye as she passed.

They were alone in that hallway with the flickering lights. Crud-smeared white tiles lined the lowest three feet of the walls to either side. Loose wires hung low like tree-slithering boas. Alina picked up her pace.

The custodian called after her, "'Ey! Where do you think you're goin', girl?"

She kept moving, stared straight ahead at the literal light at the end of the tunnel.

"Girl!" He was chasing her now. His flat-footed steps slapping the floor behind her. Gaining. "Girl! 'Ey! You!" Raggedy breaths as he closed in on her. She was about to break into a run when he said, "You headin' to the buses?"

She turned. Stunned, she couldn't answer with anything more than a nod.

He jerked a thumb over his shoulder. "That way. This here tunnel leads to Millingen Street."

"Oh. Uh, well. Thanks. Thanks so much," she said as she spun on her heels, feeling just a scooch silly. These stupid signs were too confusing.

Shaking her head, she went back the way she'd come, back into the main open area.

Eventually, she found the right curb. "Bronze line to Gladjaw Junction," she read on the old-fashioned sliding letter display hanging from a nearby post.

Her nose and the tips of her ears stung in the cold pre-dawn air. She tapped her feet against her pantlegs, shuffled in place, paced around.

The bus pulled up nine minutes late, by which point she was shivering. Toes numb, she wobbled up the three steps onto the shuttlebus, slapping her holo-ticket onto the machine to the driver's right. A click and mechanical whir followed.

She hesitated.

"Alright, alright," the driver said, scowling. His hand shot up from the steering wheel to flick a few switches on the overhead console, revealing a sleeve of tribal tattoos on his pale arm. "You're good, lady. Move on back."

She wedged herself and her bag into the back-right corner of the shuttle. The warning signs ordered her to stow her luggage in the overhead racks, but she wasn't about all that. She tucked the bag under her legs, wrapping the strap around her wrist (so she'd immediately jolt awake if someone tried a snatch-and-grab). And she figured now would be the time to get a little shut-eye, given that this nocturnal shuttle ride was projected to last three hours. Despite only covering several dozen miles. Blame the ancient fleet of buses that should have been retired years ago. They still ran on oil and used an internal combustion engine. The decades-old hand-me-downs from distant and much wealthier provinces.

Oil. Alina chuckled sleepily: she had willingly put herself in a vehicle that basically worked by exploding over and over again. That was how it was *supposed* to function. Yeah, she felt totally safe.

Having charged her phone a little at the bus station earlier, she allowed herself the luxury of a listen to her favorite band's best song: *Moon-ka-Blammo* off the album *Howling Mad* by *Billie and the Werewolf.* Unlike most of the cultural icons and artifacts Alina approved of, *BillieWere* was now popular. As in, Pop Music. They'd recently hit the big leagues, appearing on talk shows and doing radio spots. Massive sellouts. But their first album was still awesome, still raw. (Alina occasionally listened to the new stuff, justifying her guilty pleasure with the statement, "I liked them before they were cool." Her tested-and-true fandom had to be worth at least a little more than the mindless horde of Howlbots who'd begun following the band in the last two years. Idiots wearing the shirt even though none of them have heard *BillieWere*'s best work. *Dumb official fanclub is dumb.*)

The bus idled. Over the course of the next half hour, a half-dozen passengers embarked. All of them looked like serious businessmen and women headed for Puurissei, the closest city. A killer commute—two hours each way by bus—but economic opportunity had left Truct to eat its dust. The only career that could truly buy you food *and* security was that of programmer for one of the tech giants, some of which had subsidiary companies in Puurissei (because of the better tax rates). Most of the people on this bus, however, were more than likely laborers for those same companies. They'd be working long hours in the dangerous field of robotics repair and testing. The city's slogan might as well have been, "Well, We've Had A Handful Fewer Workplace Accidents This Year, So That's Nice!"

The bus driver dragged himself from his seat and lumbered outside, where he made one final check for discarded luggage or last-minute passengers. Finding neither, he got back in, rubbed his hands together, and cranked the heat up.

In the way that only public transportation servicepeople can, he spoke into the onboard communications system a long string of gibberish syllables. When Alina caught the words "Gladjaw Junction," she leaned back, closed her eyes, and was out within minutes.

She opened her eyes. The bus was dark, totally dark. She couldn't see the other passengers. Even the windows showed only solid black nothingness.

"Must be a tunnel," she mumbled sleepily. But something felt off.

The bus was moving; she could tell by the occasional lurch and shift of the huge undercarriage. But there was no sound. None whatsoever. As if it had all been swallowed up together with the light.

We're under attack, she thought, sinking lower into her seat. An Aelf must have found its way onboard. She had to catch and neutralize it.

The idea was driven from her head as she became aware of a soft rasping sound, like fingernails over sandpaper. *Scritch-scratch*, *scritch-scratch*, again and again, evenly, calmly. It was breathing, she realized. Ragged breaths in the near-silence.

A figure rose from one of the seats. A blob of shadow detaching itself. Inching forward. The breathing intensified, grew frantic.

Alina's own breath caught in her throat as the figure turned. She couldn't move.

All the details of its form and face crashed into her, all at once, and she couldn't focus on any one part without drowning in the whole. Midnight-colored cloak, silver-gloved hands reaching out from its folds. Black mask, half hidden behind hair that hung like stringy gray moss from tree branches. One golden eye, a slit of a pupil in its center. The eye fixated on Alina.

The figure advanced. The only sounds in the bus were its rasping, rapid-fire breaths, and the *swish-swish* of its cloak. Its arm was raised, silver fingers twitching as if it wanted to telekinetically choke Alina.

A mere foot in front of her now, it halted.

Its silver finger pointed at her. It leaned in, then, and said, "Go home, Alina K'vich."

6

ALINA TUMBLED OUT OF her seat and onto the ribbed rubber floor of the bus. She glanced around her. Two of her fellow passengers were gawking at her, one of them laughing. But she could feel only relief. Relief that the ghostly dream or vision was over.

It was still dark outside, but just your normal, everyday dark of early morning. And there were lights on in the bus. Everyone appeared perfectly, happily bored, undisturbed. Alive and well. No sign of the black-masked figure.

She took a few deep breaths to calm her racing heart.

The screech of the intercom system spooked her, and she yelped, then laughed out loud at her jumpiness as the driver announced, "Last stop, Gladjaw Junction. This is your connection to all inter-province and Capital-bound trains. End of the line, and end of my shift. So, if you don't want to spend the next four hours at the nearest dive bar watching me drink myself to sleep, now's your last chance to escape."

Groggy and off-balance, she stumbled to the front of the bus. She was the last to disembark. As she did, she turned to thank the driver out of habit. He cracked open a bottle filled with clear liquid that smelled like fire, ignoring her.

Outside, the sting of the chill air was lessened by the three walls of the shuttle bay. Behind the bus, Alina could see the sky was lightening to a rotten lime blue-green hue. Dawn was near.

Pulling out her phone, she confirmed the time—5:30 am. Her train was scheduled to depart in only ten minutes. An overhead projection of arrivals and departures confirmed this for her. Apparently, she needed to get to the Erovin terminal. Wherever that was.

Huffing and puffing in the cold, her bag slapping her thigh as her shoes pounded the pavement, she marched along the concrete walkway toward the center of Gladjaw Junction—a massive glass dome with fang-like steel spikes of varying length rising along its circumference. Then she saw the lights, a flash of white dots darting at a steep diagonal upward into the sky until they disappeared from view. They illuminated the tracks that linked New El, a.k.a. The Capital, with the territories below. These tracks were built into three ancient chains—Libra, Concordia, and Consortio—each link half as tall as a skyscraper. Over the centuries since their creation, the links had caught and collected dirt, trash, and other junk in their pockmarks and dents; grass, shrubs, and even some small trees jutted out in places on the lower-altitude sections of the chains.

Alina wished she had even a moment to spare to admire the view, but a wall-mounted screen chimed and announced that, "*The 5:40 a.m. to Mercy's Approach*" would be "*leaving soon.*"

She broke into a jog.

Soon enough, she came to sliding glass doors in front of which stood two watchers. They were statues, larger than life, depicting huge muscled men each holding up the severed head of a long-faced, pointy-eared humanoid with flame-like hair—Iorians, a type of sentient humanoid Aelf. The message these silent watchers proclaimed was clear as the grizzly expressions on their trophies' faces: "humans only." The statues were a clear reminder of why Alina despised history so much; the more closely you read the histories of humankind, the more clearly you understood that all stories were written in blood. She dashed right past the watchers without a third glance.

The glass doors parted before her and… there was a line. A really long one. A team of uniformed gloomy-eyed men and women wearing stun batons at their hips were checking bags and asking pointed questions. Lots of people were upset, barking at one another.

Alina glowered at the back of the head of the last person in line. Wasn't that guy's fault or anything, but she sure hadn't thought there'd be so many fools heading to The Capital this early in the morning. *Oops.* She decided to blame the late bus. For all the good it did her.

From the back of the snaking line, she did a quick head-count. A hundred people, at least.

Yep, she was going to miss her train.

Of course, to *save money*, she'd bought a non-transferable, non-refundable ticket.

She slumped at the shoulders. Her bag thumped against the mauve and cobalt mosaic floor as she made a noise somewhere between a sniffle and a snort.

Looking up in disgust, she saw a man dressed in a smart gray suit with a sword strapped to his back waltz right up to the security checkpoint. There, he flashed a badge, exchanged a few words with a station employee, and was ushered through. A chorus of boos from everyone waiting behind the checkpoint chased after him, but he took no notice.

Was the sword purely ornamental, Alina wondered, or was he some movie extra on the way to shoot an action scene? Because only in blockbusters and VR games would anyone stick a sword on his back.

Actually, there was one other possibility Alina could think of: the Aelfravers who wielded *bulanotza* (specialized shortswords). She squinted at the man's weapon as he marched off, noting that it measured roughly three quarters of the length of his arms, and the scabbard was made of steel and segmented. Her smirk at the man's ridiculous style-over-substance getup abruptly shifted to awe. Her guess had been correct: that sword of his was designed for fighting *góra'cień*—flying carnivorous Aelf—*while climbing sheer rock*. His scabbard was built to fire the weapon ten feet into the air so that he could leap up and catch it, at the end of the jump delivering a fatal blow, severing his opponent's spine at the base of its skull. Again, while scaling or rappelling down a *cliff.*

Seeing that weapon had Alina wondering if the dude was genuinely hoping to parkour and climb-fight in The Capital?

More importantly in this moment, he—an Aelfraver—had cut to the front of the line. Did he have some special privilege, or could she do the same?

Plucking her forged license from its designated pocket in her bag, with as much false confidence and determination as she could summon, she strode up to the security team. Pretty much everyone in line had murder in their hearts as they hissed at her, but she cut ahead of all of them anyway. The security guard nearest her yawned as she held out the little piece of laminated plastic that proclaimed to the world her status as a "Journeyman in Good Standing with The Gild." She nearly had a heart attack as the Public Transit Enforcer glowered at her ID. Then he yawned again, and she relaxed.

He said, "Your business in The Capital?"

That little voice called "self-doubt," that uniquely human blessing and curse, cackled from the depths of her mind, saying, *They're going to figure you out. They'll see you for the imposter you are. Hopefully there's not some secret password you don't know about. You'll be arrested.*

Alina told the PTE, "The bounty. The big one, from the Plutocrats. I'm here to throw my hat in the ring."

The enforcer looked at her critically and smirked. "You are, huh? Well, *good luck* with that." He returned her fake license.

Alina briefly considered asking the jerk for directions. Instead, she followed the swordsman. At a discreet distance.

Now that she felt confident that she was headed in the right direction, she allowed herself a few seconds to take in some of the sights along her path.

It seemed like every region of the world was represented by a food stall: kebabs from Agadur, blood sausage from Glasku, Sicacorian paella… all reminding her of how famished she was. There were shops everywhere, too, selling tiny bottles of fire water, carry-on luggage, books of the non-magical variety (importing spells was double-dare-you illegal). All the merchandise was ridiculously overpriced, of course, but that's the trade-off people had come to expect for the convenience of shopping while they waited.

Every several hundred feet, a redwood, straight and tall, reached up toward the glass ceiling of the dome, four hundred feet above. Alina was interested to know if the redwoods, and the yellow and green fireflies that danced around them, and the grass and flowers and morning dew were all products of illusion or some other kind of magic. Either way, the level of skill was impressive to say the least. She'd have to linger here, study the place more closely, upon her triumphant return from The Capital.

Ahead, the swordsman passed through another gate. It, too, was guarded by statues clutching Aelf heads. One final reminder.

Alina read the holo-text between the statues: *"Erovin terminal. 5:40 a.m. to Mercy's Approach. DEPARTING."*

Now the swordsman broke into a sprint, and, cursing, so did she. The glass doors slid aside for him, then her. There were several trains resting and people milling about, sitting on benches, chatting. One train's engines whirred to life; Alina raced along the platform towards it. The swordsman leapt onto the train just as it began to move. Alina closed the distance to the rear-most door, and the attendant grabbed her by the arm and pulled her up. She slipped inside just as the doors snapped shut.

The attendant, a young woman with short, curly blonde hair, flashed her a smile. "Welcome aboard, miss."

With fumbling fingers, Alina rifled through the contents of her bag. A pang of horror—where had her ticket gone?

Without breaking eye-contact, the attendant said, "Miss, *welcome* aboard."

"Do you not need to see my—"

Still smiling, the attendant said, more firmly, "Go find yourself a seat."

Brow furrowed, Alina glanced back in confusion and found the swordsman there, arms crossed, glaring at her. He'd propped himself up against a corner for a moment, panting.

"Thank you," she stumbled over the words and steadied herself using the handrail as the floor lurched. She rubbed her eyes. She was standing in the small, dark compartment. There were two doors she could take, left or right. She turned back toward the blonde attendant as the swordsman bumped into her. "So, can I just sit anywhere, or…?"

"Lady," he said. He was sweating profusely; his rose gold tinted aviator sunglasses kept slipping down the bridge of his nose. It looked like he'd scuffed the elbows and knees of his immaculate suit during his sprint. "Get yourself to the Econ section and move aside already. Whatever seat you want. Just keep to your kind."

Still smiling congenially, the attendant added, "Yes, you may find your own seat, wherever you prefer. In the Econ cars."

Alina scowled at the sweaty man. To the attendant: "Right, right. Thank you again."

"My pleasure."

"Um."

"Yes?"

"Which way to Economy Class?"

The swordsman slammed his fist against a button to his left (Alina's right) and the door behind her popped open. "In you go."

Suppressing the impulse to light his shoes on fire, Alina mumbled one more "thank you" to the attendant as she squeezed into the cramped car.

Blindingly brilliant, golden light tore through the train. Squinting at the rows of seats, Alina found that nearly all of them were full. Only a handful of empty ones lay toward the center of the car. But she didn't dare ask to scoot by any of the men and women seated on the wings of those rows because, as she readily noticed, they were all Gildsmen. *All* of them. She could tell by the distinctive weaponry they carried—chainwhip, retractable lance, compound bow, scimitar. None of these arms were out in the open, of course, but the bumps in the carry-on bags told Alina everything she needed to know. Even more importantly, however, were the glints in their eyes, the assured curves of their passive smiles or scowls. They were here on a mission, and they were—all of them—sizing each other up. Silently. Just in case.

Everyone had come to claim the grand prize, and no one was going to be let down easy.

Alina suspected she'd have found a very similar situation in the First-Class car. Though there probably would be more champagne and hors d'oeuvres and less obvious hostility. Still, "subtle" didn't mean "safe." "Cloak-and-dagger" still involved an unhealthy amount of "dagger."

Standing at the front of the car, where all eyes could fall on her, she felt utterly naked. All their stares, weighing her, appraising her. She crab-walked down the narrow aisle, steadying her bag with her right hand.

"You in the wrong car, sweetheart?" someone said. As she turned to locate the speaker, she saw only laughing faces.

None of the faces, so far, were familiar. Although, that didn't necessarily mean anything. Her Tahtoh had indeed trained over a hundred prospective Gildsmen in his day, but there were many, many more schools in El that prepared young would-be Ravers for The Gild exams.

Living with Dimas, Alina's childhood had been colored by a number of interesting and damaged people. If, by some fluke, any of them happened to be here, all she could hope was that none of them would recognize her. The last thing she needed was to be harassed with more questions about her Tahtoh's disappearance.

After a lengthy and awkward sideways shuffle, she did spy an aisle seat one row away from the back wall of the car. She hurried toward it, relishing the opportunity to blend once more. Get all these honed Raver-stares off her at last.

About halfway to her intended seat, however, she caught sight of the jackal-faced black mask with the mop of wispy gray hairs hanging from its top. Nestled amid the shadows of that mask, the figure's one golden eye locked with Alina's. Its blue cloak shifted, revealing nothing certain about the body beneath.

Alina tensed.

The figure picked up a magazine, ruffled it, and began to flip through the pages.

Having no idea what to believe concerning the black-masked figure—had she completely imagined that bus encounter? had she been asleep? awake?—Alina found a window seat and fell into it. Maybe her subconscious had keyed into something her over-stressed conscious mind had missed, and she'd had a bizarre nightmare about a person she'd only caught a glimpse of and knew nothing about.

Nerves, nothing more.

She set down her bag. Moments later, she gasped with relief, having found her ticket tucked it into an inner pocket of the bag. She clutched it in white-knuckled, trembling fingers.

Nerves.

Her phone buzzed. A text message from Rooster.

> Dearest M'lady, thank you ever so for your good patronage. I was charmed to meet you. Mayhap we might do it again someday quite soon? Pray, do say 'Yea!' If you do choose to acquiesce to my humble request, perhaps we could meet for a Real Date next week?

Her skin crawling, on reflex, Alina deleted the message and blocked his number.

A man approached, asking if the seat next to hers was taken. She gestured as if to say, "Be my guest."

The man sat down, pointed to her phone, and asked, "Boyfriend or dad?"

Stowing the device in her bag, and shoving that underneath the seat in front of her, she said, "I'm sorry?"

"In my experience, there are only two people in the world a girl your age could be so disgusted with. The boyfriend or the dad. Ach, maybe the brother, too. So, which one was it texting you?"

"None of the above," she said.

He shrugged. "Ah, well. Can't win them all."

The man was bald, dark-skinned. In his forties, probably. Wore a tanktop and workout slacks. Thin-rimmed dull gray reading glasses sat low on his nose. He was built like a hydraulics press: all steely muscle, no wasted space. Radiating heat. Speaking of hydraulics, embedded in his back (at the shoulder blades) were two football-sized circular implant ports of shiny black metal. Body mods. Were they for utility or combat?

Alina tried not to stare, but something was nagging at her, at the back of her mind. She'd seen this man. In the tabloids? Maybe. On the Watchbox… ? Then it clicked. The black ports on his back. The fact that he was on *this* train.

Even though he looked a lot different than his professional headshots, she knew exactly who this guy was.

"Excuse me."

With his middle and ring fingers, he nudged his spectacles higher up his nose. "Hmm?"

"You're Ugarda Pankrish," she breathed hoarsely. "The Gild Master." She wanted to add, *the man who fights with two bionic arms because his real hands are too powerful, who refuses to kill anything unless it's to save another's life, who would die rather than kill out of self-preservation, my idol,* but she grappled with the words, shoving them back down.

"I gather you're a fan of my work?"

She felt like her cheeks were melting, the goopy flesh pudding sliding down her neck. "It's just amazing to meet you."

"I'm certain the pleasure is mine. But you have me still at somewhat of a disadvantage, miss… ?"

Her mind exploded. She was having a conversation with one of her idols, and she couldn't tell him who she was. Not really. Why? Because Dimas K'vich had trained and elevated Master Pankrish's most bitter rival, the younger man who'd replaced him as the nation's number one Aelfraver and top-ranking Gildsman. She couldn't make an enemy of her hero. Also, there were the small matters of her license being a forgery and her very presence on this train being a crime.

So, instead of gushing along the lines of, *I'm Alina K'vich and I'm, like, totally your biggest fan,* she restrained herself and said only, "Stitcher. I'm Stitcher."

Master Pankrish offered one of his scarred hands, enclosing it around Alina's. They shook.

"Will this be your first time in The Capital, Stitcher?" he asked.

"Yeah. I'm here for the Rave. Which, I'm guessing, you are, too."

"Maybe."

She sighed. "It's going to be really disappointing."

"What's that?"

"When I beat you to the punch. You're a childhood hero of mine. Be a real shame when I show you up."

Pankrish laughed, his glasses wobbling on the bridge of his nose. "I'll do what I can to make bursting that bubble a challenge for you." He pulled from his bag a silken white cloth, and began polishing the lightly scratched lenses of his eye-piece. "You are not my only competition. Stitcher, I'm sure you noticed the car in which we ride is filled with Gildsmen? Any one of them may reach the goal before we do. My reputation counts for little, these days. The odds are not in my favor. It will be a melee, once we are set loose.

"Remember, you will need to treat these peers of ours as obstacles, not allies. It is in their nature to try to thwart—perhaps even harm—you. These people are not your friends."

"You're telling me."

"You understand me, I think. Because we are all here, together in our isolation, charging in, there is no single one of us you need to fear. Fear the whole, not the individual. Unless." He tapped his chin with a forefinger. "Do you have any enemies? Someone with good cause for vendetta against you?"

Alina pursed her lips thoughtfully while Pankrish looked on, amused. "Nope," she said. "Not that I can think of."

"That's a start." The Master removed his spectacles, setting them inside their case with his thumb and pinky finger. Turning back to Alina, he pointed at the window and said, "You may want to risk a glance, Stitcher. This is my favorite part." The tip of her nose brushed the glass as he said, "Cloud-break."

Alina watched the earth recede: grassy plains, snaking black roads, gray-white clusters of homes and businesses, shrinking away, shrinking… Then, a burst of white that filled her vision, causing her to squint.

"Keep watching," said Pankrish. "Look up. Here it comes." He pointed a dark finger in the direction toward which the train sped.

The clouds parted, torn asunder by the risen sun. And there it was: New El, city of eight million souls, a sphere of rock, skyscrapers spearing outward in every direction from its center, and, somehow, it floated in the heavens with all the effort of a suspended speck of dust. There were no engines, no turbines—the city flew by no conventional means, and yet fly it did. New El, The Capital of the Nation of El, had graced the skies—serene, still—for three and a half thousand years. The greatest, most powerful mystery in the world. Certainly, the greatest mystery hiding in plain sight; the eight million elite Assets who called The Capital home had no concept of how this miracle had been accomplished. They didn't need to know. For them, it was enough to build, buy, sell, trade, and backstab from the safety—the untouchable security—provided by their world-in-miniature.

"And, to think," said Pankrish, his voice only slightly louder than the hum of the engines beneath them, "those millions are now gripped in terror, an Aelf lurking among them. The creature must be quite formidable, to thwart capture by drones, soldiers, all the powers of The Authority, and—" his tone went sour—"The Sanctum."

Alina said, "The Sanctum? The cult, you mean? What do they have to do with anything?"

"Let's just say that if you *never* come across one of them, it will still be too soon."

"I'm gonna go out on a limb and guess that you're not one of the Faithful, Master Pankrish."

He narrowed his eyes. "Are you?"

"No. Don't know much about them. My grandfather wasn't too impressed by The Big Question. He used to say, 'What do I care for what happens after I'm gone? I'm far too busy.' No, gods are just a jumbo-sized question mark to me."

Pankrish appeared relieved. "Barbarians, all of them."

"I believe you," said Alina diplomatically, "but what makes you think so?"

"The Sanctum propagates a most damning fad of a belief: 'magic is a sin; monsters are the punishment.' They would have you scrape and bow to them while they tell you the Aelf are mere mindless beasts, instruments of torture sent down by their demented god. Stitcher, how long have you been an Aelfraver?"

"Three years?" she lied.

"Don't be ashamed to state that fact proudly; you've a thousand times the experience with the Aelf than most will ever have. Tell me, in your three years of Raving, have you found the Aelf to be mindless beasts?"

The answer seemed so obvious to her that it felt like a trick. "Depends on the type of Aelf. There are lots."

"Precisely. There are the bestial ones, those driven purely by primal instinct."

Alina mentally ran through a dozen such varieties: *mil'ig, k'ethr'o, Katy-tear…*

"Then, as we know, there are the Mythidim and other sentients. The Ushum are intelligent for the most part, but there are exceptions. And, of course, at the top sit the dangerously cunning Demidivines."

Vassylbrundir, Schildkrahe, Sevensin—

Master Pankrish continued, "The Sanctumites paint the world in black and white. Naturally, they consider themselves white, pure, *good*; everything and everyone else is black, evil, *unclean*. They desire that all humans kneel before their god or face the 'monstrous' Aelf. But you and I both know the Aelf are far too varied and complex to fit into such backward philosophies." He paused. "In the coming days, we will certainly not be dealing with a lowly, hungry animal. No." He raised a calloused finger. "Were I a gambling man, I'd wager we are about to be set on the trail of something very clever indeed. Cleverer than most humans. No mindless beast could blanket New El in such palpable terror. Nor could it be so elusive and terrifying." Sighing, he concluded, "One thing I know for certain: no part of this mess has anything to do with the gods. The Sanctumites' dogma will be the death of many fools."

At the end of Pankrish's monologue, Alina was stuck on one particular point. *Cleverer than most humans*. She shuddered. *Elusive. Terrifying.* She wasn't ready for this!

But she'd come too far. She'd gambled everything. Couldn't turn away now. Forget it. She crushed her inner urge to shrivel up and crawl back home.

Then, the pressure in her skull mounting, the other side of her slipped in a cruel reminder: the last time she'd tangled with a powerful Aelf, she'd been on the ropes. Osesoc-ex'calea, the Hubris demon, the one she'd "trapped" in that fragile little algorithmic prison, had *almost* gotten the best of her. (Still could, if it escaped). And that demon was merely a pest compared to the challenge of a Colossi or an Ushum. She could forget about besting a Demidivine.

The prospect of embarrassment, total failure. Building up to her untimely death. Pressure behind her eyes, pinching the bridge of her nose. That pressure continued to rise until her skull felt ready to pop, and—

She burst out laughing.

Pankrish's stern and solemn expression shifted to curiosity. "Hmm?"

"It—it's nothing." Alina waved her hand between them as her eyes teared up and she ran out of breath. "Nothing. I just—" Regaining her composure: "I just thought of a joke, is all. What do you call a personal communication device you've trapped a demon inside? A *Cell* Phone."

Master Pankrish's polite smile dampened her mood. "I'm afraid I missed the meaning. What's this about demons?"

"Nevermind."

Wafting melodiously through the speakers built into the walls of the train, an automated female voice said, *"We are nearing our approach of New El. Estimated arrival time: seven minutes. Please take a moment to locate and secure your belongings. Please do remain in your seats until the train has reached a full stop. Thank you."*

Almost there.

Her knee shaking, Alina pulled out her phone and closed any incriminating or embarrassing browsers and apps she might have left open (there were only three). She said, "Master Pankrish, would you mind if I snapped a shot of the two of us? Hope that's not inappropriate and whatnot, but my friend will never believe me unless I have photographic evidence."

He nodded graciously, and she held out her arm, leaning in a little as she did. A dozen rapid-fire pics later and she put the phone away again. "Thank you," she said.

They shook hands once more.

"Always a pleasure," he said, sitting up, "to meet a fellow Aelfraver." The next part he shouted, so the whole car-full of Ravers could hear: "And may the best of us win."

Most of the occupants of that cramped car practically flew out of their seats, kicking and punching the air, hollering at one another.

"Rowdy children," said Pankrish, but excitement twinkled in the corner of his eye.

At Pankrish's suggestion, Alina peeked out the window again, watching with awe as the train passed into the shadow of Nebuzar's Arch. Great goliaths of glass and blue steel. The occasional hanging garden or terrace nursery. Men and women in flowing white and tan robes, their thousand-gelder hairstyles—long and black, curly and red, glimmering—billowing in the wind.

"The leisured elite," said Pankrish, his bespectacled eyes fixated on his newspaper again.

So, this was Mercy's Approach. She'd made it.

The only thing left was to clear the customs inspection.

Soon enough, the train glided up the length of the great chain Consortio and passed into the monolithic shadow of the underbelly of New El.

After three musical chimes, the same automated voice announced their arrival in *"New El, Esperant District, Mercy's Approach Station. All Assets are hereby reminded that non-cooperation with The Authority is a capital offense. Enjoy your stay."*

Before the train had even pulled into the station, the early-standers reached up and snatched their luggage. They eyed each other. Their hands slipped into pockets, folds of their jackets, compartments in their bags—weapons at the ready. With all the time Ravers spent on the road, travelling alone, trying to beat each other to the decent-paying bounties, they were not naturally trusting. Especially of each other.

A little *ding-ding* from the speakers indicated that the train had come to a full stop. Moments later, a rush of air that meant the doors had opened. The early-standers were already halfway outside by the time Alina even thought of getting up.

All around her, the other Ravers had leapt to their feet, yanking their bags and gear from the overhead and under-seat compartments. The exception was Pankrish, whose jaw cracked as he yawned against the hairy back of his hand. The Ravers rushed, nudging and sometimes shoving each other forward. Within thirty seconds, the train car was nearly empty.

She froze, though, when she caught sight of the black-masked figure—whom she decided to call Mophead for lack of a better name—rise phantom-like from its seat. No bags, no belongings. Its head twisted without warning, turning nearly one-hundred and eighty degrees. Like a one-eyed owl, it glared at Alina. Then it walked down the aisle. No, it definitely wasn't floating. It *walked*, only its footsteps made no sound.

"Friend of yours?" asked Pankrish.

Alina shook her head. "Oh!" She realized she was blocking him from getting up. "Sorry."

He smiled kindly.

She said, "Do you know who that was?"

"Were I you, I'd be more concerned about my own mask, Alina K'vich."

She watched Mophead exit the train, and then her brain finished processing what Pankrish had just called her. She said, "Uh, who?"

Slinging the long strap of his bag over his broad chest, Pankrish inclined his head. "Alina K'vich. You're Dimas's granddaughter. No, please. There is no reason for you to explain. We all have our games. How else could our profession endure? I can understand why you might have wanted to hide your identity while in The Capital. In fact, I recommend you keep doing so. Your grandfather was never short on enemies. But, if I may, a friendly caution: only lie when you know you can get away with it, and make friends who can protect you when your falsehoods fail."

Alina felt nauseous. "How did you know?"

"I'd recognize your grandfather's blood anywhere." His spectacles case disappeared in his pants pocket. "And I'm not the only one. Be on your guard."

"Uh…" Alina's mouth hung open.

Pankrish calmly got to his feet, dragged his palm over his eighth-of-an-inch hair, and slung his shoulder bag's strap around his neck. He smiled pleasantly. "Excuse me." He shuffled his gargantuan bulk past her and ambled down the aisle. A few paces away, he turned. "Are you coming, *Stitcher*?" He stepped out of view. Into the light.

The same smiling curly-haired attendant form before stood at the end of the aisle, ushering her forward. "Miss? This way."

She and the attendant were the only two people in the car now. Maybe the only two on the train.

Her face flushing, Alina stamped her way along the grimy Economy Class carpet.

If she couldn't keep her identity secret for forty-five minutes, how could she expect to survive the coming *days*? Granted, the man who'd seen through her ruse had been none other than Ugarda Pankrish, a living *legend*. By Buthmertha, hopefully the average person wouldn't be so very perceptive.

Turning sharply to her left, avoiding the smiling get-the-hells-off-already stare of the attendant, she hopped over the gap and onto the platform of Mercy's Approach, New El.

Alina entered the sky.

7

HER LANDING JARRED HER stiff knees.

The train at her back, she gazed out at the cathedral-like structure of Mercy's Approach with its stained glass windows and tall statues of unnaturally, perfectly proportioned men and women—heroic figures swathed in the multicolored coats of arms of the Twelve Families.

Most of the Ravers, despite having tripped over each other to be the first one off the train, were clustered within a few feet of it. About two seconds passed before Alina understood why.

She frowned at the hunters around her and took a breath—but something was wrong. Reflexively, she slapped her palm to her chest.

She couldn't breathe.

Dragged in breath after rushed and shallow breath, she felt none of the relief that followed taking in oxygen. It wasn't like the air was catching in her throat; she could feel her lungs expanding, at least somewhat. But, rather than filling her, each breath seemed to hollow her out.

A panicked glance at the other Aelfravers showed her how she herself must have looked, doubled over, clutching her throat, panting. Some were better off than she was, sweating, gritting their teeth, but standing upright; others seemed worse for wear, a couple of them having dropped to their knees. One man—a burly, hairless-chested man with a greasy combover who carried a mace—had fallen prone. He was unconscious.

Beside Alina again, Ugarda Pankrish told her, "Stitcher, look at me. It's difficult, I know, but try to relax. This is normal. You've left the pressurized cabin of the train, and you're not acclimated to the thin air up here. Give it time. Nothing is wrong. Everything is fine. Breathe. Slowly. Good. There you are; steady." He flung his bare, muscled arm out to indicate the crowd of gasping surface-dwellers. "This is what happens to those who rush in without thinking. Remember the lesson. And, if you suffer from vertigo as I do, try not to look up." He inclined his head. "Good day, Stitcher. A pleasure meeting you."

"Good…bye…" Alina wheezed, giving a shaky thumbs up. "Huge… fan."

He smiled sympathetically, giving her shoulder a quick pat, and he walked off.

Despite her respect for that man, Alina seethed in his direction: he moved with such ease there might as well have been a skip to his step.

She slid down to a seated position, straight-backed, leaning against a pillar, and she focused on her breathing.

Yet another barrier to entry into The Capital! Almost like getting into New El was *supposed* to be difficult for a Terrie on every conceivable level. Alina stifled a laugh. Good thing she did, too. If she had so much as chuckled just then, she might have passed out.

Then, to make matters worse, contrary to Pankrish's advice, she made the mistake of looking up.

Well, "up" was relative. She used to think of El as "up." Now, standing on it, she lifted her gaze and caught, through the clouds, a glimpse or two of the purple peaks of Mt. Morbin and a few of the taller skyscrapers of Puurissei. They jabbed toward her accusingly—toward her, from the sky.

Up was now down, and down up.

Alina's mind tried to rationalize what she was seeing, but when she watched a passenger plane fly by—from her perspective, upside-down—she clamped her eyelids shut and continued to devote all her attention to hyperventilating.

A small number of minutes passed—maybe six to ten—before the waves of panic subsided and she was able to feel some amount of oxygen reaching her lungs. During that time, she watched several of the other Ravers get up and shove off. However, when she stood up, she noted that she'd pulled herself together faster than a little under half of them. Whether she should feel proud of that or not, she lifted her nose as she left the pale, cold-sweat-drenched, swearing Ravers behind.

The shadows cast by the buttresses, spires, and columns of Mercy's Approach were sliced to bits by daggers of rainbow light, refracted by the station's stained glass windows.

Scowling at Alina, hundreds of gargoyles—thin, gangly monstrosities—were locked in motionless, eternal struggle with proud, angelic-featured humans wielding swords and spears. The marble champions gazed down upon all who entered, their dead pupil-less eyes boring into the souls of the living. The weight of their judgment could be felt across the ages.

(The architects of this building had clearly had no use for subtlety. Every detail served as a reminder that New El had been baptized in the blood of the Aelf.)

Upon the station's central twelve-sided tower hung an outward-facing clock. Its minute and hour hands were a polished dragon's fang and claw, respectively. Though not of one of the Twin Dragons, the sight was still impressively morbid—another reminder to all of the fury of ancient humanity. A fury whose embers still smoldered, awaiting fuel.

With a host of other Ravers and civilians, earth- and sky-dwellers alike, Alina marched through the automatic sliding-glass doors into the station. She looked up and gasped.

Hanging from steel cables, suspended from the ceiling, were the fully assembled remains of a dragon. It was *huge*. Its segmented exoskeleton, arranged in a menacing stance, as if ready to pounce. Every black and smooth inch had been polished, gleaming in the crisp light of the risen autumn sun. Its insectoid wings, Alina noticed, were replicas—good ones, of course, but she still caught the polymer-glimmer that gave them away. Plastic.

Alina's progress was halted; she hit the end of a long, long line.

She tracked her progress using her position beneath the long-dead dragon as a guide. As she shuffled forward, inch by inch, she wondered what its name had been, where it had hunted, how many centuries it had lived—whether it had been killed in battle or stalked and butchered during its final multi-year hibernation.

Such a slow line.

A man in a black uniform worked his way through the waiting travelers, passing out clipboards, declaration forms, and pens.

Pen and paper. How retro.

As Alina took in the scarred, wildly eclectic mass of battle-hardened warriors and mages, she supposed holopads would be a bit too pricey to entrust to this particular crowd.

She inched forward. One inch per five minutes.

Ugh, customs. Unavoidable. She'd known it, right from the start. And here she was, ready to face down a full-body search, bag inspection, and any other trick these bored officers could think up.

A bubble of acidic nerves burst in her gut. This was it, the moment she'd either make it through, in spite of the odds, or get picked up like a piece of trash and thrown back down to the surface. If all those leaked videos on the Aetherthread were legit, she might even be "detained for further questioning," which was Public Transit Enforcer code for "tortured."

From what she'd heard, the pretexts for "detaining" a suspected "disturber of the peace" got slimmer by the year.

Still, the long line of frustrated Ravers and dull-eyed commuters between her and the agents in their little bullet-proof glass enclosures would probably work in her favor. After inspecting two hundred or more legally armed-to-the-teeth trained killers, anyone would be ready for a break. Hopefully, by the time it was Alina's turn, the PTEs would be daydreaming about an early lunch and forget to look too closely at her very, very fake Raver-X License.

Whenever the pins and needles came, she bounced from foot to foot. She crossed her arms. Uncrossed them. There was a lot of yawning. Her jaw cracked during one of them, and a drop or two of spit dribbled from the corner of her mouth. Immediately covering her face, she checked that no one had seen her shame. And that's when she noticed the girl—maybe ten, eleven—weave between the people in line. Something about the girl's easy, lighthearted step held Alina's eye.

The girl was swaddled in old and ratty man's-clothes. Her short black hair swished, more than a little wig-like, underneath her worn black beret. Her boots flopped back and forth whenever she moved. They must have been a men's size nine. At least three times bigger than her feet. The soles were worn-through.

She'd just finished shining the shoes of some smarmy-looking, silver-haired businessman, packing up her bottles of polish and brushes into her kit, which she slung over her back. Having collected her tip, she'd cut her way into the crowd of waiting people. She'd stopped.

Her expression shifted from *determined* to *frightened with a dash of innocence.* She tapped one of the Ravers in line on the elbow. He shooed her away without turning his head. And then, as the Raver did his best to ignore her, she plucked his wallet from the back pocket of his pants, replacing it with a wad of wrapping paper. The switch had happened so fast that even Alina couldn't be sure she'd really seen it. Maybe she didn't want to believe that anyone could be insane enough to pickpocket an *Aelfraver* in the middle of a military-controlled facility with hundreds of potential witnesses.

The girl's and her eyes met. The girl had the look of a cornered fox—unafraid, ready to fight if needed.

Alina briefly entertained the idea of turning her in. Stealing was bad, after all. That's what you were taught. Knowing and bowing to the law was the foundation of a working society… Yadda-yadda-yadda. Very rarely did you hear about the *other* side of theft, though. Sometimes you just had to take what wasn't yours. Like a few gelders for clothes. A hot mug of coffee on a cold morning. A wheat roll and a bowl of rice.

Maybe it was just the silly-big clothes, but this girl looked too thin. How had she gotten to this point? Was Alina seeing a vision of her own not-too-distant future?

Rarely were the gods kind. They favored those who helped themselves. But that didn't mean Alina needed to go out of her way to help anyone suffer. That wasn't her job. Besides, she had always had a soft spot for *misckies*—small-time criminals of opportunity.

She considered that the nature of her own arrival in New El made her no friend to the Authority. Creating a scene by outing the little sneak-thief would only make it harder for everyone—including Alina—to clear customs.

So, as she and the girl looked at each other through narrowed eyes, Alina gave the kid a smile and beamed some positive energy her way.

The thief slinked off into the shadows. If only Alina could slip in and out of security lines that easily, she'd switch from Aelfraving to robbing banks. On second thought, even the mental image of taking on one of the Plutocracy's monetary strongholds made her queasy. She'd stick to using her sneakiness to play tricks on Cal. Pick locks. Or finally catch a Jittuch before it woke up and disappeared into the ethereal plane (a pretty cool natural defense mechanism).

There were two Ravers in front of her now. Only two. With dread, her heart kicking her in the teeth, she watched the PTEs search each of them, examine their personal effects, ask questions about their professions, where they've been recently, and so on.

Only one more guy between Alina and her inspection.

Her lungs suddenly remembered just how light the air was, and her breaths became even shallower, sweat trickling from her hairline. A sharp itch tingled in her palms, her elbows, the curve of her spine. What if she had unknowingly brought an illegal substance with her? One of the ingredients in her Auggies?

She contained the jitters, attempting to appear perfectly calm. Yes, everything was going to be fine.

Sirens blared.

Well, this was it. Somehow, she'd been pegged for the law-breaker she was. Her last seconds of freedom were slipping away as she stood there, paralyzed.

Five burly security guards wearing black uniforms—the shoulder patches displaying three white stars and a tower, also white—jogged over. They surrounded the Raver directly in front of Alina and wordlessly dragged him away.

Alina held her breath.

The momentary commotion dealt with, the PTE agent standing next to a buzzing, beeping console as tall as she was, barked, "Next."

Exhaling, Alina shakily stepped forward.

The agent beamed a flashlight beam into Alina's eyes before she could blink. (Just checking for *Chernoboggles*. Standard procedure. Probably.)

A type of Liliskur, the lowest brand of non-sentient Aelf, Chernoboggles were mindless night-dwellers. Miniscule, star-shaped, with sucker-mouths, they fed off your dreams. Symptoms of chernoboggle infection included dreamless sleep, waking with a sore throat, and finding little bits of crud in the corners of your eyes. (The Sand Man was a myth; chernoboggles were very real, and difficult to shake once you had an infestation. The only method known to consistently work was gulping three cups of water upside down, your head between your knees.)

Of course, there were many other creatures who left their stamp on the human eye. The PTE could be checking for almost anything, but Alina chose to comfort herself with her original guess. Anything to keep from shivering so violently that she couldn't keep her footing.

"Name?" said the agent.

"Alina K'vich." Feeling a flare of volcanic heat shoot through her entire body, she handed over her Raver-X License.

The agent grunted, combing a loose strand of her hair behind her ear, revealing a twelve-digit serial number embedded in her neck. She tugged on the lip of her cap. "Seventeen. Resident of Truct. Place of birth?"

Noticing, but pretending not to notice the serial number, Alina answered, "Clerica Viridim. I don't remember which hospital."

"Good enough. So, Raver, huh? You carrying any weapons, uh, Alan?"

"Alina," she corrected automatically. Stupid, *stupid.* Why had she done that? Don't give them an excuse to look too closely. "No, no weapons. Just some Auggie—I mean, Augmentative Elixirs, which I declared on, on the form. The one I was given. Here." She produced the slightly scrunched sheet of paper she'd been clutching in her fist. "Oh, well, and I do have this pocketknife."

"That's nothing, don't even worry about that," said the agent, a lazy grin spreading across her tired face. "I'm talking about a Raver weapon." She accepted Alina's form. "You seriously have nothing but that little letter opener with you?"

Alina shrugged. "Um, yeah."

The agent snorted. "*Good luck*. I think I know the answer to this next question, but what are you doing in The Capital, Alina?"

"I, uh, I'm an Aelfraver. Here for the job. Like the rest of them."

"And how long are we planning to stay?"

"Until the job's done?" Alina said, her eyes wandering.

"That's funny. I bet you're a real hoot down in Truct." The agent turned to her left and indicated the white plastic foldout table. "Your carry-on."

"I can carry on?" said Alina, grinning.

The grin disappeared as the agent grumbled, "No, show me your carry-on. Your bag."

"Oh." Alina shuffled forward, pulled the strap over her head, and set her bag on the table.

"Any harmful, dangerous, illegal, or otherwise suspect liquids or other substances today?"

"No."

"And have you come into contact with any Doppelgangers in the past eighteen months?"

"No."

As the agent dragged a purple rubber-gloved hand through ninety percent of Alina's belongings, she said, "Have you or has anyone you know attempted to forge, brand, or otherwise engage in commerce with false currency—known or unknown—in excess of twenty-five gelders? Have you or anyone you know ever bought, sold, or exchanged contraband materials? Have you or anyone you know partaken of illicit substances comprised of more than five percent non-human elements?"

"Uh, no, no, and no," said Alina, not sure she'd understood every aspect of those very specific questions. Though, she was fairly confident she *had* done at least one of the crimes described.

She willed her eyes away from the phony Raver-X License.

The agent noticed the bandages on Alina's arms. "What about those?"

"Battle injury," Alina lied.

There was an uncomfortably long silence as the agent lifted one of Alina's Auggie bottles to the light, twisting it this way and that. The pink gel inside bubbled.

"As you can see," said Alina, because she couldn't stop herself, "the containers are all regulation size and none of them exceed the liquid ounce limit."

The agent frowned at Alina, saying, "Yes, I can see. Thank you for that." A holo-keyboard appeared in front of the agent's eyes. With a drawn-out sigh, she tapped a few keys. The steady stream of radio chatter being fed into her earpiece cut out. And, dropping for a moment her professionally confident aloofness, she told Alina, "Kid, I don't know why I'm bothering to tell you this because it should be so obvious, even to you: this town'll be the death of you. You came on a train full of real, honest-to-goodness killers. They're going to eat you alive. As a concerned fellow Asset, I'm suggesting you seriously consider getting back on that train and going on home."

Her nerves tossed aside in favor of irritation—who did this rando think she was?—Alina shook her head. "Yeah, I can't do that."

The holo-keyboard between them, the agent said quietly, "You're more than a little crazy, aren't you?"

"I'm sure you won't be the last to think so." Before Alina could backpedal, she doubled down: "Thanks for the warning, officer. Now, are we done here? A girl's gotta work."

"Can't say I didn't warn you. I tried." The agent's radio crackled back to life as she waved Alina over the narrow yellow line painted on the floor. The yellow line that separated her from her destination.

It'd only been a day and a half since she'd begun planning for this moment. So much had happened in those thirty hours, though, that it felt like much longer.

Her fraying nerves were probably why she almost burst out laughing when the agent said, in a rehearsed monotone, "Cleared for entry. Welcome to New El, Asset."

8

THE SANCTUM, LIKE GOD, never slept.

Within the man-made Mountain of the Mendicant—hewn of stone imported, at tremendous expense, all the way from the deserts of Kadic—three hundred voices hummed in unison the daily meditation. From their hexagonal cells, their thrumming, guttural, bassy tones gave praise to the One True God, the Author of All Creation, Who Wrote the World and made Mankind His Chosen Instrument.

The thanksgiving complete, three hundred young men and women sat, alone in their spartan cells, to sup on bowls of gruel and a lump of hard black bread. They ate in silence, reflecting on the day's deeds.

Finishing their meals just as the chiming of the sixth bell could be heard, they were free to engage in an hour of the recreational activity of their choosing. Most chose more meditation; some, physical exercise such as pushups, pull ups, and so on. Only a healthy mind and a fit body could serve The Author well.

Clutching his iron quill pendant, Tolomond Stayd sat on his shins in the darkness. Tallow candle wicks crackled and sputtered around him, as if they were spirits whispering to one another. They gave off a faint red light, barely enough to stave off the shadows.

This small alcove was a place of solitude, contemplation, rest. The bare stone floor bit at his bones, but this, too, was something to endure. Pain was a test, a measure of one's readiness. Tolomond had stoically awaited and welcomed new opportunities for pain all his life. Suffering was a product of the mind. Thriving in it marked one for greatness.

His eyes closed, his hands lay open, palms up, on his legs—a supplication, a prayer to the Author of Creation: *Rewrite my story.*

The swish of fabric informed him that someone had entered the alcove.

Before the man even spoke, Tolomond recognized him by the sound of his footsteps—this man walked on the blades of his feet, unevenly, a slight malformation present since his birth. "Disciple Stayd," said the man.

"Brother Tarus," said Tolomond, clenching his fists but otherwise remaining still.

"It's time."

"You have new names for me." It was not a question.

"Three. The last. The Hierophant promises that, with the severing of these snakes' heads, your labors will be complete." Smacking his lips as if tasting something unpleasant: "You'll fully be one of us." His fingers crinkled the parchment scrap in his hands as he approached Tolomond, who still would not face him. "Burn after reading."

Tolomond let that obvious goad slide off his back like bathwater. Of course he knew to do away with the evidence.

Tarus was a small-minded and weak-willed fool, always determining that he knew the mind of the Author better than anyone else. He hated Tolomond, who was humbler than he. *Unlike some others,* Tolomond was wise enough to go where he was needed, to speak only when it was necessary.

Tarus dropped the parchment in Tolomond's lap and, without another word, turned away. Tolomond ran his scarred palms over his clean-shaven head, feeling the ridges of scar tissue fold under his firm touch.

He unrolled the parchment and read the names.

For the first time in years, he felt excited, joyful even. Truly, it was the Author's will that he succeed in his labors, for his mission now set him against true and terrible enemies of everything he held dear. At last. This was justice, pure and unfettered. The laws of men finally gave way to the laws of God.

Rising to his feet, he felt the blood flow to his extremities. He flexed his fingers, stood on his toes. He knelt to claim his greatsword—Rhetoric—caressing its naked clove-oiled blade with love in his heart.

Having committed them to memory, he held his written orders to the candleflame.

He imagined that he could see the real people burning, burning away with their names. And he was glad for it.

9

ALINA HAD JUST TAKEN her first steps out of the transit station and now officially stood on a sidewalk in The Capital.

Towers cut beams of shadow through the fierce glow of the early morning sun. Hovercraft zoomed mere feet in front of her. Eyes spiraling, she tracked the swirling progress of translucent green and pink bubbles as they shot off in clusters, split into wildly different directions, landed on terraces, balconies, and rooftops, and deposited human beings just before popping out of existence. The individuals who'd been dropped off in this way were simply going about their business as if they hadn't just experienced something so beautifully and ridiculously dainty. Was this how Elementals commuted?

Before she could fully process any one aspect, her mind flitted to something else, like a child in a gift shop.

Everywhere there were people. Heavy talkers, covered head to toe with brass bell piercings, so that they jingled with every heavy-set step. Tall, thin women in all-gray one-piece suits, shouting into their earpieces. Dog-walkers clutching the leashes of their r0b0-d0gz, Cyborks, and Holo-mutts. There were even a few real, live, flesh-and-blood canines.

The noise—power tools drilling into pavement, utility workers cursing each other, vendors talking up their street meats—was overpowering. It sent Alina's head spinning.

At the center of her field of vision, though far off, sat the gleaming clockface of City Hall, the world's largest bank. The clock's hands were said to be made of solid gold. But that couldn't be true—they'd be far too weak, and there surely wasn't enough gold in the world to justify that much waste.

But maybe the gaudiness, the glamor was the point. Everywhere she looked, Alina saw shimmering clothes that displayed motion-picture advertisements, makeup that shifted hue and intensity depending on the light striking it, and, of course, body mods of all types. Some of The Capital's denizens sported gleaming black titanium alloy arms or legs; those of others had been spray-painted a gleaming chrome, blood red, or bedazzled with what appeared to be actual diamonds. It wasn't just limbs, though. One guy turned toward her, his glowing blue eyeballs buzzing and whirring—he licked his lips at her and whistled as his gaze all but literally bored into her. She scowled at him.

She was so distracted that she almost stumbled over a cluster of people slumped against a wall. It took her a moment to realize they had white wires running from ports in the sides of their heads to pencil-sized holes in the panel built into the concrete wall behind. Most of them looked fine, just meditative (except for their rapidly flitting eyes). One man, however, looked a little worse for wear. His eyes were half-lidded, drool dripping from his lolling orange-coated tongue, multiple overlaying pit stains on his fancy gray dress shirt. He might have been there for days.

Carefully stepping around the group, Alina kept moving.

Before gaping some more at the incredible magnitude of strangeness around her—she texted Calthin:

Guess who I just got a selfie with?

She attached two of the pics she'd snapped of her with Pankrish.

Right away, Calthin responded:

oh! holy Buthmertha—was he awesome? TELL ME EVERYTHING

it was amaze-ing, Cal. A real trip. He was a bit loopy but chalk that up to jet lag

loopy you say? How so?

Well, he was supes anti-Sanctum. Like way way overboard.

ah. and what did you say to that?

just kinda smiled and nodded along. i was def star struck. Pankrish is legitimately the only royalty i've ever met, ya know?

yeah

i mean tbh he was a smidge arrogant—a bit too far stuck up his own bum

haha!

but not bad overall!

glad ur having fun!

Ok got 2 go

keep me posted

She double-tapped her phone's screen, locking it, and sucked in a panicked breath when she saw the gold eye of Mophead reflected within those several square inches of blackness.

Spinning, neck snapping this way and that, she found no trace of the mysterious figure.

Her behavior was attracting the attention of the commuters around her, she realized. From under their wide and wavy, multicolored, multilayered hairdos the men and women of New El pointed her way and giggled, rushing off in groups, murmuring.

She really ought to get to where she was going.

The briefing at the West Precinct Station wasn't scheduled to start for another three hours, giving her a small window of time to find a filthy cheap hotel room within a reasonable distance.

On every street corner there was a watery-eyed do-gooder handing out informational pamphlets about saving the fluffy-nosed seals or writing letters to school children in the war-torn region of Lodestar. They scowled at Alina when she told them she was sorry, that she didn't have any change to spare. She pressed on as the wind plucked at her scarf.

Every few dozen feet she'd check out the way she'd come, sure that, to the Elementals, she appeared to be exactly what she was—an ignorant tourist. And the one mistake Alina wanted to avoid, especially in The Capital, was being outed as a tourist. Dodging the pamphleteers and their thousand different causes, the curb-side peddlers of illegal off-brand merchandise—even the sunken eyes of the gray wool tunic-wearing street preachers—was only as important as hiding her status as a newcomer. Because newcomers got lost. And the lost were easy prey for pickpockets and kidnappers.

Alina was broke, and there would be no one who could or would pay a penny's ransom for her life. But nobody else knew that. Calthin's jacket and her stylish new haircut made her look roughly (lower) middle-class. Which was quite a few steps up the economic ladder from where she really was. She'd done everything she could, after all, and done it well. She was iron wrapped in golden foil. If the foil tore, she'd be exposed for the fraud she was. Her grandfather's school would be lost. And—

She gritted her teeth. Okay, so maybe she *was* a grifter and a cheat, but she had every right to be here. She'd only come to get what she deserved. Why should she be fine with the world stripping her of everything she cared about, piece by piece?

People were still looking. This would not do.

She had to move through the streets as inconspicuously as possible. Time for a change in strategy.

Before setting out, she'd speed-read most of a book entitled *The 77 Must-See Sights of The Capital*, by I. N. Wixolis. The author had dedicated a whole chapter to the way New El natives walked—straight, stiff-kneed, square-shouldered, not flinching, slowing, or turning for *anything*—and now Alina could see why. Studying the way they moved, she saw the pedestrians as schools of fish, propelled in a hundred different directions by invisible streams of undulating energy. These people flowed, like bubbles traveling along undercurrents whose patterns were so complex that they were lost in the mix.

Foot-traffic, no matter the road conditions, took priority. And that fact had nothing to do with law. Alina watched the traffic light at the next intersection flash green for the hovercrafts—huge stainless steel natural gas tankers, bright blue private shuttles, personal recreational vehicles of red, white, gray—but nobody on foot took any notice. Men, women, children, tiny old ladies carrying a thousand pounds of groceries in tearing plastic bags—they just kept walking. The blaring of horns. Screams and insults aimed at the mothers of everyone involved... but nobody ever stopped marching forward.

That determination was what Alina tried to mimic, while stealthily scouting the area for hotel vacancy signs. Whenever she went too far, or took a wrong turn, she put her chin up and kept walking as if nothing had happened. Better to go way out of her way than to turn around.

Look confident.

She rounded yet another block. Her third mistake.

It didn't matter. As long as no one else saw.

Another of Mrs. I.N. Wixolis' recommendations: take on the famously blunt attitude of the Assets of New El. For the tourist hoping to survive long enough to book a *second* vacation in The Capital, a certain amount of gruffness, even rudeness, was required. Forget about your "good mornings" and your "excuse me, sirs." If you wanted to blend in New El, you had to glower into the other person's eyeballs and grunt what you wanted at them. That, if anything, would earn you some small token of respect.

For those cursed with a provincial accent (like Alina's Tructian one), Wixolis had only one word of advice: mumble. Low-talk, repeat yourself as needed. But don't—under any circumstances—reveal that you're from one of the Provinces. "The Assets of New El regard their 'Landsider' compatriots as somewhat inferior to the lowest junkyard dog," wrote Wixolis. ("Landsider" was the more politically correct term for the surface-dwelling Assets of El. Although, personally, Alina had never minded "Terrie.")

One detail the guide had overlooked, though, startled Alina: the Sanctumites were far more common a sight than she'd expected. There, again, on a nearby corner stood three of them, close to her age, one guy and two girls. As Alina had seen a few times by now, they each wore their hair real short, maybe an eighth of an inch at most. Their clothes were simple loose-fitting gray pants and tunics. The ladies' layered garments stretched from their ankles to their chins.

All three of them were shouting a chant of some kind, though they were slightly out of synch making it hard, at first, to make out what they were saying. Quickly, however, Alina figured out that they were ranting about The Author, about how everyone in El would suffer if they failed to heed the Written Word. That kind of thing.

They were really intense about it. As Alina got closer, her path taking her past them, the guy informed her, "Magic is sin. The Aelf are our punishment."

"Uh, cool?" said Alina. "I gotta go."

"No sense in hurrying," said one of the girls, staring pointedly. "You'll have all the time in the world when your soul is locked in purgatory. Accept the Word into your heart, or be forever denied the glory of Nehalennia. Repent before it's too late."

"Will definitely keep that in mind, thanks," said Alina, picking up the pace.

Magic is a sin? She rushed to put a block between herself and them.

Pankrish hadn't oversold the passion of the Sanctumites. They were hardcore. Only a couple of hours ago, the old Master's criticisms had rung over-the-top and bigoted, but now Alina had to admit she felt more than a little uneasy after only that brief exchange with the would-be saviors of her soul.

"Looking for love?" interrupted a holographic projection of a bronze-toned, oily-muscled man in a speedo.

She jumped backward, flailing her arms.

Several people grumbled before flowing around her like water around a rock. A few chuckled at her ridiculousness.

The projection continued, "Are you a cyborg tired of the same-old, same-old impersonal interfacing over drinks at some dive bar? Are you due for a love-life upgrade? We here at GoGoChat think so! For a limited time, GoGoChat by Haxis Inc. is offering cybernetic singles ready to mingle an all-expenses-paid cruise off the Requis Coast. Act now, and we'll throw in a pair of Twistr sunglasses so you can process in style. *Twistr: 'Blow 'Em Away.'* So, what do you say?"

Alina looked around. When it became clear that the projection's glowing eyes were focused only on her, she shrugged and mumbled, "I'm not enhanced."

The projection flickered as the program switched itself to a different track of the script. "I'm sorry, I didn't quite catch what you just said, friend. What do you say to a *free* luxury vacation?"

"I said, 'I'm not enhanced,'" Alina mumbled furiously through the corner of her mouth.

"I'm sorry, I didn't quite catch what—"

"I've got no cybernetic implants! None! Zero!"

With another flicker, the projection was suddenly wearing a suit with LED lapels and adjusting its digital tie. "In that case, have I got just the deal for you. Announcing *iSite*, a revolution in real-world enhanced all-in-one visual display. Now, enjoy instant access to *everything* you need, at a glance! Monitor your husband's heart-rate, track the exact trajectories of oncoming traffic, scan for ticks and flea eggs in your canine companion's fur, and much, much more! And that's not all—"

Alina backed away, circling around the projection. Her maneuver earned her more stares, finger-pointing, and chuckles.

Meanwhile, the advertisement program blathered on: "… see everything your teen sees! Never worry about your little girl going to a block party again! Omni-presence in just sixteen easy payments of thirty gelders. *iSite* by VeriTech: '*Gaze Into The Future.*'"

As she hurried away, Alina thought about how her grandfather hadn't needed any tech gimmicks to see her every move. He'd always seemed to know what she was thinking, usually even before she did.

For luck, she appealed to her Tahtoh's spirit to guide her to a suitable hole-in-the-wall motel where she could store her gear and, later, sleep. Preferably somewhere that wouldn't break the bank. The very, very small bank she had at her disposal. And, please, no bed bugs.

If fate proved exceptionally kind, maybe she'd even get to bathe in a clean tub.

Ahead, the light was red, but she crossed the street anyway, away from the crosswalk. She just followed everyone else. Made things much easier.

A few minutes later, she found a neon vacancy sign hanging beneath the feet of a slender and wavy silver crane. "The Clarion," she read. *Definitely bank-breaking.* She turned away, flowing back into the section of the crowd headed in the same direction she was.

She checked the time on her phone. *Only an hour to go.*

As Alina's time buffer grew thinner and thinner, she became frantic. With forty-five minutes left, she worked up the nerve to ask a stranger, "I'm looking for a place to stay. Got a recommendation?" He ignored her. "Hey! A little help, here, pal?" Then he gave her a *very* rude suggestion. She came *this* close to cursing his shoe-laces. But she refrained.

A crowd had gathered in front of a department store, *ooh-ing* and *ahh-ing* as a group of street performers battled each other with illusionary swords. Alina wriggled her way through the cluster of gawkers. Farther up, an unshaven and runny-eyed man with a nosebleed came up to her, muttering, "I got spells. Magic tomes, grimoires. What you need, I got. Just follow me." She told him "no, thanks" but he darted in front of her again. She avoided his gaze, dodged away. Then he grabbed her by the arm.

That was his mistake.

Before she could think of a less damaging, less conspicuous way to handle the situation, her hands wove a complicated pattern in the air between herself and her attacker. Struck on the chin by a fist-sized hunk of concrete that had soared upward from the ground, he crumpled like a puppet whose strings had been cut.

Alina cleared her throat and released the spell with a snap of her fingers. The clump of concrete shrunk, flattening and smoothing until it had fully melded with the pavement again.

Great. She'd rendered a man unconscious in broad daylight. Now she might be arrested. She had to make tracks.

She ducked into the first open door on her right.

Conveniently, it was an old motel. Tan walls, fake wood paneling, fake wood floors, and a staircase running along the wall behind the dark counter—decorations that were poorly-crafted throwbacks to last century's Art Antique interior design fad.

The man behind the counter, tugging at his long tail of wispy silver hair, said, "Welcome to the *Preening Peacock*. We haven't got much, but we're competitively priced (I can charge by the hour, if it's easier on you), and the breakfast's included."

Alina examined her surroundings, doing a bit of mental arithmetic.

"Show me your cheapest room."

Eventually, she was brought to Room 4.

First, to check in, she had to show the motel manager her fake Raver-X License. He pretended to be impressed, but he undercut his false flattery when he explained that his establishment was used to catering to down-on-their-luck Ravers ("No offense, dear.").

In fact, the manager continued, Alina was fortunate to have found the *Preening Peacock* rather than wasting her time anywhere else. There were only a select few designated places within the city that out-of-towners were even allowed to stay. Of course, none of the fancier places in town had made the cut. The only businesses Terrie Ravers could frequent were those open to wide-mouthed tourists, the rare overnight commuting businessmen, and the servant population. Basically, the mid-to-lower classes whose existences the high-born Assets of New El had to tolerate but clearly didn't feel a need to make *too* comfortable.

The extent of the Elementals' concern over the visiting Ravers' wellbeing was apparent for all to see: the *Preening Peacock*, no two ways about it, was a dump.

Proving true what she'd been told, Alina soon discovered there was another Raver staying there already. "Arrived only an hour before you," the manager informed her.

Figuring she'd make nice, she stepped just outside the lobby into the tiny walled-off garden (if that's what you could call the collection of brown weeds) wedged between this building and the next.

The woman slammed her fist against the chirruping soda machine's blown-out speaker. She grumbled, spitting a string of expletives ending with, "Stuck."

When Alina looked at this buzz-cut, purple-haired Raver with glaring emerald eyes tattooed on her bare arms and legs—this fellow person who'd been forced to stay here, in this garbage heap—she thought she'd identified a kindred spirit.

"Here," said Alina, handing the other woman a gelder, hoping it'd be just enough to buy a little goodwill because friends in new places are hard to come by. "Might knock loose the one you wanted."

If friendliness was off the table, maybe the gesture could at least make them something less than enemies.

The woman took the bill without a word and fed it into the machine. The mechanical arms clicked, popped, and whirred. The bag of chips selected never made it to the bottom, but the motion did cause a can of *Cherry Punch!* soda to dislodge and drop.

The Raver reached down and grabbed the not-quite-ice-cold can. She cracked it open, slurped the beverage, and stuck out her free hand. "Vessa Tardrop."

Alina grabbed it. The handshake was awkward. Vessa had squeezed too early, catching Alina's fingers.

"Alina K'vich."

"Not gonna lie." Vessa sniffed. "I'll probably forget."

She released Alina's hand, turned on her heels, and walked off. Her retreat was punctuated by the regular violent gulping of soda and the squeak of her torn-up formerly white sneakers.

Alina mumbled, "Nice," shrugged, and took to the streets once more.

Compared to discovering the *Preening Peacock*, finding her way to the Authority's Western Precinct Station was as easy as figuring out where you left your phone based off the direction the ringer was coming from. (It's always on your bed, wrapped in your blanket. Always.) To get to the stronghold, Alina only had to head towards the sirens, and then keep going as the hovercraft squad cars—flashing their purple emergency lights—zoomed past.

A lot of action today. She wondered if this was normal but didn't ask. She was more than done talking to strangers. Besides, it wasn't like she was required to solve every mystery in a single afternoon.

The Western Precinct Station was by no means the tallest building in its District, but it was by far one of the most impressive: a chrome-painted brick plaza surrounded by a maze garden and row after row of blue-flowering hedges. The path became a staircase of the same brick, leading up to black angular archways marked with letters and glyphs (in every language) spelling out the word "Authority." Fifteen-foot walls boxed in each of the three levels, each wall rising higher than the last. At the highest level stood the doors—twenty-foot slabs of solid steel, flanked by white marble statues depicting more beheadings of humanoid Aelf. Finally, a tower rose from the squat, two-story, walled compound. A scimitar-shaped spire of glass narrowing to a razor-point. And on that point—Alina rubbed her eyes—perched a dragon.

Its folded wings and long, crested skull gleamed blindingly against the sun, its clubbed tail swaying lazily as it stretched its hindlegs. As Alina watched it, the beast yawned, producing a sound like the world's biggest speaker dropped into a pool, blasting dubstep, volume dialed to eleven out of ten.

There was something really, terribly off about this whole situation.

Her first instinct upon seeing the dragon was to run for the nearest manhole and dive into the sewers. The impulse directly after that one instructed her to scream. Luckily for her ego, she did neither of these. Instead, she looked to others for inspiration on how to act.

No one else seemed bothered in the least. That made Alina even more worried.

How was no one else *seeing* this dragon—

The behemoth lifted its head and yawned, spouting a stream of white-blue flame.

—this fire-breathing dragon?

Dumbfounded, she simply stood there for a moment before she realized that she'd dropped her Raver-X License. She reached down to retrieve the card, but a young man beat her to it.

He looked up at her and smiled. "Rather magnificent, isn't she?"

By the look of him, he was a little older than Alina, and his sharp dark green-gray suit with tails and snappy black shoes made him look a bit older even than that. He wore two platinum rings, one on either index finger. But Alina was most taken by his hair—shoulder-length, pulled back by a hair-tie so that only a few choice strands hung in front of his hazel eyes and copper skin. His hair was the color of a lightning storm. It wasn't just any *one* color, either. Each strand *changed* colors even as she stared, shifting from lightning-bolt-white to summer-storm-pink, thundercloud-silver to electric-blue. His beautiful thick sparkly hair.

He offered her his right hand (her license remained in his left). "Ordin Ivoir, most humbly at your service."

"Stitcher." She noticed the black patch on the shoulders of his jacket depicting a white tower with three stars. Just like the ones worn by the PTEs at Mercy's Approach.

"A pleasure to make your acquaintance." He nodded toward the dragon high above them. "I see you've been admiring H'ranajaan." Ordin Ivoir held up a hand as if to cup the serpent's chin. "Our mighty protector for over a century."

As she had been since her arrival in the city, Alina was still short of breath. "She's… really something."

"Forgive my being forward, but I notice that you're new to The Capital. Concerning our defender, here, you're probably wondering, 'why?' Or, maybe even, 'what is happening?'"

"The thought had crossed my mind."

Ordin Ivoir looked both ways before leaning in and saying, in a stage-whisper, "She's not real. She's artificial, our noble H'ranajaan."

Alina snapped her fingers. "H'ranajaan… that's the Ciirimaic word for 'guardian'? But it also means 'man of clay.' A golem, basically. So, it's a pun. You named your dragon after a pun."

"You've read your way around an ancient text or two, I see. You wouldn't believe how many saucer-eyed tourist girls I've explained that to, only to have them bat their lashes at me in confusion."

"You say this to all the girls? This is your move?" Alina grinned. "Really?"

Ordin Ivoir shrugged. "Now that you mention it, it is rather… what's the word I'm looking for?"

"Lame."

He laughed. "That's the one. But, no, I don't banter when I can help it. Sometimes I *can't* help myself, though. I'm an entertainer by nature."

"And I'm in a hurry, actually. Could I have my license back now, Mr. Ivoir?"

"Please, just Ordin. My father is Mr. Ivoir, and he's a surly old grump. A barnacle I only recently managed to rid myself of. Mostly. I have no profession, though, since you ask. Because I have the distinct misfortune of being among the leisured class."

Alina's gaze passed from her license, wedged between his thumb and forefinger, and his grinning face. She didn't have time for this, but he wasn't picking up on the hint. "You're a noble?"

He held up his long-fingered hands, his rings sparkling. "Guilty as charged, I'm sorry to say."

"Yeah, it must be so terrible, being rich."

"You might be surprised. For one thing, I can't usually carry on a conversation of this caliber—open, honest. Hardly ever. Today is proving to be a day for exceptions."

Alina checked the time on her phone. "Well, I have really enjoyed this chat with you, Ordin, but I actually do have somewhere I need to get to. So…"

"The precinct?"

She nodded.

He lowered his voice. "You're a Gildsman, aren't you? I should have known, what with that flashy jacket and no-nonsense hairstyle. What luck!" He clapped his hands, entwining his long fingers. "We share a destination. Please, allow me to escort you."

"Wait, what are *you* up to at the station?"

"Nothing too alarming, I swear."

"One of your butlers steal something from you?"

He chuckled but didn't answer.

She held out her hand, and he finally returned her license. Her fingers snapped onto it like a mouse trap closing for the kill.

They walked together up the steps. Arriving at the steel doors, Alina wondered how she—or any human—could be expected to move them. Nothing happened for several moments as she stood there. Then the doors slowly swung open on their own.

"Motion sensor," Ordin explained. "Boring but functional. This one's been on the fritz for some time. They really ought to replace the system." He sniffed. "Last century. Archaic."

Inside, the marble hall opened up into a stadium-sized lobby. Cold white light poured into the room from arch-shaped windows set between obsidian columns. A staircase split off to the left and right, each way leading to a series of corridors Alina couldn't see from her vantage point on the first floor. Their footsteps and voices echoing, men and women, Enforcers and perps, traveled along the tiled floor. Overhead soared log books, en route to deliver themselves to whoever had magically summoned them.

Watching her eyes, Ordin said, "Analog. Real books. Some things about this place rightfully belong in a museum, but there is a reason for all of it. The Authority's most sensitive documents are lately handwritten and kept in triplicate. Three copies, for the three branches of government. Just in case three superfluous bureaucrats all run out of toilet paper at the same time."

"Can't hack a book," said Alina.

"Right. A computer network can be compromised. Words on paper have to be stolen by more conventional means." He leaned in close to whisper in her ear, "There was a cyber-attack a few years back. No one was ever caught. No one knows what they even took, if anything, but it had The Authority scared. For once."

"So, they adapted. It's smart, putting it all down on paper. And this place is a fortress. I don't see how anyone could physically walk in *here* and run off with a bundle of ledgers." As she said this, a quintet of tactically outfitted, shotgun-toting Enforcers marched past.

"Nowhere is completely secure," said Ordin with a foxy grin. "Where there's a will, there's a way. The books will be phased out once the firewall is patched. For a time, The Authority will think itself secure. It'll get complacent. The cycle will begin again. I guarantee it."

"You sound like my grandfather. But he'd earned the right to be cynical through years of suffering."

"I might have suffered."

"Not like my Tahtoh. He used to tell a story about how once, when he was seven or eight, he had to choose between eating his own dog and starving to death."

"Alright, alright. I surrender. He is the clear winner." Ordin shook his head. "Did he really eat his dog?"

"He decided to starve to death. He was halfway there, too, alone in the middle of that forest. Then a ranger found him." Pause. "The dog ran away less than three weeks later, leaving Tahtoh all alone."

"A real tear-jerker, that tale of yours. Your old grandfather would fit in splendidly at House Ivoir, I think. Everyone in my family is just as miserable. All of them fawning over 'the good old days' while oxymoronically trying to paint a picture of the bleakest, most deprived childhood imaginable. It's always, 'Ordin, when I was your age, I was lucky to get a scrap of cake after dinner.' Or, better yet, 'Ordin, when *my* father came home from the war, we counted our *lucky stars* that all he did was beat us bloody with the butt of his rifle.' It's particularly funny to me—in a morbid sort of way—because there has never lived a more pampered, soft-handed bunch. But if you listened to them for five minutes, you'd think they were the children of Zinoklese diamond miners."

"They sound fun."

"Fabulous, yes. You'd have to see them for yourself, to believe a group so pathetic could be real."

Ten feet from the front doors, there was setup yet another security checkpoint. Alina was beginning to think the people of The Capital must all be paranoid wrecks. (Except when it came to dragons on top of skyscrapers, which everyone seemed cool with.)

Two officers staffed the checkpoint. One stood behind a table, ready to inspect purses and handbags for dangerous contraband. The other waited impatiently just beyond an open metal pod shaped like an egg with two separate quarters of its shell missing. A metal detector?

"That contraption, there," said Ordin, waving a hand at it, "can sniff out any magical item or artifact you have on you, no matter how small. I don't suggest attempting to sneak anything in."

"Wasn't planning to," said Alina. She set her bag on the table and sighed her way through yet another invasion of her privacy.

She had brought her bag with her because there was no way she'd leave any of her personal belongings unattended at the *Preening Peacock*. The only things she'd left at the motel were her toothbrush (hopefully a choice she wouldn't later regret) and the dirty, sticky bandages she'd peeled off her forearms.

Subconsciously, she now rubbed her fingertips over her sleeves, feeling her arms, freshly bandaged from elbow to wrist.

Bypassing the inspection, Ordin was ushered around the roped off area and Niima detection pod. He looked back at Alina, having the decency to shrug apologetically.

She checked her bag with the officer, neatly folding her receipt before shoving it in her pocket. She was invited, brusquely, to step inside the pod. As soon as she had, two metal hatches snapped down, sealing her in total darkness for a few seconds. There was a whirring, like an engine warming up. Then it was over.

She thanked the officers for their time, receiving no response.

On the other side, she said, "What's the deal? Why'd you get through no problem?"

Ordin clicked his tongue against his teeth and made a quick popping sound with his lips. "I'm known here."

"Known? You catch your butlers stealing from you fairly often, then?"

"Not quite. I sometimes work for The Authority. I'm no detective or anything similar, but I've been called in once or twice to assist with ongoing investigations."

"You solve crimes?"

"Eh. It would be more accurate to say I help with the technical side."

As she wondered just who the hell this guy thought he was, he took her hand, saying, "Come on," and led her to the left of the stairs. "Diverting as this has been, we've dallied too long. We'll be late."

We'll be late? He was headed to the same briefing as she was?

Ordin led her through a series of corridors, down some steps, outside, along a paved path in the middle of a high-walled enclosure, and, finally, into a long rectangular building that turned out to be the gymnasium. An officer opened the door for them as they hurried over.

Within, Alina saw rows and rows and rows of foldout metal chairs set opposite the bleachers, and there was a Gildsman in almost every single one. There were probably two or three hundred of them in total. Each one could not have been more different from the others—tall or short, body-modded or virgin-fleshed, fully steel-armored or nearly naked—but all of them focused intently on the man standing on a small podium.

Towering over his lectern, he spoke into a slightly squeaky microphone. A white screen lowered from the rafters, then, and the speaker held up a remote, clicking a button. Electronic blinds slid down to cover all the windows, darkening the large space.

"Nice of you to join us," said the man on the podium. He patted his oiled black hair with pasty white hands, glowering at Alina with his yam-colored LED eyes. "For you two barely-on-timers, I'll repeat myself just this once. My name is Detective Ding—"

Someone in the audience snorted.

The speaker's glowing orange eyes fixed on a point in the crowd. The laughter cut off. "Something funny to you, lowlife? Let's get one thing sorted before I proceed with my little presentation, here, alright? Here's my honest to goodness, backed-by-the-facts opinion: you're all scum."

Jeers from the audience.

"Mercenary filth," said Detective Ding, stabbing a finger at random Gildsmen. "Gelder-hounds. No loyalty, no code, no honor. Were it up to me, I'd take this once-in-a-lifetime opportunity to round up all you sorry dogs and toss you in one big cell."

Boos. Hisses.

One Raver shouted, "Tell us how ya really feel, detective."

Laughter.

Ding added, "You might be asking yourselves, 'Why one big cell?' That's simple. It's so that, once the food gets scarce, and you all start getting antsy, you'll *eat* each other like the rats you are." He slapped the sides of the lectern.

"Are we clear about where I stand on the subject of Ravers?" He put on a mannequin smile, cocking his head. "Now that we understand one another, I'm going to prattle on and on so as to waste as many minutes of your time as I can. And you're going to sit there and damn-well pretend you *love* every word of it. Got me, scumbags?"

More jeers. A few Gildsmen darted upright. Shadow-washed Enforcers moved in from the periphery, hands on their stun batons. Ding held up a hand. The Enforcers stopped. There passed a tense few moments.

Ding said, "It's hilarious to me that you, the dregs of our society, think you can handle an Ushum-level threat."

That shut everyone up.

Ordin said, "Well, now."

Alina suppressed a gulp. An *Ushum*?

What had she gotten herself into? She'd bet everything on this job! Oh, sure, she could maybe take down an Ushum. If she had a tank. Or, like, a fighter jet armed with tactical nukes. She wasn't going home, though, so she'd just have to die trying.

Enjoying the silence for a moment, Ding grinned. He continued, "First reports we got of the attacks come from two weeks ago…"

Alina and Ordin stood at the left backmost edge of the assembly. He whispered, "In Ding's defense, he does grow on you. Like an infectious fungus."

Alina watched as Ding clicked through a series of grainy photographs showing sites where the beast had torn through town. It looked like the culprit had been a tornado rather than a living creature. What beast could be massive enough to leave markings like *that* behind? What could have done that much damage? Claws? Not teeth, surely?

Ding proceeded far too quickly through the important details, sometimes skipping over entire sets of images. Instead, as promised, he spent a ridiculous number of minutes blathering about unimportant side-notes, such as Authority response times after each attack.

Alina would never learn even a hundredth of what she needed to know this way.

Worst of all, the location of the very first attack in the Eleru District had been declared off-limits to non-essential personnel. Ding dismissed all follow-up questions, citing "state secrets" and "national security." The Ravers would have to work with the two crime scenes they were allowed to investigate.

"As you can see," Ding said, sounding bored, "the three sites form a triangle. We are working on figuring out why, or if this pattern indicates intelligence. Our top priority, right now, is to determine whether we're dealing with a sentient Aelf."

"And my top priority is to kill it," shouted someone. The outburst was received with rowdy applause.

"Fool!" said a colossal man dressed in what appeared to be interwoven snake skeletons. "This man nonsenses. It is Gurigan of Ranbarzi who slays your monster."

The next person to stand was small, bald, and clothed in a mango-colored robe that spilled onto the floor in a circumference reaching several feet outward from her. "I'm Cesthra Ci, favored daughter of Quartz-Ragvar, and I say this is a farce. Cease wasting our time."

A woman near Alina yelled, "Yeah, give us our badges or permits, or whatever, and go back to arguing semantics. Leave the real work to the professionals."

"Professionals? *Professionals?*" Ding threw his head back and forced a laugh.

He hurled the remote control at the front row. The Gildsman it struck—an average-looking tough guy, probably from nowhere important—pounced onto the stage and raised his fist.

The Enforcers would not have been able to act in time to prevent him from landing a punch on Ding's nose.

Alina sucked in a shallow breath. There was about to be an incident. The gymnasium would become a bloodbath, all because some overeager sword-swinging buffoon forgot to check his ego with his bag.

But the Gildsman's blow never landed. His hand twitched, inches from its intended target (Ding's face), fingers splayed, inside the airtight grip of a different Gildsman, one whom Alina was very sorry to recognize.

Beside her, Ordin murmured. "This is getting quite interesting."

The Gildsman who'd preempted the fight—who now twisted the would-be attacker's arm so hard that he buckled, his knees slamming onto the podium—was none other than Baraam bol-Talanai, currently ranked number one of all the Aelfravers in The Nation of El. The best, the most powerful, the most respected.

As with every celebrity Raver, he was the subject of many tall tales and rumors, each one more ridiculous than the last. According to legend, he was born at the exact moment that a lightning bolt split a cherry tree right down the middle; the blossoms caught fire midair, and the ashes blanketed baby Baraam, marking him as chosen by a long-silent storm god. It was said that his eyes were white as mountain snow because, as an infant, he'd sipped the waters of the River of the Dead. Baraam could cleave the earth with a word. He could fire a bullet, fly after it, catch it with his bare hands, and crush it between his thumb and forefinger, all in an instant. He was unstoppable.

The Gildsman who'd tried to harm Detective Ding was visibly terrified. Arm bent at a most unpleasant angle, the joint cracking, his face a mask of agony, he sputtered a long stream of apologies. The smartest thing he'd done all day.

Alina knew Baraam better than many people ever could. The legends about him were all pure garbage. As most legends are. But their main point was undoubtedly true: Baraam bol-Talanai was an extremely dangerous man.

Leaning over the other Raver, that dangerous man said, "We are guests here. The Detective graciously invited us to share in The Authority's intelligence." To the gymnasium at large: "All of you, acting like children—your insolence shames The Gild." He released his colleague's hand, and the man whimpered, nursing his broken fingers. He did not get up as Baraam walked past him and returned to his seat in the second row.

The offending Raver was escorted out of the gymnasium. Someone else passed Ding back his remote control, and the rest of the briefing went by without issue.

As before, everything Alina heard over the course of the next hour was filtered through Ding's icily sarcastic and dismissive point of view. She spent her time hiding her yawns; she'd already resolved to personally check out each one of the sites mentioned. That would be the only way she'd learn anything of value.

The presentation wound to a close. The screen drifted upward, out of sight. The blinds were opened, and the overhead fluorescent lights switched on.

Alina blinked as she scanned the room. Conspicuously absent was Ugarda Pankrish. She idly wondered what would have happened if there'd been a contest of strength between Baraam and *him.*

Lightly placing two fingers on her shoulder, Ordin said, "Alina, it truly was wonderful meeting you. I hope you don't mind, but I took the liberty of adding my contact information into your phone."

"What?" She pulled her phone out of her pocket, unlocked it, and tapped the contacts icon. Yep, there he was, 'The Most Charming Ordin Ivoir.' "Hah, hah," she said, locking the device again. "But how?"

"A magician must never reveal his secrets." He smiled. "Of course, with a bit more prompting, I might tell you anyway. However, we'll have to save that for our second date." Twirling his fingers as he bowed his head, he said, "I'm expected elsewhere. It is with a heavy heart that I leave you. Call me if you need or so desire. A most pleasant evening to you." He took her hand and, lightly, lightly, put his lips to her knuckles. Releasing her, he strode off.

Many of the Gildsmen had already left the gym, but a few dozen were milling, blabbing at each other. With any luck, Alina could sneak out before anyone recognized her.

She was halfway to the door when Baraam, arms crossed, appeared before her. Like, literally. Out of thin air. With a whiz and a crackle, he was there, barring her path.

She *hated* it when he did that. Way too showy.

"Baraam, my man, good to see ya." She fired a pair of finger-guns at him. "You're looking quite… thunderous."

As always, his long tunic was a miniature version of The Gild flag—teal and black with a white empty vase over his heart. His contract demanded that he constantly represent the organization, and he appeared to be as willing a foot soldier as ever.

He'd never change.

Baraam said, "What are you doing here? Shouldn't you be back in Truct, driving your grandfather's school into the dust of forgotten history?"

She crossed her arms, stared up at him. "I figured it was time for a vacation. Destroying a Master's legacy is ti*ring*."

"No respect. Will you never grow up?"

"Mighty rich coming right on the heels of your little powerplay on stage. Still need to prove to everyone that you're the baddest, eh, Baraam? That official Gild ranking not enough for ya?"

His eyelids twitched. Otherwise, he was still, like a hovering thundercloud just before the opening of the heavens. "We held a memorial service for Master K'vich a few weeks ago in Ramis. Just a few of us veteran students. It was solemn and respectful."

"That's cool." She jerked a thumb over her shoulder. "We had the real funeral a month before that. In Truct. Where Tahtoh lived."

"Some of us have jobs," said Baraam.

"Some of us cared about our teacher."

His voice was the distant resonance of thunder. "You dare?" He turned his back on her, now shouting, "The Capital will swallow you, Alina, as the serpent devours the mouse."

"Nice to see you, too, Baraam," she said, giving him a little wave entirely for her own amusement.

With a deafening bang, his body was bathed in white lightning. He became a single electric bolt which shot out through the open front doors, and he was gone.

To the slightly scorched patch of wood where Baraam had stood only seconds before, she said, "Show off."

And she followed the crowd of Gildsmen back to the main building to retrieve her stuff.

She could finally rest. If only for a little while. Time to return to the *Preening Peacock* for a nap.

Maybe later, if she could find a hole-in-the-wall cheap enough, she'd grab a bite in celebration of her definitely super successful first day in New El.

On the way, she checked her contacts again, staring at the newest entry—*The Most Charming Ordin Ivoir*. She shook her head, grinned despite herself, and kept on walking.

The titanic sentry H'ranajaan roared from his throne of glass, that tower ablaze with the light of the slowly sinking sun.

10

THE DOWNSIDE OF THE *Peacock*'s being so close to the Western Precinct Station finally hit her like a goat kick to the chest. She tossed and turned half the night away, crushing her lumpy pillow over her head to drown out the sirens.

Despite it being late fall, her cramped room was somehow overbearingly hot; sweat dripped down the inside of her knees and the bridge of her nose. She'd tried opening the window but closed it again as soon as she heard the revving of hovercycle engines and the whooping and cheering that signaled the start of a drag race.

Somehow, exhausted as she was, she failed to marvel at the brazenness of holding an illegal street race near an Authority stronghold. She just wanted to *sleep*. Please.

How was no one putting a stop to this?

After what felt like the hundredth lap, the engines finally cut out, and then came the screaming. Alina crept back over to the window sill and peered outside, watching the members of two gangs—one dressed in shades of blue, the other green—shoving and slapping each other.

She thought about calling somebody, but had no idea what was going on, or even if she was reading the situation correctly. For all she knew of Capital custom, this could be perfectly normal street theater.

Regardless of what it was—undergraduate final project or death match—it kept her awake. As did the constant grinding of machinery in the walls. Maybe that was the malfunctioning air conditioning unit, struggling futilely to provide some relief from the stifling heat. Or maybe it was an overworked heater, turned on to torture guests of the *Peacock* for some twisted psychological experiment. Well, if that was the case, it was working: Alina was ready to crack.

Sometime past four in the morning, she finally fell asleep.

A familiar dream…

She watched her grandfather shaving with a straight razor. He didn't look at his reflection in the bathroom mirror. He focused intently on her. Because this was a dream, she was simultaneously seven (as she'd been when this event had really occurred) and seventeen. For a long, long time, she simply observed him drag with care the blade across his concave cheeks. Scraping away the old, tough, and thick stubble beneath his jutting nose, just above his pointed chin, and everywhere between. He wiped away the foam, rinsed his hands and razor and face in the sink. Then, as always, a bird called in the distance—a raven or crow…

And, not knowing why, Alina snapped awake, drenched in cold sweat, breathing hard. She searched her surroundings, the darkness of her room, but found no birds.

Shifting to the other side of the bed (away from the pool of her own sweat), she laid her head down again, took a deep shuddering sigh of a breath—

And heard the voice from the bus, the voice of Mophead, saying, "I told you to go home."

Alina sat upright and raised her hands, ready to cast a spell of warding, ready to tear the whole motel down if she had to.

"I told you to go home. You are not ready."

"Who are you?" Alina whispered into the shadows.

One of those shadows detached itself, and the single golden eye fixated on her. "New El is a city of madness and rot. Corruption runs deep, to the foundations. You are not ready for the truth. A mere pawn in another's game, you are not ready to play for yourself."

"Who are you?" Alina said again, snapping her fingers, a flame now hovering an inch above her palm.

She held out her hand, extending the flickering glow across the room, and the shadow disappeared.

From somewhere, or nowhere, Mophead's disembodied voice told her, "Many are the doors that do not close once opened. Yet you will open them like a child exploring an old house: with no regard for the consequences. You run through the halls of memory and fate with abandon. You are a child; you are unready. The gods will burn down your house."

"This is a dream," Alina told herself, knowing it to be true. That's why none of it made any sense.

Slowly, her gaze drifted upward.

Now floating parallel to and directly above Alina, Mophead said, "All is dream." The gold eye flashed. "Dream is all."

Alina woke up to the late morning sun spearing her eyes. With a moan she rolled over and slept another half-hour.

Around noon she headed downstairs. She was far too late for breakfast but convinced the cook (who was also the owner, the concierge, and the greeter) to give her some leftover fried potatoes and bacon scraps. It was cold but filling. Tomorrow, she'd try for a hot meal. She was paying for it, after all.

She rubbed her puffy eyelids, contemplating ways to stuff her ears tonight.

Mentally kicking herself for starting her first day on The Big Case as late as one o'clock in the afternoon, she geared up and stepped into the streets.

She'd marked on her map the locations of the three sightings of the Bane of New El. There would be Gildsmen there. Lots of them. Maybe even Baraam. They'd all get in her way, trip over each other. Clutter the crime scene.

She'd have to be on guard. But she *could* do this. No matter what Baraam and her fitful dreams told her, she was the granddaughter of Dimas K'vich, maybe the greatest Master who'd ever lived. His strength flowed through her.

The Gild turned to murder first, always. Because, in the end, they were cutthroats. And Baraam was the worst of them all. He'd do anything to maintain his standing with The Gild. Their precious poster boy.

To a knife, everything is just meat. It has only one function—to cut.

But Alina would find the Aelf first and take care of it. Her way. She'd make it *stop*, whatever it was. And she would not let Baraam or any of the others butcher it. For all they knew, it was just some animal, lost, afraid, trapped. Leading it away from the city could solve everything.

Killing was just too… simple. Blunt. Dumb. Resolving problems without violence, now that took real creativity and effort. She'd show Baraam and the rest of them what she was capable of, and she'd do it without the bells and whistles and thunderbolts.

It'd be a long walk. Several miles. But she couldn't justify spending money on a cab. Or one of those weird pink bubble things she'd seen the Elementals using.

Passing over an arch that allowed pedestrians to safely cross a major intersection, Alina looked up: delivery drones soared in tight "v" formations overhead, leaving behind streaks of vapor from their hydrocell engines; maintenance workers hung loosely from steel cables as they patched switchboards fifty stories up; in the distance, the golden dome of the Capitol Building loomed, flying the colorful banners of the Twelve Families, the rulers of New El.

"This city is too big," she said.

Still struggling in the weak air up here, she adjusted the weight of her bag, switching it to her right shoulder, and carried on.

Under heavy scrutiny from two Enforcers in their crisp and angular lavender-colored uniforms, Alina stood between two shops connected by a large archway: the mouth of Tallendum Road, a minor offshoot from Sartorian Square.

Before approaching the scene of the crime, Alina had spent some time asking around Sartorian Square what this part of the city was known for, what it was normally like. Getting the lay of the land would help her identify anything out of the ordinary related to the Aelf. Also, it would give the crowd of Ravers plodding around Tallendum some time to thin out.

Lounging on a park bench, listening to smooth jazz emanating from their portable wireless speaker, a couple of young men in starched all-white uniforms were happy enough to answer some of her questions. They were novices with The Gild, first-year students of alchemy, they explained, and came here two or three times a week for lunch—and to get some more sensitive items, they added, blushing as they did. From this pair, Alina learned some useful tidbits.

The Square was one of three competing marketplaces in The Capital. There, merchants and tradesmen would sell their wares—herbs and spices, mysterious and semi-magical gadgetry, trinkets from the far corners of the world… It was a place of business, a haven for the Authority-tolerated black market, one of the city's many "open secrets." It was also the site of the Bane's most recent killings. Well, not exactly. The offshoot, Tallendum Road—that was where the three victims had quite literally lost their heads. The road had immediately been sealed off. But the Square remained open; the Square could not be closed on a business day.

Following a pleasant half-hour's conversation, Alina had said her goodbyes and proceeded to the crime scene. Conveniently, the last of her rival Ravers were just leaving.

Now, flashing her Raver-X License at the lavender-uniformed Enforcers, she was ushered through the amber holographic strip whose scrolling letters read, "FOR YOUR SAFETY DO NOT CROSS BARRIER." The Enforcers returned to their guard duty, and Alina, panting, walked down the vacant stretch of Tallendum Road. She turned to hear them snickering, probably at her inability to breathe this frigid and hollow Capital air. (She consoled herself with the image of the small group of Ravers she'd passed on her way to Sartorian Square, drenched in sweat and hunched over. At least she wasn't alone in her total and permanent discomfort up here.)

Tallendum Road only narrowed as she progressed. Several hundred feet in, she practically had to duck under jutting signs and weave between open manholes. The pavement was composed of cobblestones of many different shapes, sizes, and colors, from triangular cobalt to circular ash-gray. This was a place cobbled together and maintained at a rate only slightly faster than it was falling apart.

Alina could read the messages of centuries of winds and rains and human footfalls by how they'd worn down the stones, smoothed what was jagged when it had first been made.

This was an *old* road.

And, again, a *small* one. Alina spread her arms and found that here, at its narrowest point, she could almost touch her fingertips to the doors on either side. Alone there, in that ancient alley, she looked up at the rooftops hanging over her like hooded men with shadowed faces.

She examined the three glowing sky-blue outlines magically traced where the victims had fallen. The outlines had no heads. And there were no markings to indicate where the heads had ended up. The Bane *took* them, Alina guessed, and, when she trembled, she blamed it on the cold.

Three men had been killed here by one beast. Whatever it was, it couldn't have been very big to have comfortably fought in this space. Which didn't track with the huge claw marks that Ding had shown during his presentation. Either those markings had been made by something else entirely, or this mysterious Aelf could alter its shape and size.

If it could do that, what else was it capable of?

By how the bodies had landed, it was obvious that the men had been huddled together at the time of their deaths. They'd probably been terrified in their final moments. Alina, brow furrowed, stepped into the center of the rough circle formed by their outlines. Rotating slowly on her heels, she noted that they'd tumbled almost straight down. That meant that they'd been killed before they'd had much time to react. Dead before their bodies hit the ground.

Had they realized what was happening to them? Or had it gone down so fast they'd blinked and their lives were over?

In addition to outlining the corpses before ferrying them to the morgue for processing and disposal, The Authority forensics team had also magically tagged the blood spatter: sky-blue splotches on the cobblestones and mossy brick walls.

Alina heard her Tahtoh's voice, then, in her head. A lesson years past: "*Blood tells all, Lina. Where it falls, when, and how—these are stories.*"

"Stories?" she'd asked.

"Yes."

"Who of?"

"The spiller. If you can follow the blood, Lina, the truth will come quietly."

She knelt, staring into one of the glowing bloodspots.

There was a lot of it. Blood. On the road, the walls, the small windows. Blood had seeped into the large, arcing gashes in the buildings and roofs as well. Alina's thoughts lingered on those arm-width scrapes for a moment: How had something hulking enough to tear into solid stone like that ever fit into such a narrow space? Again, if Tallendum Road had to be described in one word it would definitely have been "cramped."

Shaking her head, she checked the blood again, willing it to reveal something useful, but it kept its secrets from her.

So, instead, she reviewed the facts.

Three young men. Sons of wealthy families, set to inherit large fortunes and become captains of industry. The report noted that they hadn't been robbed; their deaths had been their attacker's only goal.

This was strange behavior for an Ushum. They weren't exactly known for their precision.

Ding had been right about one thing: when dealing with an Aelf attack, you first had to ask yourself, is my target sentient? There were many varieties of Aelf in the world—an intricate hierarchy—and those Ravers who took insufficient care to understand their opponent before beginning the hunt all eventually ended up in the same place as these three victims had.

The Bane of New El was some type of Ushum, yes. Not all species of this type were sentient, but many *were*. If the so-called "Bane" terrorizing The Capital had brains to match its brawn, had it had a *motive* for killing these particular men?

And why take the heads? There were many rituals she knew of that required—she shuddered again—parts of the brain or eyes to complete. Spells of power, of far-seeing, of control…

Without more information, or a solid lead, the wheels of her mind would spin and spin without propelling her out of this mental ditch she'd fallen into.

She sighed, rising.

Nothing for it but to hit up one of the other crime scenes. For now, she'd learned all she could in Tallendum.

Leaving the trio of glowing outlines behind, she made her way back to Sartorian Square. From there it'd be about a forty-minute walk to Myrcul's Copse, where the beast had last been spotted.

She didn't get that far, though. When she stepped out of claustrophobic Tallendum Road and into the Square, two conflicting sensations swept over her. Goosebumps brought on by chilly gusts of wind. And a hair-raising heat radiating from Baraam bol-Talanai.

She stopped in her tracks, her heart in her throat.

"What are you doing here?" he said, crossing his arms. His dark face remained passive, but she could feel his disgust, his anger, crackling beneath the surface.

Ever since she'd been a little girl, she'd watched that scar on his cheek—beginning just beneath his right eye, running past his jaw and down his throat. It always twitched when he was furious. Dead giveaway.

Taking a breath, she crossed her arms too. "I'm investigating."

Humorless as ever, Baraam took one step forward. "More childish games."

Her laugh was mostly growl. "Why don't you just say what you really want to say, Baraam?"

"You're in the way. I'll ask you only once more, get out of New El—tonight—and leave the completion of this contract to a real Raver."

"Or what?"

One of his hands slipped into the pocket of his gray pants. The other he balled into a fist. Little electric tendrils sparked from his knuckles, up his wrist and the sleeve of his gray hoodie.

A crowd had gathered by this point. They'd been following Baraam, the celebrity, the big man in town. And now they were laughing, stabbing fingers at Alina, shouting all kinds of insults, slinging jokes like stones.

She couldn't back down. She'd never be anything worth talking about if she didn't stand up for herself. Right here. Right now.

As dramatically as she could, Alina threw back the tails of her coat, revealing her belt and, on it, her three full Auggie bottles. It would be an expensive shame to have to use one, but Baraam was way overdue for some humbling.

Well over a decade of him belittling Alina was about to come to a head.

The crowd swelled. People called over their friends, relatives, fellow barterers. There were even a few off-duty and undercover Enforcers. You could pick out the undercover ones by the poorly-concealed stun batons and firearms they carried under their civilian clothes. They were, apparently, prepared to let happen whatever was about to happen.

Alina didn't have to win. She just had to put up a good fight.

She chuckled nervously, delirious with excitement and terror.

The *Great* Baraam, expertly marketed people's champion… To show him up, she only had to make him look bad for struggling to beat up some novice girl from the provinces. Just make him work for it. Then someone would *have to* step in and stop him before he killed her.

Right…?

Alina felt about ready to throw up. Voice croaking, she said, "I guess we're doing this, then."

"If it's the only way to get through to you, then so be it," said Baraam. His lightning-bolt earrings tinkled as he glared down the length of his nose at her.

Thunder crackled somewhere far off.

And he was gone. No blur, no flash, no *anything*. He simply was no longer standing where he'd been a split second before.

Alina's jaw dropped. Her head snapped from left to right and left again.

Then she was flying upward like a rocket… No, not flying—being lifted. The toes of her boots scuffing the ground, she saw Baraam's body solidify before her, strands of lightning stitching themselves together until he retook his usual shape. With his left hand, he held her by the collar. Gazing up at her, his eyes alight with sheer disappointment, he simply shook his head. And he said nothing.

Alina grimaced down at him, gritting her teeth, clawing at his arm. If he felt any pain whatsoever, he didn't show it.

A deafening whistle sounded, sharp as an icepick piercing Alina's brain.

"Alright, alright. That's enough. Break it up!" It was Detective Ding, dressed in a plain brown shirt and pants, his stun baton in hand.

"I respect your Authority, detective," said Baraam, eyes locked with Alina's. "But this is not your concern."

"I swore an oath to keep the peace, and you're having yourselves a brawl in my city. This is my *foremost* concern." He inched closer to Baraam, lowered his voice, and said, "Please."

Baraam's scar twitched. He blinked. Then he let Alina go.

She fell on her backside, groaning.

"Thank you," said Ding quietly. Then, to the assembled onlookers, he shouted, "Back to your stalls and deals, gawkers. Nothing to see, here."

Baraam snapped his fingers and pointed at Alina before turning and walking away, leaving her to sulk in humiliation. She clenched her jaw, her hair hanging in her eyes. She was crying, but she wouldn't let him know that. She wouldn't give him *that*, too.

Someone said, "Pigs. Always interfering. Would'a been a good scrap."

"Damn pinkojacks," said someone else, spitting.

Alina looked up, sniffling. "Pinkojacks" was what you called an Enforcer when you wanted them to come at you. "Pinko" was the provincial word for a freeloader, any person living off a government paycheck (printed on pink paper). And when you were someone's "jack," you were a lapdog, a tool, and nothing more. To a survivor of the impoverished towns below New El, everyone in The Capital could be considered a pinkojack in one way or another. But the corrupt Authority Enforcers were the worst, so many said. Alina didn't necessarily disagree, but she knew not to shout the slur in the heart of the Plutocracy, within earshot of an Enforcer.

Ding, surprising no one with half a brain, stopped in his tracks. He cocked his head, his shoulders sliding upward. He scanned the crowd, a smile on his lips, until he found the offending speakers: two Aelfravers, as it happened. Both wore steel-studded black leather jackets with matching duct-taped scabbards, their simple worn swords nothing special to look at. Tools meant only for killing.

"Sorry, friends, I must not have heard you correctly," he said.

"If you heard me call you a 'pinkojack,'" said the first Raver who'd spoken, advancing on the detective, "then you heard right." His palm dropped to the pommel of his shortsword.

The other Raver pulled free a whip from its hook on his belt. It unraveled, slithering along the asphalt of Sartorian Square.

Detective Ding chuckled. He pensively smacked his lips and looked up, as if performing a quick line of mental arithmetic. In one motion, his thumb jabbed the button on his stun baton and he thrust the weapon's business end into the swordsman's throat—before the Raver could so much as draw.

The other one reared back, winding up his arm. His free hand twisted, fingers twitching in tandem with his lips—signs of spellcasting. But before he could complete his two-pronged attack, he fell, his nose bursting as it struck the pavement. A barbed steel wire sling had wrapped itself around his neck, seemingly tightening every time he breathed. His color shifted from healthy to various shades of sunset, all of them very unhealthy-looking. By the time he approached midnight blue, two Enforcers in civilian clothes emerged from the crowd, removed the sling, and pinned him to the spot. He gasped for air. Three more Enforcers stepped forward, two of them stooping to lash together the wrists of both downed Ravers with Niima-nullifying cords.

Ding said, "Your idiot friend will have to be filled in by you when he wakes up. It is for your benefit that I tell you, Mr. Still-Conscious Raver, you are under arrest for disturbing the peace and assaulting an officer of the law. You have the right to remain silent. Anything you say or do will most certainly be used against you in a court of law. You also have the right to continue to be stupid because it gives me a reason to hurt you. Drael, Magorna, get these dregs out of my face."

The two plainclothes Enforcers he'd spoken to saluted and dragged the prisoners to their feet.

Just like that, the fight was over before it even had time to really get underway. As the crowd of disappointed Assets dispersed, marching back to business, there remained behind three armed Ravers. Standing like lightning rods against gathering black clouds.

The three Enforcers turned to face them.

The smell of ozone hung thick in the air, coating Alina's eyelashes, cheeks, and tongue.

She could practically feel everyone else's fingers *itching*. There was a moment during which each of their lives teetered on a knife's edge…

Then the Ravers looked to Baraam, who shook his head. And they backed down.

So did the Enforcers.

They all went their separate ways.

Alina then noticed the five Sky-Eye News drones hovering overhead, filming everything that had happened. From every conceivable angle. With state-of-the-art facial recognition software, the techies at Sky-Eye could easily identify her.

In terms of her non-existent popularity, she'd thought a backward step would have been impossible. No such thing as bad publicity, right? Wrong. Her status in New El had taken a hard turn from "non-existent" to "laughing stock." The only damage control option left to her now was to flee.

Fully aware that the window of her anonymity was about to slam shut, she hid her face behind her hands, dashing from the scene.

One of the Skye-Eye drones had chased her for block after block until, finally, she'd smashed it with a cluster of bricks.

That'd been a trick, for sure. It hadn't been easy to use the reflection in the window of parked hovercar to angle her shot. She couldn't very well have smashed the thing head-on or she'd be held liable for the damages. And court fees were most certainly *not* within her budget.

So, biding her time, facing away from the drone, she'd run her hands through the complex series of flicks and twists to channel her Niima into a Geomancy spell. The magic shot from her fingers, flying backward, tearing three bricks from a nearby shop wall. The bricks collided with the front end of the drone, shattering the plastic bubble that protected both the sensitive camera's memory card and hardware essential to the machine's basic functions. The drone whined mechanically, sputtered, and, with a spark and a puff of smoke, crashed onto the sidewalk.

Alina jogged away.

The *Preening Peacock* was the only place she felt she could lie low. Right now, that scrap with Baraam felt like the biggest disaster of her entire life—and, considering the fact that she'd nearly been killed by a demon two days ago, that was saying something.

She had to consider her next move. No doubt, the Sky-Eye drones had gotten plenty of footage of Baraam handily outmatching her. Like she was nothing.

Back in Room 4, plugging her phone into the nearest outlet, she flopped onto the unmade bed and opened up her messenger app. Her thumbs blurred as she banged out a note to Calthin:

> i really messed up. i shouldn't have come here should i. what am I going to do. I'm out of money and i'm never going to make it here. u were right when u asked me to stay. maybe i'm not cut out for this. What do i do, Cal? this sucks.

She stared at that message draft for a long time.

First, there'd been the weird dreams demanding that she give up. She couldn't tell if they'd been genuine productions of her subconscious or tricks straight out of the playbook of that Mophead creep.

Then there'd been Baraam, who had, to put it delicately, mopped the floor with what had remained of her dignity.

Maybe she was the only one who couldn't see herself for what she really was—useless. Everyone else seemed to have her all figured out. What if Baraam was right? What if she wasn't ready for any of this?

Yet, how interesting it was that such discouraging dreams hadn't plagued her before she'd come to New El. And, at the first crime scene, Baraam had been right there waiting for her, ready to toss her out of town. The timing was certainly a smidge convenient. If she hadn't known any better, she might have wondered if Mophead and Baraam were working together. Or, if they weren't, why were they—separately—trying so hard to keep her away from the Rave?

Hells, maybe Baraam was Mophead. That would would be a twist.

Shaking her head, she groaned and rolled, hugging the pillow.

What would Tahtoh think of his Lina were he to see her now?

She sighed. She knew the answer. And she knew that it wasn't over. Not yet. There were still two more crime scenes to visit.

She was sore, bruised. Baraam had only grabbed her by the collar of her jacket. He hadn't touched her skin. But, even so, the electric heat radiating from him had singed her neck and curled back the tips of her hair. For the time being, she lacked the willpower to head out again. However, grounding herself for a while didn't mean she could get nothing done.

She rummaged around her bag until she found the tube of expired moisturizing and pain-relieving ointment. Applying pea-sized dots to the tender patches on her neck, she told her phone, "Iingrid, search term: 'Bane of New El.'"

Her phone's screen flared and the rotating ball-shaped loading sign did its little dance. A second later, Iingrid, the built-in V.I. said, "Showing results for 'Bane of New El.'"

Alina clicked her tongue. There were dozens, maybe hundreds, of links to blogs and chat groups on the Aetherthread where users detailed supposed sightings. In great detail, they described hearing noises, claps of thunder, scraping of metal or bone on stone and steel. Some had been outside when a shadow passed overhead, blotting out the moon for a moment before vanishing without trace. Occasionally a picture accompanied the panicked posts—deep, long gashes carved into buildings.

So many conflicting comments. Even within a single post or video. The one thing that all these accounts had in common was that no one had actually *seen* the beast. Not one clear sighting.

Of course, as always, there were those who'd *claimed* they'd caught a glimpse. But their stories were so disjointed, so poorly thought-out, that Alina had no trouble determining that they were obvious lies. Pleas for attention.

After an hour of wading through nonsense and hyperbole, she went *pfft*.

Getting nowhere, again.

Next, she turned to Tahtoh's extensive personalized database of all the Aelf he'd dealt with over the years. It was a disjointed collection of anecdotes, sketches, and methods of disposal—the direct result of decades of trial and error. There were concepts in there you wouldn't find in any official Aelf encyclopedia. Family secrets.

For ease of reference, Alina kept a copy of the jumbled notes on her phone. It had already come in handy on numerous occasions. Why not give it one more go, now?

She flipped through the categories, skipping past the lowest rungs—Liliskur ("Worms," pests and other nuisances) Then there were the medium-threat Aelf—Raccitan (dangerous in packs, clever but non-sentient hunters) and Uardini (sometimes called "Guardians," minor nature spirits, petty godlings)—which she ignored. Right on past the Mythidim (which included Elves, the Lords and Ladies, and fey folk), Legionari (demons, hybrids, and shifters), Demons, and Colossi (mountain-, forest-, or deep-sea-dwelling mammoth-sized beasts).

Finally, having bypassed countless pages of exhaustive notes, she arrived at what she called "the Big Boss" section of this unofficial guide, starring the Ushum. (There were no notes on the final two categories—Demidivines and Uult.)

Alina spent a couple hours scribbling notes, word-associations, and questions in her journal, trying to find some link or similarity between the Bane of New El and any of the Aelf with which her grandfather had previously squared off.

All her efforts got her nowhere. Slowly.

She ended up rage-quitting out of the notepad app and, with a growl, flinging her phone onto the other side of the bed.

Did she dare turn on the six o'clock news? It'd be propaganda mixed with somewhat useful facts. She might learn something. Or she might catch a third-person perspective, with full-blown commentator break-down, of Baraam completely out-classing her in two seconds flat.

Pass. She leaned back, closing her eyes.

She was exhausted. Bad night's sleep, and all this stress.

Nodding off, she mumbled, "How do you catch lightning?"

Her phone dinged, and she snapped awake. Rubbing the leftover lotion moisture from her fingers onto the bedspread, she checked her messages.

The Most Charming Ordin Ivoir, she read. Her gut twisted itself into a knot. His full text:

> I heard about your dance with the Lightning Rod today. The Media's Darling can be a real brute… Would you like to get back at him?

Shaky with excitement, she answered,

> Does a bear crap in the woods?

She kept refreshing her messenger app, holding her breath as she waited for the reply.

Finally, it came:

Could you meet me in front of *The Caduceus* in one hour's time?

Caduceus?

A high-quality dining experience on the corner of Ascoli and Tripalon.

be there soon.

Can hardly wait.

Giddy, hopping around the motel room, she ran into the bathroom to brush her teeth, changed her mind, returned to the bed to decide on what to wear, changed her mind again.

She paused.

As the granddaughter of Dimas K'vich—the eternal skeptic—there was something she had to do.

Opening the Aetherthread browser on her phone, she tapped onto the tiny keyboard the search term "Ordin Ivoir."

Five hundred thousand results exploded onto her screen. Holding her breath, she thumbed through the first few pages:

- Ordin waving off the paparazzi.
- Ordin, his arm looped around the waist of a model.
- Ordin, his face plastered on the cover of *El-viral*, the biggest tech magazine of all time, under the title "The Virtual Virtuoso: Ordin Speaks on White-Hat Hacking."

- Ordin as a young boy standing beside a middle-aged man wearing the sourest expression. They were breaking a champagne bottle on a new cargo ship bound for the colonies, the man white-knuckle clutching the small fists of the boy in his huge meaty hands. The photo bore the caption, "Ordin (left), seen here putting his first mark on the geopolitical world, as ever guided by his father Darus Ivoir (right), patriarch and Plutocrat of Ivoir province."

Alina snorted, rubbing her chin.

No *wonder* Ordin's name had rung a bell: he was the son of one of the twelve most powerful men in the entire country.

Ordin Ivoir. Yeah, of *those* Ivoirs. The ones that'd had a whole province named after them.

Immediately, she became suspicious. What did he see in her? No, better question—what did he want from her?

Breaking out of her contemplative trance, she looked to the bundle of clothes she'd lobbed onto the bed.

Alongside her suspicion ran curiosity, and curiosity narrowly edged out its competitor.

Alina reminded herself that she was an Aelfraver in all but name. She could handle herself. And, the fact remained, she needed allies in this fight she'd undertaken.

What had Pankrish said, again? "… make friends who can protect you when your falsehoods fail."

This opportunity was too big to pass up. She fully intended to find out what Ordin could possibly want from her.

The giddiness returned.

11

COLUMNS OF WHITE SANDSTONE held up a pyramidal roof whose front bore the animated projection of a slithering golden serpent. Into the columns had been nailed sconces that held blue-flamed torches. Between these, a velvety black-carpeted path lead into a dim waiting area. On the curb, in front of the building, Alina took a moment, eyeballing a small diamond-shaped bronze plaque embedded in large glass doors that read, "*The Caduceus.*"

The tiny, hard-to-spot sign sent a clear message: "we don't need to advertise; all the important people already know about our establishment."

Even the moderate effort of speed-walking in this diet New El air had Alina slumping against one of the pillars, sucking in as much oxygen as she could. She hoped her speed-walk to the restaurant wouldn't leave her too sweaty. Self-conscious, she clamped her arms to her sides.

(There'd been this one time, interviewing for some sales call job, when the interviewer had noticed the dark spots around her armpits. She never wore light gray button-up shirts again. Never. Again.)

Having correctly anticipated that *The Caduceus* would be absurdly fancy, she'd worn her Good Shirt. Technically, it was a blouse—short-sleeved, cornflower blue, ruffled around the neck. It was one of the few nice articles of clothing she owned, and she'd brought it to the city in the event that she had to put the charm on somebody. By the way Ordin had acted so far, he apparently had connections, status, money, and some kind of interest in her, which made him as good a candidate as any—and a better one than most. She'd debated over her choice of outfit for a dangerously long time: was it too forward to wear something nice; what kind of restaurant was this; was she going to be laughed at? In the end, she'd settled on assuming that a place called *"The Caduceus"* demanded that she dress up. So, she'd donned the Good Shirt and a tiny spritz of perfume. She'd painted her lips cobalt to bring the whole ensemble together.

If she'd known just how upscale the place really was, she might have had second thoughts about leaving Room 4.

The hifalutin entryway was nothing compared to the richness of what the guests were wearing. Though she remained on the curb, waiting for Ordin to arrive, Alina could see, both inside the restaurant proper and the waiting area, nothing but black suits (probably in the latest fashion) and backless flowing dresses with elbow-high white gloves. Sparkling high heels, hair done up in buns draped with silver lace or pierced by emerald pins.

Compared to these high society types, Alina—wearing the nicest article she owned—looked like a homeless person.

Meanwhile, the man sitting across from her scowled at her, exposing behind his twisted lips a pair of blindingly white front teeth. His partner polished his chained pocket watch, expertly pretending Alina didn't exist.

With her evening off to a wonderful start—almost as thrillingly as her afternoon had gone—Alina talked herself into slipping away, making up some excuse, and apologizing to Ordin. Through text, of course.

Before she could escape, there screamed up the street the most expensive looking sporty hovercar she'd ever seen (in real life or on the Watchbox). And she knew that vehicle just *had* to belong to Ordin Ivoir.

The chrome-colored two-seater gleamed as its engines hummed. Its speed dropped from forty-five to zero miles per hour in less than half a second; it came to a complete stop directly in front of, and perpendicular to, the columns and their blue flames. The door opened upward at an angle—because of course it would—and Ordin slid out of the driver's seat, his stereo booming some repetitive pop song. Sounded like *Five Years of Winter*'s latest hit. Although, honestly, it could just as easily have been their debut single or anything else by them.

A valet appeared from the shadows behind one of the columns and dashed up to Ordin, who tossed him a solid silver kwart—a coin that was worth *way* more than what the valet would make that entire night. Alina hadn't even known that coin versions of kwarts and konings were still minted. It would have been only slightly more surprising if Ordin had tipped the man with pirate gold.

Ordin flashed a dashing smile when he saw her. "My dear Stitcher," he said, extending a crimson-gloved hand that matched his suit and vest. He bowed extravagantly, his other arm swooshing backward, as he lightly kissed her knuckles. Alina found herself staring at his sparkling, ever-changing hair. He smiled again and let his eyes wander over her for a moment. "You look absolutely stunning."

"Hi," she said, folding her hands behind her back. "It's good to see you. What did you want to talk about?"

Ordin looked left, then right, and he said, "Conducting a business meeting in the street is so very... gauche, don't you think? Shall we discuss things over dinner? My treat." Alina pretended to offer to pay, so he predictably added, "No, no, I insist."

Stomach growling, she graciously accepted.

The hostess greeted him by name—"Ordin, *dar*ling"—and right away ushered him and Alina to a cozy table for two, tucked in a corner away from most of the other patrons.

After she'd sat down, and he'd scooted her chair closer to the table, she asked, "You had a reservation already?"

"No. My father has a standing arrangement with the owners. He handled their immigration papers."

"Nice of him," she said.

Ordin grinned, leaning his forearms on the table. "Now, you can't really go wrong, here, but I encourage you to consider the duck. Slow-cooked, a tangy citrus sauce to accompany it. Heavenly."

She nodded, opened the menu, and went into shock when she noticed the prices. Then she remembered she wasn't paying, and her mood lifted. She couldn't read the names of hardly any of the dishes on offer, she didn't understand half of what came with each course (what the hells was *"confit"*?), and she was pretty sure she was the only woman in the whole building wearing pants that cost less than five hundred gelders. But she decided to *try* not to care. If only for a little while.

She focused on Ordin, who told the server, "We'll try the '48 Mirac de Montagne."

"An excellent selection, my lord," said the server.

My lord. A title reserved for the Plutocrats and their families. Two little words that reminded everyone that Ordin Ivoire was literally one of the most important men in the world.

He turned to Alina. "You don't mind red, do you?"

"I've never had wine before," she admitted.

"This will be a night of many firsts, and I'm glad for it." He winked.

The server returned moments later with the bottle, uncorked it, and offered it base-first to Ordin.

As Ordin poured, swished the wine around his glass, inhaled, tasted, the server explained, "The grapes were harvested the year Mount Sanzelle erupted, lending a smoky undercurrent to complement the airiness granted by the Sanzelle Vinyard's high altitude. Only twenty such bottles were salvaged in the wake of the Piravimme Civil War of '55."

Ordin smiled at Alina, saying, "Perfect."

Alina closed her menu. "That server really knew his stuff."

"Sommelier."

"What?"

"He's a sommelier. But you're right. He's mostly a server. He's just paid more to know things about wines."

"Oh," said Alina. "Um."

A different employee of *The Caduceus* arrived, then, introducing himself as, "Hundin. I shall be delighted to serve you this evening. Have we had time to decide?"

Ordin said, "If the lady is ready, then so am I."

Alina cleared her throat. "I'll have the twelve-ounce sirloin. Thank you very much." And she handed him her menu.

Hundin accepted it, nodded, and took Ordin's order (the duck).

When Hundin left, Ordin said, "I appreciate a woman with a healthy appetite."

Alina said, "I haven't had a good meal in days if I'm being honest."

"It's refreshing to meet someone so forthright."

She gulped down a few mouthfuls of the pristine mineral water in the frosted glass set in front of her.

"You're unlike anyone else I've met, Stitcher."

She glanced up at him, her stomach growling. She hoped he hadn't heard it.

He continued, "In the most wonderful way, I mean. You're bold and direct. Unlike the great number of fools living on our little floating rock."

If Ordin could diminish the shining sky-spanning city of New El by describing it as "our little floating rock," Alina dared not imagine what he'd have to say about her working-class home of Truct.

Running a hand through his glorious head of hair, Ordin said, "You'll be wondering why I asked you out tonight."

Asked her out? Had she misheard him? Was this supposed to be a *date*?

Hundin glided over, delivering a small plate of crispy slices of bread and a gravy boat filled with a mixture of olive oil, salt, pepper, and some other spices. Ordin said, "The crostini here are divine." He drizzled a bit of the oil on one of the breads, guided it to his lips, bit down, and chewed. "I caught the news today. The big story was a rather ugly incident involving some Gildsmen and The Authority. At Tallendum Road. Our daring friend Detective Ding was there. Small world, eh?"

Alina felt a sinking feeling in her stomach. Why was he mentioning this to her? Had the drones caught her face on camera? Was her cover blown? If she became a meme… Taking a sip of water, she tried to play it cool. "What happened?"

"It wasn't pretty." He lightly cleared his throat. "I don't mean to pry, but would you like to talk about it?"

"Why would I—How did—" She shook her head, her appetite gone. "They plastered my name all over the news, didn't they? Everybody's laughing it up, right? Getting their hits in?" She gave a shuddering sigh.

"No, it wasn't like that at all. No Ravers' names were mentioned. I only recognized you because of your distinctive jacket. The one you were wearing when we met."

"Oh." So, the media hadn't been able to identify her after all. She had gotten off the streets pretty quickly, and her hood had been up. Her anxiety loosened its grip on her.

For now, she remained anonymous. Praise Buthmertha for small favors.

Relieved, her appetite returning, Alina plucked one of the breads, eating it without the oil. It had been lightly seasoned with garlic and flecks of sharp cheese. She hadn't eaten anything all day; the sizeable bite she took was so rich that her mouth hurt, sheer deliciousness overwhelming her senses.

After nearly a minute of silence, Ordin asked, "Stitcher, again, you don't have to answer if it would make you uncomfortable, but why did Baraam come at you like that?"

"Throwing his weight around," Alina grumbled, scowling at the tablecloth.

"Sorry, what was that?"

She had to be careful. Too many details about her relationship with Baraam and Ordin might guess who she was. She couldn't trust him. Not yet, anyway. "He was putting me in my place. I guess. I don't really know why. Maybe he was trying to prove something to everyone there."

Nodding slowly, Ordin said, "The oaf bullied you? That is awful."

"It's over," Alina cut in. "He made his point. Whatever it was."

"Well, I, for one, think you're brave for standing up to him."

Alina's eyes landed on his for just a moment before they drifted back to the tablecloth. "Thanks."

Ordin raised his palm in a sort of lazy shrug, the platinum rings on his ungloved hand catching the candlelight. "And, for what it's worth, Master bol-Talanai didn't come out of this affair looking too grand. A handful of the news hour commentators positively eviscerated him."

Alina perked up. "Really?"

"You're beautiful when you smile." He seemed a bit dazed for a second, then he shook himself out of whatever daydream had gripped him. "I mean, you're always beautiful. That is to say—my apologies for that comment."

She continued to smile. "No, don't worry about it. I, uh, appreciate the compliment." She wolfed down another piece of bread. "Now, please, tell me more about how bad Baraam looked."

As he poured a healthy amount of red wine into his and Alina's glasses, Ordin gave a vivid account of the footage, commentary, and criticism of Baraam bol-Talanai that day. He finished with, "The theme, it seems to me, was, 'a grown man picking on a mere girl, for shame, for shame!' You're more than 'a mere girl,' of course. Much more that. But that's the story the media ran with."

"And did he do anything in response? Baraam?"

"The Gild Council of Masters has him locked up for the rest of the night. Certainly, they'll be having a meetup right about now. I don't envy the public relations team whose job it will be to try to put a positive spin on this whole mess. Still, I'm sure they'll manage. He'll be propped up in front of the cameras as always, stiffly rambling about honor and duty or something, and he'll be let off the hook."

Sipping his wine, Ordin proceeded to mock Baraam, doing a very bad but very funny impression of him. Laughing, Alina clapped her hands. She and Ordin then toasted Master bol-Talanai and downed their first glasses. Hundin silently swept in to refill them.

And then the food arrived.

Perfect from preparation to presentation, a parsley-and-carrot garnish daintily set atop the steak, with exactly-measured dots of creamy sauce encircling it, the wonderful artistry of the dish Hundin set before Alina had absolutely no effect on her. All she saw was a big slab of pink-center meat to tear into with her bare hands. Like a starved animal. Tear into it she did (with her utensils, clumsily).

Ordin cut into his duck, sniffing with delight its flesh and the juices pooling on his plate. He carved one flawlessly square bite, picking up in one forkful each component of the dish, including a dollop of the shimmering orange sauce. He took a deep breath and nodded as he chewed and swallowed. Licking his lips, he said, "Stitcher, I have a proposition for you. No, please, keep enjoying your meal. I'll just lay my cards on the table while you dig in, if that's acceptable." He dabbed at the corners of his mouth with his napkin. "We're both aware that there is a lot of money on the line, with this bounty. This Rave will make or break fortunes, both metaphorical and literal. I won't pretend the money interests me—it doesn't. My family is so rich we could fill a thousand cannons with gold and gems, fire the valuables into space, day and night, for years…"

Alina's eyes narrowed. The money-cannon joke, that was *her* go-to. Weird that he'd used her bit.

She chalked it up to coincidence.

"… and we'd still be one of the wealthiest families in the world. So, no, for me, it's certainly not about the money." He leaned back, and she leaned in, and he said, "It's the prestige. The thrill. The ascendancy to the top of The Gild rankings. Do you know what my current ranking is, Stitcher? Go on, guess."

"Um." She didn't keep up with that junk. What were the metrics? She had no idea. "Twenty?"

"Hah! How very flattering. Thank you. No, I'm afraid I'm sitting rather impotently at forty-three. Not to sell myself short. There are, after all, hundreds of Gildsmen who (realistically or not) consider themselves in the running for Number One. But that spot's been monopolized for several years. By the same man."

This answer Alina knew: "Baraam bol-Talanai."

"Yes. And I, for one, have had enough of that." He paused to take another carefully sculpted combination-bite of his meal. "There are many ways to raise one's standing. Donating lots and lots of money certainly helps, but the best one has always been the successful completion of Gild-sanctioned assignments."

"Bounties," Alina confirmed.

"And the bigger the bounty, the more significant the jump in rank." Ordin waved his fork in slow circles near his ear. "This El-usive contract is the biggest of all. Of all time, maybe. Has there even been a threat to our civilization greater than this? Has there been one *as* terrifying since the Dragons?"

"Maybe, maybe not. But, listen, I come from Truct, Ordin. We don't live in the sky. Every other year, we deal with herds of marlok and outbreaks of Fisherman's Fright. Skin-changers and Pycts and more—we have a very personal understanding of them. Whether we like it or not, they're part of our lives. Seems like The Capital has gotten used to safety, but it's a rare thing in Truct and the other mainland towns I've been to."

Ordin nodded hurriedly. Alina found herself thinking he was cute when he blushed. He said, "Naturally. I didn't mean—I don't get down to the surface as often as I'd like—I certainly wasn't intending to—"

"It's alright, Ordin. It's fine. I'm not trying to be prickly. You're right that this Rave is a big deal. I was at the Tallendum crime scene today, after all. It was impressive. And… weird. I couldn't find any signs I recognized, any trails that even looked like—well, like *anything*. It was one huge dead end."

"Exactly," he said, setting down his utensils. "I thought the same."

Alina had finished her steak. And the side of oven-baked broccoli. And she'd even polished off the pickled radish and water chestnut palate cleanser. She said, "You texted me for a reason. So, what did you want to ask me?"

"Straight to it, then. I'd like us to be partners."

For one insane moment, she wondered if "partners" was somehow Capital-speak for "in a relationship." Heart fluttering, she chided herself for being profoundly ridiculous, and waited for him to continue.

He said, "We have a common enemy. Several, in fact. All the other Gildsmen will stop at nothing to take the beast's head for themselves. But their back-stabbing we will thwart, if we join up, form a team. What do you say? I have considerable expertise when it comes to crawling the Darkthreads. There is very little I can't find out about a target. With my resources and your bravery, we would be unstoppable—a tour de force."

She stared into his hazel eyes, searching for ulterior motives. He just smiled back at her, so open, exposed.

Though she was unsure of why he'd chosen her over all the other Ravers in New El, she recognized that he'd made himself vulnerable by posing the question. He'd done his best to make her feel as though she could crush him in an instant, if she wanted to. But she didn't want to.

"Sounds good to me, Ordin," she said.

He beamed at her. "Excellent. Amazing. Yes. Stitcher, you won't regret this. We'll divide the work and the spoils evenly. You'll keep all the money, of course. As I said earlier, I don't have any need of it."

She laughed. "No argument from me on that point."

It was around this point in time that the wine's effects hit her like a huge damp blanket. Her thoughts became foggier. Everything seemed thirty percent funnier. Whenever she moved, there was an increasingly long delay between her brain giving an order and her limbs executing it.

Hundin returned, asking if there was any call for dessert.

Alina had only just finished her third glass of *Chateau Whatchamacallit*, and it was safe to say that she was feeling pleasantly off-balance by then. She blurted, "That steak was so amazing, Hundin. How did you manage it?"

Chuckling politely, the server replied, "Well, my lady, I didn't have anything to do with it. Our head chef, who personally prepared your meals, hails from NeCay and is a gifted arcanist. Our dishes are a fusion of traditional NeCayan cuisine and thaumaturgical gastronomy."

Nodding her head to pretend that she had heard of thaumaturgical gastronomy, Alina gave him a lopsided smile.

Ordin said, "The prospect of dessert is tempting to the extreme, but no. The lady and I have an appointment to keep." Hundin ran off to fetch the check, and Ordin told Alina, "I hope you don't mind, but I have one more activity planned for us."

Her cheeks hot, she said, "Oh, really?"

"Do you know of Uleandra, the famous ice sculptress? A friend of a friend knows her. Anyway, she crafts living statues of ice using magic, and I thought—"

"That sounds so great," said Alina.

Ordin glanced at the only almost-empty wine bottle. "Ah, no, this won't do. There's still a glass's worth for each of us."

Alina nudged hers forward. "I solemnly accept."

Ordin poured. "To a fruitful partnership."

"To us," said Alina, instantly regretting her choice of words.

But Ordin breezed right past the comment, or he didn't care that she'd said it. Or—maybe—he'd wanted her to say it.

She was confused.

They clinked glasses and drank, and she felt her nervousness dissipate.

The next two hours were a warm blur.

Getting into Ordin's hovercar, speeding off (they were both quite drunk by then, so he engaged the vehicle's self-driving feature); walking arm-in-arm with him down a series of fancy boulevards; using a bronze door-knocker in the shape of a lion's head (the lion's expression made it seem constipated); unsteadily climbing the steepest and darkest staircase in the world; shaking hands with Uleandra, a stick-thin and fidgeting woman in her twenties who wore the baggiest clothing; sliding onto Uleandra's couch (she called it a "divan"); and, of course, watching her work.

Uleandra, in conversation, was pleasant but skittish and distrustful as a cat being fed by a new owner for the first time. Talking to her was more than Alina's tipsy brain could manage with any grace but seeing the artist lose herself in her passion was absolutely surreal.

Alina and Ordin huddled on the divan in that chilled apartment as Uleandra dipped her arms into a basin filled with frigid water, flinging handfuls of the liquid into the air. It crystallized into intricate, ethereal masterpieces before their very eyes. Dolphins, dragons, miniscule puckwudgies and mountain ranges complete with puffs of cloud—Uleandra sculpted an amazing array of creatures and landscapes out of ice, and every one of her creations *moved*. Fluidly and serenely.

This show-for-two was, in a word, spectacular. Such a shame that Alina wouldn't remember most of it.

The next thing she knew, she was in a cab (paid for by Ordin) returning to the *Preening Peacock*.

That night, she fell asleep easily, and dreamed strange dreams. None of which she could recall.

12

IN THE SHADOWS DRAPED across and around the columns of the *The Caduceus*, Tolomond lay in wait, stealing glances through the window at a couple, a man and young woman—barely more than girl. The couple indulged in wine, laughing and chatting up the waiter. The young woman had the latest fashionable hairstyle—an affront to every decent person present—daring to show her ears in public, as so many unfaithful females often did. The man seated opposite her, by contrast, had shoulder-length flowing hair that had been bewitched in some way to shift color and flash unnaturally—an even greater offense. The pair sipped greedily their wine, their lips stained, plump and red with sin. By their easy movements and casual, flirty banter it was clear that they had made a game of their petty evils.

Tolomond could stand no more of this. He withdrew from the windowsill, slinking a few paces back to watch the front door.

Last he checked, the couple had nearly been done with their gluttonous romp. Stuffing themselves to bursting while so many starved. Tearing into dainty platters of the most expensive foods, while many below The Capital could scarcely afford rice and beans. Well. Soon they would come out. And Tolomond Stayd, faithful servant of The Sanctum, would be waiting for them.

His earlobes twitched in time with a gentle rhythmic dripping—runoff from the verdant gardens on the rooftops high above him. More waste. The drought had obviously done little to convince the Assets of the Capital of the need to conserve resources. Water, electricity, food… The people of New El called themselves "Elementals" but knew nothing of living in harmony with nature. In fact, they seemed to stray as far as possible in the opposite direction, burning, destroying—needlessly—all the world's bounty. Their ignorance could only be described as willful. To remain so blind required *effort.* So ignorant always, and in all ways…

Soon, though—soon they will learn of fire. *Let's see how they react to that element.* Tolomond scoffed as he gripped the long-familiar pommel of the greatsword Rhetoric at his hip. Its weight reassured, as did the flat press of the dagger sheathed against his ribs.

For the most part, it was illegal to openly carry weapons in the streets of New El. There were only two exceptions to this rule: the Enforcers of The Authority, who were the dogs of the Twelve Families, and who therefore knew themselves to be above the law; and the Gildsmen, charged with hunting beasts and monsters beyond the abilities of mortal men (or so they arrogantly claimed). Even though he hated them, Tolomond chose to ignore the self-superiority of the Aelfravers: their special status was useful in its own way.

Praise The Author that the Hierophant, the holy father of The Sanctum, had in his foresight commanded Tolomond to earn his Raver-X License years before. That little laminated card now gave him free rein to walk among the unaware sinners, observing, watching. He traveled in their midst, invisible. And he would cleanse them of their wickedness. One day. Meanwhile, he could tolerate his own masquerading as a champion of The Gild. Vile pit of sorcery that it was.

Evil grows within itself the seeds of its own undoing, Tolomond remembered.

Though it committed blasphemies and created abominations daily, The Gild had its uses. It had given Tolomond immunity from suspicion. All he had to do was flash his license, and doors opened and guards stood aside. The prejudice and persecution reserved for followers of The Author were instantly replaced by awe-stricken stares and admiration. Politicians and commoners alike were blind to the crimes of The Gild. Thus, Tolomond, a servant of The Author, could move in, around, and *above* the laws of men as he saw fit.

One day, he would destroy The Gild from within. And, eventually, all enemies of The Sanctum would meet that same fate.

In service to this grand design, he'd come to *The Caduceus* tonight to deliver the next blow in the battle for the soul of the world: he would execute the heretic Ordin Ivoir.

Despite the mildness of the night, Tolomond shivered. His twitchiness had nothing to do with the gentle breeze wafting down the alley in which he stood and everything to do with his proximity to the first name on his newest list. Tolomond always got nervous just before he enacted the will of The Author; it was now, as always, an awesome honor to be chosen to serve as His Instrument.

He prayed as he waited. *Let me be as the Pen with which He Wrote the World…* Waited for his chance.

At last, there they were. The young woman with the boyish, obscene haircut, and her date, Ordin Ivoir—black magician, more maggot than man. Ivoir raised two fingers to his lips and whistled. A few moments later, one of the valets brought over his shining silver car. Ivoir clambered into the driver's seat. He laughed uproariously as the young woman drunkenly stumbled after him. The girl paused, rushed back to the restaurant's entrance, and exchanged a few words with the waiter from before. Abandoning any sense of proper behavior, she threw her arms around the waiter's neck.

Ivoir called for her. Being so weak-willed and empty inside, no doubt he grew jealous when kept waiting.

Tolomond had never seen a creature more disgusting than this spineless worm hiding behind the face of a man. From the surface of his skin to the marrow of his bones, Tolomond felt ill. Even his soul cringed at the thought of Ivoir manipulating—mentally enslaving that young woman. It proved more than Tolomond could bear.

That girl. Despite her haircut and improper demeanor and assertive smile, he sensed that she could still be saved. And it was his duty, as an evangelist of The Author, to try.

Making for the vehicle, Tolomond pushed his way through the clusters of diners as they slurred their speech and shouted obnoxiously at one another. The air around him smelled of alcohol and meat. The stench of drugs, the grinding of electronic music, and other pointless horrors hung over him like a thundercloud. A crashing in his ears. A perfume on his lips. He could almost taste these devilries on his tongue. It was all he could do to remain alert.

At last, he grabbed hold of the young woman's wrist. He locked eyes with hers. All he wanted to do was shave her head and wrap a cloak about her—shield her from the evils of the world and her own ways. But the smell of her white and blue hair struck him, and he was ensnared by her eyes. She was trying to cast a hex on him. Suddenly feeling ill, he looked away, and he barked at her, "That man over there." He jabbed a scarred finger toward Ivoir in his sickeningly shiny car. "You must not trust him."

Some of the haze over the girl's eyes lifted, and she looked at Tolomond. Her lips moved silently. She frowned but made no reply.

"You stay away from him," said Tolomond.

He watched confusion flood her face again even as two men pulled him from her. The waiters stood between him and the woman. It would have been a simple task to beat them both into unconsciousness, but there were now too many witnesses, and Tolomond knew that patience was a virtue. He would await a better opportunity.

He could not kill the girl, even though he hated her for her indecent hair and form-fitting clothing. He could not kill her yet.

Perhaps Tolomond should wait until he could get Ordin Ivoir alone—or near enough. Bodyguards and servants were no issue. If a worm or two in service to that sorcerer had to die, then so be it.

But not the girl. She could still be saved, couldn't she?

Perhaps he'd failed, succumbed to her spell… No, he had to have faith. In his judgment. In the will of The Author.

Tolomond looked on as she climbed into Ivoir's car and they sped off. He noted the vanity license plate—"MAG!CM4N."

The two waiters who'd wrestled with him released his arms as soon as it became clear that there would be no incident. They dusted off their hands and harrumphed as if they'd proven a point.

Ambling off into the night, Tolomond reminded himself of two truths the Hierophant had taught him: good things come to those who wait, and the smiting of an infidel—especially one as horrid as Ivoir—was worth savoring.

There would be other chances.

Having returned to the holy stronghold of The Sanctum for the night, Tolomond whipped himself for his weakness, and he recited the Orations deep into the night.

The words of the Prophets comforted.

Blood ran down his back.

13

ALINA'S EYES SNAPPED OPEN. She gasped and flew out of the bed. Within seconds she'd littered the floor with her clothes and most of her few belongings, flung the pillows from their cases, flipped the mattress…

"My wallet," she groaned. The *headache*. It was bad. Real bad.

She couldn't find her wallet anywhere.

It couldn't have left this room. When you guarded every penny like Alina did, when you carried every cent to your name in one little pouch, you made sure not to lose it. No matter what.

But she *had* lost it.

No, wait… the events of the previous night, they were coming back to her.

She fell onto the bed, muttering, "That little girl. With the shoes…" Slapping her forehead and instantly regretting it, "Holy Buthmertha, I got mugged."

Losing the money would have been crushing enough on its own, but it just so happened that her wallet contained her forged Raver-X License, an expired credit card she used for lockpicking (only when she needed to!), and other essentials. All that vital, life-saving stuff had been stolen from her. By some damn kid.

Alina wouldn't be getting those gelders back. That was already beyond awful. But her Raver-X License was the real reason she ran into the bathroom to puke into the sink.

Shakily, she asked herself, "What do I do?" and stared at her reflection in the cracked mirror, waiting for an answer that wouldn't come. "What do I do?"

When she pressed her fingers against her cheeks, violently rubbing her flesh, she noticed her arms—the bandages, they were caked with gray fluid. Much more than usual. More than ever before.

Hands and lips quivering, jaw locking, she fell to the ground, scrambling backward, toward the grungy bathtub. Her back thudded against it.

She held up her hands, palms facing her. Her breaths shallow, she began to unwind the dressing from her left arm. Round and round and round.

The curling, brown-and-gray-stained bandage-tail drooped to the tiled floor, and Alina slammed her knuckles against her teeth, stifling a shriek.

Her arm had gone… scaly? The skin was covered in bumps and crevices and cracks. And, every inch or so, there were black spots poking out. Too thick to be hairs.

Gingerly, she touched one with the tip of her finger. *Ah*. She pulled away, shocked. Blood welled from her fingertip. *Sharp*.

Head in her hands, she was swept up by another wave of nausea.

What do I do what do I do what do I do—

She slapped herself across the cheek. Hard. And again.

"Don't panic," she scolded herself. "Even though now's the perfect time, don't."

Slowly, steadily, she took a few breaths. And, even though she still felt completely overwhelmed, she managed to drag in a clear thought, then another. "Think. Prioritize. What do I need *right now*?" She considered her position, on a grungy motel bathroom floor, strange protrusions sprouting from her arms. Her Raver-X License, while essential, would have to wait a few minutes. "I need antiseptic, gauze, bandages." Her newly emptied stomach grumbled. "And starchy, fatty food."

Had she already eaten today? And, if so, how many times? A fog still hung over her memories of the previous night's events, and the accompanying headache pulsed angrily behind her left eyeball. Regardless, she was hungry. Bordering on *hangry*. So, feeding the beast was a definite must. First, however, she needed to clean and cover her gently oozing, cracking forearms.

Making certain that the motel's gross manager was still in the kitchen, whipping up underdone omelets and waffles and slapping some wilted, moldy fruit on a tray, Alina sneaked into the lobby. A quick glance—left-right-left—assured her that nobody was nearby. She slid over the counter, avoiding the broken bell and stacks of yellowed paper, and nudged open the door near the off-white dusty old plastic fan.

Inside the small space there was a bed, a rack stacked with unmarked and full pill bottles, and piles of pirated movie discs. Next to the sweat-stained faded-blue heap of sheets there was a closet which turned out to be a bathroom. Well, really, just a broken toilet (the bowl was entirely covered in orangish-pink slime with dots of black filth) and a cabinet with a busted and hanging door.

Careful not to step on the strips of fluffy dark green mold, she opened the cabinet. Even her gentle touch nearly took the door clean off its one surviving hinge, but she managed to hold the thing in place and check what was inside.

Pills. Lots and lots of pills. Some tablets sat in small neatly labeled orange bottles with blue caps; others had been cut or crushed and poured into plastic baggies. Also stuffed into the corners were a few loose meds of various sizes, shapes, and colors.

After silently noting that the motel manager was either deathly ill or a drug dealer, Alina's attention focused on what lay stashed behind the pills. She reached in, her fingers closing around a roll of bandages. The outer layer seemed to have gotten a bit wet, so she unraveled the first few feet of the stuff and, using her pocket knife, cut away the useless length.

Under the sink she discovered some moonshine which would work in place of rubbing alcohol. She poured the clear liquid over her spiky forearms, wincing and grunting at the icy, fiery flares of pain. Lacking medical tape, she just wrapped the probably-clean-enough bandages tightly around her arms, once more hiding the gray, scaly, oozing skin from view.

A quick inspection of the manager's dusty mirror showed her that she could use a few more hours—or days—of sleep. But there was no time.

She crept out of the bathroom, away from the manager's sleeping space (it would be a stretch to call it a bedroom), and over the counter into the lobby.

With priority one sorted out, she felt her stomach drop again. How in all of creation was she supposed to find the person who'd stolen her wallet? Everything that had happened last night had gotten twisted in her head.

She had to retrace her steps. This was just like a hunt. She had to think her way through what had happened.

Last night. The skies had been clear. The late hour had meant the airways and roadways had been mostly empty. Only a handful of hovercraft had zoomed past overhead, following the floating lane-lights, emitting their fluorescent pink and blue afterglows. To Alina—especially in her inebriated state—it'd seemed like a free light show.

Then she'd gotten into a cab. Yes, that's right. That much was clear.

What had happened after that?

Being intoxicated had been a new experience. Like her brain had been replaced by a dry luffa and she was seeing the world through the wrong side of a pair of binoculars. Everything sort of glowed. Even the streetlamps seemed comforting, warm.

And she was, of course, giggly. She could still feel the heat of Ordin's hand on hers. A steady, soothing fire under his skin that she'd leaned into as her breath fogged in front of her nose and Uleandra's ice sculptures took shape around them.

Ordin had hailed her a cab and paid the bill, wishing her a good night. The cab took off and, the entire way back to her motel, she'd babbled at the cab driver about Ordin—how handsome he was, how confident, how quick-witted and perceptive. "And I bet he's a good kisser," she'd finished, blushing as she said it.

Having reached his girlish-excitement limit for one night, the grizzled cab driver had finally pressed the button to raise the transparent plastic screen between them. Alina had stuck her tongue out at him. The rest of the journey had been quiet, and she'd counted the street lights below as they zipped by.

The Capital had glimmered with a thousand different hues of neon, blending into a rainbow of car-sized blue hologram cats leaping after orange salmon, yellow mice dancing their way into a mousetrap, an octopus clutching seven bottles of green soda in its tentacles (doffing a top hat with its eighth limb)… Everywhere Alina had glanced, something was being bought or sold, or the idea of buying and selling was being implanted in her brain. In that moment, however, all that complexity had bubbled and frothed and evaporated. The colors, the cartoon-voices blaring from billboards and wall-displays, faded.

Floating on the pink puffy cloud of a lovely encounter, she'd barely even noticed the chill to the air. The Adamantine Tower had boomed two notes—two o'clock in the morning.

Alina had gazed at the tower, its clock face glowing emerald in the night. The structure was home to the D'Hydromel, one of the Twelve Families. It loomed over Chinquator Way, one of The Capital's largest streets, reminding every Asset of that family's strength.

Apparently, the Twelve Families sure did love their giant clocks.

(Wasn't the current Consul—the head of the Plutocrats—one of the D'Hydromel…? No, no, it was a Xaveyr, pretty sure… Alina's sleepy mind had had trouble dredging up her slim knowledge of politics.)

Surrounding what had happened next, her memory got especially hazy, but she did know that she'd flopped out of the cab only to realize that the cabbie had gotten the address wrong. Or something. There'd been some mix-up, anyway, because she was, in fact, not standing in front of the Preening Peacock. *It had taken her some time to get her bearings, at which point she'd realized she'd been several blocks north of where she'd needed to be.*

As late as it was—woah, two a.m. already!—New El never truly slept. Fewer people were out on the streets than during the daytime, but plenty still crowded the sidewalks and balconies of bars and other after-hours businesses. Alina had tried to keep her wits about her, but she'd drowned them in alcohol. So, easier said than done.

The moments blurred. Humming happily, stumbling with every other step, she'd been thinking about how she should try for at least a solid six hours of sleep.

The cold air eventually had helped to clear her mind a little, and she'd begun to walk at a brisker pace. Then she'd bumped into something.

The "something" had actually been a "someone"—a girl, about ten years old. Maybe twelve. And the girl had said, "Check yourself, old bag," before running off.

Alina had made a rude gesture—wasted effort, because the girl was already long gone.

The little twerp had looked familiar, but Alina'd had trouble placing where they might have met. After a few moments of thought, she'd snapped her fingers and exclaimed to the brightly lit nighttime street, "The shoeshine girl from the train station!" And only then—remembering the most relevant detail about that particular misckie *girl—had Alina thought to pat her pockets.*

"Oh no. Ohnonono…"

The thief had taken her for everything she'd had. Spinning, trying to figure out which way the girl had gone, hyperventilating, dizzy, Alina had heard the voice of her Tahtoh in her mind. He told her to close her eyes, and to listen.

Aided by the sobering stress of the situation, the effects of the booze had really begun to wear off now. She'd sucked in a breath, then, closing her eyes, listening…

There! Just around the corner. Footsteps. Tip-tap, tip-tap. *Little feet slapping puddles on the street.*

Alina had dashed off after the girl. And she'd almost instantly found herself out of breath. This useless Elemental air—no matter how much of it she gulped down, it wouldn't take. It leaked out of her lungs like water through a sieve, leaving her shaky and weak.

The lactic acid had washed her muscles, like she'd dragged herself through a field of stinging nettles. Nevertheless, she persisted. Through the pain and well past the point of exhaustion.

She'd passed by a solitary couple holding hands, an old man pushing an overloaded cart onto the curb, and a trio of green-and-gold uniformed Authority Enforcers patrolling the neighborhood. To that last group, she'd shouted, "Stop that girl! She stole my wallet." And not one of them had lifted a finger. That much she remembered clearly.

Alina had then caught sight of the girl in the middle distance. She'd started to gain on the little thief, whose gray and tattered clothes flapped like sails behind her as she ran. Her dark ponytail had swished back and forth hypnotically, like a pendulum slicing away the seconds.

A stitch in her side, Alina yelled, "Hey, you!" and felt like she was going to be sick.

Her sense of equilibrium chose that exact moment to completely fail. Nauseous, tipping to her left as she lost her balance, Alina had made one last effort to close the distance between herself and the thief. A swirl of arcane energy—colorless, because it contained all colors—had enveloped her. Releasing a stream of Niima *from her heart on down through the soles of her feet, she had leapt forward. As she did this, a wave of concrete and rock had risen like a springboard to launch her up, up, up into the air.*

For a few seconds, she'd flown.

And then she'd flailed her arms, falling, falling, spinning in the air. A bird with a clipped wing.

She'd landed. Headfirst. In a back-alley garbage container.

Bang. Lights out…

… When she'd opened her eyes, Alina had seen only light, blinding light. Pink, white, green… She'd wanted to cover her face with her hands, but she couldn't. She'd been imprisoned, locked in a cell only slightly larger and longer than she was. A cell made of pink-hued crystal.

She'd screamed, but that accomplished nothing other than making her ears ring. No sound could escape the crystalline walls. She'd floated inside her shining coffin, oppressively few inches of air between her and the gleaming, faintly singing faceted walls, each reflecting her terrified expression.

She'd only wanted to be free again.

She hadn't known where she was. Her surroundings—those chairs, desks, bookshelves she hadn't been able to touch because she'd been immobilized—had seemed wholly unfamiliar to her.

For a long, long time, she'd waited.

Then, a visitor. She'd recognized this person. It was herself.

Alina had banged on the mirror-walls of crystal cell with her elbows; she'd slammed her heels into them. She'd made almost no sound, though she'd screamed and screamed and screamed for help. "Help me, Alina! Help me!"

But the other Alina hadn't heard her, even though she'd stared right at the crystal. Stupidly.

"Make things right," the trapped Alina had pleaded with herself. But her self had merely kept on gaping upward at her, mouth open, droopy-faced, dopey-eyed.

Inside-the-crystal-Alina had grown furious. Outside-the-crystal-Alina had continued to fog up the facets of the crystal with her breath.

"Free me!"

Outside-the-crystal-Alina had done absolutely nothing.

Hold on, that last part couldn't have happened!

Alina shook her head violently, dispelling whatever crazed fantasy her hungover mind had just been feeding her. She must have been confusing real events with half-remembered booze-fueled nightmares.

There was something else, though: a flash of memory. The image of a scarred-up guy with a buzzcut harassing her after she'd gotten out of *The Caduceus*. He'd had a greatsword strapped to his hip…? Was that real? And she hadn't been able to understand a thing he'd been saying.

Alina pinched the bridge of her nose. She couldn't remember climbing out of that dumpster and returning to Room 4 at the *Peacock*. Even though, clearly, that had happened. Well, at least now she could explain her headache. The fact that she'd even woken up at all was a good sign.

Who'd have thought that getting sloshed and hitting your head could mess with your memory so much? The swordsman who'd spoken nonsense at her, the crystal-twin situation… It'd all been one big, old wacky dream.

Glad and more than a little relieved that that burst of mini fantastical nightmare was just that—fantasy—she closed her foggy mental window and fully returned to the present: shaking, sweaty, and folded over a rusty metal chair in a crappy motel lobby.

From her journey down recent-memory lane, she had learned two things: the little shoeshine girl took (and possibly still had) her wallet; and she and alcohol did not mix well.

The light hurt. Sitting hurt. Lying on her side on the crumbling old couch hurt. Lying on her back made her woozy. Everything was bad and terrible. And, on top of it all, her Good Shirt now smelled like garbage. Literal garbage. She swore she would never drink again if *this* was the result.

"I'm sick of being broke," she complained to the peeling wallpaper.

Again, that unhappily familiar roiling and angry wave rose up in her. She flipped off the chair, tumbled onto the floor, got up, rushed into the nearby bathroom, and was intensely sick. All over the floor, in the sink, in the shower stall, *around* the toilet. Basically, she barfed everywhere except where she'd been meaning to.

Panting over the bowl, she considered for the millionth time that she only had a couple weeks left to pay off Mrs. Qamasque or she'd lose The School. The life's work of her Tahtoh.

She was sick some more. It was loud and awful.

After a while, she felt a little better. She could tell, because the idea of drinking water and eating salty food became appealing again.

Sniffing the air, she smelled an *almost* appetizing aroma wafting from the kitchen. She was just in time for the motel's complimentary breakfast.

Over the next fifteen minutes, she put down a couple of eggs and three strips of bacon that didn't quite taste like pork (and, no, she really didn't want to know where the meat had come from). As she ate and gulped down glass after glass of lukewarm tap water, her stomach settled somewhat. Enough for her to realize what she had to do.

She didn't like it. But there was only one option.

Alina had three Auggies left. Three. She *hated* having to use one up just to fix a stupid mistake. She could almost hear her grandfather's disapproving click of the tongue. He'd say, "Tut-tut, my little Cabbage. I taught you better than this."

Yes, Dimas *had* passed on a fraction of his knowledge of brewing Ability

Augmentative Elixirs, but it hadn't been nearly enough. Maybe if he'd taught her more, things would have turned out better for her. Longer-lasting, more potent, and with far fewer side-effects, his private recipes had been highly sought-after by The Gild and other buyers, but he'd refused to sell his secrets. Even though The School had been in dire financial straits for years already.

Still, as a consolation prize, he'd brewed and bottled a couple dozen just before he'd disappeared, leaving these for Alina. Well, he'd left them where she could find them easily. And he hadn't been around to tell her *not* to use them, so…

Whatever! He'd abandoned her, so the Auggies were Alina's property now, anyway. After all, she was the one who'd been stuck with managing The School. No one *else* had stepped up when it mattered.

It had been better. For a little while.

The first couple weeks, she'd taught martial arts and Aelf theory classes, just as she'd done when Tahtoh had still been around. She'd been assisting him for years by that point, taking over a lot of his work. But the students saw things differently. They reacted to the transition with dismay and anger. They all left when they finally figured out Master Dimas really wasn't coming back. They left when they were faced with the prospect of being taught by "some girl who didn't even have her Raver's license."

On her own, Alina had had to make do. She'd taken on all sorts of jobs, culminating in the hunt for Truct's murderous demon. And over the course of that lonely panic-inducing year, she had steadily had to consume Auggie after Auggie. Sparingly, carefully, and only in those moments when she'd just needed a little bit of a boost.

Maybe she could have learned to make her own, could have replenished the stock. There were, however, two complications: they'd never be quite as good as her grandfather's work; and the ingredients were prohibitively expense. Like, it was ridiculous. Made sense, given that the roots and leaves and all that came from all over the world. *Still*, though, how was anyone supposed to afford to run a business with all these *costs*? How had her grandfather managed for so many years on, apparently, a shoe-string budget?

At an alarming rate, Alina had whittled down her supply. And now she had three Auggies left. Three.

She was about to have to consume another. But if she didn't bet it all on this one chance, this one Rave, she'd be finished one way or another. She'd already invested all her money—why not all her elixirs as well? This was, after all, *it.* Do or die.

She knocked back the bright, glowing, viscous liquid. It went down like molasses but burned like pure vinegar.

Without that Raver-X license, she would be discovered for the fraud she was. At best, she'd be booted from The Capital. At worst, they'd fling her in the caverns beneath the city and throw away the key.

Remaining at the tiny crooked table near the kitchen, she waited about a minute for the Auggie to take effect.

She exhaled, long and loud, until her chest hurt and she heard something pop, until there was no whiff of oxygen in her lungs. Then she took a deep breath and—gagged.

This particular Auggie—*Hogsnout*—enhanced her sense of smell far beyond that of all humans and most dogs. She could now *see* scents in vibrant color. And, not only could she discern all the colors but she also knew intuitively what the source of each was. The air inside the motel, for example, was dusty, poorly ventilated, and distinctly greenish brown. A pungent yellowish waft told Alina that the only other guest in the motel (upstairs) was about to cry because she'd just received bad news. The motel manager/breakfast cook had used rancid peanut oil to prepare the eggs she'd just eaten. Too easy. Also, yuck.

The people just outside the motel were a couple, they were holding hands, one of them had just gotten his nails done, and the two of them were sharing chocolates. Chocolates *and* caramels.

The rat that lived inside the kitchen walls had just begun to nibble at the hunk of cheese rind with which it had made off moments earlier. The rat was pregnant.

The man who'd just stepped into the motel lobby had only recently arrived in town. The unwashed dry-sweat stink of the train station hung about him, floating into the kitchen in tendrils of dull gray. He'd eaten hotdogs with mustard and relish for lunch. The hotdogs had been vegetarian, actually. Tofu.

She could go on if she had the luxury of a free afternoon, but there was work to be done. She focused and tried to filter out all other scents except the one she was looking for—the nose-hair curdling tang of shoe polish.

Because even shoeshine girls who are secretly scam artists must carry shoe polish, if only to keep up appearances.

Alina quietly got up and left the motel. Occasionally she'd pause, close her eyes, sniff, and home in on her target.

It was slow going at first. There were so many unfamiliar smells in New El—hovercraft fuel, the burnt-oil reek of lubricated ad-bot joints, the vanilla of flowers blooming on rooftop and balcony gardens. What was most confusing of all to her senses was the clear impression of clockwork, gears, and magical power cores within individuals who otherwise looked human. She realized these must be what the Elementals called "androids," synthetic people. Alina felt way too far out of her comfort zone on that front, so she quickly skipped out of the way of the young woman (human) with the black dress and parasol and her tall pale gray-robed companion (non-human) who followed closely behind.

Wasn't it against the law to own an android? She blinked. Well, no time to worry about that right now.

Finally, she isolated the stinging white thread of shoe polish that cut through the other smells like an axe through a block of wood. She latched onto it firmly, tracing it along the street, through an alley or two, into a secret doorway hidden behind some empty dog cages and a stack of boxes, and into a nook. The space was too small for her to stand fully upright, and it was cramped, covered in knick-knacks—silver spoons, cracked computer monitors, a porcelain doll-head missing an eye, egg cartoons with cartoon animals scribbled on them in black marker.

Before Alina could investigate further, her nose crinkled as she detected whiffs of cherry-sour candies, stained and crinkled paper money, and old-man-coat. The coat was too big on the girl—its ends were caked with mud from dragging along the ground. The coat's pockets were stuffed with lint, wads of cash, and—metallic tang—a pocket knife. Maybe a switchblade. The girl was about ten, as Alina had suspected.

Alina knew all this about the little thief before even turning around.

The girl stood there in her frayed old tweed coat and fingerless gloves. Her gray cap rested at a jaunty angle on her ear-length, thin, straight black hair, held in place by her big ears.

A hard, pink candy fell from her open mouth, thwacking against the ground between her and Alina. The sweet rolled down a drain, tapping a metal grate before slipping into the sewer.

Lunging forward, Alina grabbed the girl by the shoulders.

The girl, understandably, screamed.

Alina clamped a hand over her mouth, saying, "I'm not gonna hurt you. Not gonna hurt you. Just came to talk about you giving my stuff back." Before she could get half the sentence out, however, she felt little half-grown front teeth dig into her palm. Yelping in pain and surprise, Alina let go of the thief, who dashed back the way she'd come.

Shaking her stinging hand, Alina ran after her, growling and lifting her unwounded hand. She gestured in the air, a swooping rise and fall, ending in a left-to-right slash.

Before the girl had made it ten feet down the alley, with a flash of amber light, the wall to her left stretched and expanded. The bricks and pipes and drywall all had shifted and reformed in a matter of milliseconds, blocking the thief's escape. The girl smacked into this new obstacle, slapping it a few times as if to make sure it was really there.

Reflexively clenching and unclenching her bitten fist, Alina approached. "Kid, I really hope you didn't give me rabies or something just now. But I'm not angry with you. I won't do anything to you, even. I just want my things back." She held out her hands in a gesture of peace.

The girl turned on her heels to face Alina, drawing her pocketknife and extending the blade in a jerky, one-two motion.

"There's no need for that. Look, I don't even care about the money," Alina lied, taking another step forward. "You can keep the gelders. But I need the other stuff back." She sighed. "My name's Stitcher. What's yours?"

Scowling, the girl asked, "How'd you do that?" She tapped the blade of her knife against the barrier Alina had made.

"Um." Alina considered lying, but something about this fierce, four-foot-flat girl made her take pause: she smelled *trustworthy*.

Alina knew enough about the ingredients in the Auggie she'd taken not to doubt her nose's conclusion. On instinct, a dog could sense who would feed and who would kick it. The level of perception Alina temporarily enjoyed was ten times stronger even than that. And, right now, her nose was telling her that something about this girl—something her conscious mind couldn't quite process—was… what? Worthwhile? Kind? Even friendly?

Pointing at the wall she'd reshaped, Alina said, "My grandfather taught me." She took another step.

The knife-point flicked up again. A warning. The girl said, "Was he a Raver too?"

Alina put her hands in her pockets. "Yeah, he was. He's gone now, though. And I have to continue where he left off. Which is why I need that license you stole from me. Without it, I can't work." Somewhat embarrassed by this whole situation, she stared at the ground. She noticed that the girl's shoes were falling apart—the soles were peeling off, and the sides were tearing, revealing the blades of her feet. The tips of her big toes poked through. "Those shoes," Alina tried, chuckling. "They've seen better days, haven't they? What's a shoe-polisher with no shoes? That's no good."

The girl frowned. "How'd you know I shine shoes?"

Alina tapped her nose. "I took a magic potion. It lets me sense things."

The girl's knife-wielding hand dropped a few inches. "Like what kind of things?"

"Hmm. Well, I know you had noodles—no, noodle soup for lunch."

"Eew, you're smelling my burps?"

"Hard not to, honestly."

The girl didn't take the comment well.

"Just kidding. Bad joke. Sorry. Um. I can tell you didn't get enough. You're still hungry."

The thief said nothing, but she screwed her grimy face into a grimace. Hard to read.

"You never did tell me your name."

The girl pursed her lips. She scrutinized Alina with a lazy-eyed stare for a few moments. Then she pocketed her pocketknife, saying, "It's Cho."

"Nice to meet you, Cho. Do you want something to eat?"

"I'm fine."

"Okay. Now that we know each other a bit better, how about we make a deal, you and me?"

"What kinda deal?"

"How about you give me back my wallet and license, and I buy you some food and a new pair of shoes?"

"Nice try, but I can just use your money to buy my own food."

Alina smiled. "You're right. That was pretty dumb of me. So, yeah, you probably have a lot more money than I do. How about this, then: I bet you can take care of yourself out here, but one thing that has to be tough is keeping clean, right? I'm staying at a motel not too far from here. If you want to take a shower in my room, just say the word."

Cho squinted at her. "You're literally just trying to kidnap me right now."

"No, I'm not." Alina flushed. "I—I was just—"

"You think I'm gonna follow you somewhere so you can kill me or sell me into slavery? Nope. If I cared about taking baths and stuff, I woulda gone to the orphanage. Or stayed with—" She clamped her lips shut mid-sentence.

Alina nibbled her lip, trying to find a way to steer the conversation back toward her recovery of her personal belongings. Turns out, she wouldn't need to.

Cho reached into one of her overstuffed pockets, rooted around for a few seconds, and pulled out Alina's Raver-X license. The shoe-shiner flung the ID card at Alina, who fumbled the catch.

As Alina stooped down to recover the item, Cho said, "Have it back. I can't sell that anyway. I checked. Mauldo said it's not even real."

"Mauldo?" Alina swallowed. "He's not, like, an Enforcer, is he?"

"Pawnshop guy. Knows a lot about a lot. Anyway, that piece of plastic is worthless. But I'll be keeping your money." Cho grinned. "If you want, though, I'll buy *you* something to eat with it. And maybe I *will* get myself some new shoes. Thanks, old bag."

"It's Stitcher."

"I heard you the first time." Cho passed Alina's wallet—emptied of all her gelder bills—back to her. "Y'know, what with your card being fake and all, I didn't think you were really a Raver. Guess I was wrong." Cho grabbed her growling stomach.

Right around this time, the effects of the elixir wore off. Alina shook off the mental haze that always followed her use of an Auggie.

Cho said, "Come on, let's go eat. I know a good cheap place." Under her breath she muttered, "Where there'll be lots of witnesses." Raising her voice again: "Ya like sandwiches?"

"I do." Alina flicked her wrist at the wall extension. It retracted, grinding and scraping back into place.

"Woah."

"I know, right?"

The two of them walked off together, Alina following Cho's lead.

Fortunately, the alley they were leaving was just neglected enough that no one seemed to have noticed the accordion-wall business.

They made their way to a sandwich shop off Seleusyk Street, owned and operated by a forty-year-old chain-smoker named Vittakovin. His sleeveless white shirt was smeared with grime and dotted with sweat stains, and his hands were gnarled, calloused, filthy blocks—the same consistency and color as blood sausage. But he was friendly, and he gave Cho (and, by extension, Alina) a solid discount.

"Decent guy," said Alina, as they sat down at one of the metal tables in the courtyard between all the shops.

"Yeah, Vitt's alright," said Cho matter-of-factly. "He woulda been a concert cellist if the Walazzins hadn't broken his fingers."

"What?"

"That's what he tells me most times I'm here." She deepened her voice, made it raspier, saying, "'Cho, I coulda been great man, famous man; instead, I here, making sand-vishes for ungrateful girl who rob me blind.'" In her normal voice, she added, "I always tell him that he should go talk to the people who hurt him. But he says it's too late for that."

Alina nodded. "Do you know who the Walazzin are?"

A peculiar expression passed over Cho's face. Her eyes narrowed, and she cracked each of her knuckles, slowly. She seemed about to say one thing but, with the resetting of her default frown, she switched tracks at the last second. "They're the bosses of this city."

"Some of the bosses, yeah," Alina corrected. "One of the Twelve Families. And, Vittakovin's right: sad as it is to hear, he'll never get justice for what was done to him. It's horrible, unfair. The government treats a lot of us like garbage. My family, too." She cleared her throat. "I used to think everybody up here was so much richer than me and my grandfather. Meeting you, well… If there are people like you and Vittakovin even *up here*, the system really does only benefit the Twelve."

"Who cares about all that stuff—systems and junk?" There was anger behind her words, anger Alina assumed resulted from her place in their world, in the shadow of the Twelve Families. They'd made her into a stereotype, the street urchin, the orphan. She continued, "I care about this sandwich. It's good! The sauce is soaking through the bread, see? That's how you know you've got yourself a good sandwich." Cho took a hearty bite from her meatball sub.

After that, they spent a while sitting around, talking. The subjects of their conversation ranged from cartoons to music to fast food and back again. Cho was also a *Billie and the Werewolf* fan, although she called it "vintage," which made Alina wince. In the end, though, they spent most of half an hour geeking out about lockpicking.

Cho had said, offhandedly, "This one time, I was thirsty and didn't have any change, so, guess what, I picked a busted old vending machine and used a popsickle stick I found on the ground to *pop* the lock."

Whether or not it'd been intentional, the pun had Alina chuckling. "That's cool. I forget my keys all the time. A bobby pin and one minute are all I need to fix that."

Cho playfully waved her hand, shooing the idea away. "Baby stuff. Try using a piece of soda can to get into shiny briefcases.

"Huh. You *could* use a thin strip like that to rotate the three wheels. That's really smart." Then, pretending to sound stern, Alina said, "Cho, have you been stealing from businessmen?"

"It's almost stupidly easy. Couple minutes tops."

Alina smiled. "You know, a soda can shim works on handcuff, too. If you get it between the teeth just right. Or, so I hear."

"But *I* tried it once."

"Really?"

"Oh, yeah. Had lots of practice 'cause they keep arresting me. Maybe twice, eh, three times by now."

"Wow. Well, it's at least nice to know the soda can trick is legit."

Cho licked her lips. "Okay, lady, what's the most ridiculous thing you've ever broken a lock with?"

Alina thought about it for a moment. "A tennis ball."

"Nope. No way."

"I'm not joking. Burn a small hole into the ball, press it against the lock on the car door, then hit it—hard—and *bam*. The mechanism is forced to unlock by—"

Cho clapped her hands. "The air!"

"Yeah. Air pressure. Yeah, that's right." Alina shook her head in satisfied surprise.

People were staring, she noticed. They were ogling her and Cho, no doubt commenting on their ragged appearance. Alina didn't look nearly as haggard as the shoeshiner with no shoes, but the difference between them wasn't too dramatic. After all, Alina had been living off scraps for months, and her water and electricity had been turned off for half that time. Soon enough, she could very well become a slightly bigger, much grouchier version of Cho.

Unless…

Doing her best to ignore the nosy stares of the well-dressed, well-mannered upper-middle- and upper-class gentlepeople around her, Alina methodically devoured her roasted red pepper hoagie, contemplating an idea. When she was done, she looked Cho dead in the eye and said, "Cho, you're a good thief. Maybe the best. Right?"

"Definitely the best. No one's ever caught me."

"Well, I did."

"That's not fair. You got magic."

"Actually, you're right. Point taken. But you said you've been arrested a bunch of times?"

"That's different!" Cho snapped. "They grab me when I'm asleep. Throw me in a cage on account of my vibrancy."

"Vibrancy?" Alina repeated. "You mean 'vagrancy.' You're arrested for just being in public places?"

She nodded, glaring at the table.

"That happens a lot where I'm from. It's—Cho, I want you to know that's not your fault, okay?" Alina imagined how frightening it must be, being woken up by a bunch of armored guys with big guns. Being thrown into the back of a truck, then into a dark cell. And do it all again a few days later.

"I know that. Like I told ya," Cho said, taking an angry bite of her sandwich, "I was *asleep* under a bridge or truck or whatever. They got me cornered. I still almost got away. I've never been caught for stealing." Her pride was as obvious as the pasta sauce smeared on her cheeks. "I'm too fast."

Alina made up her mind. "Okay, then. I have a proposition, if you're interested."

"You don't have anything I want."

"I don't, that's true. But I know someone who does."

"Who?"

"Someone I used to know. Someone wealthier than either of us could ever imagine. He could probably buy all the businesses on this whole block—" she waved her arms all around her— "and everyone in it. Without breaking a sweat. I bet that, with just what he has in his wallet, you could live comfortably for weeks. No, *months*."

"If he's that loaded, why's he got a wallet still? Wouldn't he have all his money synced with his Eye-D? The uber rich don't gotta carry *anything* these days."

"Body mods are against his religion."

Cho frowned. "He a Sanctumite?"

"No, *way* different. He's an Éëtionian."

"A what?"

"It's a whole thing. They revere the desert, water, and blood. I don't know much about it honestly, and it's all besides the point."

"Whatever. So, if I pick his pocket, what's in it for you?"

"This guy I'm talking about, he has something I need for a job. It's his license. Just like mine. Except much better. *Much,* much better. Without boring you with the details, it'd—"

"That's fine. I'm already bored. Don't explain about it, because I don't care." She dragged her sleeve across her mouth. "Is this a trick? You tryin' to trap me? Why do you care about me?"

With a shrug, Alina said, "You already know my license is fake. I know you're a thief. We could hurt each other, or we could both get what we want."

"And you're not magicking me right now? Mind-controlling my brain?"

"I'm not a Revomancer."

"A what?"

"You saw what I can do. I've got a few handy little spells on tap, but I'm mostly just a Geomancer," Alina explained. "I can shape earth, stone, that kind of stuff. I'm being real with you. Promise."

Scratching behind her ear with her pinky, Cho said, "I can keep everything except the dumb card you need?"

Alina smiled. "Deal." She held out her hand.

Cho hesitated, but then—with the speed of a striking rattlesnake—grabbed and shook it with cheerful violence.

A ding from her phone notified Alina of a message. Her eyes flicked downward, to the table.

It was from Ordin. He wanted her to meet him at his place.

She cleared her throat, wiping her own face with a napkin she'd dipped in the dregs of her cup of water. "I, uh, I gotta go for now. Can I meet you back at your hideout later tonight? To discuss plans?"

Cho shook her head. "That's okay. I'll figure it out on my own. Just tell me who the guy is."

Alina blushed. "The guy who just texted me?"

"Why would I care about that? No, the guy you want me to steal from. I don't wanna know about your boyfriends."

"He's not my—whatever." Alina wiped the beads of sweat off her forehead. Composing herself, she flipped through the photos on her phone, stopping when she got to a fairly blurry shot she'd snapped at the Authority's Western Precinct Station, where all the Ravers had been assembled for Detective Ding's briefing.

Alina showed Cho the picture—a dark-skinned man, with lightning earrings and a constant scowl. His hair was a strip of curly black with close-shaved sides, little lightning bolts carved out of it.

"Baraam bol-Talanai," said Alina. "He's always angry and has got *really fast* reflexes, so be careful. Just don't get caught."

Cho went, "Pfft. He doesn't look that tough. Not gonna be a problem."

"I admire your confidence." Truth be told, Alina wasn't quite so sure of Cho's chances of success. But she was willing to take the risk. Whether Cho's mission went off without a hitch or failed spectacularly, Alina would adapt. She always did. (For the record, she did feel bad, using the girl like this. But high reward comes with high risk.)

She parted ways with Cho, who left a decent tip—using Alina's money, of course. And they agreed to meet back at Cho's hideout tomorrow morning.

Alina rushed off to join Ordin at his apartment—to discuss strategy.

The knot in her stomach was probably just indigestion and nausea due to all this running after a big, greasy meal.

14

AS ALINA WANDERED A winding greenway in the Iuscat District, she muttered to herself, "Number 1500 Jin a'Luge Boulevard. Where are you?" She sped-walked, mentally retracing her steps, wondering where she'd gone wrong…

To reach Iuscat, Alina had taken a tram across the city. Due to the threat of the Bane, which continued to lurk somewhere out there, Alina's Raver-X license granted her free access to specific public transportation options during limited daytime hours. Her destination had lain on the other hemisphere of New El, the skyward-facing one, far from Mercy's Approach, the *Preening Peacock* motel, and the Western Precinct.

She'd had to admit, it was somewhat of a relief to no longer have the trees, fields, and mountains of the surface "above" her. The basic positions of "above" and "below" being so relative in The Capital still gave her a headache. Or, maybe that was just the empty air up here.

It was strangely funny how the Elementals managed to look *down* on the Terries when so many of those same Elementals had to literally look *up*—every day—at the homes and lands of the people they considered their inferiors.

Speaking of resentment, the looks she'd gotten on that tram ride!

She'd had every right to be onboard. And yet, even with an Aelf of unknown origin and description prowling about town, even with her risking her life to hunt that very monster, she could feel the seething judgment of the other passengers burning into the back of her skull as she gripped the overhead rail. They'd all beamed their hatred at her, wordlessly communicating that they'd thought she was garbage. They could smell the Terrie on her, and their stares told her that—in their eyes—even the lowliest Asset of New El would be forever superior to the likes of her.

How could they hate her so much when they needed her, and those like her, to save them?

Alina again thought of her meeting with Cho, of the girl's story about Vittakovin the vendor's broken fingers. They were two of several sad cases Alina had stumbled upon during her fairly short time in The Capital. Until now, she'd assumed absolutely everyone in El was rich beyond counting. Having caught a glimpse of the truth, however, she set aside those assumptions.

The truth was the upper class simply had to have its laborers. She'd been foolish to think otherwise. It wasn't like the Elementals lived on clouds, drank rain water, and lounged all day. They needed people to do things for them. The young, the elderly, the dispossessed, the indebted, the servants—they were tolerated and otherwise ignored by the "real Elementals" because they represented a useful underclass. Because of these non-noble bodies, the essential work in The Capital got done. Such flesh-and-blood drones weren't respected, but—being necessary—neither were they hated.

By contrast, what made Alina and the other Terrie Ravers so despicable was their status as interlopers: they weren't servants and they certainly weren't the Elementals' equals; they didn't belong. At best, they were a momentary inconvenience; at worst, a threat. Good enough to die for New El, but never worthy of living there.

During the tram ride, Alina had gazed out the window, squinting against the flashes of sunlight glancing off zooming delivery drones, pink bubble transports, brand-new hover cars, and sparkling towers of glass and steel.

Finally, her stop had been announced by a hologram projected from a display pad at the center of the car, most of its translucent form blocked by passengers, its head jutting eerily from the shoulder of a yawning man.

She had gotten off as soon as she could, ignoring the hateful glares boring into her from all sides. On the street, she'd taken a moment to do the tourist thing: she'd gawked at what she saw—trees. Real trees. Above the clouds, in the middle of a metropolis. And they were huge. And weird. Longer-limbed than trees on the surface, with semi-translucent bark. The red and orange leaves glowed like embers, reaching finger-like from white branches. Between the high-rises, the sun fell in sheets upon these fifty-foot giants.

Alina had held up her phone, trying to orient herself using its map. GPS hadn't been working, though. Interference. Probably to protect the residents' privacy.

No doubt about it, Alina had arrived at that part of town only the very richest Elementals could afford to call home. The lofty, rounded, tall apartment complexes on either side of the boulevard were each set on one-acre plots. An incredible luxury on New El, where space was so limited.

She gaped at the physical evidence—the spaciousness, the largesse—of the Elemental elite's majesty and influence. Then she found the real jewels of the district: there were several independent fortified towers at the heart of wide, flat stretches of grass, surrounded by meticulously ordered and ornamented greenery and stone gardens. At least she knew she was headed in the right direction: beyond a doubt, Ordin's family wouldn't be sharing a wall with anyone. They'd be living it up in one of these high-walled castles.

If it hadn't been apparent before that Ordin was absurdly wealthy, it certainly was now.

According to I.N. Wixolis's guide, which Alina kept tucked in her back pocket, Iuscat Disctrict was also famed for its lawcourts, record houses, and associated offices housed in tall, stately white-bricked buildings. Wixolis further noted that many of the original deeds, certificates of ownership, and legal codices going back to the first Plutocrats were there maintained by highly trained clerks and protected by a full brigade of Jaandarmes (the Nation of El's supreme military branch). Keeping these historic documents was an almost sacred duty. In more ways than one, Iuscat was where the power lived.

Now, Alina asked herself for the tenth time, where was number 1500? It must have been close.

No, that was 1640.

Maybe if she cut through that stone path in that little park area.

She got turned around, popped around a corner, looking for more street numbers for reference, stopping abruptly before bumping into a blindingly bright beacon of light. The beacon was actually a woman; she and her flanking friends wore frame-skirts that looked like bird cages. From these cages hung reflective strips of metal. Behind the women stepped servants whose apparent job it was to hold mirrors angled in such a way as to beam sunlight directly at their mistresses. The sunlight thus bounced in all directions off the frame-skirts, and the women were like lighthouses, like living flame trapped in ephemeral human bodies.

The nearest of the ladies smirked at Alina, who—blinded by their dramatic fashion statements—tripped and fell. Alina caught herself on a wall as the illuminated women laughed lightly, passing her by. Trailing them and their servants were a pair of men, who had servants of their own and who wore frame-kilts of similar design.

Alina blinked the patches of blue from her vision, muttering, "Must be real easy to sleep here at night. Yeesh." She picked herself up and found the brass number "1500" pinned to the wall against which she'd slumped. "Nice. Nice."

Her gaze drifted upward. The house was made of marble and real wood—both incredibly valuable resources up here—but bore a distinctly modern look. It was all right-angles, its dozens of half-floors jutting out at irregular intervals. The whole structure reminded Alina of the last few turns of that game where you remove the wooden blocks from the middle of the block tower to stack them at the top. As precarious as it seemed, Ordin's home must have been a feat of engineering.

She scooted up to the front door and knocked. After a brief conversation with the doorman and security guard, and after standing in front of the security camera (for identification purposes), she was allowed upstairs.

The elevator ride took forever. It was *thirty* floors, and the guard gave her the stink-eye the entire way up.

When the doors opened, she was greeted by a short, round butler. No way was his bald dome naturally that shiny. Surely, he waxed that bad boy.

"Miss Stitcher," said the butler, his pencil mustache twitching. "Master

Ordin has been expecting you."

"Sorry I'm a bit late! I—"

The butler talked over her: "If you would kindly—" He jiggled the brass handles of the big double doors and nudged the portal open—"step inside. The Master is in his office. Take a right, then a left. Fourth door on the left. I will see to tea."

"Oh, I'm alright, I don't need—"

The butler gave a bow and stiffly walked off. Alina watched him. His knees didn't bend once.

She mentally recited the man's directions, nearly getting lost once or twice. She passed a lot of exciting and curious sights as she moved deeper into the loft.

Its walls and floors and furniture and even most of the wall-hangings were colored—as a magazine she'd once read had called it—"Agreeable Gray," silver, or (if made of wood) a kind of rust-gray. One room she skipped past was covered, floor to ceiling, in black wallpaper painted with lidless white eyes. There was a library packed with gilded wooden globes, brass telescopes and other scientific instruments, and shelves upon shelves of silver- and gold-filigreed books—books of law and religion, encyclopedias, classic works of fiction. And there were other rooms holding tricked-out super computers and wall-to-wall monitors—red, yellow, and green wires running out like anacondas, pinned to the baseboards.

Arrived at the closed door she thought was probably the right one, she knocked.

From within, shuffling, drawers being slammed shut, a roller chair rolling. Throwing the door wide, Ordin said, "Stitcher! What a thrill you could make it."

"Yeah, sorry I'm late—I had a—There was this—"

He combed back his luscious, glimmering, color-shifting white-lavender-midnight-blue hair. "Please. It's no bother. I've only just gotten started. Had some family business to attend to. Horribly boring stuff. Ghastly."

Alina took in the fairly small room. Unlike the other nooks and crannies she'd peeked into on her way here, this space seemed disorganized. Papers were scattered about the floor or piled up in corners; there was only one computer and monitor, and these had been shoved against the wall opposite the door. Five rolling office chairs crowded the center of the room. Hanging from hooks hammered into the walls were these strange, off-putting octopus-shaped devices—bulbous headsets, numerous wires dangling from them.

Ordin followed her gaze. He said, "It's a junk pit, sure enough. Now you know my terrible secret: I'm an irreparable slob."

"It's not that bad," Alina said with a chuckle.

"Oh, who are we kidding? I'm like a human wastebasket. My being the first-born is the only reason my parents haven't disowned me. They can't; it would take too long to grow a new one of me."

Alina laughed. "Are we alone?" As soon as she heard herself say it, she quickly corrected: "I mean, is your family, here? I mean, you were saying something about family business."

"I was." Ordin took a seat in front of his computer, flicking the omni-pad on the desk to wake the monitor. The screensaver—a silver spider's web being spun across a black screen—disappeared. He gestured for her to sit, continuing, "As it happens, my parents, uncles, cousins, and everyone else who usually fills this place with hot air and pomposity are gone. Vacationing in the colonies. Well, nothing is really a vacation for father. He's found a way to combine business and pleasure in all things, so this trip of theirs is all about seeding future enterprises. Something about a diamond mine. Frankly, I was only half paying attention."

Alina took a seat. "And they left you here alone?"

Ordin snorted. "If only. I'm here to manage the house and our affairs. But my armed bodyguard is always alarmingly nearby, and I believe you've already had the pleasure of meeting Fulipe, our major domo. He's a fourth-generation servant and can therefore be a bit prissy." He leaned back in his chair, sighing. "This moment, with you, is honestly the most privacy I've enjoyed in—ah, I can't even remember. Isn't that something?" He shook his head. "Anyway, let's get on with our own project, shall we?"

"Absolutely."

"So, stop me if you have a better idea, but I propose that—before we dive into the Bane itself—we first size-up the competition."

"Sure, I'm game."

"Wonderful. Pass me those contraptions over there. On the wall." He pointed to the octopus-headsets, and he tapped a few commands on his holographic keyboard. "Put one on."

"What are these things?" said Alina.

"Never seen a Loom before? I take it you haven't tight-rope-walked the mysterious twists and turns of the 'Threads?" Ordin gave a wry smile. "Don't worry. I'll be with you, and I've been Thredding since I was three. Maybe even earlier, but I don't recall."

"You're talking about the Darkthreads?"

Ordin nodded eagerly.

Alina had heard all manner of unsavory stories surrounding the information network called the Darkthreads. You could find anything there, you could lose yourself anywhere—buying, selling, trading yourself away, one byte at a time.

The Darkthreads were the seedy shadows of the state-endorsed Aetherthread. Just about anything you could ever want was obtainable through listings hosted on one of the millions and millions of Aetherthread Threads. But everything else—anything of a less disclosable nature—could be found, too, if you only knew *where* and how to search for it.

Enter the Darkthreads.

However, if you dug deeply enough, if you lost yourself too thoroughly in their strands, someone or some*thing* else might just find *you* instead. Through its far-reaching networks, the Darkthreads connected most of the human nations. But, rumor had it, they reached out much farther even than that. Supposedly, there were other… *entities*… watching, silently traversing the infinite cyberspace…

Ordin prattled on about the technicalities of the network for a while, and Alina let her attention drift. He mentioned that the mainframe—the actual hardware used for all the computing of El (including the Aetherthread and the Darkthreads)—was housed in a man-made cloud supercluster high above the city. The tremendous heat generated by all that processing was counteracted by the dry subzero temperatures at 20,000 feet. The "computer" itself was made of the *powder* of many precious metals (beryllium, platinum, palladium, gallium, etc.), with each speck acting like a single cell in a humongous brain. These particles were strung together on thousands of lines of nanolattice—a metal coated in aerogel to make it seven times lighter than air. In turn, the nanolattices were tethered to hundreds of ship-sized air buoys, monitored and repaired by remote-controlled bots.

Ordin had a lot more to say, but he lost Alina for most of it. He finished with, "And that's cloud-computing. Astounding, really."

"Yeah," said Alina, tuning in again. The extent of his geeking out about the topic was amusing. Maybe even cute.

"The real breakthrough, which allowed for all sorts of advances, was the realization that binary code is outdated. Why limit our machines to ones and zeroes, yesses and nos? So rudimentary. No, when we figured out that the key is that moment *before* the switch is flicked to the 'on' or 'off,' state—the 'maybe-moment,' if you will—that's where all the real power is. Theoretically limitless storage and unbound possibility, all because a small group of geniuses discovered that you can have a 'yes' and a 'no' at the same time. And from there arises, naturally, true artificial intelligence, the billions of sub-worlds of the Darkthreads—even the quantification of the human mind or soul, or whatever you want to call it…"

When he finally winded down, Alina interjected with what she'd been waiting to ask: "Then, you're not worried about—" What were they called again?— "the Collectors? Aren't they a thing?"

"Soul-snatchers scouring the networks for unsuspecting fools to kidnap? Never seen one. Doubt they exist. *I* would have encountered them by now. An urban myth designed by The Authority to discourage participation in the black market. If the Collectors are real, they're probably just undercover Enforcers—grabbing anyone they don't like."

"It's weird to hear you, of all people, say that."

"How so?"

"Well, aren't you—Sorry, it's just—You're an *Ivoir*."

An undercurrent of sadness—no, disappointment—filled his smile. "Is that what you're worried about? That I'm the scion of one of the Twelve Families? You believe I have The Authority and all its Enforcers in my pocket, is that right?" He shook his head. "The circumstances of my birth aren't all that make me what and who I am. I'm no patsy of the oligarchy." With thumb and forefinger, he rubbed his eyes. "I live in the thirty-sixth century, just like you, you know. Yes, my family has profited from the Elemental empire, but don't think I agree with everything done in our name." Combing a lock of his luminescent hair behind his ear, he added, "What people do on the Darkthreads isn't all bad. Certainly, there're some incredibly vile, scummy losers out there, but the Threads are so much more than that. They're a chance to innovate beyond limitations through the unfettered sharing of ideas. Think on it—unlimited and free communication across borders—the unification of humanity. It's within reach. And maybe, when I take my father's place as patriarch of the Ivoirs, I'll be in a position to change some of our government's less enlightened laws. For now, I live in this country of contradictions, and it's expectedly, well, complicated. Isn't everything, though? Aren't we all children of two worlds in some way? I'm not a carbon copy of my father. I had hoped you of all people would be able to see me as just a tad more complex than that."

Alina was surprised by the suddenness and passion of Ordin's monologue. She wondered what she'd done to set him off like that. Was she seeing real shame arising from his family's past actions, or was he putting on a show for her benefit?

He looked embarrassed. "My apologies. I usually try not to get so heated. I suppose I'm just a bit excitable today, what with the Bane of New El killing off young noblemen." He chuckled, gazing at the floor. "Maybe I am afraid after all."

Unsure of whether she should apologize as well, Alina said, "I didn't mean to imply anything about you, Ordin. You've been… particularly cool to me, so far. Guess I'm nervous. I've never Thredded it up before."

His grin returned. "Just you wait, we'll make a ThreddHedd of you yet. All you have to do is trust me and put on the Loom." He put the octopus-looking contraption on his head. The solid black visor flipped down to cover his eyes. "These things are state-of-the-art. Designed them myself. Utterly hack-proof." As he spoke, the loose black cables hanging from the helmet crawled up the length of his body and then slithered along the desk behind him, finally plugging themselves into the black ports built into the walls. He leaned back. "Do you trust me?"

Alina hesitated. Then she sat down and put on the Loom.

She cringed as the tentacles crawled up her arms and shoulders, pulling her and her chair closer to the wall. A few disconcerting pops, clicks, and whizzes, like power drills driving screws home.

"That's just the Aetherthread cables sliding into the jacks."

Alina cleared her throat. "Does it take long to turn on?"

She blinked, and suddenly everything was different.

Alina and Ordin were standing, visor-less, on a balcony overlooking a still gray ocean. The wind tugged thunderclouds across the sky. Just on the horizon, a few faint rays of green sunset poked through the cloud cover. Alina looked behind her, where a six-foot-tall fire raged on the other side of a black wrought-iron cage.

She yelped and backed away, bumping against the railing at the edge of the balcony. Looking down was a mistake. Her stomach lurched. Vertigo.

She managed to hold down her breakfast. "Where are we?"

Ordin chuckled. He was holding a wine glass, sipping its dark blue liquid. "The Ordin Airy."

"It's a lighthouse. Oh, 'Ordin-ary.' I get it. Cute. How did we get here?"

"We're in a lobby, a sort of waiting room." He tossed his glass over the edge. As he did so, a massive wave crashed against the rocks dozens of feet below with such violence that the foam splashed onto Alina's feet and she reflexively skipped backward. Ordin continued, "I made this lighthouse, the waves, the sun, everything. What do you think?"

Alina looked around, mouth hanging open. "This is virtual reality?" She'd played some VR video games back in the day, at the old arcade in Truct before it closed down. But that was kiddie stuff—ancient, one-note nonsense—compared to *this*. She could feel on her cheeks and fingertips the gentle misting of rain and wind-carried sea-spray. The distant rumble of thunder on the horizon vibrated the stones beneath her feet.

"'VR' is such a limiting term: it implies that nothing here has substance. And, while it technically isn't 'real'—in the sense that the birds, cars, people, and Aelf of our world are 'real'—unlike games and films, any actions taken in the nearly infinite worlds of the Darkthreads have real-world consequences."

Alina watched the seagulls on the lighthouse roof stir, squawk, and fly off. "Like what?"

"Injury," said Ordin. It began to rain, sudden and fierce. "Death." With twin flashes of emerald light, a pair of silver-handled black umbrellas appeared in his hands. He deftly opened one and held it out.

Accepting his offer, Alina said, "But our bodies are still safe back in your office, aren't they?"

"Yes, of course, but you have to understand that the 'Threads were wrought by magic. Niima flows through every synthetic strand and figurative fiber. The Collectors may only be a myth, Stitcher, but by inserting your consciousness into this tangled web, you do run some risks—however small. There are influential folk out there, and some less-than-scrupulous types. But I'm here with you. I know all the tricks. As long as we don't dive too deep, and we retrace our steps, we'll be just fine. Oh, and don't tell *anyone* a *single* real fact about yourself. In fact—" He waved his hand in front of her, wiggling his fingers, which flashed again with green light. Holding up to her face a mirror he'd materialized, he asked, "What do you think? Disguise-wise?"

Alina saw reflected a tall woman with overly large black eyes, a crooked, thin-lipped frown, and plaited silver hair. Her skin pale and translucent, indigo and pink veins crawling along her neck and up her chin. Her ears were leaf-shaped, pink and throbbing with blood. Thin black straps dangled from her shoulders, flowing into a tight-fitting dress that brushed her ankles.

Alina recognized the features, of course, from the many, many accounts she'd been forced to read as a child. Her grandfather would stand over her with a light, jabbing his finger at highlighted passages, thumbing through earmarked pages.

She frowned at Ordin. "You've made me an Iorian."

His smile held a bite to it. "You impress yet again. You've learned some lore, I see."

"My grandfather, he made sure I never had any fun as a child. Working or training all day, studying all evening." Alina looked out over the artificial ocean. "I don't do dresses, though."

"It's only temporary. I didn't mean anything by—"

"Just change it, please."

"Done." Ordin waved his hand again, and Alina found herself wearing much more sensible traveler's clothes—scarf, tunic and cape, knee-high boots with slightly pointed toes. She looked like she'd been pulled out of a fantasy novel, but it would do.

Clearing his throat, obviously trying to change the subject, Ordin said, "He must have been a great man, your grandfather. I was sad to hear of his passing."

"Disappearance," Alina corrected, still showing Ordin her shoulder. Her frown deepened. "There was a funeral, but I never found any, um, remains."

"I am sorry. That all must have been quite difficult."

Alina sighed, facing him again. "Ordin. If we're supposed to be partners or whatever, we have to be completely honest with each other. I'm not going to work with someone I can't fully trust."

The lighthouse's fire flared, casting off a series of sparks that were whisked away by a stiff gust.

"Of course," he said.

"How did you know about my grandfather? How did you find out who I am?"

"I admit, after I met you, I ran a search on you. It doesn't look great for me, and it is an invasion of privacy. But you have to believe me when I tell you that it was done, if anything, out of paranoia: my family has so many enemies, Alina—can I call you Alina?"

"I'd prefer Stitcher for now."

"Stitcher, then." He spoke quickly, hurrying through the words as if hoping that, just by saying everything he had to say, he could fly past her doubts. "You talk of trust. Well, mine has been abused before. I have been duped. And it's always my family that suffers the consequences. I can never have that happen again. It wasn't about *you*. For all I knew, you—a stranger to The Capital—had orchestrated to meet me at the Western Precinct the other day. Just to get to me, to use my connections."

"Which I never asked for, but you freely offered."

"Once I knew who you really were, yes. Gladly. And I still do."

Alina had done a few minutes' research on Ordin, too, just before heading to *The Caduceus*, so she couldn't exactly fault him for running a background check himself. For being cautious. His status as a celebrity didn't make him any less of a real person, a human being, with all the fears and insecurities that accompanied that condition. It made sense that he'd been thinking about his family's security. The bigger they are, the harder they fall. And the Ivoirs were titans.

No, she decided, she wouldn't hold this against him.

"So," she said, meeting his digitized eyes, "what did you learn? How far did you take this little investigation of yours?"

"Only as far as knowing your name, that you really weren't an agent of one of my father's rivals. And I found out you were the grandchild of the great Dimas K'vich. I'd always wanted to meet him. I never knew he'd had children."

Alina crossed her arms. "Did you learn anything about my parents?"

"The accident? I only saw that they'd passed. At that point, I had figured out that you'd been telling me the truth. So, I didn't pry. Correction—I didn't pry *further*." He stepped closer, his eyes just the slightest bit red at the edges. "I truly am sorry for my invasiveness. I can return the favor, if you'd like. To you, I'll be an open book, I swear."

"Not necessary." Despite herself, she smirked. "Besides, I'm not sure we'd be able to work together if I *really* saw the weird stuff you get into on here."

"She jokes! Does this mean I haven't completely blown my chances with you—Ah!" He scratched the back of his neck, flushing. "Partnering up with you, that is to say."

"Tell you what, show me *how* you found all that info about me, and—as promised—give me the scoop on our toughest competitors for the prize."

"And then you'll forgive me?"

"And then we'll *see*."

"If I do this, though," he said, transforming himself into a three-foot-tall sunflower with big googly eyes and a shiny, white-toothed grin, "will *this* expedite the forgiveness process?

Alina laughed. "Stop. Agh, you're so creepy like that." She covered her eyes. "Turn back and we'll be square."

"As you wish." Ordin changed shapes again, this time wearing the appearance of a cloaked and hooded figure.

"Definitely nothing suspicious about that getup."

"Everyone on here, regardless of intent, is a colossal introvert. Believe you me, I will blend." He offered her his black-gloved hand.

She looked where she thought his eyes were, hidden behind all that edgy shadow. Within the cowl, she saw his face was in fact covered by a rounded mirror—she was staring at her own reflection, warped, distorted, disguised.

One more time, she hesitated. Was it worth the risk? Could she find another way to get what she wanted? Up to this point, she'd always acted on her own, and that's the way she'd liked it.

Who was using whom, here?

She took his hand.

The Ordin Airy fractured, exploding into giant chunks of stone and storm cloud that flew in all directions, catching in the air as if against an invisible net. They fizzled, grains of sand buffeted, blown away. Where these stone-and-mortar pieces had been, there was now only white space—gaping holes in the fabric of this unreality.

Still holding her hand, Ordin led her to one of those bright white gaps. "One of my best kept secrets," he said, stepping through.

She followed. They began to fall.

Over the rush of air, Ordin shouted, "Don't worry. You're safe. This is a shortcut to my hideaway. The disguise was necessary because others occasionally use this route. But we'll be there—"

With a lurch, and the jarring realization that she'd stopped moving, she found herself standing in a bank vault, the vault door ajar. All around her were rows and rows of lockboxes and filing cabinets.

"—soon," he finished as he landed. He pulled out a ring of brass keys. "*Hide in plain sight*. That might as well be the Ivoir family motto. Many have tried to break into my strongbox." He kneeled, tossed aside an area rug, revealing a trapdoor. "They were all taken care of before they got here. No one's ever gotten past my Exxy." Lifting the heavy door by its latch, he gave a bow and let Alina go first.

"Exxy?" she asked as she descended the steel ladder into the dark.

"My sentry program—'Guard_dog.exe.' 'Exxy' for short. She's modeled after an *einharthrak*, a hellhound."

Alina knew well what an *einharthrak* was, but she didn't feel like telling Ordin about the time she'd nursed one back to health over the course of a summer. That pup had come in the size of a purse and left as big as a pickup truck.

She thought that her real-world experiences with that species of Aelf would have prepared her for what she was about to see; she was wrong.

At the end of the stone passageway rested, curled up, a bear-sized white-maned, green-eyed creature with the ears, snout, and upper body of a direwolf and the skin-flaps of a flying squirrel. From its fist-sized nostrils curled plumes of blue smoke. As it yawned, a red inner glow illuminated its throat.

"I made a few modifications, naturally," Ordin said, leading her along the dark passageway just wide enough for her to stretch her arms, "adding rocket launchers and an acid breath-weapon. Couldn't resist."

The simulated *einharthrak* blinked sleepily at the them as they edged past it and around the corner.

Ordin said, "Ah! Here we are." At the dead-end, he tapped a stone that looked in no way different from the others. His dark-cloak disguise momentarily flickered as a bright light pierced his entire digitized body. "Avatar code scan," he explained. "The password is my genetic signature. "To the wall: "Ordin Ivoir and guest."

A computerized woman's voice said, "Welcome, Master Ivoir."

The wall slid away, revealing a comfortable parlor with red wallpaper, a plush umber carpet, a pair of recliners, and a fire pleasantly crackling in the fireplace. Ordin tossed a log onto the fire, and Alina shook her head because there was no point in doing so.

The place certainly felt cozy.

How many girls had he brought down here?

He sat down in one of the chairs near the fire and sank deep into its velvety cushions. Steepling his fingers, crossing one leg over the other, he said, "I'm still sensing some discomfort. I assure you, Stitcher, you can leave anytime you'd like. We came to this admittedly remote hideout of mine only because here—of all places—can we be sure we aren't being spied on."

"Still. Isn't this place just a little bit too dramatic?" Alina pursed her lips.

He chuckled but did not answer. A wave of his hand and the fireplace rotated, shifting into the wall, revealing a flatscreen Watchbox.

Alina said, "I just can't get over the idea that you could have made *literally anything* but you chose a goofy old-timer's smoking lounge. It's like the waiting room for the waiting room of some stuffy country club."

He dropped the cloak-disguise, becoming instead a handsome salt-and-pepper-bearded man with small gold-rimmed spectacles on his nose. He scratched his nose. "You wound me. Honestly, my reason is simple, if somewhat silly. I loved spy novels as a child. Behold the unholy result. But are you going to take jabs at my bad taste all night, or can we get down to business?"

She fell into a chair, leaning forward, fingers interlaced. "Ready!"

"I've prepared a little slide show. Please do interrupt if you have questions." A remote control appeared in his hand, and he clicked its single big red button.

The Watchbox displayed the still image of a light-skinned, scarred, scowling man with short-cropped hair and only one ear. The tattoo running along the right side of his face was nothing more than a series of hatch-marks, like he was keeping score.

Ordin narrated, "Thorios Teninten, native of Cantus-Senta. The ticks on his face represent the number of Mythidim bounties he's completed. This man is bad news."

The second image was of someone Alina recognized. "Ugarda Pankrish."

Ordin drew in a sharp breath. "You know him?"

"No way. But I met him. On the train a couple days ago."

"Then you're aware of how dangerous he is."

"Yeah. Supposedly, he can't actually fight for real anymore because his punches are just *too* powerful."

"I can't tell if you're joking, but even if his legend isn't wholly based in truth, he's slain more Aelf than the next thirteen Ravers ranked beneath him. A betting man would wager everything on him."

"Your vote of confidence is overwhelming," Alina said flatly.

Ordin flashed her a grin. "Good thing I'm not a betting man." He clicked the button again.

The third image was a mugshot.

"What kind of name is 'Scranvurry'?" said Alina.

"A pseudonym. His real name is Hens Popjay. He'd be unremarkable if not for the fact that he recently popped up in the news—in connection to a triple homicide. All three victims were Ravers, and no slouches, at that."

"A Raver of Ravers. Huh." That was… unusual.

Next was another familiar face. Ordin said, "You'll recall Cesthra Ci of Quartz-Ragvar. The honor code of her people dictates she never use modern weaponry. No firearms, grenades, or anything of the sort. She's stuck with her greatclub, which you'd imagine would be a hindrance in this day and age. But she's apparently killed a *lemlar* with it."

"No freakin' way."

"Believe it. I found her secret, though—the club is studded with shards of an unidentifiable metal. On contact, it poisons carbon-based lifeforms."

"Don't you mean 'unidentified metal'?"

"No, I do mean *unidentifiable*. As in, neither I nor anyone currently alive seems to know what her club is made of."

Alina bit her lip, nodding. "Noted. Who's next?"

They ran through image after image, file after file, for hours, skipping over the small fries, lingering on the big fish. They discussed all the heavy hitters. The nature of Aelfravers, and the wide variety of schools that trained them, made each of Alina and Ordin's case-studies stand out in one way or another. There were snipers, grenadiers, acrobats, fencers, professional wrestlers, soldiers, assassins, and every type of scary individual imaginable.

"Why aren't any of the Top Ten on here?" Alina rubbed her eyes. "Other than Baraam, I mean?"

With a shrug, Ordin answered, "It's only a rumor, but I heard they all moved on once they found out bol-Talanai had accepted the contract. They didn't want to waste their time."

Alina shook her head. "Yeah, okay. He's the favorite. We get it."

Even after that reality check, she was still riveted by this chance to adjust the playing field ever so slightly. Knowledge is power.

Eventually Ordin yawned, tapped his feet, cracked his knuckles. He began to flick through the pictures faster and faster, drastically shortening his descriptions.

"Stop," said Alina, as Ordin was about to skip one Raver entirely. The visage had snagged her attention. "Who's that?"

"These are the bottom-feeders, Stitcher. I think we've reached the point of diminishing returns. We should take a break. Aren't you hungry? I'm starved."

"Go back one." When Ordin complied, she said, "There. That's him—or her." Unlike most of the other Ravers, this one's file contained only one photo. And it was no mug shot or driver's permit or Raver's license. Alina squinted at the grainy black and white blur of a cloaked figure lurking around a warehouse in the dead of night.

Mophead.

This single still-frame from some random security camera was, apparently, the best evidence that the cloaked, stringy-haired, coyote-masked entity even existed.

"That... person was with me on the bus from Puurissei. Ordin, you have to tell me *everything* you know about them."

"Oh, her? She's either the world's best-kept secret or—more likely—nobody of consequence. No record to speak of. Barely even made the list of unmentionables." He yawned again, and he leaned back in his chair, stretching his arms above his head. "She calls herself Morphea—the Queen of Dreams. A bit self-important, and that's coming from *me*."

Morphea, Queen of Dreams.

"So, she's a woman and, by the sound of her name, a Revomancer. Great.

That's *all* you've got on her? *I* could've told you that much."

Ordin shrugged and swiveled the fireplace 'round again. The Watchbox disappeared behind the wall. The open fire sputtered. He fed it another log. Alina was aware that he was speaking but understood none of what he said.

Fixated for another few moments on the afterimage of Morphea, Alina finally blinked and shook off her lingering uneasiness. She had to ask Ordin to repeat himself.

"I said, I think we've done all we can with one night. It's incredibly late—or quite early, depending on one's lifestyle choices."

Torn between the desires to learn more about Morphea and stay the hell out of her way, Alina asked, "Fine. Now that we've seen them, our colleagues, how do we beat them?"

Leaning back, stretching like a cat, Ordin said, "We outsmart them. Whether they rely on Niima or missiles, they're all brutes in one way or another. Brutes often have simple weaknesses—their egos, their honor—and we have only to identify and exploit them. My ViiCtor has already been set to the task of running millions of scenarios and combat simulations, filtering events through the relative skill sets of the Ravers we've covered."

ViiCtor. An Integrated Intelligence like Iingrid, but one not watered down for public consumption. Alina had never had the opportunity of playing around with one, but supposedly it had enough processing power to handle space exploration missions or run air traffic control for any major airport. Basically, a military-grade multimedia operating system.

On reflex, she tried to slip her hands into her jacket pockets and brush her knuckles against her obsolete phone. Only, she couldn't because her phone was with her real body—physically within reach but, practically speaking, a universe away.

"Regardless," Ordin continued, yawning again, "ViiCtor should be done analyzing by—hold on, let me check—midday tomorrow. Shall we resume then?"

"That quick, huh? Yowza." She mentally slapped herself across the face. *Yowza?* Had she really just said that? She might as well flush herself down a toilet right now. Aloud, she said, "Sure thing, we'll pick it back up at noon. I just had one more question."

"Absolutely."

"This might have been a just weird dream I had last night, but, after our… dinner, I think some guy came up to me. Close-shaved head. Carried a big sword. Scars on his face and neck. Looked really rough, now that I'm remembering him more clearly."

"This man, did he say anything to you?"

"Just to stay away from you."

"Me?" Ordin laughed. "Well, he's not wrong. I'm quite excitingly dangerous. Still, he was scarred? Let me guess, he had on a gray woolspun shirt and pants, heavy black boots with a big iron buckle, and he looked like he hit every branch falling down the ugly tree?"

"I try not to be too judgmental about people's appearances, but, yeah, your description's not far off. He was wearing that exact getup. And he walks like someone who's lived a hard life. Who is he?"

Ordin locked eyes with her. "Tolomond Stayd. As of last year, a Raver. If you want to live to see twenty, you'd best avoid him like you would a vlindra during shedding season."

Alina crossed her arms. "If he's a Raver, why wasn't he on the list? What's his deal?"

"Try as I might, I can't get access to his file. It's sealed."

"Even for someone with your resources?"

Ordin pursed his lips, shook his head. "I can only infer that he's being protected by someone with impeccable connections. If I had to guess, it's The Sanctum."

"The Sanctum? I thought they were just a fringe group." Alina clicked her tongue. "I saw a couple of their people screaming in the streets. I didn't know they had any real power."

"Appearances can be deceiving," Ordin said. "The Sanctum's been around for three hundred years or so. At first, they were persecuted. And it's only been a hundred and fifty years, give or take, since they graduated from small-time cult to recognized religion. And they're gaining an alarming degree of favor lately. Just look at that massive eyesore of a stronghold they built right here in The Capital—the Mountain of the Mendicant. That drab slag-heap wasn't there in my grandfather's day." He gritted his teeth. "And, even more than before, everything's been coming up roses for them since they managed to convert Wodjego Walazzin."

"Walazzin—one of the Twelve?"

Ordin nodded. "The Sanctum's been up to an awful lot of mischief in the past eighteen months or so, and the beginning of their more ambitious 'holy work' conveniently coincides with old Wodjego's baptism."

Unable to fully care about all the political interconnections, Alina summarized the points she found most important: "Stay away from Tolomond because he probably works for a shadowy branch of a powerful church. Gotcha."

"Close enough." Ordin stood up, walked over to her. His fingers found her elbow—a gentle, light, and reassuring touch. "Stay by my side, Stitcher, and you'll come to no harm. I promise. Together, we'll prevail."

She looked into his mirror-face. It fell away, then, revealing his eyes, like pinpricks of light at the end of a long, long tunnel. "I believe you," she said.

His form shifted; his features becoming his own again. "I have something I want to show you. Do you have a little more time?"

"Um, yeah, sure."

He smiled, snapped his fingers, and everything went dark.

"What is this place?" said Alina.

She gazed along the infinite sea of roiling black and silver static, listened to its distant steady buzzing. Glinting, colorless sand beneath her feet. Above, a pitch-black void of sky.

A stone appeared in Ordin's hand. He whipped it. It skipped along, bouncing over gentle waves. Wherever it struck, a kaleidoscope of color rippled outward, and voices could be heard—so many of them that what any single one said was lost.

"The Sea of Deleted Comments," said Ordin, facing the waves. "I come here sometimes. To think. To maintain perspective. This place is humbling."

"What do you mean?"

"Everything anyone has ever said that they regretted and removed, every nasty remark flagged by a moderator, every unreturned telephone message… They all wind up here. Lingering for all eternity, the ghosts of the forlorn, the loveless, the tortured souls who scream into the void." He cupped his ear with his hand. "You can almost hear them, their 'Where are yous,' their 'Well, actuallys.' And you figure what they were all really saying was, 'Please. Please, someone, tell me I matter.'"

"But they didn't," said Alina. "And now their echoes are here. Stuck. Just like they were."

"Life is a shout. What we create—friends, family, legacy—is the echo. We remain as long as our echo, and no longer. By our words and deeds, we try to brush up against eternity. Only to fail."

For a few moments, they watched the waves—each drop of the "water" another memory or bungled connection. Heartbroken parting words, tender admissions of love, lively invitations to party. Every time a wave crashed against the shore, the foam and spray hissed, ebbing and flowing. Each bubble a picture or video clip—dogs, cats, accidental shots of someone's thumb or wall or nostril, couples kissing, news footage that didn't survive the editing room…

"Not gonna sugarcoat it, Ordin. That's one lame poem you just quoted."

He turned towards her, his heels grinding in the sand of forgotten chain digimails and birthday e-cards. "That was no poem. It's my own thought."

"Ugh, that's so much worse," she said, grinning. Looking up: "Stars."

"Those are closed accounts—investment funds, shopping credit lines, dating apps. Fees, foreclosures, inheritances, product subscriptions… These tell the true stories of people's lifetimes: buying their first homes, losing everything, finding love."

Sidling up to Ordin, Alina placed a hand on his shoulder. "Why did you bring me here?"

"I find its serenity soothing—and terrifying."

A wave crashed much more forcefully than expected, the waters gliding upward along an invisible wall before falling, falling down again and flowing outward into oblivion once more. As the wave hit, Ordin's face contorted into an agonized grimace.

Pulling her hand away, Alina asked, "What's wrong? Ordin?"

"If I tell you, can you promise to keep it between us?"

"Yeah, of course."

"Promise me."

"I promise, okay? I promise."

He sighed. For what felt like a long time, he said nothing at all. Then he sat down and pulled off his boots, rolling up the legs of his pants. Arms wide, embracing the stark shadows of sea and sky, he waded into the water.

His eyes were closed; he was listening for something. When he opened them again, the pain had fled his features. In its place, there was emptiness. And Alina knew, for one foreboding moment, this cold serenity Ordin claimed to fear.

He said, "When I was nine, my father left me alone in the Thredds. He told me it was for my own good. I had to learn to be strong, self-reliant. He abandoned me in a busy marketspace. The frantic screams—buy, sell, buy—and what they were negotiating *for*—the things I saw, then…

"I don't know how long or how far I ran to get away. Distance and time, after all, are hard to pin down in the Darkthreads. But I eventually found my way, here, to this sea.

"I waited and waited. I thought father would come back for me. 'It's just a joke, a cruel joke,' I told myself. But the silence, the indifferent glare of the stars—I was driven mad with boredom, with panic. The sort of terror that comes only from knowing that there is no escape and you just have to… sit there, alone with your thoughts.

"The waters began to look quite inviting, I remember. So, I worked up the nerve, stripped myself bare, and swam into the open." He pointed straight ahead. "That way. No idea for how long. Again, distance here is a measure of threads of data, not any physical dimension.

"I lost myself, became one with the water. And I couldn't distinguish between my own voice and the voices that formed the waters of the sea and the sand of the beach and the clouds and stars of the sky.

"The next thing I remember is the island. Exhausted, I slipped onto its shores like a dead fish. When I gathered the strength to stand, I wandered it. Until I found others. I wasn't alone. At last, I wasn't alone. We became friends—I knew them all so well. I knew everything about them, and they everything about me. We were very close. I—" He cleared his throat. "I cared for them."

"Were they real?" said Alina.

His brow furrowed and he smiled sadly. "Couldn't tell you. Not now. It's been too long."

"What happened?"

"We fished, swam, played, laughed, sailed. I lived a whole life there, with them." The forlorn smile faded. "My father returned. Like the hand of a soulless god, he reached down and plucked me from my home. In that moment, I felt willing to kill him.

"But I awoke in my chair, on the same day that I'd first entered the Darkthreads with him. Hardly any time at all had passed in the real world, I was told. Still, I felt I'd aged a century. It was so bizarre, sitting down to dinner with my family that night. Rising early for my tutoring sessions the next morning.

"Father forced me to swear not to tell anyone of what happened. What I had suffered because of him."

Alina said, "Did you ever try going back? Finding the island again?"

"A hundred times or more." He threw back his head and laughed, a sudden and violent storm. There were no tears in his eyes, on his cheeks. The laughter subsided. "I'll never see any of them again, even if they did exist. And, as time flowed ever onward, cruelly and callously, I forgot almost everything about them all—their faces, the sounds of their voices, their names. All I have left is how I felt back then. That is all."

Speechless, Alina wondered what she was even supposed to say to all that. "Ordin." She reached for his hand. He let her take it. "Ordin," she said again.

He tugged at her hand, drawing her in a little closer. They stayed there, silent, inches apart, for the span of a moment or two. Alina pulled him, gripping him in a fierce hug that lasted just a second too long.

They separated, fingertips lingering for a heartbeat.

There was nothing but the waves, and the hiss of unintelligible whisper-screams—humanity's weak and unremembered defiance in the face of inevitable annihilation.

At length, Ordin said, "Maybe, when this all over, we could go Thredding together again. For fun. There's much I'd enjoy showing you."

She looked at him. He stared straight ahead, scanning the waters for the island he'd never see again, the island of his youth.

There were a million things she could have said. She settled on: "I'd—I'd like that."

15

BY THE TIME ALINA had exited the Darkthreads, left Ordin's home, and boarded the late-night expedited shuttle bus (minimal stops), it was well past midnight.

Experiencing a sudden pang of guilt for having forgotten about Calthin, she shot a quick message his way, filling him in on the broad strokes of the day—her adventure into virtual reality, her and Ordin reaching an agreement, and so on. She left out the bit about the Sea of Deleted Comments and what had happened there.

She then stowed her phone and watched the neon rainbow of lights and the occasional bubble transports bounce by.

Because it was practically on her way back, and even though she was exhausted, she hopped off at Vitternitu Station, Dyrex District, and walked the three blocks to Mycul's Copse—the site of one of the Bane's three massacres.

Mycul's Copse was so-named because of the architecture's arrangement and design: the shops and buildings had been made to resemble willows, their "weeping" leaves fashioned of lights that drifted with the wind; they formed a ring around a courtyard with, at its center, a platinum statue of the man named Mycul—a legendary hero who supposedly had done this-or-that in such-and-such year. Too lazy to consult Wixolis's handy guide, Alina yawned her way past the monument, noting that the droppings on the shoulders of the statue had probably been left by a vippersnüp, a semi-ethereal, winged, omnivorous meerkat-like creature that fed mostly on human garbage.

Alina had always believed New El to be completely free of Aelf. Whoever had told her that, apparently, had been grossly exaggerating. It seemed that, no matter how high they lived above the clouds, and no matter how tight and draconian their security, the Elementals would never quite get rid of those Others with whom they shared this planet. A fact that the Elementals were finally having to come to grips with, now that the Bane prowled about, unchecked. Small parasites could be ignored, but the Bane of New El…

According to the official report, the last massacre had been the worst of all—a quadruple homicide. (Could you call it a homicide if the creature's not sentient? Alina wondered.) She had to see it for herself.

With it being so late, dark, and cold, she'd expected to find the Copse vacant. To her surprise, someone was hunched over the fountain. A tall man dressed in moldering clothes. She hesitated, considered backing away, but then he turned around and gave a vigorous wave.

She approached the figure, her fingers wrapped around the handle of her hidden pocketknife.

"Hey, there, miss," said the man. He was even taller than he looked: he hunched at the shoulders, shaving a few inches off his height. "What are you doing out here so lonesomely? This part of town isn't unfriendly, but nighttime's no time for a gal to be moseying about by herself. Never know what you might bump into." He ran a hand through his scruffy red-and-gray beard.

"Thanks for the advice." She kept a good six feet between them. "Just passing through, really. Looking for information."

"About the *Thaal*?" said the man, a glint in his bloodshot eyes.

"*Thaal*? No such thing."

He snorted and looked around at an imaginary audience. "Oh, she knows so much, eh? 'No such thing as *Thaalene*', you say? Well, how do *you* explain the Bane's habits, then?"

"I'm looking to find out what those habits are in the first place," said Alina.

His expression turned grave. "The *Thaal* has a terrible glamor about it—it shines as only darkness can, flitting from shadow to shadow, growing in size, changing shape." He edged closer to Alina, hoarsely hissing, "It *feeds* on our waking nightmares, I think. It wants us to be afraid."

Alina inched backwards. "It changes shape? How?"

"I was here when it attacked those four poor fools the other night. No one knew I was watching, waiting for my chance to come aboveground and hunt for vittles and supplies, odds and ends and such. The four youngsters were having themselves a grand old time, hooting and drinking. They were dressed up mighty nice, too. Born into wealth, I'm sure of it." He cleared his throat. "When *it* came, it was small as a mouse, first, hugging the edge of this fountain, right here, like this." He bent at the knees, resting on his shins, and crawled around the circumference of the fountain. "Then, in the blink of my bleary old eyes," he said, leaping to his feet, stretching up his arms, "it was massive, a great swirling storm of shadows. The youngsters, how they screamed—each one crying out a different name. Perhaps they were calling to their mothers. But it was all over so fast. They cried, turned tail, and ran—and they were dead before they reached the edge of the courtyard."

Alina tried to make some sense of what she'd been told.

A shapeshifter with a shadow affinity? Could the Bane be an umbrite? That couldn't be the case. They weren't usually nearly as powerful or confrontational as the Bane. In accordance with their nature, umbrites tended to cling together, glomming onto a host body, maintaining control through careful administrations of images that frightened the host. Except for the lurking-in-the-shadows part, the creature this man was describing didn't fit the bill at all.

Alina needed more information. "How did it attack them? Did you see?"

The man shook his head. "I remember a flash of yellow lightning, though the skies above were clear, I thought. Next thing I knew, I was dreaming of my wife and children back home. And, when I awoke, I was standing where I'd been hiding, slack-jawed, my tongue lolling for all the world to see. And the four young men were sprawled on the ground—torn apart! I can't have any more trouble with the Elemental law, so I fled."

A few yards away from the fountain, a ten-foot square had been cordoned off, the holographic yellow barriers reading "CAUTION—NO UNAUTHORIZED ENTRY." A warning from the Enforcers not to tamper with the scene of the crime. Craning her neck, Alina could just make out the glowing outlines that marked the placement and position of the victim's bodies at the time of their discovery. (The bodies themselves, of course, were long gone, carted off to the morgue.) Alina noted the outlines were missing their heads. Deep, curving gashes had been carved into the fountain and pavement. Whatever had made them must have been huge and frighteningly strong—a fact that didn't line up with the way its victims had fallen, all in a neat little row, rapidly, like dominoes. A creature capable of striking with such speed and precision had to be slim and agile.

So, either the Bane was actually at least *two* Aelf that differed greatly in size and power, or it could indeed shape-change at will.

Alina returned her attention to the stranger. While the yarn he'd weaved certainly was interesting in its own right, what she keyed into was the way he'd said "Elemental law." As if he didn't belong in The Capital at all. Yet another person trapped on this floating city, caught between the Terries and their masters.

She wondered how many more like him lived up here.

"Do you live alone, mister…?" she asked.

His demeanor shifted instantly; he leaned back at the hips, raising his backpack between them as if it were a shield. "Who's asking? You a bootlicker? A pinkojack?"

"Not a chance," said Alina quickly. "I'm just curious. New to this town myself. I just didn't peg you for one of these hoity-toity types I've been seeing all day now."

"Don't look too carefully, miss. I'm not someone either one of us needs you to know. For both our sakes, I think you'd best be getting on, now. I've been out too long. Feeling exposed."

He picked up his backpack, his plastic bags, and the sack into which he'd been stuffing gelder coins he'd retrieved from the fountain. The instant he'd collected his things, with not so much as a glance over his shoulder, he sprinted off.

"Wait," cried Alina.

But the man had ducked between the strands of the artificial willows of Mycul's Copse. She lost sight of him amid the gently swaying lights, and she was left alone to wonder why the Bane had come here and where it had gone.

Why kill four young business bros? Why here? And why leave the red-bearded dude alive?

She stopped herself, suddenly questioning her own questions. Clearly, her gut had decided that the Bane had acted with purpose, but her grandfather had always taught her never to declare anything based on incomplete data. Accordingly, she checked herself.

All she *really* knew, at this point, was that the creature—whatever it was—had seemingly attacked at random. Emphasis on "seemingly." The killings had occurred in different parts of the city, places that were unrelated except for the fact that they were business centers. That could be coincidence. After all, even a mindless night-stalker might accidentally lash out in similar locations. That's chaos for you—from high up enough, it could look perfectly ordered and sensible.

No, the worm that wriggled in Alina's apple wasn't the setting of the crimes but the killing method. The description she'd just heard from that strange man didn't match up at all with what she'd seen for herself at the first crime scene at Tallendum.

Was she the crazy one?

She'd been learning to Rave from her grandfather since shortly after she could walk and talk. But, for the first time, she felt truly uneasy. More than usual. This feeling was far more intense than the typical existential dread that, like a prairie dog, occasionally popped out of the mud stacks of her mind to squeak "hello." Something was horribly wrong, something she couldn't quite put her finger on.

Besting that demon back in Truct had been dicey, sure enough, but the only consequence she'd risked that day was death. Death was simple, easy, understandable. No, she didn't want to die, no way. But dying was by no means the worst possibility.

There were Aelf out there who could imprison your soul, draining it slowly, sometimes over centuries. There were Aelf who were known to chase their prey through looping, mazelike nightmares for what felt like an eternity. Dying, at least, was quick. Even a slow, agonizing end seemed a mercy compared to the tales Alina had heard from veteran survivors of Raves conducted at the edges of civilization.

This hunt for the Bane was giving her all sorts of the most unsettling vibes. The same goosebumps she'd felt when, as a little girl, she'd listened to the ghost stories told by Tahtoh's students.

The way this unknown creature had everyone shrinking beneath its fear-wave… Well, Alina had come to New El and seen for herself how rich, powerful, and self-assured its Assets were (for the most part). To see them terrified of something no one had really gotten a good look at yet—it was not just unusual, it was unheard of. She had grown up hearing and reading about the Elementals, how they didn't bow for *anyone* or *anything*. Yet, here they were, plain before her eyes, confused and scared almost out of their wits. Oh, sure, they kept quieter about it than Alina was used to (people down below were blunter about their emotions). But the Elementals—high, proud, noble, supposedly unshakable—had been reduced to dodgy-eyed, jittery, gelatin-skinned blobs of fear. She could see it on their faces as they walked by, as they bought things, as they talked to one another.

The creepy red-bearded man from a few minutes ago had only been the latest and most obvious example of this festering panic. From him all the way up to the flashy-skirted noblewomen she'd seen earlier that day, Alina could read the paranoia on their faces as easily as she could the street signs.

Elementals weren't any better than Terries, after all. And now, faced with a real, live Aelf for the first time in who-knew-how-many centuries, some of them were beginning to confront that unsettling fact.

Alina thought again about Detective Ding's clashes with the Ravers, in the gymnasium at the Western Precinct and at Sartorian Square. The growing tension had already claimed a few casualties, breaking bones and landing at least three Terries in jail. These violent flare-ups made a lot more sense once she realized the Detective and his colleagues had been acting out of fear. Simple fear.

Like any other bully, The Authority hurt people to stay in control. Because the one thing more frightening than the unknown is powerlessness.

How many more incidents like the one at the Square had there been? And, if Ding and others like him continued to maim and punish to bury the evidence of their own terror, more Elementals might follow their example.

A dark hypothetical hung heavily in her mind for a moment: was this what the Bane *wanted*? To spread the rot of panic to everyone in The Capital, forcing them to despair? Tearing the masks of civility and self-superiority from their faces?

Deep in thought, she had been standing around, like an idiot, alone in the dark. Not paying enough attention to her surroundings. Practically begging to be robbed like the tourist she was.

Dragging her fingers through her wavy hair, she spent some time reexamining the magically-traced outlines where the four dead men had been recovered.

She learned nothing she hadn't already gleaned from Tallendum Road.

Not having too much farther to go, and not wanting to wait around for an hour for the next shuttle bus, she hoofed it back to the motel.

Back in Room 4, she fell into bed.

But sleep just wasn't in the cards tonight.

Making the best of her insomnia, as the pre-dawn sky brightened, Alina canvassed the areas surrounding Tallendum and Mycul, where the beast had struck. With a few hours to kill before her agreed-upon meeting with Cho, she knocked on door after door, asking for interviews with anyone who'd seen or heard anything unusual in the past week or two.

Mostly, she spoke with curt butlers and manservants who shoved her off their respective masters' properties. Sometimes literally with a broom, like she was a rat or a clump of dog hair. A couple of shop-owners did give her a moment of their time—until they found out she had no money and wouldn't be buying any of their wares, and she was promptly shooed away.

She did manage to gather a handful of peculiar accounts that simultaneously helped her understanding and confused her further. The stories these witnesses told supported what she'd learned from the *Thaal*-obsessed man from before: the creature had not yet been positively identified or even clearly seen. The descriptions were so frustrating; the details didn't point toward anything Alina had ever heard or read about. The single element they had in common was their complete lack of sense. However, that fact was of some slight use to Alina: the one thing she knew beyond a doubt about the Bane of New El was that it had some means of protecting itself against prying eyes. Whether it could momentarily blind anyone watching or scramble their brains—whatever its defense mechanism might have been—this Aelf knew how to cover its tracks. That indicated intelligence, just as she'd suspected. And intelligence might mean that the killings weren't random.

Riding the bus back toward the motel, she idly flipped through the apps on her phone, endlessly refreshing her Phys-i and Niima displays (both almost, but not quite, full). And she hate-listened to BillieWere's newest album, *Perfect Pitchfork*. Poppy. No soul. Tired lyrics.

She knew what she had to do next. She wasn't happy about it.

And she'd need top-level Gild clearance. By Buthmertha, Alina hoped Cho could deliver.

A notification in the bottom-right corner of her phone's touchscreen showed her she had an unread message.

Not now, Calthin. Not now.

Fifteen minutes later, she was standing outside of Cho's cramped corner hideout. Eventually, the thief herself shuffled up to Alina.

"You're late," said Cho, pulling back her hood. She'd gotten a black eye since Alina had last seen her.

"I was here before you," said Alina.

"Hah! That's what *you* think. I was just waiting around to make sure you weren't followed or tryna nab me."

"Don't trust me yet, huh? That's fine. But, hey, what happened to your face? Who hurt you?"

"It's nothing. I, uh, bumped my head and fell. I'm square."

Alina balled her hands into fists at her sides. Unwilling to force the issue, she switched topics. "Were you able to get that, um, thing I asked you for?"

"From that weirdo with the lightning earrings? Nah. I tried. Couldn't get close enough."

"Oh." Alina sighed.

"But I can totally do it, you know. Totally. I just need, like, a distraction or something."

"You want me to help you?" She didn't like the idea at all, but nothing better came to mind.

"I wouldn't say that. Like, but if you talk to him, if he turns his back, I can get in there. Do my thing, quick as a cat."

Alina thought about giving Cho grief over having come back empty-handed. She also considered demanding that Cho show her more respect, or at least stop being a total grouch-ball. But she did neither. Instead, she simply said, "I can do that."

"I know where he's gonna be next. He's giving some kinda talk pretty close to here."

"Great. Lead the way," said Alina. She took a moment to examine Cho's flashy rust-red shoes with swooshes of turquoise and white soles. "By the way, you look downright snazzy in those decked-out kicks. Your shoelaces are untied, though."

Cho pulled her hood up. "Yah, I know."

"Probably should fix that. You never know when you might have to run."

"I know!" she growled, shoving her hands in her pockets. "I just don't feel like doing it right now, okay?" She field-goaled a rusty can down the alley.

Alina absentmindedly fiddling with one of her thumbtack ear-piercings. "You don't know how, do you?"

"I do, I said. I just don't care about it. Get off my back, ya nag."

Alina shrugged off the jab. "Okay, gotcha. But, well—tell you what, consider this a favor in exchange for the good intel you've brought me."

As Alina approached, Cho reflexively took a half-step backwards, but after that brief stumble she stayed put. Alina bent down, slowly, deliberately looping the laces, pulling them taut, tying the knots. Single, then double.

When she was done, not wanting to hurt Cho's pride, she said nothing besides, "I'm right behind you. And, I appreciate all your help, Cho."

The girl didn't meet her gaze, instead scampering away from her hideout.

There was a slight skip in her step as she proceeded toward the main street. Barely perceptible, but Alina caught it.

Not too far from them lay Rafleugar Square, home to the Rhetoricum (a debate hall for the richest and most influential men in the city) and the second biggest private library in The Capital. (The only larger one was The Gild's Labradorite Dome). It was a wide expanse of flagstones, each one a piece of a colossal, jaw-dropping, hand-painted illustration—the visual history of New El, from the war with the Twin Dragons all the way up to the laying of the foundations of The Pecunia, the original house in which the founders of the Twelve Families had determined the destiny of all the nation's Assets more than three thousand years ago.

The Square was a place of gathering: years before, there'd been a demonstration here, a protest. Alina had always been hazy on the details, but it had had something to do with the introduction of a new Loyalty Law. All she could remember on the subject was a snippet or two flying from her father's worry-twisted lips.

"They'll never leave us in peace," he'd whispered. "We have no choice."

That had been the last night Alina had seen her parents alive.

Rafleugar Square was also a meeting ground, a space where the Elementals could sit on cushioned cast-iron benches or beneath cream-colored parasols. Wide, open, sun-lit. Peaceful.

Alina looked up and experienced that familiar jolt, her stomach squeezing. "Above" her glided the surface world of the Terries—her world. All its trees and mountains and warehouses and city streets unfurled like a dream. Up here, it was easy to forget that she stood upon a planetoid chained to and magically suspended from the mainland. Head buzzing as if filled with angry bees, she gripped the nearest dainty silver lamppost, clutching it as if it were the only thing preventing her from tumbling into the sky.

Beside her, Cho grumbled, "Oh my gods, could you at least *try* to blend even a little?"

"Sorry," said Alina through gritted teeth. She wiped the back of her hand across her clammy brow. "Suddenly so dizzy." Taking a few unsatisfying breaths, she said, "I'm good now. I'm good."

Ahead, a crowd had clustered before a podium which had been set atop the steps leading to the entrance of the *His Merciful Blade Library of the Elemental* (bit of a mouthful, yeah). Some of these people were upper-class Assets, come to see what all the to-do was about. Many, and especially those nearest the podium, were journalists and camera operators and sound crews and other agitated professionals in tight-fitting business suits.

A deceptively real-looking dog scampered past Alina, the bells on its collar tinkling chipperly. The illusion was almost perfect; as the shaggy-haired dog crossed her path, panting, there was only the barest flicker of pixilation around its lolling tongue. A distortion in the image due to the shedding of excess heat: the tongue was its exhaust pipe, essentially. Alina had read about that stuff in a magazine once, while waiting to make a meager withdrawal from her grandfather's bank account some months ago. To pay for his funeral.

"Everything here is so fake," she complained, rubbing the back of her neck. "Except the sun. The sun is still bright and annoying."

The chatter around the podium dissipated as someone in sunglasses and a sharp black uniform performed a mic check. The little mic drone zoomed a few laps around the podium, buzzed some scales—*do-re-mi-faaaa*—at different frequencies and levels, and then flashed the blue "all systems optimal" indicator light.

The gilded brass doors to the library swung wide, and out stepped pale-eyed Baraam bol-Talanai flanked by his flunky entourage of Gild bootlickers.

"Speaking of fake," Alina mumbled.

The tails of his aquamarine tunic swishing dramatically behind him, his lightning earrings catching the glare of the sun, glinting like coins reflected in the eyes of a pauper, he walked right up to the podium, pressed his palms onto the edges of it until the skin surrounding his knuckles whitened. His lips pursed. The bozos on either side of him crossed their arms and stood around, desperately trying to seem even the least bit relevant.

"Good afternoon," said Baraam. "Gildmaster Ridect called this conference today to alleviate concerns about the hunt for the Aelf at large in our city—the so-called Bane of New El."

Alina clicked her tongue. So, she'd have to stand here and listen to him deliver propaganda. Hopefully the speech would at least be over quickly.

She was about to make a joke for Cho's benefit, but the thief was nowhere to be found. Blended with the crowd, a ghost. A ghost with awesome shoes.

Baraam was saying, "While we haven't yet uncovered the lair of the monster, we can without a doubt lay to rest the rumors that it is a *yuorgith*, *drualoniok*, or *Thaal*—physic or sanguine. I will say this *one more time* for those here and at home who still don't get it: *Thaalene are not real.*"

Having already figured that much out, Alina nodded with satisfaction. She'd been right. Unless, of course, this was some kind of coverup by The Gild. Stating the obvious truth as if it were a ridiculous lie—it was an old trick, but a good one.

She crossed her arms, pinching her chin between thumb and forefinger, thinking. No, it couldn't be a Thaal stalking the city. She had to stop doubting herself.

She tuned out most of Baraam's speech because it was highly repetitious and uninspired. A lot of platitudes like "Don't panic," "Everything is under control," "Our best people are on it," "Wrapped up in no time," and so on.

At one point, a deafening roar tore up the sky over the Square, and every head swiveled just as the shadow of H'ranajaan darkened the library steps. The automaton imitation-dragon circled Rafleugar a few times, and then flew toward the opposite side of town, off to go "keep the peace," "defend and serve," or whatever euphemism The Authority was using these days. The roar and the flapping of its razor-sharp semi-translucent wings were so loud that Baraam had to pause mid-sentence for half a minute waiting for the giant machine to move on. That made Alina chuckle.

The press conference wrapped up, and Baraam posed awkwardly for some photos. He stood there, on his little stage, glaring at the cameras—left, right, center, right, center, left. Stone-faced, iron-jawed, as if he were an automaton himself.

To Alina, just for a moment, he looked every bit the teenager that colored some of her earliest memories. The way the rapid-fire flashes of the cameras made him squint, bare his teeth just a little, hunch and squirm—he seemed entirely out of his element. Awkward. Like he was sitting for a class photo while wearing a sweater he absolutely hated. This struck Alina as weird. Wasn't he, the Number One Raver, supposed to enjoy the spotlight?

When the last pictures were snapped, the audience and members of the press began to disperse. That left Alina standing there in a thinning crowd, in the open, vulnerable.

Baraam immediately spotted her. "Why haven't you gone home yet?"

"Nice to see you too, Baraam. And, I don't need to dignify your very personal question with a response, but I'll tell you this much: I'm not going anywhere until I'm done stuffing into my pockets and bag the fat rolls of gelders I'll be earning once I close this Rave." Alina knew she was blathering, but she had to keep his attention; Cho swiftly approached him from behind. "I'll get it done. Before you. Because you're gonna fail. Because I'm gonna win. It's gonna be me. Because—well, you get it."

Cho waited behind a pillar supporting the arch over the stairs on which Baraam stood.

Unsure of what else she might do, Alina kept talking, "And when I get that money, Baraam, I'm going to make sure—sure, I tell ya—that you never step foot in The School *ever* again."

Baraam smirked down at her. "It will be quite a trick if you can keep me, The School's soon-to-be legal owner, off my own property."

She was about to blurt a comeback when the full gravity of what he'd just said struck her. "You're buying The School?"

Baraam's smug expression said it all.

Bile burned in her gut.

In that moment, she wanted nothing more than to hurt him, yet she knew she couldn't. It was still there—the eternal, useless frustration of knowing your bully is so much more powerful than you.

So, this must be why Mrs. Qamasque's efforts to push her out had gotten much more forceful recently. Sure, Alina had missed rent a couple times—alright, *more* than a couple—but she'd been paying what she could. And she'd thought she and the Qamasques had had an understanding. They knew she was trying. They knew she was giving them everything she could.

But it was like Mrs. Qamasque had told her the other night, *"You're like family to me, but I have a business to run."*

That exchange had happened only three or four nights ago. The very night Alina had decided to embark on this insane quest to salvage what was left of her life. Three nights. Four tops. And, now, here stood Baraam, telling her that he was prepared to destroy her one chance. Because he could.

Alina sputtered, "Mrs. Qamasque promised I had two weeks to get my business sorted out." She watched Cho edge closer, the thief mirroring in perfect time the drifting gazes of the bodyguards flanking Baraam. Staying out of their peripherals. Unseen, so far.

Cho's nearness to her goal ignited within Alina a spark of furious defiance, and she rallied. "Know what? Doesn't matter. When I get the money—when—I'll pay Qamasque double what you're offering. I don't care. The big bounty's as good as mine, Baraam, face it. By Buthmertha, I swear it. And with my cashflow problem resolved, The School will stay in my name. Forever. You hear me? Who even *are* you, anyway? Just some pretender."

Her ears popped. The tile beneath her boots cracked. Around her, slivers of terracotta drifted upward. "*I'm* Dimas's granddaughter."

"You're nowhere near the minimum recommended rank for this job. You're not even a real *Raver*!" he barked. "All you ever do is charge childishly into the unknown. There's only one way this can end, can't you see that?" His arms, resting on the podium, flashed from within, emanating a white light that shot up and down the wood. The podium exploded into glowing splinters.

On instinct, Alina shrunk away, shielding her face with her arms.

Standing over the crackling, red-hot ruins of the podium, Baraam said, "I'll be taking *my* property from *you* sooner than you think. I just got off the phone with charming old Mrs. Qamasque. She remembers me well, always liked me better than you. And I offered her a deal she couldn't dream of refusing. I signed the paperwork last night."

"You're lying," said Alina plucking a smoking splinter from the back of her hand. "You've always been worthless at lying."

"Call her, then," said Baraam, smiling without the barest trace of joy. "Ask."

Cho lunged forward, a blur of motion and energy. Alina didn't see what she did, but, a split-second later, she sauntered off, a satisfied smirk on her lips.

Perfect timing.

"I will call her," Alina said slowly, turning to walk away. "And I have nothing left to say to you."

Refusing to look back, she speed-walked as fast and as far away as she could.

Before she knew it, she was back at Cho's hideout, and her fingers numbly slapped her phone's screen, dialing Mrs. Qamasque's number.

The restaurant owner picked up almost immediately, answering in her fanatically rehearsed tones, "Traditional Kadician Cuisine. This is Mrs. Qamasque. How may I help you?"

"Is it true?" said Alina, her voice cracking.

"Alina is that you? I can hardly hear—Where are you?"

"Is it true about Baraam?" Fighting back tears. "You're giving him The School?"

Silence. Then, "Alina, my dear, I am so sorry. But my husband and I have to do what is best for family. If someone comes in offering much more money than we ever ask before—we had to take the chance. I am sorry. I know it's not easy to hear, but I am so unhappy about this for you."

Scraping and grinding furiously, the cogs and bolts and other pieces of Alina's brain tried out idea after idea. Finally, she said, "I'll pay you double what he's offering."

"You don't have no money, sweetheart."

"But I *will.* That's why I'm here—in The Capital—to make money. I'll have it all for you, and more, Mrs. Q. Please," she rasped through the tears, "don't take the last piece of my grandfather from me."

"I have sympathy for you. Really, I do. But my decision is made. Have your things out by next week."

"You can't do this to me, damn you!" Alina shouted into the phone's tiny overworked mic.

"I know you're feeling bad, so I will ignore that last comment. Goodbye, Alina, dear. I hope all—"

Alina crushed the pad of her finger against the "hang up" icon, bending the nail back. She felt no pain, only rage.

Something tugged at her elbow—a hand, a small one. It was Cho's. She said, "Having a bad day? This should cheer you right up." She clutched something in her hand.

Wiping a small snot bubble on her jacket sleeve, Alina cleared her throat.

Cho spun on her heels, wide-eyed like a cat tracking a particularly chubby goldfish. She tossed Alina what she'd been holding.

Alina caught it and did a double-take: she was holding a weathered leather wallet. Flipping it open, she saw great big wads of cash stuffed into its folds and compartments. Not only that, but Baraam's arrogant smirk was staring back at her—from the photo on his Raver's license.

"Cho. Cho, you did it, you beautiful rascal, you. I'd hug you, if I weren't afraid you'd stab me for trying."

Cho nodded. "Smart. You're learning." The grin on her face, however, displayed nothing close to anger or even her usual irritated impatience.

Alina wasn't done singing her praises. "You were amazing! Ah-mazing. I barely even saw you sneak up to him. And I knew you were coming. Your talent is—I gotta tell ya, it's something *else.*" She held Baraam's license up to the light. "And do you know what this is? Like, do you even *know*? It's a Raver-S license. It's got the highest security clearance." She laughed. "Agh, you fantastic, creeping highwaywoman. I love it."

Alina leaned against the mound of garbage that was Cho's makeshift home. What a rush the last twenty minutes had been. She felt confident that she'd never before moved so quickly and fully from annoyance to despair to joy.

But she clamped down on all these emotions, bottled them up for future tasting. Now that she had a Raver-S badge on hand, she could initiate phase two of her research into the mystery of the Bane of New El.

"El-beast," she mumbled to herself distractedly. "*Hell*-beast! Hah. That's a good one. I hope the news ends up calling it that."

Her phone buzzed. With a vocal and sharp exhale, she flicked the screen with her thumb. Another message from Calthin.

Again, bad timing. Making a mental note to catch up with him later, she focused on her big plans for that night.

But first, to Ordin's place for more information-gathering.

Alina glanced at Cho. "Your laces came undone again. How did that even happen? Do you enter a parallel dimension when you go all thievy, a dimension where knots untie themselves?"

Cho looked at the ground for a moment. She seemed to be carefully choosing her next words: "No one ever taught me. Will you?"

Alina was checking her phone to see if Ordin had texted any updates. "What? Oh, yeah. Sure." She knelt and repeated the procedure from earlier, slowing it down, repeating it a few times so Cho could take note of the steps.

"Why aren't all shoes zip-ups?" said the girl, thumping her heels against the ground.

"You know what, that's a reasonable question. Seems like it would save time." Alina stood. "Speaking of time, gotta go for now. Maybe practice on your own before I get back."

"Now you're patronizing me."

"You're right. Sorry. I've only ever had to worry about adults. Guess I don't know how to talk to kids."

"But I'm not a kid."

"Okay, yeah. Sorry again. Um. Anyway, where did you learn that word, 'patronizing'?"

"A book," was all Cho would say.

"You really are full of surprises."

Cho shrugged.

Alina broke the silence with, "Well, thanks a billion and a quarter, Cho. You're literally a life-saver. You've given me a chance. Time to go make it count."

"Sweet. You know where to find me." And Cho ducked into her trash cave, a few orange-flavored cola cans tumbling from the heap to roll into a puddle of muck.

Alina left her there, in her private space, as private a home as anyone could hope to make in the sprawl of New El, where the skyscrapers were densely packed and ringed by rails, dotted with solar panels, and home to all sorts of prying, judgmental eyes.

Alina left her there, promising to return, and headed straight for Ordin's.

One way or another, Baraam would get what was coming to him.

16

C*LUB MORIBUND.* THERE COULD be no name more appropriate for this den of sinful abandon.

Tolomond staked out the front entrance, assessing the relative strength of the two guards there, watching the flashes of white teeth, bling, diamond-crusted glasses, globules of spittle flying from mouths twisted in gluttonous revelry. Alcohol sloshed from plastic cups, the cups flying from hands and into gutters, the gutters overrunning with vomit.

And in the naked light—a parody of the light The Author wrote into existence at the dawn of time—Tolomond shivered at the frigidity clinging to his soul, this shudder an involuntary, instinctive response to the sweaty, hot, writhing devilry unfolding before him.

If this was how bad it was outside, he dared not imagine the carnality occurring within. The sheer, nauseating moistness of it all. The images dancing before his tightly shut eyes threatened to overwhelm him.

Soon enough, the quaking in his abdomen subsided, and his fear was replaced by a rigid-spined, ice-pillared anger. He leaned into this coldness, let it numb his heart for what lay ahead.

The noise—the vapid *thump-thump-thump* of the droning club "music"—it made a mockery of The Author. This brazen, blaring, manic assault on the ears burned the last shreds of serenity from Tolomond, scorching the fields of his mind.

He'd come here for that Ivoir wretch, but he'd hesitated again. Hesitated—Lord forgive him—when he saw the girl. The tall one from the other night. With the white and blue hair. She'd linked her arm with Ivoir's. Ivoir's arm. She'd smiled. The empty-eyed gleam of one who nods along but cannot understand.

She was lost.

So, it *was* too late. The hourglass sands had fallen like so much rain; the storm had passed, leaving behind only ruin.

The reprobate, the heathen. Ivoir had tangled her in his web of lies, of hypocrisy. If indeed she could *ever* be saved, her reunion with the light must await the separation of Ordin Ivoir's head from his shoulders.

The spotlights, strobe lights, the multicolored and flickering halogens… They blinded Tolomond, and he shrank away from the line wrapped around the block three times.

He despaired at what he saw: hour after hour, night after night, all the sheep marching eagerly to the slaughter of their souls.

He slapped himself across the face. None of that was important now. His holy charge was all that mattered; there was only the mission.

There were many reasons Ordin Ivoir had to die, but the greatest of these was the simple fact that The Author had decreed it. It was Written. And there was no law above the divine.

So Tolomond waited. And waited.

Hours passed. The sun began to crest the horizon, spilling itself over the beauty of The Author's work—all the little separate doings of man and beast, perfectly orchestrated in grand celestial harmony… The interconnectivity of all things was just so much more evident at dawn. He felt such a strong sense of renewed peace that he momentarily forgot about why he'd come here in the first place.

Perhaps he'd better try again another night. There would be more chances.

His targets hadn't come out all night. Was this a test of his patience?

"Patience is a virtue." He sighed.

Shaking the stiffness from his limbs, grasping the reassuring solidity of Rhetoric's pommel, he pushed off the wall, ready to leave.

He would be ready for the moment The Author saw fit to test his faith.

This dawn was an eruption of purples, pinks, blues, and fiery whites. Streams of molten sunlight converged like a slow-moving but inexorable wave of magma, engulfing him.

A tear rolled down Tolomond's cheek. All this beauty.

But his rapture was cut short by a loud, nasally voice. There approached a man in a tight blue full-body suit with a yellow jacket over it. The shape of the blue suit made it clear that he was wearing a tactical vest underneath. He had a stun baton and gun clipped to his belt, another sidearm strapped to his calf. Arrogantly walking up to Tolomond, he placed a hand on his shoulder. "Sir, what you are doing out here? Sir?"

Tolomond said, "Enjoying the miracle that is this life by singing the praises of The Author of Creation."

The man in the blue suit looked to his two colleagues, one on either side of him. Both wore translucent plastic suit jackets, revealing gray dress shirts and various sidearm holsters strapped to their chests and hips. Their ties had been clipped with the Ivoir family crest in gold. The three of them shared a chuckle at Tolomond's expense.

Plasticks, Tolomond noted. Guns for hire legally required to wear clear clothing to display to one and all their lawfully carried armaments. Hence the name. But there was an additional meaning: just like plastic, these mercenaries were possessed of the most malleable of moral codes, easily adapted—or discarded—in serving their employers.

No surprise that the cowardly Ivoir had sent his flunkies to pester Tolomond. "What's it to you," he said, taking a step forward, "where I stand and what I do?"

"We've received a complaint is all. Nothing personal. It's our job to take care of… any issues that may arise."

"I haven't done anything." He gave the speaker another critical glare. "And you're not even with The Authority."

The man in the blue suit licked his lips. "That's almost true. We are, in fact, *higher* up the food-chain than the run-of-the-mill cops. My advice? Play nice."

Tolomond grimaced. "Did you rehearse that line?"

"You're being awfully fresh, friend." The blue suit brushed his yellow jacket back, revealing a chrome-plated handgun. "Why don't you come with us? Have ourselves a nice little heart-to-heart. One religious man to another. Even if you follow that wacky new Author trend, I'm sure we can find some common ground. What d'you say?"

"I say that there is no god but The Author Who Wrote the World. All our stories are His purview. His is the ultimate power in the universe." Tolomond rubbed his jaw. "That is all."

"Let it not be said I didn't try." The man in the blue suit sniffed. "You fanatics sure do make me chuckle. It's like we're not even speaking the same language." His two underlings stepped forward, their clear plastic suits rustling as they unclipped the straps on their holsters, their fingers twitching. The one in the blue suit continued, "I'm going to have to ask that you vacate the premises, sir. Our employer needs to feel he can safely exit the building. And you've been acting far too bold for comfort. Don't think we haven't seen you watching for him tonight."

"You're nothing more than dogs, yipping for scraps. As I told you, I'll stand wherever I please." Tolomond's gaze slashed across all three of their faces, and their hands drifted ever closer to their weapons. "Try it. Go on. I've been hoping you would."

The sun had risen. The crowd thinned. Giggling and belching and stumbling, the revelers began to return to their respective homes after their night of moral degeneracy. That meant fewer witnesses. A sign from Above.

I hear You, Lord.

The sun had risen, and it was at Tolomond's back. The lapdogs squinted at him. He had the advantage.

I hear You, Your Voice crystalline in Its clarity.

"Awfully cocky, aren't we?" The man in the blue suit scowled. "I wonder, did your god make you bulletproof?"

Tolomond loosened the blade in its scabbard at his hip. "Would you like to find out?"

The three men shared a final chuckle, which they cut short with practiced timing, drawing their handguns almost in unison. Their weapons free, they lifted their arms, lined up their shots—but Tolomond was faster. He kicked the ball of his foot into the blue suit's knee, fracturing the cartilage with a *pop* like wet wood burning. The blue suit went down howling as Tolomond spun around him, pirouetting between the two other bodyguards. His greatsword flashed in the brilliant light of early dawn, the flat of the blade thwacking the gun from one hand and bouncing to smash the jaw of the other. Multiple bones broken with each strike.

Next, Tolomond swept the legs out from the one with the busted hand and wrist, catching him with a punch to the gut. The mercenary was out cold before he hit the ground. The one with the shattered jaw moaned and backed away, but Tolomond grabbed him by the ears, yanked down hard, and delivered a knee to his chin. Knock-out number two.

To deal with the blue suit, Tolomond delivered a steel-toed roundhouse to the side his head, efficiently silencing his agonized screams.

By the frantic voice coming from the communicator on each of the bodyguards' wrists, Tolomond assumed he'd been made. But The Author had now given him more than one sign that the time had come to prove himself. To the Hierophant, to all The Sanctum.

"I am Your Instrument," he said, striding toward the emptying club.

Stragglers filtering out of *Club Moribund* glared, wide-eyed, at him, muttering, tripping over each other to give him as wide a berth as possible. Some sobered up enough to whip out their cellphones and call The Authority.

It wouldn't matter, however. The Authority would not arrive in time to stop Tolomond.

He brandished Rhetoric, and proceeded inside…

When he'd finished, there were a handful more maimed and dismembered Plastics scattered around the dance floor and strewn across some bar stools, and he had Ivoir cornered in the VIP lounge. With the girl.

About halfway through the fight, the music had cut out; the last of the staff, the final DJ, had fled the scene.

Give or take three minutes before The Authority arrives, Tolomond thought, flicking droplets of blood from his blade.

Soberly, he looked up at them—Ivoir and the corrupted girl. They were standing on top of a floating bar, hovering about three feet over a bean-shaped, heated indoor pool. The water bubbled. The two sinners blubbered, clinging to each other. Their tears and snot fell like a tiny localized rain shower.

As he approached the red ropes that divided the jacuzzis and gravity-defying enchanted bar from the rest of the club, he called out, "If you come down, I swear to the Lord I'll make it quick."

They continued to weep and wail. Tolomond hated to admit it, but he grew impatient. He walked over to the pool's edge, picking up a wooden lounge chair. Testing its weight, he nodded. Then he hurled the piece of furniture at Ivoir and his companion.

They were thrown backwards, off the bar, splashing into the pool. Seconds later, they broke the surface, flailing, sputtering, crying, choking.

Tolomond intercepted them as they clambered out of the water. Wrenching two fistfuls of hair, he shoved them back down, thrusting their heads under.

Calmly, forcefully, he held them beneath the frothing water for a minute. Maybe a little less. Until there were no more bubbles. No more ripples.

It was only after he pulled their still bodies out that he realized his mistake.

Without emotion, he asked his god, "Are You testing me yet again, Lord?" But he knew the answer. Of course this was a test.

Everything was.

He knelt, inspecting the bodies. They reeked of that all-too-familiar tangy ozone scent—*magic.*

After he'd drowned the man and woman, the illusion spells cast upon them must have faded. They no longer looked much at all like Ivoir and the girl whose name he didn't know. They were too tall and too short, their hair black. Wrong color, wrong sinners.

Tolomond sighed heavily. He'd been duped. *Mages and their devilish tricks.*

He wiped his blade off on the jacket of one of the dead or unconscious mercenaries just as he heard sirens in the distance.

Sheathing his sword, Tolomond left *Club Moribund* through the kitchen.

Thank you, Lord, for giving me another chance to serve as Your Instrument.

The sun greeted him as he exited the building. He'd had to flee this scene, but it wasn't over. He would not stop until his mission was fulfilled.

It was a new day, a good day to tremble in awe of the majestic wrath of The Author.

17

IN ORDIN'S OFFICE, HE and Alina sat across from one another on his expensive swivel chairs.

It was supposed to have been a fun, productive conversation about how the two of them were going to divide the labor surrounding their shared hunt. But there had been news. Awful news.

Alina didn't know how to respond to what Ordin had just told her.

She finally settled on "How?"

"A sword, apparently," said Ordin.

"A sword?" She scrunched up her face. "No, I don't mean *what implement did he use*! I wanna know *how this happened.* What were they all even *doing* there in the first place?"

Ordin couldn't meet her gaze. "Precautions had to be taken. We both read his file. Tolomond Stayd is—to put it far too mildly—unstable."

"But you brought me into it," said Alina.

"I certainly did not. How do you figure?" He dragged a hand through his glimmering, multicolored, ever-changing hair. "I didn't tell you because I didn't want you involved. I would never dirty your hands with this."

"But you still had someone *who looked like me* in there. And now they're dead." Alina grimaced at him. "You're taking this way too well. I feel sick."

"You think I feel no guilt about what happened? The events at the *Moribund* were not the plan. He was supposed to harass the body doubles and my men would step in and take care of him. I never wanted anyone to get hurt. At most, I'd hoped Tolomond would be turned over to the Western Precinct. Make him the problem of some downtown flunky."

"Yeah, well, that clearly worked out great."

Rubbing at his eyes, Ordin said nothing. His default smirk had long-since cracked and fallen from his sharp face; his brow wrinkled with worry, like the jagged blades of a plow had been dragged across it.

Alina softened. "Hey, Ordin. Hey, I didn't mean to sound like I was making this your fault. I'm just—I'm in shock."

"So am I. Now I have to clean this up." He tapped one of his three or four wristwatches and a green hologram popped up. He keyed in a few commands, twisting it this way and that, before it disappeared. "And hire new Plasticks."

"I wish you'd have run your plan by me first. Aren't we in this together? Wasn't that the deal?"

He finally met her gaze. "You're right. You're so right. And I'm very sorry. About all of it." He stood up, walked over to her. "I should have consulted you. I should have told you everything. But you have to believe me when I say that, flawed as my logic was, my motivations were pure." He fell to his knees in front of Alina so that she sat above him. "I only wanted to protect you. And me, of course—I definitely am not ready to die anytime soon. But you, also. I will not let you come to harm."

Looking down on him, despite everything, she had to stifle a smirk. "Get up, Ordin. You're being ridiculous." She got out of her seat, offered her hands, and helped him stand. Realizing they were now well within each other's personal space bubbles, she took an awkward step back. "Where do we go from here? About Tolomond, I mean."

He said, "I assume I'll not be able to convince you to have an armed escort at all times."

"Not a chance. Anyway, they didn't much help those two random people who just got murdered."

"For the record, they were all my father's employees, soldiers for the cause. They knew the stakes." He paused, thinking. "If you refuse protection, the next best thing would be to keep to populated areas, and don't go anywhere alone at night. I can't say if he's independently interested in you or if your body double was killed because she was with mine. In other words, he may have made both of us targets, or he simply doesn't care how many bodies he stacks up while working his way towards his objective." Ordin cleared his throat. "Me."

"Stick to the light and don't get cornered alone," Alina recapped. "No sweat. I do that automatically."

Ordin gave her a quizzical look.

"Used to get bullied a lot," she explained.

"This is nowhere near the same as bullying, Stitcher."

"Yeah, though, it is. The risks are higher, but Tolomond's still just a disturbed, jumped-up schoolyard tough who takes his self-hatred out on others."

"Just keep away from him. Please."

"Why's he after you, anyway?"

"I have no clue." Ordin turned his back on her, heading to the walk-in storage closet opposite his many computers and other digital devices. "A vendetta against my family, maybe? Tolomond's deep in that Sanctum business, so, for all I know, it could be some kind of holy war against my father and his legacy."

Alina stared at him blankly.

"Right, I forgot, you are not plugged into the political foolery of The Capital. How I envy you." He shrugged. "Among my dear father's many responsibilities is serving as High Priest of Plutonia. Given that she's the state-recognized chief Goddess of El, I can imagine how a fanatic like Tolomond would take offense. According to Sanctumite doctrine, besides this Author of theirs, all gods are illegitimate. It's no secret. They publicly denounce the pantheon every day. And if they're willing to call Plutonia a false goddess in the streets, I shudder to imagine what they're doing in the shadows."

"I see," said Alina. "I'll be careful. Couldn't we still get The Authority to lock him up?"

"If he had hurt anyone other than Ivoir employees. Or, if there'd been any witnesses other than my personnel. The problem is that we live in a world in which the government is run according to different interests. These interests often conflict with one another because the Twelve Families do not always get along."

"No kidding. You're really pulling back the curtain for me," Alina said dryly.

"My point is, I was acting on my own, using my own enforcers." Opening the closet doors, he stepped inside. "Here's a truth for you: what we call 'The Authority' is made up of security and military personnel funded by a common pool of resources that belongs to *all* of the Twelve. The Enforcers and army can do nothing without the consent of the majority. And, no matter what my family and others might think of the religious zealots infecting this city, there's consistently been one powerful voice that has stifled—time and time again, I am telling you—any attempts to investigate the dubious deeds of The Sanctum and their agents."

Alina recalled something Ordin had told her last time they'd met up. "Lemme guess, Walazzin?"

Ordin poked his head out of the closet to nod. "So, you can see our predicament, here. The Authority is held in check by Walazzin's backdoor scheming. For all we know, he may well be the one protecting Tolomond. Maybe he's even the one plotting to have me killed. Who can say? But I need proof before I can move against him. And, until I know for certain, please, please, please be careful."

Alina crossed her arms, leaning most of her weight on her right leg. "Kinda cute that you're so worried about me."

"At least take a weapon with you. I have some really outrageous ones that can—"

"No weapons." A wave of her hand dismissed the suggestion. "I don't do weapons."

"You are impossible," said Ordin, but there was a glint of humor in his eyes.

"Wait, Tolomond's an Aelfraver. Maybe The Gild could step in. They have their own procedures for punishing bad behavior."

"Huh," said Ordin, cupping his chin. "True. I got so entangled in the politics I almost forgot about our profession's governing organization. Yet I doubt they'll do anything in a hurry."

"Ugh." Alina groaned, rolling her eyes. "Why's that?"

"The man who runs The Gild? Gildmaster Covenant Ridect?"

"I've heard the name."

"Great. Well, his brother's name is important, too. The Sanctum—you know, the cult that's got Tolomond running around murdering people like it's nothing?—it's headed by a man named Pontifex. Pontifex *Ridect*."

"Wow. Any chance you're kidding?"

Ordin's laugh petered out. That was all the answer Alina was going to get, and all she needed.

"I have got to get started cleaning up this disaster however I can." He returned to the closet, ducking out of sight. She heard him rummaging around in there for a moment. When he returned, he was holding a large, overstuffed cardboard box.

"*In the meantime*," he said, setting the box in front of her feet, "it would be oh-so helpful if you could go through these."

She tapped the box with the toe of her boot. The lid slid off. "What the hell are they? Files?"

"Non-digital data points concerning our host of competitors. There's bound to be good stuff in there, information that hasn't been shared anywhere else. Not even on the 'Threads." He grinned. "I pilfered these beauties myself, right from under The Authority's nose."

Alina said, "So, that's it? That's what you want my job to be? What about surfing the 'Threads for rumors about the Bane? What about knocking Baraam out of the race?"

"I wouldn't ask if I didn't think it would be useful." Ordin scratched his neck. "I would do it myself, but, unless you think you can impersonate me well enough to fool my staff—and run my entire organization for a few days—maybe we should keep to our respective spheres of usefulness for now."

"You're not serious. You can't be." She glared at the dusty old box full of papers. "Can't you just, like, run a search for this info? Comb the 'Threads, or whatever the expression is?"

"Afraid not." He shrugged. "Not all information is digitally accessible. Some work must still be done by hand, and, well…"

"Yeah, yeah, I get it."

"You're not happy."

"Of course I'm not happy. I hate reading legal and historical documents. If I wanted to read academic, hifalutin crap like this, I'd have shot for college."

He placed a hand on her shoulder and smiled innocently. "For your sacrifice, I thank you." Gesturing towards the closet, he added, "There is a whole lot more where that came from, by the way." As he headed for the door: "I'll have my manservant make you some supper. Anything you'd like. If you need a break, there are fully hooked-up Watchboxes in—well, in every room, come to think on it. Call me if you need me. I'll be back as soon as I'm able. And, if you have this done when I return, let's go out together. For dinner."

He was out the door.

Alina shouted after him, "Thanks, Ordin! So stoked about all this."

"I knew you'd love it," she heard him yell.

Staring at the wall, Alina waited a full fifteen minutes after he left, just to be sure he'd really gone.

Shooting one last bemused glance at the box overflowing with stacks of papers and folders, she pointed, said, "Oh, no, ma'am."

"I'll have my manservant make you some food," he'd said to her. As if she were a lapdog. Or his eighty-year-old great-aunt.

Well, Ordin would soon find out that she most certainly was not all about that busy work, and she would not be swept under the rug.

She walked up to the nearest wall, the one with all the desktop computers. Pulling her phone out of her pocket, she glanced at her Niimameter. *Half-full.* All the excitement had really taken it out of her. But 50% should be enough to get the job done.

Pressing her palm against the solid wall, she let her senses drift beyond her body, eyes rolling back into her skull. She felt bricks beneath the wood paneling, the steady pulses of electricity traveling along the wires buried within. Her perception melded itself with the inside of the wall, and then she was there, moving through the bricks as if she were walking underwater.

Luurkeyari's Material Phase-Shift. No simple spell to pull off, but Geomancy—of all the magical disciplines—had always come most naturally to Alina.

She passed between rooms, skirting the families of mice as best she could so as not to disturb them. She swam over the kitchen, glancing down at Ordin's balding butler as he busily chopped chives.

The front door, she reasoned, would be more closely watched. Especially now that Tolomond was after Ordin. So, she opted for a sneakier exit.

Down and down she went until she reached an unlit room in the basement. From there, she could creep out the back door, or a vent or something.

She clawed her way through the exterior wall. Solidifying her hands again, she used them to pull the rest of herself into the open.

She shivered—well, her particles vibrated—as damp, chilly air passed through her. A few steady breaths of stale basement air and she regained her normal physicality.

Seconds after she'd returned to her usual, fully solid state, the hanging naked lightbulb above her head flickered on. Her luck was as good as ever.

No time to think—she dived behind a rumbling icebox, a huge spark of static electricity spearing her fingers as they brushed the machine's metal shell.

Three people entered, dragging three-legged wooden stools behind them. They were dressed in tight black pants, the sleeves of their white button-ups rolled up to the elbows.

One of them, a big, hairy-armed brick of man, his bionic eye glinting by the incandescent light of the single bulb above, immediately spotted Alina.

"Best come out, girl," he barked. "It's three to one, and Tevriend may be old and slow but even he can't muck up these odds."

"Yes," said the graying, lanky, leather-skinned man. "I may not look it, but my smacks pack quite the wallop. Just ask the Young Master. He remembers." The joints of his legs creaked. Gears grinding.

"It's alright," said the woman with them as she pinched the bridge of her crooked nose. The scars on her forearms and knuckles sang a saga of many a night spent street-fighting. There was a scar on her throat as well, right over the larynx. Maybe that explained why her voice sounded just the faintest bit as if she were speaking into the whirring blades of a fan. "You're Alina, aren't you? The Young Master's… friend?"

Grumbling, Alina stood. So much for her daring escape. "Yeah, you caught me."

"She's a guest, guys," the woman told her colleagues. She cracked her knuckles, and then jabbed a thumb into her chest, saying, "I'm Mystlin." She clapped the square-shaped man on the shoulder. "This is Jaggos." She flicked her nose toward the older man. "And Tevriend."

"You're… servants?"

Mystlin gave a nod, her muscled shoulders and neck tugging at her starched white shirt.

"Ah. Pleasure meeting you, miss," said Tevriend, setting his chair down next to the wooden table in the center of the room.

Jaggos shrugged. "Any friend of the Young Master's a friend of ours. If there's anything we might do for you, only say so." He set his chair opposite Tevriend's.

Mystlin completed the triangle, sat down, and produced a set of playing cards. "We were just about to fan the flames of our hatred for one another over a game or two of Blind-Eye. Care to join?"

Unsure of how far she could push her luck, Alina said, "Actually, I'm in a bit of a hurry, so…"

Nodding, Mystlin said, "Another day, then. Servant's entrance is that way." She pointed before tossing her cards to Jaggos, who shuffled.

Tevriend rubbed his nose. "Am I mistaken, or was it the Young Master's wish for his charge to remain indoors today?"

With a twisted smile, Mystlin said, "I don't recall that exact order being vocalized."

"'Charge'?" Alina bristled. "I'm not his 'charge.' We're partners. Equal partners."

It was Jaggos's turn to grin. "Don't mind us. We're nothing but a buncha gossiping busybodies." He shot Tevriend a knowing look. "Seems to me, old friend, that this one can handle herself. How she got down here without setting off a single one of the silent alarms we set, without being caught on any of the cameras—quite a trick, I'll say. Might be for the best she don't want to play with us, Mysti. Probably got the devil's own luck in cards."

"I expect she knows what she's doing," Mystlin agreed.

Alina waited a beat. The three servants remained seated, relaxed. None made a move to grab her.

"So, you're letting me go?"

"I wouldn't call it 'letting.' You're a guest here, and we're the help. You can do as you please."

"Can't say as I'm thrilled about this situation," said Tevriend, scooping up the cards he'd been dealt.

"Your hand or the girl?" Jaggos asked.

Tevriend scowled at him. "Oh, wouldn't you like to know?"

Alina pursed her lips and took a tentative step toward the door behind the old man, a door that creaked slightly, opening up into the kitchens and the direction Mystlin had indicated.

As Alina moved away, the woman spoke up: "Don't ever let anyone tell you you're wrong to do things your way."

Alina paused mid-step.

"Eh?" said Tevriend.

"Just musing. Pay me no mind," said Mystlin, but she let her meaningful look linger on Alina, who'd glanced back over her shoulder.

"Thanks," said Alina, then, unsure of what exactly to make of this exchange but certain that she'd either accidentally passed some kind of test of initiation or she'd been vouched for—probably by Mystlin with her patchwork of scars and her machine-supported voice.

Had it been Alina's imagination, or had Mystlin's eyes touched on Alina's arms? The ends of the bandages poked out from the sleeves of her jacket, slowly staining a faint gray. Alina flexed her fingers, balled her hands into fists.

"Won't you get in trouble for this? I'm grateful, don't get me wrong, but—"

Jaggos chuckled. "What's he gonna do, fire us?"

Still fixated on his hand, Tevriend snapped his fingers at Alina. "I'm third-generation. Mystlin here cut her teeth on the bones of the Patriarch's enemies. Buthmertha knows, Jaggos *delivered* the Young Master. And my grandad was wipin' the Young Master's *grandad's* bottom when he were just a babe. We was born acclimated to The Capital. Help like us is hard to find on El. Hell, help like us is hard to find anywhere."

"Oh, sure," Jaggos said, blowing emphatically into a handkerchief, "the Ivoirs could find *someone* else. But quality, time-tested help is worth its weight in jewels, no mistake. So—"

"So, bugger off, girl," said Tevriend. "The triumvirate have spoken."

"You're covered." Mystlin winked.

"And come back and play with us sometime. I'm bored with only taking these two fools for all they're worth," said Jaggos.

"Thanks," Alina blurted, and she left.

Skirting sideways around wooden islands covered in cutting boards and pristine knives, ducking under hanging ceramic, stainless steel, and cast-iron pots and pans, she found the servant's entrance.

Before anyone *else* was the wiser, she was off, jogging over the Ivoir compound grounds.

She'd been putting it off too long. It was high time to do possibly the stupidest thing ever.

But first, on her way to her destination, Alina stopped by Cho's hideout.

The girl wasn't there, so Alina left a note—an apology. Short and sweet:

> *Sorry I bailed on you earlier. I had to go meet someone. Not like that. Just important.*
>
> *If you get this in time, I need another favor. Can you meet me outside the Aelfraver's Gild HQ after midnight? I promise I'll find a way to make it worth your while.*
>
> *I could use an extra pair of eyes for what I've got planned.*

She wasn't sure what else to say, so she added the sign-off:

> *Thanks.*
>
> *S.*

She folded the note and tucked it under the top-most piece of junk—a leaning bucket. Hopefully it would be conspicuous enough to someone looking for it. Cho was clever; she'd notice.

Whether she'd respond, though? That was a little iffy.

18

THE PROBLEM WITH BREAKING into The Gildhall, the business and educational headquarters of The Gild, was obvious enough: the place had been designed and built by Aelfravers. The walls, windows, doors, arches, pillars, columns, and even the grounds themselves, were imbued with so many charms and countercharms that to even make the attempt was supposedly suicide. The second an uninvited toe touched down on Gild property, its owner would be rooted to the spot, wrapped up in thorny vines, set on fire, or teleported directly into the holding cell of the nearest Authority precinct. Sometimes all of the above, all at once.

Luckily for Alina, although she hadn't been invited, neither would she be breaking and entering.

She tapped Baraam's Raver-S card against her forehead, grinning to herself.

Anything less than S-level clearance would require sign-in at the front desk. Even with Baraam's badge, to say nothing of Rooster's forged license, she probably never would have gotten past the attendant. After all, she and Baraam looked about as much alike as a needle and a sword. However, because Baraam was so Very Important and Exalted among Ravers, he could enter and exit The Gild at will through the faculty's private entrance. No fuss. And that meant now Alina could do so as well.

It was a mystery why The Gild bigwigs would allow such a glaring security risk *until* you remembered that only the Gild Grandmaster, select faculty members, and the Top Ten Ravers were granted this privilege. Also, it was rightly assumed that, whoever *could* steal anything from someone like Baraam probably deserved to. (Ravers were an extremely competitive bunch. "Merit" they valued above all else. Losing his wallet would probably cost him a lot of political points with the other Gild Masters. Not that Alina cared.)

Alina made a mental note to ask Cho just *how* she had managed to pickpocket the man the media called "Living Lightning."

Anyway. For once Baraam's fame and fortune were serving someone other than himself: Alina made her way toward the faculty entrance, Kwurdla's Bridge, which lay on the eastern side of the outer wall.

Even from a mile away, The Gildhall was a humbling sight. Before this moment, Alina had only ever seen those fifty-foot white alabaster walls in photographs. Millennia of being beaten down by the elements had not significantly reduced the fortress's luster.

She'd waited most of her life for this chance, to touch the walls, try to pick out the spots where Tahtoh had once studied, played hooky, stolen his first kiss. What kind of trouble had he and his friends gotten into while they were here...? But now she didn't have that kind of time.

Working from memory, cobbled-together anecdotes Tahtoh had told her over the years, she wandered the precipice of the moat surrounding the outer wall. Eventually, she discovered a bronze plaque set into a stone at the moat's edge. She could see the faculty entrance on the other side, but the Bridge must've been invisible, if it were even there at all.

Nothing was ever easy with The Gild. It's all shadows and ceremony and robed men twirling their long fingers ominously.

The plaque's inscription read, "From blinding ignorance."

What seemed like a random trio of words, an innocuous phrase, rang a little bell in Alina's mind, summoning a memory.

It was a line from the Aelfraver's Creed. Well, a first snippet of one.

Alina held up her hand, palm facing down, spreading her fingers. She cleared her throat, her voice croaking a little as she recited,

Let my hand grasp and hold

a Lightless lantern and guide

the blind along Unlit ways,

from blinding ignorance, ensnaring gnosis,

to the mystic shade of science and truth.

She didn't know what she'd expected, exactly. Had she thought the plaque would start to glow with magical light, or that a celestial guardian would glide down and ask her three riddles?

Nothing was happening. Had she messed up the verse? Was there something else she should try?

After a moment of feeling foolish, however, one of the stones beside the plaque slid away, and from the hole shot up a long, thin steel pole with a console on top of it.

Crossing her fingers, Alina pressed the barcode on Baraam's Raver-S license up against the touchscreen. A flash of gold let her know that the identification had been accepted. The pole retracted; the stone slid back into place.

She took a step forward, gazing down the twenty feet into the waters of the moat. They began to ripple. She backed up.

One after another, a series of octagonal stepping stones rose up. Step by step, they formed Kwurdla's Bridge. Named in honor of Uzimsar Kwurdla, the first Grandmaster of the Gild, known for her fondness of trickery.

Alina took one more lingering look at the sheer abyssal drop, her confidence falling to a new low—just as she might be doing in a minute.

What a ridiculous series of hoops to jump through just to get in the building. Did the Top Ten really have to bother with all this nonsense every time they wanted to sneak out the back? (Baraam, at least, could fly.)

Her mouth dry, the hairs on her head stood on end. Maybe there was a detection spell up that had recognized her for the fraud she was. Maybe she was about to step out onto nothing but air. An illusion designed to drop a would-be intruder to her death.

She swallowed. Only one way to find out.

She tentatively lifted her foot and set it down on the closest stone. She leaned a little more weight on it. Finally, she worked up the nerve to begin walking.

As she proceeded, the eight-sided stones beside her dropped, and new ones appeared in front. Always two paces ahead of her progress.

Once she'd cleared the moat, she reached the outer wall itself, the first of two huge triangular barriers. The outer wall pointed roughly north, while the inner—set around the crown of the hill—pointed south. Her goal was to enter that innermost section of The Gildhall. The path she walked led her to an archway illuminated by glowing orbs floating at eye-level.

The orbs disappeared.

She gasped. There was a young man sitting cross-legged there, beneath the archway. He was floating, too.

Alina considered turning back, trying a different approach.

"Who's there?" said the man. He wore a teal tunic, a white vase embroidered on its breast—the mark of a Journeyman Raver.

"Uh," said Alina.

He floated forward, still seated on thin air. His forehead was shiny with sweat, his eyes closed. He gritted his teeth, gliding closer and closer. He'd been holding his breath, apparently; he finally inhaled, touching down first with one foot, then the other.

He opened his eyes. "Who're you?"

"Ruqastra bol-Talanai," Alina blurted. Why that name had sprung to mind, she hadn't the faintest idea. But there it was, as if it hadn't been ten years since she'd last seen the woman it belonged to.

An orb hovered just above the young man. Eyes half-lidden, his lips twisted into a tired smirk. His hair had been buzzed practically down to the skin, the standard for Ravers-in-training specializing in the martial arts. His eyes, however, set him apart. They were pupil-less, gleaming fluorescent green. When he glanced to his right, Alina could just make out a trademark—TETA-TETA, INC. Artificial eyes. But unlike the one belonging to Jaggos, which had appeared close to natural, this stranger's eyes in no way pretended to be anything like those of a human. They were something more, rune-integrated. Imbued with an enhancement for spellcasting, possibly.

"Bol-Talanai, eh. The Great Baraam's little sister, is that so?" he said.

Alina licked her lip, nodding quickly.

He stared off into space a moment, his eyes whirring back and forth, up and down. "Nope, as I thought: you're definitely not on the list of people cleared for entry." He crossed his bare arms, the tight black shirt under his teal tunic stretching taut. "What are you doing here?"

Alina decided to play dumb. "Baraam gave me his, um, pass so I could pick something up for him. It'll only take a sec."

"And just what are you looking to pick up, Ms. 'bol-Talanai'?"

"Um, *excuse* me?" she said, mostly to buy herself a second to think, disguising her dismay as disgust. "Who do you think you're talking to? Just who are *you*?"

"Lonami N'dalte, Third Year, and third unwanted son of my father. At yer service." He curtsied.

"Well, Mr. N'dalte," said Alina, clapping her hands, "when my brother hears about this, he's going to—"

"Do nothing at all?" said Lonami, laughing. "Because he's not really your brother, isn't that right? Oh, don't look so shocked. The tiny twitches of your facial muscles gave you away. Most people would have missed it, but I've got it down to a 98.7% certainty that you're lying through your teeth, Ms. Sneak-thief." He lightly kicked off the ground, hovering again, crossing his legs. He closed his eyes, their unnatural light once more hidden from view. "But I'll tell you what, I don't really care. If I had to guess by what you've told me, your demeanor, and your stated reason for being here, you're probably trying to mess with Baraam in some way. And, honestly, I'm cool with that."

"You—you are?"

He shrugged, drifting away from the arch. "Yeah, why not? I never asked to be here. And, here I am, guarding a door no one ever uses. Except you. At least maybe now something interesting might happen."

Alina couldn't help herself. She asked, "Aren't you afraid of, I dunno, getting in trouble?"

He only chuckled.

On guard in case this was a trap of some kind, Alina dashed past Lonami. He made no move to stop her. His eyes were closed.

She paused. Over her shoulder: "You're not going to call anyone as soon as I'm in, are you?"

Without turning, he said, "All communication is blocked here. Everything except good old face-to-face. I suppose I could make use of one of the thirteen secret passages I know of, get ahead of you, and make sure you're caught." Another chuckle. "But that's a chance you'll have to take, whoever you are."

"No matter what happens in there, I'll remember you, Lonami N'dalte."

No response.

Alina clenched her fists. This was her best chance to get a one-up on all the other Ravers. Why was she hesitating?

A thin trickle of gray fluid ran down the back of her hand, her knuckle, her finger. By the time the droplet struck the floor, she was already moving forward.

She caught a small snippet of Lonami muttering to himself—"'You lack control, N'dalte'; 'Focus, N'dalte'; 'You must learn to drift as the lotus petal over still waters.' Yeah, well, I'll quietly drift over your grave, Master Iazar. How'll you like me then, huh?"

After ninety feet or so, the long triangular passageway cutting through the outer wall ended, and Alina stepped into the light of the moon again. Ahead lay the inner wall. To her left, a one-hundred-foot-tall iron ring as big as a coliseum.

The Gildhall itself consisted of six parts: the Azurite Alchamer, where research into potions, spells, and Aelf anatomy were conducted; the Iron Wheel, where were studied the martial arts; the Adamantine Manor, in which the instructors and staff resided; the Stone Keep, a quartet of towers that served as the students' dormitory and common room; the Labradorite Dome (affectionately shortened to "Labradome"), where all business and contract registrations and divvying of official assignments occurred; and, finally, the Crystallarium.

Tonight, Alina was interested only in that last one. Above the artificial candleflame of the Adamantine Manor's central tower was suspended the Crystallarium.

To call it merely a "library" would be criminally inaccurate. The records kept there brought to life thousands of years of history, going back to the days of Kwurdla and the other "Reapers of Elves," those human mages who'd founded The Gild almost two thousand years ago.

The Crystallarium was a massive, jagged crystal that flashed pink, green, azure, gold. The amount of Niima consumed to re-up its levitation spells was staggering. Dozens of students emptied their reserves daily in service to this tradition.

But Alina wasn't here to comment on the aesthetic preferences of The Gild higherups. She had to reach and enter the crystal.

The next obstacle was a twelve-foot-tall set of double doors, the front entrance to the Manor. They were made of pink ivory wood, every plank of which was worth more than the Qamasques' entire restaurant. Carved into the wood were reliefs depicting the conquest of New El by twelve human warriors and mages. Supposedly, these were the ancestors of the Twelve Families.

The doorknocker and handles were solid platinum, carved to resemble dragon talons. Alina approached, took a deep breath, and pushed with all her might. She winded herself, broke a sweat. Nothing happened.

Leaning against the doors, she steadied herself, tried pulling this time. Nope. They would not budge.

Thumping her back against the wood, she sat down.

"You're seriously gonna let yourself get beat by a door?" she panted, her forearms and shoulders burning. "After all this?"

When the mess of pink and blue dots cleared from her eyes, she noticed a shape standing not too far in front of her.

It was slender, spiky, strangely curved. Two glowing amber eyes in a swirl of concentrated darkness.

The sight triggered a cold sweat. Alina's breaths became hurried and shallow. It was fear unlike any other she'd ever felt, the fear of the caveman staring into the night, hearing the baying of wolves. The fear of all things that slither, crawl, or claw. Primal. Unstoppable.

She actively fought against the panic; even though every muscle in her body tensed with the instinct to leap up and sprint away from this *thing*, she forced her breaths to travel to her stomach, to look the shadow in its eyes.

The more she tried to make sense of it, however, the stranger it appeared: it was a slender silhouette of a man, head cocked to the side, arms akimbo; then it was a many-tentacled, spinning, pirouetting lump; a spiny worm, bobbing its upper half up and down; an ape scratching its haunches, hopping left to right. It was all these things, and it was none of them.

A fishhook of a migraine tore through her head as she looked at the thing, growing more intense by the second, until she broke eye-contact.

Almost immediately, the headache lessened, but the terror remained. And, even in her panic-poisoned mind state, she knew what it was she was seeing.

"The Bane of New El," she rasped, a stream of sweat coursing from her scalp, matting her hair.

The creature twisted like a wrung towel, recoiling. Its form squirming, breaking apart, reconstituting itself, it took a step toward Alina.

She pressed herself up against the doors. She knew she had to run, but her will had drained away. Her moment had passed. Her chance had gone.

Her time was up.

Knees knocking together, she dug her fingernails into the wood.

The creature drew closer and closer. Alina's scalp tingled, her nostrils flared.

And closer.

Her skin burned, like she'd stuck her arms into an oven. She stared into the smoldering stars that were the shadow's eyes.

And closer.

It reached out thorny arms, thick and coursing with blood-like shadow. Ichor dripped from it now—pools of shadowed fluid glimmering by the light of the stars and the Adamantine tower's arcane candleflame.

It was just about to touch her. All she could see were its eyes. Like gazing into twin suns.

A flash of golden light blinded her to all else…

19

THE REASSURING WEIGHT OF her father's hand on her head and the flutter of her mother's toe-tickling fingers. The girl felt their loss, every night, as she curled up on the dusty floor under her bed. That year, she cried herself to sleep.

One afternoon, she spied a gray cat, tail up, chin up, prancing down the street and away. At first, she thought nothing of it. Then whatever the cat carried in its curled mouth caught a glint of sunlight—a metal object? And there was something else, too. Something white.

She dashed upstairs, stumbling on the third step, banging her knee. In her room, she threw open her bedside dresser.

Her needle and thread. Gone!

The cat must have it, she realized. But how?

She ran after it, down the stairs and out the door and into the street, breathing heavily by now.

When it noticed her, it picked up its pace.

Cheeks burning with tears, chilly wind stinging her lungs, she gave chase. All the way to the fair that had rolled into town a few days before.

She shot right past all the happy families and their stupid smiles, ignoring the jugglers, fire-spitters, bullet-catchers, the merry-go-round with magically animated plastic horses, and the ferris wheel made of completely translucent steel. She stayed focused on the gray cat.

Winding between people's legs, flitting between stalls and men on stilts, it darted into the hedge maze.

At the mouth of the maze, she hesitated. Tahtoh wouldn't want her to go in by herself. But her needle and thread! He'd have *to understand. Better yet, if she hurried, maybe he'd never even find out she'd run off.*

The hedges were in bad shape, the leaves all brown and withered, the twigs and branches brittle as slivers of hard toffee. The sporadic tufts of grass underfoot had been winter-bleached the color of a horse's teeth.

When she made up her mind to go in, her knees were stiff. They just wouldn't bend. Her legs wouldn't move. Her body wouldn't obey.

An eerie whisper of silence hung over the tall, tall hedges. She could see between some of the branches—the gray cat with the white thread in its mouth!

Clenching her fists, she forced herself to take first one step, then another. Before she knew it, she was inside the labyrinth.

Without paying much attention at all to where she was going, she wandered deeper and deeper into it.

The cat was nowhere to be found.

Eventually, she reached the center of the maze.

She'd looked everywhere for the cat.

She couldn't remember the way back.

And the fair had closed for the day.

Hours passed. The sun set. It got cold. Her voice was hoarse from shouting.

In the middle of the night, Tahtoh found her. He scooped her up, wrapped her in a blanket, and brought her to his home above the restaurant, where she was supposed to live now, too.

She cried to him about the cat, about what it had stolen from her.

He told her that she could cry all she wanted, that there was no shame in it. But if she ever wanted to do something about it, he could teach her how.

"What do you mean?" she asked.

"I can teach you how to track and hunt. How to find anyone or anything."

"I want to find that cat," she said.

"If you are a good student, it may be that you will. Maybe you will yet, my little Cabbage."

20

WHEN SHE CAME TO, SHE heard a grinding and a heavy thud behind her. A bar slid into place with a hiss and the hollow, noisy friction of wood on wood.

It took her a few seconds to realize she'd been the one to close the doors and drive the bar home into its bracket.

She looked around. Portraits of stuffy, self-important-looking men were hung up on the walls all around her, framed by curtains of the highest thread-count. That confirmed it: she was, in fact, inside the Adamantine Manor. Somehow.

Had she opened the doors? She couldn't remember doing so.

She inspected her hands. They were pink, and they felt tingly but also numb, as if they'd been scalded.

The last thing she remembered before blacking out was the creature—the Bane of New El. Its aura, its mere presence had deeply shocked her; she'd simply shut down, as if it had flicked her brain's on/off switch.

Just how, exactly, had it invaded The Gildhall? The place was supposedly protected by dozens if not hundreds of protective charms and arcane shields.

No Aelf should have been able get within a quarter-mile of these spell-warded grounds, but the Bane had managed it.

Was it still out there, right now, on the other side of this door? Alina backed away, Niima welling in her fists.

She was afraid, but she imagined her fear evaporating from her body like lake water on a warm afternoon. She released the magical energy. It disseminated throughout her system again.

As long as it refrained from killing her in the next few minutes, in a weird way, the Bane had done her a solid tonight. Secondhand accounts were one thing, but experiencing the thing's mind-warping effects for herself would certainly help her focus her research. Having had her own thoughts and emotions scrambled like eggs—or grinded up like sausages (she was starving)—she could eliminate the category of parasitic Aelf as a possibility. All the usual suspects of the blood- or soul-siphoning variety could not bend a person's perceptions the way the Bane had done. Unless it really was a *Thaal.* But that wasn't possible. Because the *Thaalene* had gone extinct hundreds of years ago. Were that not true, they'd still be ruling the world.

With a significantly shortened list of contenders in mind, Alina listened for any sounds of movement beyond the double doors. Hearing none, she turned around and got her bearings.

Randomly interspersed white and blue orbs dimly illuminated the interior of the Adamantine Manor's grand entryway. The ceiling was so high that it was blanketed in heavy shadows. Those walls that bore no fancy oil paintings were made of some kind of green rock, maybe jade. On one side, there protruded busts carved to resemble animal heads—boars, goats, yaks, antelopes, hippopotamuses—anything with horns, antlers, or tusks, really; on the other, human faces of all different races and ethnicities.

Alina didn't know enough about architecture to tell the difference between the parts of The Gildhall that were the original structures (built by the Twin Dragon Kings' human slaves) and additions created by later human conquerors. Maybe these animal and human carvings represented all the Dragons' snacks over the years? A statement about who's in charge?

She came to a crossroads. On either side, the white marble floors led to the personal quarters of the faculty and key members of the staff. Ahead, an archway, behind which there was nothing but a small circular stone space. She moved into it, looking up. She was standing in essentially a long stone shaft. High above her, maybe four stories up, there was a platform. Above it, another. And another. And so on. Above all of these would be the access hatch leading to the tower's ever-burning candleflame. And above *that* floated the Crystallarium.

Now, how to get *up*?

There'd be no signal anywhere on Gild property, but her phone was still good for something: the beam of its flashlight flicked all along the circular walls. No clues. Then she checked under her feet. The floor mosaic depicted a stylized Raea, a primordial wind spirit believed to bring good luck (though, to Alina, they'd always looked like fat-bodied, bald, and flightless birds). Yet another species the Ravers had driven to extinction, now remembered only as something to walk all over.

Wind spirit, she thought, clicking her tongue. Maggos loved their riddles. Must be a hint.

An idea struck her. She held out her hands parallel to the floor, gazed up, and willed herself to fly.

And she did.

It was just like the wizards' towers she used to read about in fairytales. Apparently, imitating their fantastical counterparts, the Gildsmen also couldn't resist flaunting their abilities at every turn.

Though initially a bit uneasy, she soon got the hang of it. Calmly drifting upward like a clump of cat hair caught by a puff of air conditioning, she passed balcony after balcony, the railings of each bearing the name of teachers and honored residents of the Manor.

Finally, she reached the ceiling, found and fiddled with the latch, flung open the hatch, and the touched down on the roof.

She was standing in the middle of the whale-sized purple candleflame. Good thing it was just an illusion, or she'd have been flash fried.

The shimmering pink base of the Crystallarium hung a stone's throw above her now.

Feeling no need to fix what wasn't broken, she willed herself just a little farther upward. The flight enchantment continued to nudge her toward her target.

She began to pick up a bit too much speed for her liking, so she tried to stop but found she couldn't. She was being pulled—drawn in by the crystal. She threw her hands in front of her, braced herself for impact.

It never came. She moved through the crystal walls as if they were nothing more than a curtain of warm water, and she emerged, standing on the floor, perfectly safe.

Her heartbeat slowed over the next minute or two she spent observing her surroundings. Everything was tinged violet due to the magical candleflame coming from below. The moon was the only other light source, and the clouds did away with most of that, leaving an eerie dark glow to settle over the Crystallarium. The floors were stone, composed of complex and irregularly shaped interlocking pieces. Each pathway joined at the sprawling chamber's center, where she stood, and snaked out in all different directions. Wedged in nooks carved into the pink-green-purple crystal were weathered and cracking scrolls, some crumbling from repeated review, some time-yellowed but with their seals still intact.

Alina walked right past all that old junk, finding the simple mahogany staircase that led to the second level. At the top step, her breath caught in her throat.

She was not alone.

The telltale flickering of orange candlelight emanated from up ahead. And where there was a candle, there would be a librarian.

Cursing, Alina watched the light, trying to guess if it was coming nearer or moving farther away. Why couldn't this old dingbat, whoever it was, go to sleep like everyone else?

The light seemed to be retreating, so she risked inching forward. At the top of the steps now, she saw rows and rows of bookshelves. Dusty old tomes bursting with knowledge. But this *still* wasn't where she needed to be. She wanted level three, the highest section of the library, where the Lorestones were kept.

She tiptoed behind the nearest bookshelf.

Humming. Coming from nearby. Maybe two shelves down.

Holding her breath, Alina peered between the books. What she saw very nearly made her gasp and give away her position.

Impossible. It had to be that she was exhausted. Or maybe her encounter with the Bane had knocked more than one screw loose. In any event, her brain protested having to interpret the evidence presented by her eyes.

The being clearly wasn't human. The halfway-too-long neck, the arms that hung too far past the hips. Narrow, iris-less, pupil-less, blue-veined white eyes. An upturned nose. Cornflower-blue lips. Spear-shaped ears. And turquoise hair that was on fire—scratch that—hair that *was* fire.

No way. Alina blinked, hoping that would dispel the image. No such luck.

She was looking at a sentient Aelf, but that wasn't all. This Aelf was of the Mythidim class, an Iorian—a terrifying ancient enemy of all humanity. What was this thing doing in the Crystallarium of all places?

The Iorian glanced in Alina's direction. Alina carefully placed a hand over her mouth to muffle the sound of her breathing. The Iorian's eyes narrowed. Alina thought she caught a smile dance across the Aelf's blue lips, but that must have been a trick of the light.

A candle hovered just above the Iorian's pale outstretched palm. Its turquoise tongues of flamelike hair danced down the length of its back. It shuffled away, the hem of its dress and tassels hanging from its braided belt swishing against the floor.

There was a table set in front of an obsidian door. The Iorian waited near the table for a moment or two and halfway glanced over its shoulder, back in Alina's direction. Then it moved on, heading left, out of sight.

Alina heard a door swing open, and then it closed with a click.

The Iorian had taken its candle with it, and the Adamantine tower's magical purple light was now obstructed by two floors and sets of walls (not to mention all the book- and display shelves). Alina was left in pronounced darkness. Holding her breath, she sidled out from her hiding place, peering around the low-lit library.

Eventually—after making sure that the door through which the Iorian had gone was well and truly shut—she worked up the courage to check out the table. On it, she discovered a deck of divination cards, all face down except for three—the Fool, Death, and the Ace of Wands, in that order. Beside these rested an obsidian triangle with an ivory handle. Teeth had been carved into the triangle. A key.

She looked to her right, considering the nearby obsidian door.

She picked up the key, went up to the door, and slid it into the identically-shaped keyhole. There came a series of clicks. By the handle, she turned the key, and the door shifted upward, surprisingly quietly, disappearing into a slot in the ceiling. Taking the key with it.

There was no obvious lever or switch that would return the door to its previous position. So much for leaving no trace.

A troubling thought struck her. Why hadn't the Iorian just taken the key with it when it had left the room?

Her proximity to her goal, however, cut short her puzzlement. With a hop, skip, and a jump, she made her way through the revealed passageway, up the top of the final flight of stairs.

She was surrounded by Lorestones. Emerald-esque, fist-sized, they gleamed from within. Row upon row upon row of neatly stacked, perfectly smooth stones set into brass and glass cases, each one inscribed with a unique legend. The one nearest Alina read, "LIGEIA." The inscriptions flanking that one—"SU'MYN HAR-ERVAI" and "BRYNDT FAEHN-CLAN"—made clear that the Crystallarium's organization wasn't alphabetical.

Most of what she knew of this massive store of knowledge had come straight from Tahtoh. She thought hard, remembering what he'd told her.

The Crystallarium's primary purpose was to preserve records of important deeds and memories from the era after humanity defeated the Dragons. Three thousand years ago, of course, the ancients hadn't had cameras and computers, but they had found a workaround: they'd used polished Chrononite to record a copy of the verbal accounts and perspectives of those who'd witnessed or made history.

Chrononite was a mineral of very peculiar properties. Nearly indestructible, this pistachio-seafoam-colored material simultaneously existed both inside *and* outside of space and time. Essentially, it was a time-traveling rock. Maggos all over the world had had many reality-defying uses for it, once. Most of these adventures ended horribly. Now the only surviving examples of Chrononite could be found right here, in the Crystallarium. Obviously, the stuff was utterly priceless.

Without Chrononite and its unique properties, the Lorestones could not have been created. These feats of magical craftsmanship had never been matched, and likely never would be—no matter how far technology progressed. Memories preserved for all eternity would be a hard achievement to beat. Furthermore, the Lorestones didn't contain only the *words* spoken into them—they also captured the *thoughts, feelings, motivations,* and innumerable other facets that characterized the speaker. A Lorestone, in a way, entrapped the very essence of the memory-maker. A moving-picture copy of their soul.

Alina had only to walk up to one—"ADRAM & HAGAAR"—touch it, and—

She found herself on a grassy hilltop, and she felt dread. So, this was the end.

It felt so real. She had to remember that it was not her body kissed by rain, nor her emotions sinking like beads of iron in a deep pool. She saw through another's eyes. There were eight of them, huddled on the hill. Six were human. The other two…

A tan-skinned, orange-haired, ape-shaped hulk of a man-like creature. He gripped a short sword in both of his studded-leather-gloved ham-hock hands.

At his side, a dark-haired, dark-eyed, horned Child of the Undermoon.

Ahead of them, an army of undead, charging uphill.

The end—their *end. And after so long a road. All eight companions would die on this hill and on this day.*

Death, however, would have to put in the work to claim them.

Foam spurted from between the taut lips of the orange-haired one. The last battle-frenzy of Hagaar Wrothbone.

Strider Adram, his dark-haired companion, unsheathed his longsword. On its blade were inscribed runes. On its hilt, the word "VIGIL."

The horde—

Alina snapped out of it, but only barely. She fell to the floor, panting. Breaking her connection to that alien memory had required effort, like pulling apart two particularly stubborn magnets.

By Buthmertha, she'd had no idea the Lorestones were *that* intense.

Hagaar and Adram. Even the few seconds she'd seen of their story had been far more thrilling than any movie or VR game she'd tried. Her curiosity would have made it easy to ride that wave to the end, but she had to move on.

With urgency, she got to her feet and kept scanning the names on the display cases. She didn't know exactly what she was looking for, only that it had to be in the Crystallarium, if it even existed.

For all its mysterious and long-forgotten powers, the Bane of New El seemed to her to have burst straight out of the distant, mythic past—when trickster gods and titans still walked the earth. She'd reasoned that her best hope for finding the Bane's weakness would lie in a Lorestone as old as the war between humanity and the Aelf itself.

There had to be *something* useful in this library. If not, why would The Gild have gone to such lengths to protect it?

The display cases were arranged so that the only way to proceed through the collection was to follow the spiraling path toward its center, where—according to Tahtoh—lay the oldest and most valuable stones.

Alina passed dozens of the artifacts, each with its unique label. No dates, though. That would have been too precise and convenient. The library's interior designers must have believed that magic wasn't an exact science and the "organization" of the Crystallarium had to reflect this theme of uncertainty. Alina agreed to disagree, but, given that she was in their sandbox, she would play by their rules.

"THE BLACK VEIL SURVIVORS," she read to herself, fingers trailing through the air.

"NARSHEN YN ARSUNA."

"EL-WOKE."

"MACHINAMANCER."

"KNIGHTS OF THE RIDDLE, ORDER OF THE ENLIGHTENED."

"ACHEMIR."

How far back did these stories go?

Her gaze then locked onto one stone in particular. A piece of it had chipped off and was nowhere in sight, neither in the case nor near it; a crack ran down the length of the Chrononite, from crown to heart. The case was labeled, "WANDERERS OF THE ELDER ISLE."

Elder. That seemed promising.

She reached out for the Lorestone, but, before she could touch it, her consciousness was consumed by a vision even clearer and more visceral than the last.

An Iorian, a Prince—his flaming hair tied to one side, his clothes weathered from years of isolation in the wilds—stood upon the mountain as it roused from its eons-long sleep. Magma boiled up from the bowels of the earth, and great clouds of yellow smog were belched into the sky. His bones ached, but there was one more battle yet to fight. His veins would be emptied on the rock of this far-off place, and he would never see home again.

Icy fingers on Alina's shoulder forcibly pulled her out of the vision. The fingers swiveled her around, and she found herself staring up into the veiny, iris-less eyes of the Iorian from before, the Aelf's cornflower-blue lips pursed in a frown. More than a foot taller than Alina, it just stood there for a moment, its eyes creepily taking in every inch of her.

Alina's scalp crawled, the hairs on her arms and neck pricking, bile rising in her throat.

"The Wandering Age. Prince Aroukana. I knew him well, may he rest in the star-lit halls of his forebears," said the Iorian in a voice like the falling of small stones from an open hand. "Is that the one, do you think?"

Her head lolling, Alina's own sight remained unfocused. Familiar panic set in. She'd been caught. The Gild's punishment would be beyond severe. If this Aelf didn't kill her first.

Yet, the Iorian's touch was firm but surprisingly gentle. Two hands, one on each of Alina's shoulders. As if to reassure her. "Girl, you must hear me now. That Lorestone holds not the answers you want but those you need. It has been damaged, sabotaged decades ago. But you will find a way to unlock its secrets. You may be the only one who can."

Pulse slowing a little, Alina began to think rationally again. The Iorian had had at least one chance to capture her or worse, and it hadn't done so. Instead, it was speaking to her now. Nothing it said made sense, true, but it looked her in the eye. Its serene expression was soothing. Alina seemed unable to fear it any longer.

Clutching the stone in her hand, she shook off the stupor. "What are you doing here? Who are you?"

The Iorian smiled, its forked blue tongue licking both corners of its mouth at the same time. "Why, I've lived here since before the birth of your nation, human. I also happen to be the rightful caretaker of this repository of memory. I might've turned your question back at *you*, but I know already the answer. And you are out of time."

"What?"

"A silent alarm was triggered the instant you accessed the Lore of Adram and Hagaar. As we speak, a response team of Ravers is coming. The Authority have been notified as well."

"Are you… trying to help me? Why are you telling me this?"

"I always imagined that I understood Dimas K'vich. Though far too serious a boy, he was kind at heart. A rare find." The Iorian breathed in deeply. "I sense his passion in you. Temper it with wisdom, Alina, or—in this world of ours—it will do you far more harm than good."

Alina started *freaking out* again. It knew her name. She was about to ask, "You knew my grandfather?" but would not get the chance. As soon as she'd raised a hand and opened her mouth, she felt her stomach lurch.

A roiling wave of nausea, and then she was no longer inside the Crystallarium.

She'd been transported outside, some several hundred feet away from the Adamantine Manor. Just ahead was the archway through which she'd entered The Gildhall and, beyond it, Kwurdla's Bridge. She couldn't think of a reason not to leave that same way.

Teleportation, that was some seriously powerful magic. Then again, she'd expected nothing less from an Iorian. If you believed the stories, they'd been the ones who'd taught humans magic in the first place. Or, had it been the Monrainians? She might have paid closer attention to Tahtoh's history lectures had she known they would become so relevant to her personal life.

Shouts from behind her, near The Gild's main entrance. More coming from the windows of the Adamantine Manor. The Gildsmen were waking up; it was high time to go.

She jogged through the passageway and found Lonami N'dalte still there, though he was no longer showing off his stationary floating abilities.

"Caused a bit of a ruckus," he said, slightly out of breath. "Get what you came here for?"

"I hope so," she said. "Hey, listen, thanks for not ratting on me."

"How do you know I didn't?" he said with a wink. "Kidding. I didn't see anything, 'Ms. bol-Talanai.' But if you do get caught and happen to squeal on me, my ghost will haunt you for a thousand years. You think I'm joking."

"Nah, I believe you." Glancing back toward the archway, she saw a shadow glide across the tunnel. A flash of white eyes and lightning bolt earrings. She'd recognize that silhouette anywhere.

Alina froze, clutching the Lorestone behind her back.

The dark figure of Baraam stood there, watching her. She couldn't make out his expression, his body framed from behind by moon- and orb-light. Knowing that it was over—she'd come so far, only to fail—she waited for him to make the first move.

Then he left, headed back the way he'd come, shouting that he'd found nothing.

Lonami gulped. "Wait, *are* you actually his sister?"

She thumped her fist against the meat of his arm. "It's been real, man, but I gotta go."

Lonami nodded and he palmed a stone next to him, saying, "They locked the bridge, but I just hit the manual override."

"Thank you," she said, and ran for it.

Octagonal stones rising to meet her feet, her mind raced with questions even as she raced across the bridge. Had Baraam seen her? How could he not have? Why had he let her go? What was the true nature of the Bane? What was that Iorian doing up in the Crystallarium, the dusty old heart of all Raver knowledge?

She leapt off the bridge, sprinting along the exposed path toward the nearby apartment buildings. Flashlights sliced through the darkness ahead. The footfalls and clanking of metal joints—armored men were converging on her position. She threw the hood of her jacket over her head, sliding into an alley.

"What are we lookin' for, Sarge?" said an amplified voice coming from just around the corner.

The rustle of leather gear. "Suspect is dangerous. Broke into The Gild. Anything that can tangle with wizards is trouble."

"Weapons free?"

The metallic shuffle of rifle parts. They were checking their firearms, chambering rounds.

"Keep it non-lethal, Scorton. That goes for the rest of you lot, too. But shoot first, and shoot often."

The distinct whir and fizz of Niima-nullifying cuffs could be heard in between their words.

Alina held the pomegranate-shaped Lorestone up, rubbing her thumb over its smooth but dusty surface. If one of the search parties caught her with stolen Chrononite, she'd get the death penalty. Guaranteed.

She had to stash it. Come back for it later. Still, she couldn't leave it behind so close to The Gild, where it would likely be recovered.

It had been a long and eventful night; she could feel her Niima reserves draining the longer she pushed herself. But she need one more push.

She jabbed her fingertips against the brick wall behind her, pressing, prying. Her flesh entered the wall, and she gritted her teeth, wrenching it to either side, splitting it.

Brick dust everywhere, the spurting of busted water pipes. The new opening was just wide enough to sidle through.

Then the beam of a flashlight slapped her in the face.

She shoved her body through the gap she'd made.

From behind, "Hey, you! Sarge, I think I found 'em."

"Sew 'em up."

Of course, Alina didn't pause to listen in on the rest of the exchange.

She wound up inside a storage room filled with boxes of plastic figurines. Half-consciously, she noted that the toys represented a number of big-name Aelfravers. She must have ended up in a gift shop.

The door was locked; she kicked it once, twice. It flew open, and she dashed into the store proper, which was overflowing with cheap knick-knacks—streamers, vuvuzelas, VR "training" programs, instructional and documentary video series, scaled-down toy weapons, copies of *My First Aelf Bestiary*, and other overpriced garbage.

Alina hopped the desk, kicking the register onto the floor as she went. It fell with a *ding* and the drawer popped open, but, of course, it was empty.

A squad of Authority officers had congregated by the front doors, its members doing their best to hide from sight. But the façade was mostly glass, and Alina could easily count the Enforcers by the streetlamp light bouncing off their visors.

She checked her surroundings, finding no other exits.

She cracked her knuckles. *Going up.* Raising her hand and clenching it into a fist, she yanked down in a curving motion. The ceiling and floor above her turned to putty, forming into a steep incline. In this new shape, it solidified. She ran up this cracked and crumbling ramp.

Below, breaking glass. Shards tinkling.

"Did you see that?" shouted one of the officers.

"Get after them," yelled another.

By the bed, fridge, couch, lamp, and other homey touches, Alina could tell this second floor must have been the living quarters of the toy store's owner(s). Alina could hear whimpering coming from the closet, the door still ajar. She ignored the tearful sniffles and made for the window.

The high-altitude of New El was once again taking its toll. Wheezing, fighting for oxygen, she told the room and whatever occupants might be hiding in it, "Sorry for the disturbance," as she spent another burst of Niima to collapse the outer wall, glass and all, and reshape it into a bridge to the adjacent building. Instead of entering it, however, she only broke the window with her elbow. Then she jumped down to ground level, rolling as she landed.

Hopefully that would confuse the Enforcers, throw the heat off her tail just long enough for her to escape.

They thudded around upstairs, shouting "Clear" as they moved through the apartment. The frightened screams of the owners could be heard, and Alina was grateful for the distraction this caused.

Running into the night, huffing shallow breaths, she almost collided with a second and third team of Enforcers, but she ducked out of sight just in time. Exactly how many Authority goons were after her was hard to tell, but they were out in force, for sure.

Only when she'd put about five blocks behind her and The Gild did she take a breather. Her reprieve was cut short, however, by a cry from above. She looked up to see a flaming projectile blast across the sky. It took her a second to realize that the comet was a person—a Raver, flying around, searching for Alina.

Alina flung herself into the nearby steel trash container, flipping the plastic lid shut on top of her. The Raver roared overhead, crisscrossing the skies, each of their passes sounding like the scream of a jet engine followed by a thunderclap.

Cold sweat seeped from Alina's face, arms, and the small of her back. Hopefully no one would ever dream of looking for her here, in her cliché hiding spot.

When the echoes of the supersonic Raver had faded, Alina opened the lid an inch. Spotlights from hovercraft high above combed the streets and alleys. Her only hope was to slip past the cordon. And she'd never be able to do that with the Lorestone in hand.

Doubting herself even as she did so, she thrust the Lorestone as deep as she could into the garbage piles, gagging at their stench. Then she waited for the spotlights to pass by and spun out of the dumpster.

She checked her phone. Niima at 10%. Yeah, that sounded about right.

Niima Deficit Sickness was no joke, but neither was spending the rest of her life locked up. Just a little more, she promised herself, then she'd rest.

The sewers were her best shot. Sure, besides hiding in a dumpster, escaping through the sewers might just have been the oldest trick in the amateur criminal's handbook. The Authority, therefore, would definitely think to check down there. However, Alina had one advantage: they didn't know what she was capable of yet.

There was a manhole in the nearest alley. With a wrench she found leaning against the wall beside the dumpster, she pried the cover off and climbed down the ladder into total darkness.

She now had to decide which rapidly shrinking resource—her phone's battery or her Niima—was most important to conserve. Figuring she might need to make a life-or-death phone call at any minute, she decided to use up what was left of her Niima.

With a snap of her fingers, a little yellow flame flickered to life on her palm, which she held forward to light her way. For a few minutes, she proceeded without meeting any obstacles.

Then she heard the officers up ahead, even before she saw the glow of their body flashlights. They were coming her way.

She pressed her cheek, body, legs, every part of her against the slimy sewer wall, focusing for dear life.

The officers, three of them, moved around the corner, leading with the sights of their handguns. One of them slipped into the gray water. The other two laughed.

They kept going.

Alina waited half a minute longer before she sighed, released the spell, and let herself fall out of the wall. She flubbed the landing and skidded, almost failing to catch herself.

Even though she could have fallen asleep right there and then, she got up and continued along the path in the direction the Enforcers had come from.

For an untold number of minutes, the only sounds she could hear were the steady gush of rank-smelling water to her left, the skitter of rats, and the patter of her own heartbeat in her ears. Gradually, a new sound blended into the mix. It made her stop in her tracks, listen carefully.

Harsh breathing, but from something that was either very far away or tiny. Her suspicions faded: this felt way too clever to be an Authority trick.

She searched the cistern. And found nothing.

Ready to give up, she made to continue her trek. Then she heard the words: "Human. Help. Human: me, help." A scratchy voice, barely audible above the rushing water. But then she saw it, the lump of blue fur and cloth, about five inches long.

On her knees now, Alina used her middle and ring fingers to gently roll the thing over.

It had matted fur, big floppy mouse ears, muscular forearms ending in jagged yellow claws, and mini goat-like legs, with hooves and everything. A doll-sized bandolier, loincloth, and shoulder cape were all it wore.

She was in the presence of a Pyct.

Another Aelf. Apparently, New El was crawling with them. You just had to know where to look.

"Hey. Hey, there, fella," she said, keeping any and all edge from her voice.

"Hurt: I," said the Pyct, grimacing, revealing rows of triangular teeth, like a shark's. It squinted up through its half-lidded mouse-like eyes.

"Where are you hurt? How can I help?"

"Hunger: I." It posted itself on its elbows, squinting up at Alina. "Destroyed: hive, mine. Help me: you. Help you: I." Wobbling, it fell on its black button of a nose.

Alina tapped the little guy's shoulder. No response.

She considered leaving it there. Only for second.

This was going to be a royal pain, she could already tell. But she couldn't leave the Pyct to die down here. Not like this.

Deciding she must be the worst Aelfraver on the planet, she scooped the Pyct up and tucked him into her left inner jacket pocket.

Harboring an Aelf was another way to earn a capital punishment, but what was one more crime piled on top of her lengthening list?

21

PIECE BY PIECE, INCH by inch, and cut by cut. Ever did Tolomond Stayd labor in the name of The Author to reclaim the night. He scouted and searched, wandered and watched for any trace or sign of those whom he was destined to punish.

This city, though it floated above the clouds, had sunk far below heaven's reach. Built upon a foundation of lies, kept aloft by the promises of false idols.

Once upon a time, it had been a blood-wash—Dragon's blood—that had cleansed El. The lives of the Twin Tyrants had gushed forth, a deluge, a torrent that blasted away the filth and wretchedness of generations of weakness. By divine decree, such was the fate of any heathen prophets who would lead humanity away from the light of truth.

That glorious history needed repeating. But, this time, it was no Dragon that herded mankind toward its wholesale destruction. This time, the enemies of the righteous wore the faces of men, yet these mages most certainly were not *men*. Magic was an Aelf weapon; no true *human* could wield it.

For too long had such scum operated in the dark. Well. Tolomond's sword, Rhetoric, was the scalpel with which he'd cut out the arcane cancer festering at the heart of New El. He was the Instrument of the Lord, the weapon of the holy Sanctum. It was he who would—

He stopped in his tracks: ahead, haloed by the glare of a streetlamp, there walked one more target to scratch off his list.

Ugarda Pankrish.

Rumors circulated among the infidels—the Aelfravers and their abettors—that Pankrish was invincible, that his fists were the very fingers of Death.

To Tolomond, he appeared perfectly mortal. Could this man in his simple shirt and trousers and white sneakers, carrying a rolled-up newspaper and wearing wireframe spectacles, a hat covering his balding head—could *this* old fool truly be the legendary warrior Tolomond had heard so much about? Tolomond snorted, his nostrils spasming at the whiff of sewage creeping up from the gutters.

Yet, looks could be deceiving. Was it not said that the Enemy moved in mysterious ways, employing artifice and lies in its attempts to undermine the faithful?

Then again, no one was immortal or unbeatable. No one save The Author, Who was the One True God, and His chosen people.

Pankrish abruptly turned a corner, heading down a darkened alley. All the blinds along his path had been drawn, lights out. The streetlamp at the mouth of the alley bore a shattered bulb, like twisted glassy teeth, the globules of mercury within having long-since disappeared. Even the rats parted for Tolomond, whose breath fogged before his night-adjusted eyes.

He grinned a chapped-lip grin: no witnesses.

This was the hand of Providence at work. The Author was surely with Tolomond tonight, as always.

He loosened Rhetoric in its scabbard which he'd lined with the softest civet fur to silence the unsheathing of his blade. The naked steel glimmered like the quicksilver waters of a moon-stricken river.

Ready to capitalize on the element of surprise, Tolomond swung around the blind corner.

Pankrish, staring directly at him, said, "May I help you, young man?"

The Author held Tolomond's tongue.

"Why were you following me?" with his knuckles, Pankrish nudged his spectacles higher up the bridge of his nose.

"You're a—a heretic," Tolomond stammered. "Enemy of God."

"Whose God?"

"The only One."

Pankrish shook his head. "This tired nonsense again." He took off his hat and spectacles, setting them on a nearby concrete windowsill. "You're the one who went after Alina K'vich, aren't you?"

"I'm unfamiliar. Another infidel, I'm sure."

"The young woman with Ordin Ivoir. You made an attempt on both their lives."

"*Her.* Yes, I know of *her.* And I would have succeeded in my labor, but the tricks of the devil Ivoir are many."

"I can see this conversation is headed nowhere." Pankrish rolled his shoulders, wincing as they popped. "Did you come here to kill me, eh?"

"My Father taught me to only ever draw a blade when I mean to end a life with it." Tolomond raised his sword until it was level with the infidel's eyes, tracing tight *exes* with its tip.

"You're not one for idle threats. That's something." Pankrish's right leg swung in a backward arc. He now showed Tolomond his side. "I must tell you, I have no desire to fight you."

"I can't shame you for your fear of me, old man. But there is no other way. Ugarda Pankrish, you've failed to live an upright life. The only hope for your soul's redemption is the purifying crucible of battle. Behold now your every sin brought to Light."

Pankrish tucked his chin, nodded, and gestured for Tolomond to approach.

The younger man lunged, seeking to deliver a decisive first blow. He was, however, blinded by a cascade of papers; Pankrish had flung his newspaper at Tolomond's face.

Growling, Tolomond swiped the sheets aside with his weapon, then pivoted all his weight to the left in an upward thrust. The blade was caught between shiny, black, metallic palms, pressed together as if in prayer. Tolomond looked up into Pankrish's eyes, catching the glint of amusement in them. Tolomond yanked back, freeing Rhetoric from the other's grasp.

Two robotic arms had burst from Pankrish's shirt, resting below his human ones. The artificial appendages' armored plates trapped the soft light of the moon as the Master Raver assumed a low-centered fighting stance, each of his flexed fingers bunched and pointed downward.

Rushing in, Tolomond slashed left to right, right to left, and back again. Pankrish deflected each strike with a minimalist tap of his fingers to the flat of Rhetoric's blade. On the third deflection, he drove two knuckles into Tolomond's gut.

Winded, Tolomond staggered backward.

"I'll finish you if I have to," said Pankrish. "I won't enjoy the act." He took a few steps forward. "Still, I cannot leave you free to do more harm." In his fighting stance again, his two metallic arms curled behind him like rearing snakes poised to strike: "Get up."

Grinning, the taste of hot copper on his tongue, Tolomond skipped forward and spat a mouthful of blood at Pankrish's eyes while aiming a sword-swipe at his thigh. Pankrish—impossibly fast—closed in so that he stood shoulder-to-shoulder with Tolomond and delivered a chop to the back of the younger man's neck.

For a second, Tolomond's vision went white. Next he knew, he was lying on his chest in a puddle of stagnant wash-water.

"Give up," said Pankrish. "Surrender."

Tolomond rolled onto his side, hooking his legs to sweep his enemy onto the ground. Pankrish hopped over the kick, landing with his shins on top of Tolomond's upper back and shoulders. He grabbed Tolomond by the back of his skull, pressing his calloused fingers into the other's flesh.

Groaning, Tolomond looked sidelong up into Pankrish's darkened expression framed by the tall concrete and steel buildings. His bright eyes contrasted starkly with the blackness of the sky behind. Pankrish held up one of his organic fists, which twitched and fizzled and glowed with an otherworldly aura.

The very air between them smelled of burnt meat. And Tolomond knew then that, if he took that punch, he would meet his Maker.

"I yield," he rasped, blood trickling from his mouth and split lip. "I yield."

Pankrish cocked his head. "Good." He got up, throwing the greatsword out of reach.

Tolomond rested on his knees for a moment, breathing hard.

Pankrish leaned over, offering him a hand. Tolomond accepted the gracious gesture—

—and from under the skin of his other arm there burst forth, in a gout of blood, a barbed steel chain with a razor-sharp flame-shaped hook at its end, a chain that whipped toward Pankrish's face and looped around his neck—once, then twice. Tolomond hauled him down to his level, Pankrish gasping and struggling.

There was a moment when the veil of fear slipped away from Pankrish's eyes, and he looked neither terrified nor shocked, only saddened. This confused Tolomond. But then he knew it to be a ploy, and the Author commanded him to erase that expression from his enemy's face.

Before Pankrish could recover, Tolomond kicked his legs out from under him, dragging him into a rear naked choke. The barbs dug deep into Pankrish's neck, drawing blood. His eyes bulged; he pushed off the ground with his artificial arms, flailing. Locking his ankles around the other man's midriff, Tolomond held firm. Even when he was slammed against a wall, a dumpster, a fire hydrant, Tolomond would not let go.

Several seconds later, Pankrish let slip his last gasp. He fell to the ground, face-first.

Tolomond stood up and toed the back of Pankrish's head, making sure he really was dead, that this wasn't another trick.

No movement.

Certain of his success, he recovered his sword and—with one quick stroke—separated Pankrish's head from his body.

Keeping the head as proof of his triumph, Tolomond tossed the corpse in the dumpster.

Late in the night, returned to the Sanctum, he set about the rituals of absolution.

First, with soap and frigid water, he washed the dried blood of Ugarda Pankrish from his hands, his arms, his neck and face. Next, he retracted the chain and its hook into the cavity in his wrist, biting the sleeve of his tunic. Growling, a hot tear rolling down his cheek, he cauterized and bandaged the wound. Thereafter, he partook in evening prayers with the utmost zeal. And, after his meal, during leisure time, he removed from the oaken chest at the foot of his mattress his cat-o'-nine-tails.

For half an hour, he cleansed himself of the sin of murder, knowing that—though what he'd done was indisputably right—it was always the gravest of deeds to take a life. And, so, he whipped himself. Again. And again.

As he bled, from his body and soul flowed all the rage and evil of his sins. He nursed his ravaged flesh, the sting of the rubbing alcohol such sweet agony. He heated a knife over the braziers in the great hall. Pressing the orange-glowing blade to his skin, he cauterized these fresh wounds, too, groaning through the blinding, rapturous pain.

The blood-letting allowed him to sleep well that night. Better than he had in all the months since his last assignment.

This is my purpose, he thought as he closed his eyes.

Praise The Author. Praise be.

22

A KNOCK ON THE door threw Alina backward and off her perch on the corner of the bed. She rushed to answer, but only opened the door a crack.

Her heart leapt out her throat and danced a frantic jig on top of her head. "Ordin," she said, trying to sound calm.

His ever-changing fuchsia-purple-midnight blue hair was wet, dangling over his furrowed brow. Looked like he hadn't slept all night. "Can I come in?"

She resisted the urge to glance over her shoulder at the street urchin and five-inch-tall Aelf tangled in her sheets. As Cho scrambled to escape, Alina spoke loudly to mask the ruffling of the bedspread and the creaking of rusty springs: "Listen, it's a complete disaster in here. Let's talk downstairs."

"We really ought to keep this private."

"Have you seen the lobby? It's a pit. No one would hang out there, trust me. It'll be fine."

"Is everything alright? You're acting… peculiarly." He tried to poke his nose into the room.

"More than usual?" She pressed a hand to his chest, nudging him back into the hall. He gave more resistance than she'd been expecting, and she stumbled into his arms. She was the first to break eye-contact; he, the first to break their accidental embrace. "Come on," she said and led him down the steps.

In the lobby of the *Preening Peacock*, she flopped onto the crappy brown armchair. Ordin appeared visibly disgusted by everything around him. "You don't have to stay here, you know. I could have a bed made for you—"

She held up a hand. "I'm fine. I need my independence. Helps me think. What did you want to talk about?"

Taking care to touch *nothing*, he squatted down beside her. A quick few flicks through his diamond-bejeweled cellphone and a hologram popped up between them. The footage was grainy and green-tinted, probably captured by a night-vision camera.

When Alina realized what the footage was *of*, she tried her hardest to hold her poker face.

The video was only nine seconds long. But those nine seconds of street camera footage showed someone in a coat that looked an awful lot like Alina's magically tearing open a wall and jumping through it. Six armed Authority officers rushed in after the figure. And there were flashes accompanied by what sounded like the blasting of grenades and gunshots from off-camera.

"Woah, crazy," said Alina. "And weird."

"Stop." Ordin lowered his voice, leaning in. "I know that was you."

Alina gasped theatrically. "Me? I would never. To behave so recklessly? Perish the thought, sir. Perish it."

"Yes, yes, hilarious." Flicking off the video, he pocketed his phone. "But you have no concept of the scope of the events your little stunt has set in motion." He got up, started pacing. "Why didn't you just stay in my office? You would have been safe. There was a mountain of paperwork to sort through. That I *asked* you to sort through. Asked very nicely, I might add."

Alina crossed her arms. "Something came up."

"You are one lousy liar. Drop the act, please. I am owed more respect than this."

Her cheeks were burning. "Yeah, see, I don't know if you were showing *me* a ton of respect yesterday."

"It was research," he hissed. "We need all the information we can get. Why can't you understand that?"

The red-hot tingling spread to her ears. "Ordin, I know when I'm being condescended to, okay? That was nothing but busywork, and we both know it."

He opened his mouth to retort but stopped himself. Half turned away, he told her, "You might remember that Detective Ding took into custody a handful of Ravers the other day."

"So?"

"Some of their comrades are demanding their release. At the moment, the situation between The Authority and The Gild is tense, to say the least. And, so my sources tell me, your midnight jaunt has only thrown fuel on the fire. The Authority, and most vocally men like Ding, are crying foul, claiming the for-now unidentified Raver *attacked* a group of Enforcers. They're claiming it's part of a massive Gild conspiracy to undermine the peace."

Blowing a raspberry, Alina muttered, "Knew that guy's a bonehead."

"Indeed he is, but his assumption is not that ridiculous, given the evidence. Wouldn't you agree?"

"So what? He's got nothing. Nobody saw my face."

"Are you absolutely certain of that?"

"Yeah, yeah, I am," she lied.

"Thank Plutonia for that small favor, at least. But I haven't even told you the most inconvenient part of this whole mess. The Authority commanders are pressuring the Plutocrats to evict all the tourist Aelfravers from the city. All of them."

"What?" Alina leapt out of her chair. Her stomach dropped to her toes.

"It's not a done deal yet by any means, but the Consul is expected to hold an emergency council meeting this evening. And, in my father's absence, the duty of representing the interests of the Ivoir Family falls on my shoulders." He sighed. "That is all I know. I thought I owed you fair warning."

Slumping back into the ratty old chair, Alina shook her head, saying, "I didn't mean for any of this to happen."

"But it has. And we have to adjust accordingly."

"What about that… other thing… about Tolomond? Did you find anything out? Was it, um, Walazzin?"

"Of course it was Walazzin," Ordin snapped. "Only, I can't prove a damned thing, and now I have another huge problem to deal with, thank you very much."

"Ordin, I—"

"There's nothing for it. What's done is done. Just promise me that you'll refrain from running any more errands today. For the love of Sulla, *lie low*."

Alina couldn't tell if Ordin was more concerned for her wellbeing or his own. For her part, she decided a remorseful nod was the way to go. "Okay," she said.

That seemed to placate him. At least, he stopped chastising her, which was a win in her book.

He glowered at his phone, silencing it just as it began to chirrup a plucky synthesized version of the national anthem. "I will be in and out of meetings all day, but, if you really need something, text me." Combing his hair back, he asked, "By the way, what was it you were after at The Gild?"

Shaking her head, Alina said, "Stupid mistake. I thought I'd find something useful, that'd help us fight the Bane."

"Did you?"

She seriously considered telling him about the Lorestone. For a split second. Then her brain threw out two great reasons not to. First, he wouldn't exactly be thrilled about her having left a witness to her trespassing—the librarian. And, second, there was the fact that she'd abandoned the stone in a random trash bin.

Better to say nothing of the Lorestone, at least until she'd recovered it and there was something worthwhile to report. Then Ordin might actually thank her, see that she could be an invaluable member of the team.

"No," she said. "Nothing useful. Sorry."

He clicked his tongue. "Excuse me a moment." He stepped outside, promptly returning to shove a couple of full plastic bags into her arms. "Thought you might need—well, some of these things. I will call you tonight." And, without another word, he left.

Outside, the engine of his million-gelder silver sports car whirred to life, and the vehicle peeled off.

The motel manager walked in at that exact moment. "He seemed pissed. Trouble in paradise?"

Alina ignored him.

Ordin would come around. She'd show him exactly what she was capable of, and then he'd learn to appreciate her talents. He and Baraam and all the other Ravers, she'd prove them all wrong.

She peeked into the goodie bags Ordin had brought, finding bandages, cotton swabs, toilet paper, paper towels, energy bars, antiseptic.

He'd made her a care-package.

Ignoring the jeering manager, she returned upstairs.

Back in Room 4, Alina said, "Coast is clear," and Cho appeared from inside the cabinet under the bathroom sink, saying, "That bro your boyfriend, or what?"

Breath catching in her throat, Alina waved the comment off. "He wishes."

Cho opened the mirror above the sink, carefully scooping the still-unconscious Pyct onto her palm. She set him back down on the bed.

"What is this thing, anyway?" said Cho.

"A Pyct. A type of Mythidim Aelf. They're territorial. Live in hives."

"Like wasps?"

"Sort of, yeah, but Pycts can talk with each other telepathically. They're like one big tight-knit family. This one's a male. You can tell by the coloration of the fur and the size of the fangs." The little creature's purr-like snores slipped from between his gnashing teeth as his chest rose and fell.

Cho examined the tiny blue comatose mouse-man. "So, where's his family?"

"I don't know. With how I found him, probably nowhere great. If they're alive at all."

"That's so sad."

"Yeah." Alina scratched her neck and knuckles. "So, uh, Cho, I need a favor."

"What a surprise." Cho rolled her eyes. "*Another* big ask."

"You didn't happen to get my note I left you?"

Cho nodded. "This morning. Too late to help out. Sorry."

"Not a problem. But the favor I need does have to do with last night's adventure. I had to drop something important. Something insanely valuable."

Cho smirked, leaning in. "You have my attention."

Alina described the location of the dumpster that now contained the ancient and priceless Lorestone, an irreplaceable artifact from the dawn of the Nation of El. She provided as much detail as she could. Cho listened intently.

"So that's it," said Alina. "Need me to write it down for you?"

"Nah, I'm good. My memory is amazing."

"Almost as amazing as your humbleness."

"You want me to help you or nah?" With a toothpick, Cho scraped some dirt from under her fingernails.

"Yes, please, thank you," Alina said quickly. "I need that Lorestone. I will literally give you whatever you want in exchange."

"There's the problem, though. I already have a ton of money—more than you, by the looks of this rat-hole you're staying in. What would I be sticking my neck out for this time?" She blew on her nails.

"Name your price. Seriously."

"Seriously, huh?" Cho looked up, quirking an eyebrow. A glint from the window—the headlights of a passing hovercraft—flashed across her eyes. "Alright, *seriously*… I want you to take me to the mainland."

Alina scrutinized Cho's face, gauging if she was joking.

The girl shrugged, and she drummed her fingers on the bedpost. "I'm telling you, that's my price. I can't be up here anymore. I wanna get off this rock."

"Become a Terrie? You know, you've had it rough up here, but it's not going to be any better—"

"You don't know my situation," Cho snapped. "Maybe it will suck down there, too. But I *know* that up here it's summer-cooked garbage, from sunup to sundown and after. And I'm sick of it. Would ya just trust me? I have a really good buncha reasons to wanna leave, 'kay?" She paused for breath. "We got a deal, or what?"

"Where are you gonna go, though? As you so kindly pointed out just now, I'm flat broke, so you can't stay with me. What's your plan?"

"Don't worry about it. My can-do attitude's gotten me this far, hasn't it?"

"That it has, that it has." Alina paused, thinking. "Why can't you buy a ticket yourself? You have the cash."

"I can't—I don't have any of the docs I need."

Alina scrutinized Cho's fidgeting fingers and hunched posture. "You talking about citizenship papers?"

"Yah." She scowled. "It's… complicated, okay? And you don't gotta know all the details. Just get me past the scanners and pinkojacks and onto a train. I'll figure the rest out as I go. I'm good at that."

It was clear that Cho was either lying or leaving something out. Something important.

The *misckie* had claimed to have been arrested by the Enforcers on at least a couple of occasions. Would they really have released a little girl if she didn't have any legal documents to prove her identity? She'd mentioned an orphanage, too. Was she being held in The Capital against her will?

Also, exactly how *had* she gotten so very talented at stealing?

Alina wanted nothing more than to confront her. What was she hiding, and why?

However, Alina happened to need Cho's unique set of skills.

Alina considered her options. She couldn't think of a valid reason to deny Cho this promise. How she would ever manage to smuggle Cho off The Capital, though, she had no idea. Stuff her in a carry-on bag? Transmute her body into a gas and seal her in a pickle jar? Alina would have to think of something, but she could only handle one impossible puzzle at a time.

First, she needed that chipped Lorestone.

She held out her hand. "Okay, Cho, you help me out today, and I'll do whatever I can to bootleg you off New El when it comes time for me to leave. And if you do change your mind, no problem at all. You just let me know and—"

"Eh, you're annoying me. You always doubt people this much? Stop it."

Alina didn't know what to say to that. She stared at Cho's judgmental grimace—Cho, who was like a feral cat perched on a tin roof, sneering down, snidely flicking her tail. All purring and sandpaper licks one second, and next thing you knew, her claws were inch-deep in the meat of your leg.

Thankfully, the girl focused her attention on the Pyct again, asking, "You're gonna help him, right?"

"I'm gonna try."

"No, don't *try*. Just *do* it. He's sick. You have to give him some medicine. What do Pycts like to eat?"

Alina sighed. The pages of her mental encyclopedia fluttered open, her thoughts like rifling fingers, flipping through, searching for the relevant entry. She found it, answering, "Radioactive rocks. But I'll need something strong to heal and wake him up."

"Like what?"

"Cho, as fun as it would be to school you on Pyct physiology, I need to get started. He's in bad shape. And, you, honestly, have a job to do. Every second that passes with that Lorestone just chilling in a trashcan leaves me more and more ready to hurl. I will blow absolute chunks, do you hear me? If it falls into the wrong hands—"

"Relax, alright? I'm on it. See? I'm headed out the door." She paused at the threshold. "Just fix the little guy, 'k?"

"Bye, Cho."

"'K, bye, lady." Having thudded halfway down the stairs, she shouted up, "Remember your promise!"

Cho had been kind enough to leave on the pillow a wad of cash she'd withdrawn from a nearby ATM (thanks to Baraam's credit card). Armed with these emergency funds, Alina whipped out her phone, hopped onto its Aetherthread app and ordered breakfast from a nearby coffee shop. While waiting for her lox bagel and tall spiced mocha to be delivered (living a life of luxury up in here), she searched various trading pages for a few essentials.

To nurse the Pyct back to health, she'd need a small healthy house plant, about ten gallons of distilled water, three sticks of green chalk, a charged lithium battery, and an empty fuel cell. All these items were easily purchased from Gogadrop.thr—buyer, seller, and shipper of "Over 1 Billion Quality Products!"

Within fifteen minutes, the goods arrived by drone delivery. Alina had only to open the window, reach out, and sign the hovering drone's touchscreen with her pinky finger. The drone zoomed off to its next drop, and Alina closed the window, shuttering it.

She took a pillow from the bed, fluffed it, and laid the unconscious Pyct upon it. Tearing open her packages, she littered the floor with bubble paper and shredded cardboard.

Then there came a knock, and she leapt over the junk in the center of the room. The delivery guy was apologetic for being late; she told him it wasn't a big deal, handed him a generous tip, and, as soon as he'd given her the food, flung the door shut.

The Pyct was running out of time. If he didn't perk up soon, the coma he'd slipped into would become permanent. He needed to be juiced. Fast.

To his species, radioactive material was as nutritious as protein was to humans. Radioactive material was, however, not exactly easy to acquire. No way was Alina getting her hands on plutonium, nor did she have any desire to try boosting one of those fancy new mini-nuclear-reactor-powered cars she'd seen parked outside. Fortunately, she wouldn't have to.

While not as potent as other elements, pure tritium (a radioactive isotope of hydrogen) did have impressive regenerative effects for many radiotrophic species. In other words, if you were the type to eat radiation, tritium was like a nap, chicken soup for the soul, and a steaming cup of ginger tea all wrapped up in one hot little glow-in-the-dark package.

A shame she couldn't just buy a full hydrogen fuel cell. Would've saved her a lot of time and trouble. Sure, she could've turned it into a bomb with only basic chemistry and engineering skills, but—other than that—what was the worst that could happen?

Alina had other ways of getting what she needed, though.

She knelt beside the Pyct, cracking open the package of green chalk and drawing a triangle around him and his pillow. At each of the triangle's points, she drew a circle, and in one of these she placed the small potted plant (after removing the plastic wrap covering its leaves). It was young and she could feel the vitality spilling from it. Good.

Into the second circle, she shoved the ten-gallon jug of water. Her working fluid. She unscrewed the cap and dropped the lithium battery into the liquid. It sank quickly.

The fuel cell she set within the third circle.

The atmosphere naturally contains roughly five hundred-thousandths of a percent of hydrogen. If the world were a nearly empty gymnasium, the hydrogen would only amount to the slimy particulates of a single person's sneeze. In water, the hydrogen ratio is much better—two parts per molecule, of course. But separating it required laboratory equipment.

… Or magic.

Another wrinkle: she wasn't after any old hydrogen; she wanted tritium, which was even rarer. To produce it, she'd need to add two neutrons to her pure hydrogen. This could be done a couple different ways, one of which would be to detonate a nuclear device. Since she was short on atom bombs these days, she'd have to go with option two: slamming the lithium battery with radiation.

It just so happened that Niima, the force that flowed through every Maggo, was radioactive. That was the dark side of spellcasting: the more you relied on it, the likelier it would be that you only lived a half-life. Disease, injury, cancer… there were creative ways to minimize these risks, but they required detailed knowledge and special materials.

Since Niima was radioactive, why not simply soak the Pyct in it? Well, a Corpromancer—an expert in the art of transitioning between life and death—could have managed it, but Alina didn't have that gift. Her specialty was Terramancy, with her area focus being Geomancy (earth-based magic). She knew a smattering of specific spells from other disciplines, but none of them would be useful now, and *all* of them had a chance of simply killing the Pyct in his sleep.

So, no, she couldn't bathe him in radiation directly. She needed to feed him something radioactive.

Alina was about to improvise based on an old theory she'd read once. A long time ago. But it should work. If she could summon enough of her inner power, borrowing from her reserves, drawing a surge of that ethereal energy into the material world and shunt the extra energy away from herself, she… should be fine?

A whispered prayer to Buthmertha, and she was ready. Ready as she'd ever be.

Cracking her knuckles, she sat cross-legged in front of the Pyct, her thumbs and fingers forming a triangle. Focusing her Niima, she unleashed a surge of power from her core, felt it vibrate and course from her gut through her chest and down the lengths of her arms, exploding from her palms. The invisible wave crashed into and *through* the plastic jug of water, enveloping the lithium battery resting at its bottom. The fluid began to bubble and boil, the lithium fizzing, and the water level within the jug dropped dramatically. Separated from the oxygen, a puff of colorless hydrogen gas wafted upward.

She held her breath, telekinetically nudging the gas toward the empty fuel cell.

The strain was enormous. Her vision blurred, grew dark around the edges. The veins in her neck bulged, her ears popped, her lungs ached.

The gas blew into the cell as she condensed it into liquid, at which point she flicked her wrist and the cell's cap sealed itself.

Energy can neither be created nor destroyed. It must come from somewhere. She had used her own body to channel a huge amount of power, and the cost was immediately apparent. Tasting bile in her throat, blinking through the pain, she fixed her attention on the houseplant.

For one lifeform to shove aside destruction and death, another must take its place.

She imagined the life-force within the plant like a steady river in the shape of a Mobius strip, flowing on and on and around, contained within the leaves and stem and root—but it also existed outside these, mingling with all the energy rivers of all living beings, everywhere. She mentally redirected the flow of the plant's river, siphoning it from its wooden trappings.

As clearly as she could feel her own heart furiously beating within her chest, she felt the life drain from the plant. It withered, faded.

Energy can neither be created nor destroyed. It must go somewhere. She merely gave it a nudge: the excess radiation from her spell coursed upward in a roiling wave, pouring into the houseplant. She, in turn, received the plant's essence, that calm, steady, growing vitality that flowed into her through the crown of her head, spilling across her being like steaming spring water.

She allowed the Niima to drain, a receding tide. And she felt her equilibrium returning. Long, deep, lung-expanding breaths.

When she opened her eyes, the plant was nothing more than a few twigs in a pot of gray dirt, and the ten-gallon bottle of water was empty—well, that wasn't quite true. It was empty of water but full of oxygen.

The lithium had been the catalyst, a helpful focal point for her as she shuffled the neutrons in the oxygen into the hydrogen, transform that hydrogen into tritium. The tritium, then, had drifted upward through the jug's open cap and been deposited inside the hydrogen cell.

She checked the chrome-colored fuel cell. Three blue bars. Max capacity.

Success. She'd made pure, high-grade tritium. For the Pyct, it would act like an adrenaline shot.

Wiping the sweat from her brow, she scuffed the green chalk markings with the heel of her boot, breaking the magic circles and dispelling any lingering power. She then placed the cell beside the Pyct, making sure the metal touched his skin. His species absorbed through osmosis, so the energy would automatically be pulled into his body. (That natural ability could sometimes be problematic. In Alina's hometown, for example, car shops, fuel refineries, fill-up stations, and other businesses set Pyct traps. Otherwise, these "pests" would siphon any energy emitted, to great annoyance of business owners and customers alike.)

"Here you go, buddy," Alina told the Pyct. "Drink up."

Her throat parched, she got herself a glass of water. And waited.

Over the next few minutes, the blue bars flickered and slowly turned off, one by one. The Pyct's little mousy face eventually scrunched up; he rolled onto his side, wings spasming.

His eyes popped open. Before Alina could say anything, he vaulted backward and was airborne, ricocheting like a bullet across the motel room.

"Hey, relax," Alina shouted.

The Pyct landed on top of the bathroom sink and picked up a cotton swab, gripping it like a spear. "You: who? Where: I?"

His words confused her already addled mind; he wasn't speaking but beaming the words directly into her head. And they either weren't arriving in exactly the right order or he had a very peculiar speech-pattern.

By the expression on his face, he didn't seem too comfortable conversing in her language. Although, admittedly, she didn't know very much about how a Pyct's face should look under ideal circumstances.

"My name is Stitcher. I found you in the sewers." She tried to sound soothing. She didn't want to spook him, so she kept her distance. "You were hurt, so I gave you some medicine."

"Do: you, why?"

"You were in bad shape, buckaroo. I couldn't leave you there to die."

He lowered his cotton swab. "Thanks: me, you."

"What's your name?" Alina took a step back, giving him his space. He was, after all, a feral creature and—from his point of view—abducted and trapped in an unfamiliar place.

Thumping his pec with his fist, he said, "Pyct'Tsi: Mezami."

"Nice to meet you, Mezami. 'Tsi,' is that your clan tag?"

He nodded, baring his sharp fangs. His clawed hands brushed the bright crimson sickle-shaped tattoos on his chest. "Destroyed: clan, mine."

"You told me that last night. I'm so sorry for your loss."

"Crave: vengeance, I." He slapped his fist onto his flat palm. "Demands: honor. Demand: dead, people mine."

Although his face was hard to read, his posture wasn't. He was suspicious of her.

Alina sat down at the table in the corner of the room. Away from him. "You don't mind if I eat this bagel, do you? Take your time in there. But I'm starving."

She bit half the bagel off in one go, slurping down the capers and smoked salmon, chasing it all with a gulp of spiced coffee.

By the time she'd finished, Mezami had gained enough confidence to fly over to her. Several inches shorter than her to-go cup, he stood between it and the now-empty plastic food container, muscular forearms crossed. He seemed to be sizing her up.

"Other humans: unlike, you."

"I'll take that as a compliment." She downed the cool dregs of her coffee. "You must have had some bad experiences with my kind."

"Fire: shadow: rage." His wings fluttered. "Last Tsi: I."

Alina wiped her hands and mouth with a napkin. What could she say to something like that?

After a couple of minutes, she asked, "What will you do now?"

He shook his head, adjusted the strap of his bandolier.

"Well, no need to decide right this minute." She smiled despite how depressed she suddenly felt. "We've got some time to kill before Cho gets back."

"Second smell: gone, girl?"

"She's running a quick errand. For me. It would be dangerous for me to go outside, so I'm sort of under house-arrest."

Mezami didn't seem to understand.

"I can't leave for now," she explained. "Figure I might as well take advantage of that and switch on the Watchbox. See what these Elementals up here are into, entertainment-wise. Between my grandfather calling them 'Idiot-boxes,' and being so broke I can't afford food, I almost never get to just watch. So, that's what I'm gonna do for a bit. You're welcome to join. Hang out a while, until you decide what your next move is going to be."

She fell onto the stained couch, snapped up the scuffed remote, and started flicking through the channels.

Eventually, Mezami perched on the edge of the armrest, lying on his belly, posted on his elbows.

They watched a reality cooking show in which the contestants had twenty minutes to make cakes that would normally take an hour minimum to prep and bake. The only way for them to pull it off was to manipulate the laws of physics using magic. Alina laughed when one of them set their workstation on fire. "You have to account for the friction, fool," she shouted at the screen, clapping her hands between each word.

Cut to commercial. Some ad for a lawyer offering his services for hover-cyclists who'd been in an accident. Even if they were the ones at fault. *"It's no big! Call the Zigg! Billed per hour, three-hour minimum."*

The next commercial was an ad for *Thunderbolt*, the chain of martial arts schools owned by Baraam. Sterile, identical. With energy drink sponsorships and private cafés and genetically altered personal trainers. Branded to death. Alina knew that, if he got his way, he'd turn The School into that same type of soulless, money-grubbing garbage studio.

Then Baraam himself popped into view, scowling at the camera, challenging the viewer to "rise to new heights, reach for the heavens, and strike with the power of a *Thunderbolt*."

Gagging, Alina immediately changed the channel to a zany sit-com about three sisters and their son/nephew. Their gimmick was that all three of the sisters were teachers at the private school the boy attended, and they kept an overbearingly watchful eye on everything he did. Each episode, he enacted a new plan to escape their smothering. Hijinks ensued.

Mezami actually chuckled a few times. Alina couldn't tell if he got the jokes or if he simply enjoyed the copious hand-waving and over-the-top delivery of the lines. Maybe it was the laugh-track.

A couple more hours went by. The novelty of mostly-guilt-free Watch-boxing had begun to wear off, and Alina was left wondering what could be taking Cho so long.

23

AS TIME WORE ON, Alina started making excuses: Cho had stopped for a bite to eat, she'd gotten turned around, she'd had trouble finding the correct dumpster because it had been moved.

Three hours had passed since the girl had left, three hours of sitting around, and Alina could no longer tell herself that everything was *definitely* fine. No more, "Oh, this is the earliest Cho could have gotten back, so there's still time," or, "Traffic must be a nightmare right now."

Eventually, the very real possibility that something had happened to Cho became increasingly difficult to ignore.

What if she'd been picked up by The Authority? Or worse?

Holding out his arms, Mezami balanced on the edge of the squat Watch-box. "Away yet: friend, yours."

"Yeah." Alina nibbled on her lip until she tasted a tinge of blood on her tongue. "Yup."

"Worried: you."

"Right again." She paced from the door to the window and back, stopping every now and then to stare out at the street.

The Pyct fluttered in front of her face, waving. "Help: I, you?"

Pausing mid-stride, Alina blinked at him. "You'd do that?"

He nodded, gripping his left shoulder and rotating his arm, as if to say, "You bet." Although, Alina wasn't yet one hundred percent confident in her comprehension of Pyct body language; he might also have been indicating that he was still in pain.

Alina scratched her bandaged elbows, watching him. "Why do you care?"

Seemingly confused by the question, he said, "Help me: you. Help you: I." He flexed. "Idea: I."

"Maybe there is something I can trade you for or—I just—" She couldn't figure out why this Aelf was offering assistance. She'd patched him up, sure, but she was still a human—his enemy. After what he'd gone through, having been so savagely abused, how could he trust her?

Alina narrowed her eyes, weighing Mezami's mousy expression. It wouldn't be unreasonable for him to assume she was playing him, working to get him to lead her to other Pycts so she could collect a bounty. Aelfravers had done worse.

She tapped her forehead with her forefinger, suddenly aware of the ridiculous spiraling dive her thoughts had taken. There was no point to imagining an alternate universe in which she was a shifty, backstabbing, untrustworthy slimeball.

So, she failed to understand Mezami's motivations. Right now, though, there was only one fact that mattered: Cho had to be found because Cho could very well have the Lorestone.

She sat down at the table, backwards on the chair, chin resting on her hands. "Okay, Mezami. I accept your offer. Let's do this. I'm all ears."

He examined her carefully. "Incorrect: you. Ears: not. Non-ear limbs: ninety percent, you."

Caught off-guard, Alina laughed. "Was that a joke?"

"Understand: not, I."

"Never mind. Let's hear your idea."

Pycts must have displayed emotions very differently than did humans because whatever Mezami's expression was doing right now—a wrinkling of the snout, stretching of the lips, and fluttering of the eyelids—it didn't look like a smile; nevertheless, his tone was almost smug. He tapped the bridge of his snout. "Track: girl. Trail: follow. Hunt: we."

"You can smell her? You were unconscious when we were all together, though?"

"Smell: no. See: yes."

Alina snapped her fingers. Of course. She should have remembered sooner: Pycts' eyes had undergone a unique mutation; they could, to a limited degree, see into the Ethereal Plane. The leading theory explaining the evolution of this trait was that this "Ethersight" was a defense mechanism against more powerful and intelligent predators. Since all sentient creatures have souls, and all souls leave a stamp or footprint in the Ether, Pycts could use their sixth sense to distinguish between and escape the emitters of strong signatures. By that same token, they could hunt down less impressive Ethereal creatures. Guided by soul imprints.

Grinning, she said, "What do you need? To trace her, I mean. Something she touched?"

"Scent: not," he reminded her. "Trail: already, I. Easy: it."

The back of her chair clacked against the table as she shot up. "Yeah? Right. Okay." She rushed to and fro, flinging pillows and boxes aside, searching for her sweater.

This was great. With Mezami's natural ability, she'd be able to find Cho and get that Lorestone off her. Then it'd be just a hop, skip, and a jump to unlocking what was sure to be extremely valuable information about the Bane of New El.

She just had to have faith. Faith that Cho hadn't gotten bored or lost, or been apprehended. Faith that the Crystallarium librarian had been telling Alina the truth with her hint about the Lorestone's contents. (Yes, Alina was aware of how strange that last part was.)

She paused halfway into the process of throwing on her jacket. Even if they hadn't identified her just yet, The Authority was looking for her; Ordin had confirmed as much. And, speaking of Ordin, he'd be disappointed—maybe even disgusted—if Alina broke her promise to lie low a mere five hours after making it. Especially after last night's escapade. Really, he might never speak to her again. The thought popped bubbles of fire in her gut, but what could she do? She needed that damned lump of Chrononite.

According to the annoyingly mysterious librarian, it had been her grandfather's. Well, he'd mucked around with it, anyway. She figured it had to contain some juicy secret or other.

Anyway. Remaining cooped up at the *Preening Peacock* would do no one any good. She made up her mind.

Sorry, Ordin.

She pulled her arm through her jacket's sleeve, saying, "Well, Mezami. Do your thing."

Forty-five minutes later, right around four o'clock in the afternoon, they found the end of the ethereal trail.

"You're kidding me. Cho's in *there*?"

Alina stared across a crowded street at a multiwalled, red-brick fortress. The walls were fifteen feet high, mainly designed to keep out the rabble. The watchtowers, however, were forty feet tall. She counted twenty-two of them, each manned by a pair of riflemen wearing garish red leather jackets with twinkling gold buttons.

The riflemen's uniforms complemented their surroundings: from the towers hung red banners bearing gold lions with viper tails. Thanks to her conversation with Ordin the other night, Alina easily recognized the standard of House Walazzin. She was standing in front of a compound belonging to one of the Twelve Families.

She cupped her mouth and muttered into her hood, where Mezami was hiding, "You're sure this is the place?"

He tapped her shoulder. Once.

She was glad he was adhering to the code they'd established in the hotel room. Once for "yes," and twice for "no." The last thing she needed was for him to speak out of turn with any of the Elementals within earshot.

Her appreciation of his subtlety was overshadowed, though, by the impossibility of the task ahead. Would she really have to wriggle her way into this fortress? She hadn't even begun to recuperate from her jaunt into The Gild, and reviving Mezami had taken another heavy toll.

Why were the cruel gods tossing all these stealth missions her way? She was a hunter, not a cat burglar. The irony of the situation was not lost on her: she was about to attempt the daring rescue of Cho, who would have been a much better fit for the job.

"You're absolutely positive?" Alina whispered.

Mezami tapped her noggin. Once. Affirmative.

There simply were too many sentries. She couldn't sneak inside in broad daylight. On the other hand, if she waited until night, who knew what would happen to Cho in the meantime? Who knew what these creeps wanted with her?

It crossed Alina's mind that maybe Cho had *intentionally* gone into the stronghold. Maybe she'd sold Alina out. It would've been a chance to get off the streets, make a little money for turning in the one who'd robbed The Gild in the dead of night.

It didn't matter, though. Recovering the Lorestone was Alina's priority. She could not let it fall into the Walazzins' hands. Besides, Tahtoh had taught her to trust, above all else, her own instincts, and her gut told her that Cho wouldn't be caught dead in a place like this, with its foul aura. Something about it felt wrong.

No matter how she looked at it, though, she was stuck. She couldn't afford to wait till nightfall because the Lorestone might be discovered—assuming it hadn't already been reported and shipped off to the Western Precinct Station. But she couldn't simply rush in before dark because she'd be shot down from any of a dozen different angles. Those riflemen up there weren't Authority; they were private mercenaries. That meant they were subjected to even less oversight and accountability. They could do whatever they wanted as long as the action could be justified as defense of their master's property.

As all her hopes were about to be swept away by a great big flood of despair, she sucked in a breath, remembering something useful Ordin had told her about The Sanctum. Hadn't he said that Walazzin was tight with The Author's people?

"Mezami," she said. "I have an idea. It's going to take a bit to put together. Just be cool for now, yeah?"

One tap.

"Nice. Thanks."

The Walazzin guards were giving her funny looks as she approached the main gate of the compound. She could tell. Even from under their obnoxiously ornate, eagle-headed helmets made of steel gilded with red-gold, they were eyeing her and snickering behind their metal-gloved hands.

She didn't let her lack of confidence show. She couldn't. She had to be totally convincing.

Half an hour ago, she'd located a group of gray-robed acolytes preaching the good word of The Author of Creation. A brief, one-sided, and guilt-trip-heavy conversation later and Alina made off with one of their pamphlets.

Well, it was more like a three-sided card, and it didn't have any writing on it. Only pictures. Stylized, hieroglyphic-like images of humans in gray robes throwing themselves at the feet of a massive white man with squiggles coming out of him. (The squiggles represented beams of light or divine energy, Alina guessed.) The third panel showed a perfectly triangular mountain spearing out of the black earth, a red setting sun behind it. This, Alina had been told, was the principal earthly sanctuary of The Author, which the faithful called the Sword of Saint Sahni Savandar, or the Mountain of the Mendicant. It was the primary temple of the entire religion, located right here on New El, in the Fidae District. You couldn't miss it, you had but to look to the huge stone peak spearing upward, a filed nail scratching heaven, a smooth and ominous obelisk that jutted like a gigantic black splinter among the modern glass and steel skyscrapers of The Capital. The solitary, austere monument was a shadowed, light-drinking void among the infinite tangles of flashing, buzzing, beeping neon advertisements that choked the downtown sky.

When Alina had asked the acolytes why there weren't any words on the card, you know, to help people figure out where to go, the Sanctumites had laughed condescendingly, telling her that the writing and reading of letters is forbidden to all but The Author—for was it not true that He had Written the World into Being, and were, therefore, Words not Power? Yes, surely, they were a Power far too pure and perfect for human hands or minds to ever grasp.

Alina had nodded along, and the Sanctumites had chided her for "the defiant glint" in her eyes and the "form-adhering nature" of her pants. They'd pleaded with her to act now, join them, save her soul.

She'd promised she'd get right on that, and then she'd asked them for a set of their gray robes, but they'd wanted a blood oath in exchange. No, really. They'd been serious.

That's when Alina had left.

No robes then. The colorfully bone-chilling card depicting the masses prostrated before a blindingly shining, towering, white-bearded man with black wings would have to do for what she had in mind.

She had spent another fifteen minutes practicing some of the phrases The Sanctum acolytes had used. Imitating their tones and inflections, the widening of their eyes, the dramatic waving of their arms. She had to sound authentic enough to pass for one of them.

Now, to be clear, Alina was all for diversity of religion. She herself was a proud polytheist, as were the majority of the Assets of El. For generations her family had worshipped Buthmertha, a Truct favorite, and patron deity of the hearth and home. The goddess of simple folk, protector of those who lacked the means to protect themselves. And, again, she was completely tolerant of beliefs different from her own; Aelfravers were a diverse lot, coming from all parts of the world, and so believed in all manner of unique divinities.

That being said, this Author guy sounded like a real piece of work.

According to his doctrine, you weren't supposed to *read.* Reading! How do you live without that? And why would you want to?

That was all she really needed to know about The Sanctum to make up her mind, and she felt not one single pang of remorse for how she was preparing to use their name to further her own purpose.

She'd cracked her knuckles, gently slapped her cheeks to stave off a panic attack, and marched straight for the Walazzin compound's northern gatehouse.

As she neared the gates, the red-gilded guards played a quick three games of rock-paper-scissors. The loser's shoulders sagged, and he walked over to intercept her, blocking her way forward. In his shining breastplate, with pauldrons made to resemble a lion's paws, he looked like a toy soldier.

"Your business, girl?"

Alina found herself thinking this would have been so much easier had she ever been to drama camp. But Tahtoh would never have sent her. Even now, she could almost hear him saying, *"Acting is lying, my little Cabbage, that's all. You want to learn to lie? Visit a law firm. Or a bank. Heh-heh!"*

With no formal training, and hardly any practice, she knew nothing of acting as an art form. The range of characters she could play was limited to "Alina" and "Hangry Alina." However, she had been on the receiving end of so many lectures from the likes of her grandfather and other elder Ravers. Even Baraam had joined in the fun when he'd felt so inclined.

In summary, she'd learned by example how to act all self-important. And she'd benefited from the recent trial run with Lonami. (Sure, he'd seen through her bluff, but she blamed those crazy eyes of his for that.)

Channeling Baraam's dark thundercloud charisma, her brow wrinkled like sunbaked tree bark as she stepped right up to red soldier number one and declared, "I am here to take the Lord Walazzin's confession. I was told he'd be in and that I would have no trouble seeing him tonight."

"Who are you?" said the guard, but his voice quavered. Alina's unyielding demeanor was a chisel, her words hammer blows; doubt began to wriggle its way into the crack she'd bashed into the façade of his confidence.

Clasping her hands until her knuckles whitened, she smiled and said quietly, "Why, I am only a servant of The Author of All that is Good in this world. Take me to your master *immediately*, or I swear that I shall tell him *exactly* why I was detained from my holy ministrations."

"Dreadfully sorry, miss, but we weren't expecting visitors this evening."

"Haven't you heard of emergency confession? The meaning of the word 'emergency' too much for you? *Well*, I have a concept you might actually understand—'fired.' Would you care to try that on for size? No? Then let me in—" She decided to gamble for everything she was worth—"or I'll have you excommunicated from the congregation."

Guard number two, who had said nothing up to this point, chimed in, "You can… do that?"

"Do I seem like someone to be trifled with?" said Alina, lifting her chin just a little higher, hoping her question didn't seem too genuine.

A few more rounds of back-and-forth, of her verbally pummeling the two numbskulls, and she'd parlayed her way inside. The guard who'd done most of the talking led her through the gate and into the central courtyard. He hurried ahead of her, red steel armor clanking with each step, shooting a glance over his shoulder.

The courtyard was abuzz with activity; men and women wearing over-starched, rigid crimson cloth uniforms smacked blunted iron swords against practice dummies fashioned of birch logs. The trainees' foreheads and necks and arms glistened, sweat droplets flying from them as they practiced ground-fighting techniques on one another, disarmed one another, threw one another over-shoulder into the dirt.

What were they preparing for? Were they headed to frontlines of the war, to Ozar?

Alina didn't have long to ponder; guard number one led her to the nearest building, the one with a domed roof, and opened the front door for her. He shut it behind him, announced this was the foyer, and was all too happy to hand her over to the fancy butler who appeared behind her.

"You may *go*, Ralfus," said the butler.

An almost tangible weight lifted off the guard's shoulders, and he walked away, a little straighter and taller. The butler, meanwhile, stared at Alina like an exterminator might a rodent's corpse—professionally interested, but ready at any minute to dispose of her remains.

Getting into the rhythm of her assumed character, Alina went on a tirade about the guards' disrespect. The butler mentioned that perhaps their confusion was due in part to her having come in plain garb. She puffed up, snapping that she'd left her robes at The Sanctum in order to spare Walazzin any gossip that might have arisen in response to a young Sanctumite woman's appearance on his doorstep. Without a chaperone. What would people think? Would he really want that sort of scandal tied to him and to The Sanctum? Except for his continuously simmering distaste, the butler lost all interest in her. Mission accomplished.

Leading her through the halls, but not upstairs, and into a sitting room with several ornate, gold-leaf-covered, plush-cushioned chairs, the butler asked her to please make herself comfortable. He retreated, closing the door behind him.

Alright, then. Realistically, she had maybe ten minutes before they came to their senses and hauled her off to jail.

She balled up and tossed The Sanctum pamphlet, examining the room. The butler had locked the door, the paranoid jerk. Solid call on his part, of course, because she was most certainly up to no good. But she was still irritated. With only a small window of time, she whispered to Mezami, "Can you lead the way? Tap left shoulder for left, and right for right. Middle of the back for 'yes' and 'no.' Got it?"

One tap, middle.

On her way into this sitting room, Alina had noted two key details about the compound: number one, most everyone was in the courtyard, and there seemed to be few-to-no guards inside the main structure; number two, this place had only a few countercharms here and there. It was no Gildhall, that was for sure. All the Walazzins had thought to drape over the place were a few basic anti-snooping spells and a couple of nullifiers—every one of them focused on preventing offensive magic, which wasn't Alina's style anyway.

Her keen Niima-sniffing nose homed in on the nearest exit. It bore a magical lock. That might have been a problem, but, fortunately, its design was hit-or-miss. Walazzin's architects had had the foresight to install a spell-proof door, yes. The hinges though? Different story.

Well—she wiggled her fingers—who'd go to all the trouble of putting up arcane protections if what was behind this door wasn't important? They could have just hung a sign that said, "In here, thieves!"

Alina made a finger-gun at the gaudy gilded hinge and said, "Pow," once for the bottom and again for the top. "Pow." The brittle metal burst, and the door fell forward, clattering on the hardwood floor.

She thought one more time about Ordin, what he'd say if he were here. For a moment, she felt nauseous, betraying his trust like this; he had a good heart. Buried under all that showiness and styling gel, he was a decent guy, and he'd seemed really worried about her. And with good reason, given what she was about to do.

"Ah, well." She shrugged. A little late to turn back now.

She stepped over the downed door and into the hall.

The whole place was soaked in shadow; only in narrow slivers did the sunlight creep inside to stamp the gray walls and thick, dusty stillness protected by the heavy curtains and blinds covering every window. Following his ether-sense, Mezami guided Alina through the dimness. She dashed past the kitchens, the servants' quarters, the broom closets, and up some stairs. She stopped whenever she heard voices or footsteps. At one point, she flung herself behind one of those fancy fainting-couches—what were they called? divans?—just in time to watch the butler hustle past, a couple of red-armored guards in tow. She slipped behind them, unnoticed.

Everywhere she looked, there hung pretentious landscape paintings, portraits of long-dead Walazzins, with their big noses and bigger mustaches. Plenty of marble busts, too. Men and women, their stone eyes and lips locked in grimaces from beyond the grave. The whole place smelled musty, from the carpets to the exotic pelts strung up on the walls and ceilings. The glassy eyes of mounted animal heads—zebras, elephants, mountain lions—glared down at her. There were one or two stuffed Aelf up there, as well. Varieties of Raccitan, by the look of them, but she didn't linger to inspect these trophies more closely.

The second floor of the compound was a maze. Each hallway was indistinguishable from the last. There were no big rooms with clearly defined purposes that Alina could see into. Almost all the doors were locked, begging the question, "why so much secrecy?" She was, however, too focused on finding Cho to think about anything else.

Too bad that Mezami could only indicate direction; he couldn't foretell which paths would be barred, or where the walls were. The monotony of the gray halls with their gray carpets and gray portraits of pasty old Walazzins threatened to hypnotize Alina, but her tenseness kept her alert.

She was forced to skirt multiple hindrances, sometimes taking a turn down a different hallway or two, often doubling back, each time trying and trying again until she found a way around the obstruction or dead end.

After what felt like years of running, but was probably closer to eight or ten minutes, Mezami stopped her with a tap at the base of her neck.

"Here?" she whispered, stomach twisting.

Confirmation tap.

She fumbled with a loose brass handle until it fell off and the door creaked open.

Inside, a bedroom. Four-poster bed with big red drapes, gold ropes tying them back. Curtains had been drawn across the windows so that only a narrow crescent of light sliced the wood floor. In the corner, a makeup stand—no, a vanity. The mirror was cracked.

Alina's heart skipped a whole measure when she noticed someone sitting on the bed. Someone fairly small and… puffy? A child with her back turned, neither stirring nor making a sound.

Silence. Dust swirling between them. Alina's skin crawled in the disquiet.

"Close the door," said the girl.

"Cho?" said Alina.

24

CLOSING THE DOOR BEHIND her, Alina went over to the window and drew back the heavy curtains. Light burst into the bedchamber like a mother tearing the blanket off her oversleeping child.

It was indeed Cho, sitting at the edge of the bed, hugging a green pillow with frilly orange tassels. Although, she was almost unrecognizable, half-buried inside an oversized pink and white dress with rounded shoulders and way too many ruffled skirts.

Alina noticed the stack of wigs—red, brown, blonde, and black—hanging from the vanity. One of them, a brunette one, was collecting dust in the opposite corner of the room.

"Stitcher? What are you doing here?"

"Rescuing you, of course. Also, you wouldn't happen to still have that Lorestone on you, would ya?"

"I hid it. But they found it anyway."

Alina's shoulders sagged. She frantically began combing her hand through her hair.

"I'm sorry." Cho stayed on the bed. "I tried to keep it safe. But they took all my stuff." She cocked her head. "Where's our little friend?"

Mezami poked his head out from Alina's hood.

Cho waved. "Happy you're doing swell, cutie."

"He's been amazing. Never would have found you without him. Seriously." Alina's curiosity got the better of her. "Gotta say, this wasn't the way I expected to catch you. What are you doing *here*? And why are you dressed like that? When I saw where you were, I assumed you had to have been kidnapped."

"I *have* been kidnapped. I don't wanna be here at all!" Cho threw her pillow across the room, Alina ducking out of the way.

"What's going on, Cho? Is it Walazzin?" When she saw the cut over Cho's right eye, she swallowed. It was like an iron ball had caught in her throat. "Has he hurt you?"

"No, not yet. But he's going to."

"You're bleeding, though."

"That was an accident, when the guards got me off the street. They didn't mean to. I ran away. It was my fault."

Alina didn't know what to say to that.

"He says I'm supposed to live here until I turn thirteen. Until then, I have to stay. I shouldn't have left. It was stupid."

Crouching in front of the bed, Alina looked up at Cho and said, "You can tell me what's going on. You don't have to, but you can if you want. Do you wanna talk about this now?"

Cho shook her head.

"Do you wanna put on some real clothes again?"

She nodded. "My stuff isn't here, though. It's with the stone you gave me."

"Okay. Let me show you a trick, then." Alina pulled out her pocket knife. "I'm just going to make your pink-cloud outfit a bit more manageable. Hold very still."

With a few quick but careful strokes, Alina had sheared off the puffy shoulders and the outermost layers of the skirts, which seemed to amount to about seventy percent of the dress's fabric. What Cho was left with was a much less bulky, if not ideal, hacked-up frock.

Spinning her arms to test her range of motion, glancing over her shoulder, the backs of her legs, and her heels, Cho grunted her approval.

Focused on the cut above Cho's brow, Alina clenched her fist. "I'm going to get you out of here." She folded and stowed her knife in her pocket. "Sound good?"

Cho didn't answer at first. She stared at the floor for a minute, then her eyes met Alina's. "Thanks," was what she said, but she wasn't just talking about the improvised tailoring of her dress.

Alina choked, moisture welling in her eyes, but she passed it off for a cough. Forcing her voice to assume a positive, confident timbre, she said, "Let's go get our stuff."

The three of them, Mezami back in the folds of Alina's hood, left the bedroom. Alina made straight for the stairs down the hall, but Cho grabbed her by the wrist. "Wait. They're coming up. Three of them."

Alina stopped. "I don't hear anything."

Dragging Alina away from the stairs and into a nearby linen closet, Cho pulled the door closed. "I can *see* them," the girl whispered. "Through the walls."

"What do you mean you can—"

"Shh."

Sure enough, a trio of people—nervous voices and erratic footsteps—charged up the stairs and into the bedroom where Cho had been only moments before.

"Where is she?" That was the butler from before speaking.

"Why did you let that misfit in, Brannis? She was obviously playing you. She was far too tall to be innocent. You know what they say about tall women."

"Enough. She was not *playing* me, Niver. I left her in the foyer because the master prefers to handle these sorts of situations personally, especially when they hit so close to home. Not that I need explain myself to the likes of you."

"Touchy, eh, old man?"

The third voice, a raspy, soft one, said, "Be still, the both of you. Split up. Shout your lungs out if you catch either one of them. Whatever this may be, a snare set by our enemies or one of the girl's prior servants experiencing a sudden undue sense of loyalty, we *must* find them. Brannis, rouse the others. Niver, get some guards in here with us. If you fail me now, may Plutonia pauperize the both of you."

"Yes, ma'am," said the butler and the other man.

Two sets of footsteps retreated down the stairs. The third came closer and closer to where Alina, Cho, and Mezami were hiding. Through the downward angled slats of the linen closet door, Alina could see the back of a middle-aged woman's head, her graying hair done up in a scalp-tearing bun. For a breathless moment or two, she hovered in front of the closet. Then she trundled off.

Alina exhaled. To Cho: "It's implants, isn't it?"

The girl looked up at her, nodded. "My family wanted me to survive, so they hired doctors to mess around in my head. They made me a freak."

"You're not a freak," said Alina. "There is nothing wrong with you." She gripped Cho's shoulders tightly. Squeezed. "You hear me?"

So many questions swirled around Alina's head that, for a second, her thoughts grinded to halt. She respected Cho's right to privacy; Alina had plenty of secrets of her own. But it was exactly this kind of detail that would have been good to know *before* she attempted her daring rescue operation. Still, the answers would have to wait.

She released the girl's shoulders. "Right now, your super-vision is our best chance to get out of here in one piece. Can you take point and keep us out of their sights?"

"Yeah."

"Good. As soon as we get your clothes and my stone, we're outta here."

"How?"

"Man, I dunno. I'll, like, shift us through a wall or something. We'll have to improvise."

"Why can't you just do that now?"

"I *am* improvising. That's what this whole debacle has been, so far."

"No, ya idiot, I meant why don't you magic us out of here right now?"

"'Kay, one—I need what's in that stone. Two, my Niima's not doing too hot right now, so I can only do it a couple times tops before I pass out. Three, we don't have time for me to think of a three." She placed a hand on Cho's shoulder. "Don't worry. We got this. You ready?"

"No." But Cho pushed the door open. "I saw that gross old sack Walazzin go into the library. Looked like he had my stuff with him. He spends a lot of time there, usually."

How did Cho know all this?

Alina asked, "How long have you been here? Before today, I mean."

Cho didn't answer. Instead, stopping and recalibrating her chosen route as needed, she led Alina back along the paths Alina had already taken. It was disconcerting to watch Cho stare not *at* the walls but *into* or *through* them, her eyes following moving bodies she alone could see. Sometimes, judging by the lack of noise, they must have been quite far off.

Infrared vision and stealth upgrades… Alina wondered what other goodies had been loaded into Cho's bionic body.

Was that the right term, "bionic?" Whatever you were supposed to call her, Cho certainly was impressive. And efficient. She wasn't just noticing where the search parties *were* at any given time. Even as the number of people rooting around for them increased one hundred percent, Cho deftly led Alina this way and that, *anticipating* the movements of the prowling servants and guards. Alina could see it in the girl's eyes: she was analyzing in real-time the paths that the butler and others were taking—*would* take—*could* take. Cho was predicting their behavior based on factors only she could sense.

In no time flat, she'd led Alina through a dozen hallways to stand in front of a pair of doors whose brass handles resembled snarling lions with forked tongues.

Cho skidded to a halt and shivered. This must have been the place.

Fear twisted her face. She blinked up at Alina, silently asking what their next move would be.

"How many?" Alina mouthed.

Gazing through the door, Cho gulped and held up seven fingers.

Seven? Alina face-palmed. She was going to get herself shot.

She didn't want to die. She feared it, dying.

Her mind fed her images of Tahtoh's School, back when it had been full of students and life; Tahtoh teaching class; Tahtoh sharing tea with Alina in front of a rainy window. It'd all be gone if she didn't get the money from this job. Baraam would take away her home and—what?—probably do nothing at all with it. Because that's who he was—he either built lifeless, unchanging monuments to the past or he paved over the old to throw up some awful shiny gym with his face and logo slapped on it. Either way, guaranteed, all the joy would be sucked from everything he touched.

To Baraam, memory and tradition were everything, and progress meant revering the past. His way.

Tahtoh had taught Alina to value the here and now, and to look to the future, always.

For the millionth time since she'd arrived in The Capital, her fight-or-flight response kicked into overdrive, demanding she run for her life. But the second half of her continuously reminded the first that, without the money, the K'vich name would be just another footnote in some back-of-the-stacks history book that no one would ever read. Alina and her grandfather would be nothing but memories, shadows cast across Baraam's cold mind. Unless she did something about it. Right now.

She got mad.

Just who did these Walazzins think they were? Taking Cho? Just grabbing a little girl off the streets?

Digging her heels into the floor, Alina slammed her palms against the door the library. The carpet and floorboards beneath her feet tore and cracked, and the ornately carved wood was scorched as she flung the portal open.

To the groan of metal hinges, she stepped into the room.

"Good evening, liar-girl," said the man sitting in the armchair directly across from her.

There was a table between them. On it lay various articles of clothing—Cho's jacket, her shirt, her new shoes, and some other more sensitive articles. Meticulously folded.

The man who'd spoken wore a bright red cap on his head, his graying hair curling into wild wings above his ears. His earlobes were studded with dangling diamonds, his puckered lips cracked and dry as the caky white skin on his beardless neck. As he spoke, he took out a tiny porcelain comb and tugged it through his bushy mustache.

This was exactly the kind of pervert Alina could picture using The Sanctum's faithful like attack dogs…

"I am Wodjaego Ivnovu Walazzin," he said, steepling his fingers.

… and he was exactly what she'd always imagined the heads of the Twelve Families must be like. A wad of pale skin stretched, balloon-like, around an over-inflated ego.

Alina fumed. Through gritted teeth, she said, "And *I* am the one who'll be leaving with Cho and her things. So." Her eyes watered, a red-hot stone sinking in her gut. She shoved her hands in her pockets for fear of lunging at the smirking oligarch and strangling him where he sat.

To Walazzin's right there roared, bright gold, an open fire, above which hung a portrait of him on a rearing horse. The airbrushed facial features and epic pose had clearly been one hundred percent faked. (Whatever the artist responsible had been paid to transform this disgusting old creep into a passably gallant figure, it hadn't been enough.) In front of the fireplace were three red-armored guards, each cradling a submachine gun. Opposite them were another three guards, these waiting in front of the huge bay window, framed by the pink light of sunset.

"I will ask you this but once, intruder: why did you *lie* your way into my home?"

Frowning, scratching her neck, Alina said, "Didn't I just say—Was I unclear? I said we're leaving."

Walazzin's smug smile was so wide it must have closed his earholes because he completely skipped past everything she'd said. "Your misstep wouldn't have anything to do with this—" He held up in his sweaty, hairy-knuckled fingers the Lorestone—"now would it? I can't fathom how a low-life like you ever came into possession of something so exceptionally rare. And, look," he added, rubbing his oily palms along the crack in the stone, "you've damaged it." He paused to listen to a full six seconds of his own hoarse, wheezing laughter. "Would you care to enlighten me as to how you came by a Lorestone hewed of gen-u-ine Chrononite? By the look of it, it appears to be Gild paraphernalia. How large a reward do you suppose the Bursar and Gildmaster would be willing to put up for the safe return of their priceless property… and the capture of the thiefling responsible?"

Alina fired back with, "Uh-huh, well, how do *you* think it would look if your habits were exposed? Abducting little girls? I don't care how deep your pockets are, or how corrupt the system is. That comes out, and you're done." But she wondered how much truth there was in her words even as she said them. This—she hesitated to use the term—man was one of the Twelve. He *was* the system. Would the other Plutocrats really hold him accountable?

His eyes narrowed as he keyed into her doubt. "Were I you, I would not be so self-assured. If I worried over the potential of this story coming out," he said, lazily raising his left hand, the soldiers on that side cocking their guns and aiming down their sights at Alina, "I would already have had my Chimaera Guard erase you." He lowered his hand, resting it on Cho's wrinkled and worn jacket on the table in front of him. The red-armored gunmen relaxed. "But there is no need for such brutishness. You seem to be under the misconception that I 'abducted' young Choraelia, here? Nothing could be farther from the truth." He leaned back. "I am her legal guardian."

Alina was about to ask Cho if that were true, but the girl's expression answered for her.

Unsatisfied with the level of smarminess he'd already achieved, Walazzin continued, "Choraelia was in dire straits. *Alone* in the world but for one cousin. Tragedy compounded by tragedy: this cousin wished her dead. Were it not for my timely intervention, he might have had his wish fulfilled. I, however, stepped in and saved Choraelia's life. Is it so wrong that I should expect some reasonable recompense for my efforts?"

"Why are you telling me all this?" said Alina.

Walazzin grinned, displaying inhumanely white teeth. "Because I want you to know the whole truth before I have you hauled to The Gild for judgment. And, after you've served your decades-long sentence, and paid back your debt to our fair society, I want you to run around the little hovels your kind frequents and tell the other members of the Terrestrial underclass—as many as you can convince to listen—that what you regret most of all in life is the day you challenged House Walazzin—the day you challenged *me*. You will tell all your ilk of your folly in plucking fruit from the gardens of the gods. But only *after* you wallow in a hole half your life, weeping to yourself that you never should have tried to steal the great Wodjaego's bride from him."

Alina's fists clamped onto her phone and some lose change in her pockets. Enraged, she couldn't keep herself from spasming, the vibrations rising from her toes to her neck. "Bride?"

"Indeed! Choraelia and I are to be married in a short span of years. On the eve of her thirteenth birthday. And then all that she is entitled to—" He winked at Cho—"will be mine."

Fighting to contain herself, Alina dug her teeth into the inside of her cheek.

Walazzin laughed. To his Chimaera Guard, he said, "Take the intruder away. Do not dare fire unless you must. I would hate to see any of these priceless artifacts or my wonderful hunting trophies damaged in the fray."

One of the red guards pulled a chain from his belt. A pair of manacles. Another approached, holding ankle shackles.

"Struggling will only make it worse," Walazzin advised, yawning onto the back of his hand.

Alina glared at the cradle-robber. "Mezami," she whispered into her hood, tucking her chin, "get the stone."

A hissed reply: "Threat: humans?"

"Yes."

The two approaching guards hesitated. "Who are you talking to?" said one of them.

"Personally, I hate violence," said Alina, rolling her neck. "Unfortunately for you, I can't always control how others handle their business."

The hood of her jacket was torn from her shoulders as a bright blue blur rocketed into the air above them all. Even as shreds of fabric drifted down, like a mortar shell, Mezami dived for the nearest guard, denting the man's helmet with a *clang*. The man collapsed, and Alina snatched the manacles from his slackening grip. She clapped them around the wrists of the second guard, who, in confusion, dropped the ankle shackles.

The other four Chimaera Guard exchanged glances before looking toward their master. Walazzin roared, "What are you all gaping at? Kill that white-haired cur!"

"Mezami," Alina yelled.

A lot happened all at once: she pointed her right hand at the fire, snapping her fingers, and the flames exploded outward, throwing the guards forward; with her left hand, she made a fist, and the glass of the bay window shattered, the shards falling on top of the remaining two guards. In this sequence of split-second actions, Alina made sure to note that none of them were hurt—too badly. And then Mezami had grabbed hold of the Lorestone, which was twice his size, and certainly more than twice his weight. Still, biceps and triceps and neck and shoulder muscles bulging, he pried it away from Walazzin's slippery hands—thrusting his little blue heel into the man's eye—and hauled it over to Alina.

Clutching his head in his hands, Walazzin shrieked. Alina hugged Cho close, reaching with her other hand for the Lorestone.

Leaping forward, Walazzin swatted at the Pyct.

The guard with the bound wrists fell and banged his head against the desk. The four left standing lifted their submachine guns, took aim, and—

As soon as Alina felt her fingertips brush the cool surface of the Lorestone, she wrapped herself, Cho, the stone, and Mezami in a swath of her Niima. With all her heart, all her strength, she willed herself and them to become lighter than air.

Her rage subsided, leaving in its wake only fear. They were all about to die unless she could form the spell in time.

Time, it stretched before her, every second crawling by, lengthening like an uncurling worm. Alina absorbed it all in painful detail: the twinkles of firelight caught in the breastplates and gauntlets of the Chimaera Guard, the panic in Cho's eyes, the spittle glistening on Mezami's fangs, every growl and sputter of all their raised voices.

In that moment, the Pyct cried out as Walazzin's fingernails dug into his head and back, Cho screamed, and the guards opened fire.

But then Alina, Cho, and Mezami were carried away on the wind, whisked out through the shattered window and into the night.

The Chimaera Guard rushed over to the ledge and peppered the sky with lethal rounds, their guns' muzzle flashing like receding sparklers or fireflies as their targets glided ever higher into the darkening twilight.

Lighter than air, thin as mist, barely held together by the force of Alina's will, they were flying, the three of them—over the red-brick watchtowers and beyond the wall, past the moat, and now among the zooming hovercars in their air-buoy-lit lanes.

After ninety seconds or so, Alina's will finally faltered. No matter how she strained, she couldn't hold the spell for much longer.

Controlling their course as tightly as she could, she managed to tow all their loose assortments of molecules between apartment building balconies, and dodging the satellite dishes and potted trees. When they were six feet above the ground, the spell dropped—and so did they.

Alina belly flopped into a thorny bush, splintering its lattice of twigs. Cho landed on her spine.

Mezami fluttered gracefully onto a ledge, and there he perched.

Just before she passed out, Alina moaned and said, "I'm sorry, Cho. We didn't get your shoes."

25

LEANING ON ONE KNEE in a dingy bathroom, his back braced against the door, Tolomond clasped his hands and prayed. The fluorescent light above him flickered in counterrhythm to his heaving breaths. Icy tongues of sweat licked his abdomen, soaking the waist of his tunic.

He prayed for continued faith, for guidance. Most of all, he prayed for forgiveness for his dark-winged dreams of Brother Tarus. Tolomond dared wish for little, but one outcome he longed for more than most was to witness Tarus's fall. Tarus must be punished for his arrogance, his infectious hubris.

However.

To hate is a sin. It is Written. One must love one's neighbor, especially one's brother in service to The Author. Tolomond knew this, yet he could not find within himself the strength to let go.

Grant me the will to let go, please, Lord.

Even as he asked, his awareness swelled, and he grew to understand that this would be his life's burden, the shedding of his hate. As when Saint Llarmas, hearing the Voice within himself, tore the first Chapter from the Book. So far, such courage lay far beyond Tolomond's reach—forever unattainable—for he was weak, born to sin, a pale reflection of divine glory. How could someone like him ever dream of dwelling in the grace of The Author's love?

No, he must not let it control him, this rage; he could not let it take hold. Not now.

Tolomond pleaded with The Author for the necessary fortitude to see the upcoming trial through, for tonight would prove critical to The Sanctum's future: the invisible Hand of the Lord had caused the third—and most elusive—of Tolomond's targets to reveal herself at long last.

Brother Tarus had learned the whereabouts of that Many-Named Witch who so rarely appeared in any one place long enough to receive judgment. Her mobility—her ability to travel in secrecy and shadow—had made cornering her impossible. Until tonight.

No shadow could long escape enlightenment.

Even now, the witch sat at the bar, just beyond the door to the bathroom in which Tolomond readied himself for holy battle. She imbibed rice wine, her chosen poison of mind and body.

Her final drink.

Again, Tarus had proven himself reliable. This irked Tolomond to no end, but he must not dwell on it. White-knuckled, he felt an intense pressure behind his eyes, and he clenched his jaw. "Lord, forgive me," he told the grimy bathroom mirror, "but I loathe him."

Again, he wrestled with himself, forced himself to focus on the task at hand: *slay the witch*, that most persistent thorn in the Hierophant's side. Thereafter, he could focus all his attentions on Ivoir—and the girl with the white and blue hair.

What had Ugarda Pankrish named her? Ah, yes, *Alina K'vich.*

Tolomond heard now, clear as choir-song, the will of The Author, who had so far prevented his most faithful servant from slaying Ivoir.

There was always a reason.

He pressed the pads of his fingers against the mirror, the cracks in the glass spreading outward, as he said, "I now know, Lord, that You have held my blade at bay so that Ivoir might be the final of the three to die. Must the girl, too, be destroyed, Father? Can she not be saved?" He waited for the answer, and it came: a knock on the door, a persistent banging. It was time to act. "Yes, Lord. I am Yours to Write."

He got to his feet, turned on the hot water tap, splashed his face a few times. Wiping his cheeks on the sleeves of his gray tunic, he leaned against the door. From a loop in his belt, he pulled a long, thin, barbed blade.

Rhetoric wasn't quick or subtle enough to be useful in the crowded interior of the bar. The knife, by contrast, was ideally suited for such close quarters, and it had been designed to break off inside the target's body, ensuring that—no matter the outcome of this battle—the witch *would* perish.

Tolomond took a few more deep breaths, and then opened the door. With a blue-ink-tattooed arm, a surly young man shoved him aside, slamming the bathroom door behind him. Tolomond gave this wastrel not a moment's thought, instead gazing toward the bar.

The establishment was packed with well-dressed hedonists. Loose women dangled on the arms of their lascivious men, laughing shrilly into their glittering rainbow drinks, into the dazed and drug-addled faces of their shallow friends. High-cut dresses twirled as dancers spun circles on the floor in front of Tolomond; the musk of alcohol-laced sweat and cologne hung heavily in the air. Saliva flew freely; beer sloshed over rims, pattering in puddles on the sticky black floor. All the while, the one-note, machine-vomited music thumped, vibrating the walls, the soles of Tolomond's feet, his skull.

The one he sought was easily spotted in this crowd. Midnight robes somewhat shabby and tattered, a hood over her head, and no company to fawn over—her back to him, the Many-Named Witch sat at the bar, idly sipping the icy dregs of her fiery red beverage. At least, each time the glass disappeared within the shadowed folds of her hood, once reset upon the counter, there was within it a little less of the drink.

Sending a tingle up his spine, a voice—perhaps his—told Tolomond, *Have a care. She is the cleverest of all you've faced thus far. Strike first; strike true.*

Whether it was the Voice of The Author or his own, he obeyed the directive, picking up the pace, skirting a game of light-darts, the holographic dartboard momentarily distorting his vision.

He came to within three feet of his mark, and only when he raised his knife on high did anyone nearby take notice. By the time he heard the screams, he was driving his blade into the witch's neck, piercing fabric and flesh. *Yes.*

Before he could perform the ever-satisfying twist, however, all resistance disappeared. The midnight blue cloak fell limp, hanging from the point of his knife, the edges of the fabric brushing against the barstool and soaking up a puddle of beer froth.

Tolomond heard a thud. He tossed the cloak aside and looked to the floor.

There should have been a corpse, vacant-eyed—there should have been blood, at least! Instead, staring back at him, dead-eyed, was a black animal mask. It had a long snout, the tips of fangs pushing out from under its taut upper lip. Long ears curled back over its sleek head.

A jackal mask? How like the enemy to hide behind two faces.

With a growing sense of unease, he scanned the rapidly emptying space once more. The last of the patrons were fleeing the bar. The hovering holo-dartboard flickered and played a grating electronic tune, now easily heard in the sudden disquieting stillness. Only the bartender—a hapless young man in a tight sleeveless sweater vest, loose tie swinging from his neck—cowered in the corner, behind an empty liquor box. Tolomond might have laughed at him, but confusion gripped his vocal cords.

Where was she?

Thinking the witch had made herself invisible, he slashed all around him, lunging, striking nothing but air.

"Where are you, coward?" he shouted.

And that last word—*coward*—echoed throughout the bar, growing in volume and intensity. Like the rhythmic music that had been playing only moments before, it vibrated the walls, the floors, and rattled Tolomond's ribcage. He heard it again and again—*coward, coward, coward*—until it seemed his heart would burst.

The knife fell from his hands, which he pressed over his ears as he screamed.

All at once, the droning noise ceased.

Tolomond opened his eyes—just in time to take a punch from Tarus. Only, Tarus was ten years old again and, somehow, much taller than Tolomond.

Tasting his own blood on his lips, Tolomond raised his hand—the hand of a ten-year-old—and cried for Tarus to stop, please. But the others, crowded in a circle, were laughing, closing in, and Tarus enjoyed having an audience.

"Coward," said Tarus, closing his fist. He hit Tolomond again, two knuckles carving into the smaller boy's eye.

The blow was so forceful that it cracked the concrete beneath their feet, and Tolomond fell through. Into darkness.

Falling, he pitched and tumbled and whirled, but there were no handholds, no lights, nothing to distinguish one moment from another as he fell ever deeper into the abyss.

He landed in water—the wind crushed from his lungs. The fall should have killed him, but he lived. Though, quickly, he began to regret this.

Rough hands tore him from the pool, twisting his boyish arms. A boot planted itself between his shoulder blades, and he tumbled down a flight of stairs.

Fading in and out of consciousness, his mind finally cleared in time to see a man dressed all in white, gazing down at him. The man pulled a paper face-mask over his mouth, tapped the side of his head, and his gray mechanical eyes glowed and whirred like electric drills, dilating, focusing and refocusing. "Hold still, Tolly," said the doctor. "This is really going to hurt."

"No," Tolomond wailed, dragging the syllable out for as long as he could.

Searing pain in his left arm. Everything went black. That was good; he wished for death. Anything to stop the *hurting*.

It felt like a mule kicked his chest. And again.

He awoke, gasping.

The electric wave running through his limbs caused him to spasm and jerk. He wretched. Acid on his tongue.

The doctor was laughing hysterically. He leaned down, pulling aside the face mask, grinning his broken-toothed smile at Tolomond. "Lost you there for a hot sec, Tolly. Don't go dying on me again, now." He turned around. The sound of metal tools rolling and clanking. He came back clutching a wrench and a box cutter. "You were out for half a minute. Tell me, was that enough time to see The Author's face?"

Hot tears streamed down Tolomond's cheeks, but he was too weak to cry out for help.

No one would be coming for him.

"Never mind. Don't you dare tell me," said the doctor, waggling his eyebrows. "Faith isn't faith if you *know* for certain… Besides, I like surprises." He stabbed the box cutter into Tolomond's arm.

Tolomond's brain backflipped, his every muscle burning, as suddenly he was no longer on the operating table. He was lying on the grungy street, looking up at Ugarda Pankrish. The Aelfraver was offering Tolomond his hand, helping him get up—offering mercy—and Tolomond, unable to control himself, strangled the other man with the chain. The chain twisted around and fused to Tolomond's arm bones.

He was made to relive every second, every brutal second, of that kill. Midway, however, his perspective shifted. He became the victim, bucking and tearing at the chain constricting his throat, gasping for air, slamming his attacker against the walls, the dumpster, the ground. The man on Tolomond's back was now the doctor, who yanked at the chain around Tolomond's neck with all his might, his white coat flapping behind him like the wings of an enraged goose.

Tolomond's vision blurred, his world brightening until he was blinded by the light. He fell to his knees, crawled forward. The doctor was dancing around him now, pointing, laughing. Tarus was there, too, as were the other children. Pointing, laughing.

Tolomond crawled until his arms gave out. He slumped. And he died.

And he waited a long, long, long time. But there was nothing there, on the other side, nothing waiting for him.

Only empty white light.

For forever, he waited for something to change, and, just when he finally began to contemplate—for the briefest of instants—uttering the feeblest curse against his Creator, his God, The Author—

That's when everything went dark, and there appeared before him a pair of glowing yellow eyes in the blackness. The star-like eyes were deep-set in a jackal mask, the midnight blue cloak merging with the infinite nothingness.

Weightless, Tolomond drifted closer and closer to those eyes which loomed over him like twin suns—fiery, all-consuming.

Then sounded a voice like thunder, like hell, like the last crack of the earth's crust before it belches forth gouts of magma and obliterates entire ecosystems.

It said, "I see. You have known hardship. But, rather than rise and grow, you chose to emulate the evils of your world. Mired in the falsehoods of your backward cult, you stagnate. You forsook your chance to be worth something, becoming a copy of the very men you hate most. And they taught you to call the pain they gave you 'love.' Here you are, then, in your entirety. So very small and pathetic.

"Your god reflects you: greedy, frightened, and with so much to lose. You strain, both of you. And, one day yet, you will break. One day, I will come for you. I will shatter your body; I will tear down your temple as easily as I could snap your brittle bones. Until then, remember me. Remember, you live because I allow it. Watch for me in the night, for I'll be watching you. Sweet dreams, Tolomond Stayd."

The jackal face grinned.

Tolomond floated towards it, unable to do anything but watch as the mouth opened, its glistening fangs like twin peaks before the void.

He was swallowed whole, his soul torn to shreds, and as he twisted in spiritual agony, he was encircled by coyotes. Their gold eyes were wreathed in shadow; they yipped and cackled at him, drawing closer and closer. Wolves bayed at the moon above, which was purple and far too large.

He lay on the banks of a lake whose waters bubbled and boiled, fish and frogs floating to the surface, white and bloated. The moon spun around, revealing its dark side—a face that laughed down at him as the very stars fell from the sky in great gouts of explosive green flame.

Tolomond watched the apocalypse unfold before his eyes—the end of everything he'd ever wanted to love and be. He was burned to a cinder, and knew only oblivion forevermore.

Tolomond threw himself off his straw mat, flailing with his fists, kicking at shadows, swiping candles off their ledge, scattering hot wax everywhere. His foot struck one of the four pillars in his small room. Only in response to this pain—palpable, real, familiar—was he able to shake himself fully awake.

Covered in cold sweat, he panted, sinking to the floor. Resting on his arms, he drooled on the stone between his hands.

Some number of minutes passed. He lost count.

He looked up to the familiar spartan surroundings of his room within The Mountain of the Mendicant.

The witch was nowhere to be seen.

Had she cast a spell over him before he'd had the chance to finish her? How had she managed to catch him unawares? Had someone tipped her off?

Or, had it all been a nightmare? Had he never really encountered her?

Shuddering in the wake of the onslaught of half-remembered childhood terrors, none of which he could be certain was real, he leaned against the pillar, hugged his knees, and rocked himself until his sweat dried.

Hours later, Brother Tarus opened his door.

Before Tarus could open his mouth to announce himself, Tolomond said, "I need to see the Hierophant. Now."

Tarus folded his arms and sniffed. "He's quite busy today. Perhaps next week."

With his fist, Tolomond slammed the stone floor. "Next week, tomorrow, even an hour from now will be too late. I need to confess. Immediately." Veins popped in his neck and arms as he strained against the panic. "Please, Brother." He curled up on the floor and shouted, "Please."

Tarus stayed where he was. "What's gotten into you?"

Dribbling saliva, Tolomond shakily said, "I confronted the witch. Where you said she'd be. I did everything you told me to. I was silent in my approach, had her pinned. But she bested me." He rolled onto his knees, punching the floor. "I don't know how, but she did. She had me."

"Pull yourself together. What are you even saying? *Who* had you?"

"The witch you sent me after. Last night. At the bar. The Many-Named. Morphea, some call her."

"Morphea? Nonsense. Tolomond, I didn't speak to you last night, and certainly not about her. My agents have no clue where she is. I told you I'd inform you as soon as I'd found her." He sniffed, raising his chin. "Which I haven't as of yet."

Tolomond glared up at him, wiping away the tears. "You're lying. You told me where she'd be. You gave me the knife."

"Knife?" Tarus narrowed his eyes. "I did no such thing. That's not my function, even you know that. I'm an information broker. You're the weapon." He scoffed. "Whatever it is you're experiencing, don't dirty my name with your careless words. And you *will not* mention any of this to the Hierophant. Of late, he has more than enough troubles to concern him." He turned his back on Tolomond, making to leave the room. "I'll return later, when—I hope—you'll be of sounder mind." He slammed the door.

Alone in the gloomy room, Tolomond sobbed. The candle burnt out.

As he neared the edge of total despair, he heard a voice saying, *Tarus is lying.*

He gave you the knife.

He's lying.

Snot running from his nostrils to the corners of his mouth, Tolomond searched for the source of the voice.

Tarus is lying, it said, *and* you *must continue to fight for the truth.*

No one else will.

"Who are you?" said Tolomond.

No answer.

26

ALINA WOKE UP ON the bathroom floor. She clutched her head in her hands, gripping her skull as if worried it might sprout legs and leap out the window.

There was a toilet right there. Convenient.

She proceeded to be noisily sick.

When she finally felt she was done, she shakily got to her feet.

Cho and Mezami had somehow gotten her back to the *Peacock*, Alina realized; she was safe and whole in Room 4. She left the bathroom.

The Watchbox was on, set to one of the thirty-five shopping channels. An infomercial kept outdoing itself with rapidly changing deals for a compressible hovercar, a vehicle that, once parked, could fold itself in half, allowing for hassle-free storage. ("Yours today for just forty easy payments of one thousand gelders! Act now and we'll throw in the bulletproof gel windows and air freshener for free!")

Ignoring the droning advertisement, Cho and Mezami were on the bed, playing cards.

"Eights: you?" said the Pyct, holding up a card almost as big as he was.

"Nope, don't got any eights. Go swish."

"It's 'go fish,'" Alina rasped, her throat raw.

"Not the way I play it." Cho snapped her fingers. "Swish-swish, behbeh."

The two of them put down their hands, shifting to face Alina.

She said, "What happened? How'd we get back here?"

Cho pointed to Mezami. "He carried you all the way back. I just steered your legs a little."

Grimacing, Alina shuffled over to the sink, stuck her head under the faucet, and gulped down some lukewarm tap water. Gasping, she wiped a hand across her mouth.

She felt terrible, but not deathly ill. It seemed she'd once again dodged a bullet, stopping just short of burning away all of her Niima. If she'd pushed herself even a little more, she might have gotten the Nids—Niima Deficit Sickness, or NDS. And she'd seen what that could do to a Maggo. Understatement: it wasn't pretty.

She sat down on the bed, slapping the off-button on the Watchbox remote.

"What happened back there was… Well, it was *insane.* I don't know about either one of you, but I had no idea what I was doing even as it was happening. I was scared out of my mind, and—" She sighed. "Look, there's clearly some stuff we need to talk about. We will probably *all* be better off if we know even a little more about each other, so I'll start. My name—my *real* name—is Alina K'vich. I'm the granddaughter of Dimas K'vich, a famous Aelfraver."

Mezami hissed. "*Aelfraver*?" He bristled, wings fluttering, and he crossed his arms.

"But we're not like *that*," Alina added. "At least, I'm not. I'm a pacifist."

The Pyct went off to huff in a corner.

"What's that?" said Cho.

"Pacifist? Means I don't hurt anyone."

"That's stupid." Cho hugged her knees. "Sometimes you gotta."

"Maybe that's true. But, in the moment, when everyone's angry and pointing fingers, how can you be sure to tell the difference between a good fight and a bad one? Mistakes get messy real quick. I'd rather avoid the fight to begin with."

"*Chuh.* You picked a dumb job for that."

"I get why you'd think that. But Raves shouldn't *have* to be wall-to-wall killing. I really think—Um." Alina shook her head. "Never mind. Anyway, now you know some stuff about me. Your turn, Cho. What's your deal?"

"I don't wanna talk about my family," she snapped.

Alina inhaled sharply. "You don't have to tell me anything that'd make you uncomfortable. Just give me something to work with, here. I can't plan for danger I don't know about. All three of us were almost killed in that mansion."

"Yeah, getting something *you* wanted."

"That's fair." A pang of panic had Alina's eyes darting around the room. "Where is it, by the way?"

"Take your pill, grandma. Your stupid rock's in the pillow case."

Alina rushed to the bed. Feeling for the telltale hard lump of Chrononite, she sighed when she found it. "Okay, sorry. Just had a meltdown. Couldn't have all that effort be for nothing. I'm fine now. Anyway, like I was saying… I just wouldn't mind knowing how you ended up on the streets with implants like yours? You were pulling some really crazy stunts back there."

Cho's fingers brushed the base of her skull. "They were a gift. From my parents. But I don't feel very lucky at all to have them."

"Your parents?"

"Yeah."

Alina wasn't dumb; she knew pressing Cho would only drive her away. She knew that much because it's how *she* herself treated people who pried into her business.

To receive, you must first give.

"I know what it's like to lose your parents, Cho," she said. She could still hear their screams at night, feel the walls of earth pressing down on her, the air squeezed from her lungs and all she could do was stare blindly into the dusty darkness. "My parents were killed in an accident. Well, that's not quite true. It was a robbery."

Cho gaped. "What?"

"Yeah. They were thieves. Desperate." Alina was surprised at how easily the words came to her. As if she'd been rehearsing them to herself for years. "They were cleaning out a bank. Digging a tunnel under the vault. I was with them. I don't remember why because I was young, about five. Can't imagine what made them bring me along. Later, I was told they were drunks, addicts, that they always made brain-dead decisions like that. That that night was just the one that took the cake... So. When someone—The Authority probably—dropped explosive charges down the shaft, when the roof came down, I thought that was it for me. I thought I was going to be swallowed by the earth, lost and alone, forever."

"And they died."

"The cave-in." Alina cringed, the dome of her skull tingling.

"Why? Busting into a bank, that's just dumb. Why did they do it?"

"I don't remember." Alina's knee bounced up and down. "No one ever told me." She swallowed. "Even though everyone says they were trash, I miss them. I miss them all the time."

A long moment of silence. Cho was mulling something over, closed lips shifting as if she were chewing on something.

Then, softly, "My name is Choraelia Rodanthemaru Dreintruadan Shazura-Torvir."

"That's—I'm not gonna be able to—" said Alina, shaking her head. "Alright if I still call you 'Cho?'"

Cho chuckled. "Yah."

The truth had not so much rung a little bell as sounded a blaring alarm in Alina's mind. She shifted uncomfortably. "Torvir, huh?"

"Yup."

"As in, one of the Twelve Families?"

"Yup."

The sheer force of the revelation scrambled Alina's thoughts. Try as she might, she couldn't form a coherent response. She wanted to say something, anything, reassuring, but there didn't seem to be any way to get this *gahool* back in the bag.

In light of this new information, that disgusting perv Walazzin's interest in Cho made a lot more sense. She wasn't just some random little girl but a member of the elite, the overclass. The most Elemental of Elementals. And this made her one of the most dangerous people in all of El.

So many questions. Where were Cho's parents? How had she slipped through the cracks like this? What had happened to the rest of the Torviri?

How could Alina keep her word to Cho now that she knew who and what Cho was?

Alina was so far out of her depth. She'd crossed the line so long ago now that she couldn't even make out where it was.

Mezami interrupted the ebb and flow of her roiling waves of conflicting thoughts, saying, "K'vich: Alina. Strong: heart, yours. Fight: with you, me. So. Story mine: share, I." Hovering, he crossed his legs. "Nights ago: many. Hive attacked: swordsmen. Gray: clothes, theirs. Shaved: heads, theirs. Clan mine: gone."

"That's horrible," said Alina. "Mezami. I'm so sorry."

Shaking his fists, the Pyct hopped onto the deck of cards and kicked a few away. "Vengeance: quest, mine. Rest: not, I. Until: bald man destroy, I."

"A bald man? Would you recognize him if you saw him?" said Alina.

Mezami nodded, lips pulling away from his yellowed fangs, tattooed muscles rippling.

"I hope you find him. And I'll help however I can."

A drop of blood fell from Cho's forehead onto the off-white comforter on which they all sat.

"Cho, this whole time, you were just sitting there, hurt?" Alina rolled her eyes. "Look at the three of us. It's like we're in a competition to be the biggest mess." She leaned forward. "You gotta let me stitch that cut."

"Okay."

"No, really, because—" It took a second for Alina to realize she wasn't being argued with. "Oh. Okay. Come over here, where the light's better."

And Alina pulled from her pack some needle and a spool of thread. From the bathroom, she grabbed the bottle of antiseptic Ordin had brought over earlier.

She gently tilted Cho's head, saying, "Hold still. There." And she got to work. "That's good. Just a few more. Not too bad, right?"

"No, not too bad." Cho giggled. "You look goofy, your tongue poking out your mouth like that."

"Be grateful. If I'm making a stupid face, it means I'm concentrating on you and not me."

Alina worked the needle—up, down, in, out. When she was done, she dabbed the stitches with a dry cotton ball. She threw all the waste in the trash, washed her hands.

Turning back to Cho, Alina said, "Let's get you out of what's left of that ridiculous dress." Alina opened up her back and pulled out an old *Billie and the Werewolf* T-shirt and jeans, passing these to Cho.

Cho hesitated, squinting at Alina.

"They'll be a little too big, but it's nothing *this* can't fix," said Alina, handing her a belt.

Cho admired the shirt for a moment, said, "Sweet," and took the items into the bathroom. She got changed and reemerged, rolling up the legs of the jeans to uncover her legs up to the knees. "I look like I got blasted by a shrink ray," she said, wiggling her toes.

Alina chuckled, and then cleared her throat. She had to ask: "Um. I was just curious. How high up the Torvir flagpole are you sitting, exactly?"

Cho folded her hands on her lap, gazing at her navel.

"We talking minorly important distant cousin, or…"

"Walazzin knew I'm the heir."

"To what? A manor somewhere? A sizeable fortune?" Alina's eyes widened. "Not the *whole thing*?"

Slowly, almost imperceptibly, Cho nodded.

"You're the Torvir heir," Alina whispered, hardly believing the words escaping her lips. "You're, like, the rightful governor of the province I grew up in! Holy Buthmertha."

This changed everything.

As if reading her mind, Cho reminded her, "You made me a promise."

"I know."

She did know, damn it. And this, right here, this sort of ridiculousness was generally why she avoided making promises like her life depended on it. Because now, suddenly, it did.

Just look at where she'd ended up! Go around owing people favors, and, before you know it, you're abducting little girls destined to inherit one twelfth of the entire country.

With one quick anonymous call, Alina could still turn Cho in to The Authority. There probably would have been a fat reward in it for her, too. Besides, it was what was required of her, demanded of her, as a loyal Asset of El.

Yeah, right. *As if* she'd do that. Were she to report Cho's whereabouts, the girl would be steered right back into the arms of Wodjaego Walazzin—that wretched, oozing old monster who'd somehow been appointed her legal guardian.

Alina shuddered.

Society had failed Cho. She deserved better.

No matter who she was, the girl deserved better.

"Well, I'm not sure what to do, Cho, or how exactly I can help you, but I won't let you go back there. Not ever."

After Cho had fallen asleep, Alina made an online order from Gogadrop. (To her surprise, the payment went through. Why hadn't Baraam cancelled his credit card yet?). Even at this late hour, within thirty minutes a drone buzzed over to the window, which Alina gently opened. She set the slim package down on the floor, and closed the window, latching it. Using her knife to cut through the tape, she then pulled out a small, dark gray, plastic-wrapped coat. Removing the plastic with care, she set the garment on the floor, laying it out flat, smoothing its wrinkles.

From her sewing kit, she brought out her needle and thread and a gray patch with a bright green feather at its center.

Over the next half-hour, give or take, Alina hummed to herself as she stitched the patch into the inside of Cho's new jacket.

As she worked, she swore the Walazzins would never hurt Cho again.

And she hummed. Old songs. Songs of healing and of shelter. She murmured the notes even as she twisted the needle, gently piercing, weaving the thread and the notes as one.

Faces aglow by the light of the muted Watchbox, Cho and Mezami slept. The Pyct had propped himself up against the girl's elbow, and he snored, kicking his little cloven hooves every now and again.

Alina sat cross-legged on the bed, the Lorestone resting innocently in front of her. Taunting her with its tantalizing glimmer. Catching glints of street and traffic light coming in through the window.

By turns, the two feet of space between her and that lump of Chrononite felt like an infinite expanse or no distance at all.

She couldn't understand why she was stalling. This thing, this little damaged stone, was what she'd been fighting to claim for almost two full days. Why wasn't she cracking it open like an egg to slurp all the wisdom out of it?

Her hands were shaking, she realized.

What was she afraid of? They were only memories after all. That was the sum of what the stone contained—the memories of those long dead. Long, *long* dead. She shouldn't be scared.

But she couldn't do it. Every time she reached out to touch the Lorestone, her trembling fingers stopped as if blocked by an invisible forcefield.

With a soft growl, she turned once again to her old friend *procrastination*. Always there when you needed him, eternally ready to provide any and every alternative to whatever it was you should have been doing, procrastination never judged. He didn't help either, and he certainly was a waste of time, but he'd never put you down for desiring a few moments of escape from dreading that particular task, that little nagging chore that would probably have taken all of twenty minutes to accomplish, if you could only bring yourself to make that phone call, roll that trash barrel to the curb, write that paper. Whatever was slowing you down, procrastination would be there for you, as he was for Alina now. Always changing shape to suit your needs, always inviting and overly friendly.

This time, he took the form of her phone, which she grabbed in order to check her messages, half-expecting there to be one from Ordin. There wasn't.

But there *were* texts from Calthin. About twenty of them. She skimmed the messages, checking the time stamps. On average, he'd fired one off every hour or two.

She'd had her phone on silent during her infiltration of The Gild and forgotten to switch it back. Whoops.

Her immediate reaction was guilt.

She and Calthin had been friends since they'd figured out how to walk. (They'd met when she'd tripped him in front of the swings at Gratchette Park.) This had been the longest they'd ever gone without communicating.

His clear concern touched her at first. When she read the messages in greater detail, however, her reaction shifted to "What the hell?"

Over the course of the past forty hours or so, Calthin had written:

hey, are you okay? Your last text worried me a little, not gonna lie. You doin ok up there?

Haven't heard from you in a minute. Hope everything's alright.

Kinneas says he wants to show you a picture when you get back home

Let me know if I can help at all…

If you're in trouble call me. if youre dead call me anyway

if youre pissed at me thats fine. I don'tt know why that would be but I'm fine with it

Just please let me know you're not hurt at least please

Okay Im not overreacting. For all I know youre dead in a ditch and I cant do anything about it

do I need to call somebody, Alina?! HULLOOOOOOOO

by Buthmertha, answer me dammitt!!!

…?!?

guess ill watch for your name on the evening news

Wow.

Just, wow.

She would not have described Calthin as paranoid. Certainly, he'd never acted like this. All she could think was that something about their most recent conversation had primed him to go full-cling on her.

Did he not know she could take care of herself?

Her annoyance was then overshadowed by her concern over the increasing franticness of his tone. She couldn't leave him hanging like that.

Her thumbs dancing across the touchscreen of her phone, she fired off a reply:

hey, im so srry I didn't get back to you earlier. Ive had the craziest couple days ever. Didn't mean to make you worry, pal.

She set her phone down, noting how ridiculously late it was, figuring it'd be a while before he caught her message.

Calthin answered almost instantly.

Alina I thought you were dead

Im srry. i ran into some trouble. Its fine now, but I had to figure some stuff out. Like seat-of-my-pants quick.

That's all I get? Youre not gonna tell me what happened???

Trust me when I say that A) you probably dont want to know and 2) this is more a face to face kinda convo

A few minutes passed.

Is this about that guy Orphan?

What??? NO

And it's O R D I N
btw

I D C
btw

Whats really bothering u?

Oh my gods EVERYTHING is bothering me! I dont get u. ur treating me like trash

HOW exactly? Like… I had my phone off for a while. Whats the big deal?

You know that's not it

Then what is?!

You really dont get it. You just dont. You cant see how your actions hurt the people who care about you. you act like your life doesn't matter but it does. It does to me

But you insist on throwing it away

your off, running around up there, doing Buthmertha knows what

And you don't care one iota how it makes us down here feel

My dad

Kinneas

Me

We care about you but that's really hard to do when you don't seem to care about yourself

You done finally? Or you gonna keep being a butt about this? Am I gonna have to mute you?

Know what? What. ever. I wait for 2 days to hear back from u, the whole time thinking my best friend is dying and im powerless to help. Then u finally answer back with some lame "I cant talk about it right now" nonsense

And its like are we even friends at all? Do u trust me even a little?

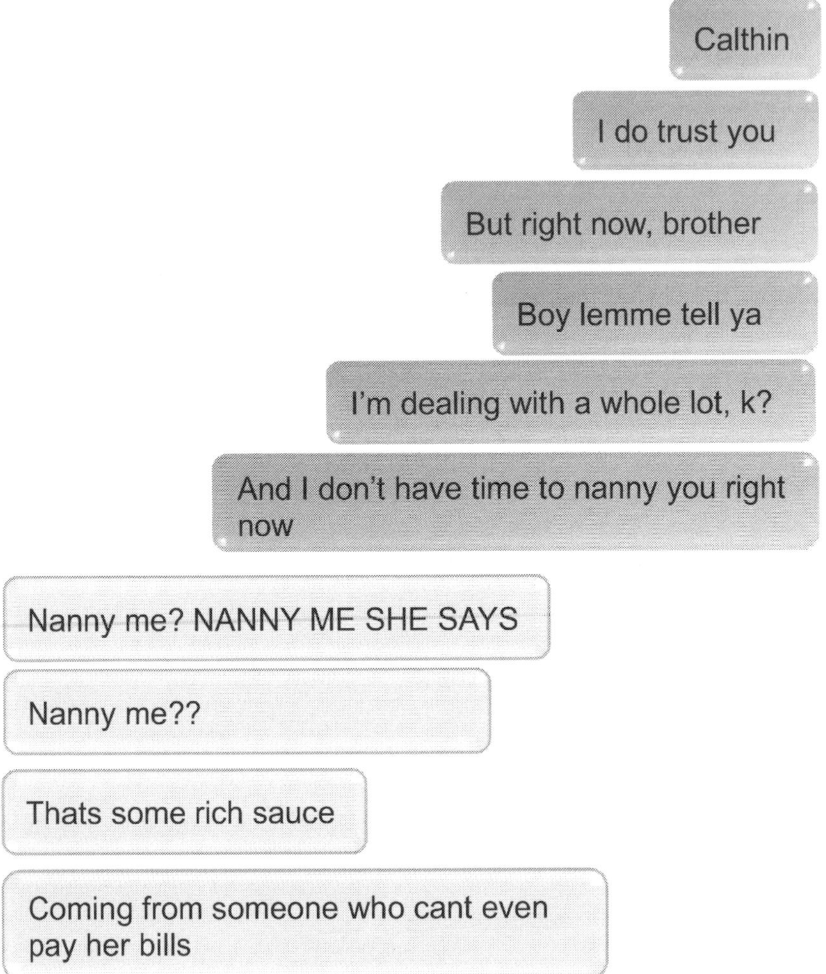

Calthin
I do trust you
But right now, brother
Boy lemme tell ya
I'm dealing with a whole lot, k?
And I don't have time to nanny you right now
Nanny me? NANNY ME SHE SAYS
Nanny me??
Thats some rich sauce
Coming from someone who cant even pay her bills

Alina would later be proud of the restraint she demonstrated in that moment. The massive amounts of willpower required to hold herself back, to prevent herself from crushing her phone like a tin can…

Taking a breath, collecting herself, she typed:

Hey cal

U can go ******* yourself and then *************, got me?

Stupid profanity filter

But I think u get the picture:

Dont contact me til uve pulled ur head out of your *** you *************

Then, in the heat of the moment, she flipped to his contact icon and blocked his number.

What had gotten into him? How could he have acted so cruelly dumb?

Did Calthin resent her for leaving him behind, for actually trying to fix her life? Had he thought she was going to carry on as his little pet project forever?

Was he *jealous* of Ordin?

Stomach acid boiling, she stretched her legs, leaning back. She was so flustered that she didn't notice her bare toe straying perilously close to the Lorestone.

Her skin contacted the smooth, slightly warm-to-the-touch Chrononite—

27

—and she was staring at the reflection of Dimas K'vich, her Tahtoh, his face lathered with fluffy white shaving cream. His back to her, he hunched over the small white porcelain sink, a straight-razor in his hands. The hot water running from the tap made the mirror all steamy.

Every twenty seconds or so, Tahtoh would wipe his palm across the glass.

He did so again, now. His reflected eyes locked onto Alina's.

"Cabbage, what are you doing? You should be outside practicing your forms."

Alina looked at her hands—the hands of a younger version of herself. She breathed in a lung-full of steam. "Is this a dream?" she asked.

Tahtoh chuckled. He lightly dragged the razor up his leathery cheek. "What a strange thing for a little girl to say. Do you *think it's a dream?"*

"Yes," she admitted. "It has to be. You're dead."

He wiped the straight-razor's blade on the towel. "But, Cabbage, can't you see me right here?" Still holding the razor, he waved his extended pinky. Tight circles. "Eh?"

"But you've been gone. No one's seen you for a year."

"A whole year? Hmm. Was no one planning to tell me?" Up-down with the blade. "How have none of my students noticed in so long? I must punish them for such poor perception."

Alina remembered this moment. The way it had really happened. Back when she was about six or seven.

The scene as it was unfolding now was wrong. This wasn't how it had gone. Close, but not quite on the mark. Still, the setting, how she felt, the crinkled skin around Tahtoh's dark-shadowed eyes—it seemed so familiar. Like déjà vu. And that's probably how she knew he was about to tell her something, something important…

Tahtoh's face became serious again. "Run along and practice your forms, Alina. I will come check you when I'm done."

… Or not?

She'd felt certain a revelation had been forthcoming, a warm word, a warning, anything a grandfather might tell his grandchild to keep her spirits up after he was gone.

He should have told her whatever—whatever it was.

Maybe this was a dream after all.

A sliver of her conscious mind pierced the veil of this vision out of time, allowing her a moment's clarity: maybe she had to phrase her questions a certain way.

She tried a different approach. "Tahtoh, I'm using a Lorestone. From The Gild Crystallarium. That's how I'm seeing this right now."

"Who taught you all those big words, Cabbage? Have you been reading my history books?"

"Tahtoh, please, just answer me if you can. Lorestones are filled with recorded memories, right? Why does The Gild have this *moment in their library?"*

Now cleanshaven, he put down the razor, but he would not face her. "That's simple, Cabbage. When I was young—younger than you are in your *present—I stole the Lorestone you speak of and modified it. It does not show memories but* truth*."*

"But this is *a memory—I mean, I* remember *this conversation. You're about to tell me—"*

"That your parents aren't coming back for you. That they are dead. You will find it hard to believe. You'll argue with me, so sure that you are right. But—" His scraggly brows drooped as he smiled sadly, the mirror slowly fogging up again. "In less than a week, you'll run away into that hedge maze. And I will find you, and we will set off together on

the decade-long road that leads to where you are standing now." He paused. "Could I know all that, were I a memory?"

"No, I suppose you couldn't." Alina looked at her small child's feet. "Where does my road end?"

"That is not for me to tell, Alina. You stand as if at the front door of a great house. Your toes touch the threshold of this place that has sheltered you, but it is a barrier to your progress, and you may not linger. You must take the next step. To the road beyond. A road that wraps itself around all horizons, seen and unseen. One that will not end until you do. Yet, always be certain that whatever happens, wherever you go, from here onward—every step shall be your choice."

"Could you just be straight with me? Please."

"But how can I be? I am not real, my little Cabbage. I am part memory, part imagining, part prophecy. I am your creation. Everything I might say or do is entirely conjured by your own mind." He grinned in that perfectly self-satisfied manner of his, the look he gave when he knew that whatever he'd just said was immensely clever. "You made me and this place. Which means…? Go on! Which means…?"

"That I already know the answer," she breathed. The bathroom was filled with so much steam now that she could hardly see him anymore. He was no more than a whispy outline. She thought about reaching for him but stopped herself. "I know what the Bane of New El is."

Her Tahtoh's voice drifted toward her through the white sheet of steam: "I have always been, and am still, so very proud of you."

She began to cry, the tears evaporating even as they flowed from her welling eyes.

He continued, "You're going to have to decide one thing more. The creature—will you spare or slay it?"

Empathetically, she said, "I'm not a killer."

"By your inaction, others might die."

"I can't take a life. I won't do it." She shook her head. "It's not who I am." Clenching her fists. "I'm not a killer."

"I hope you're right."

She heard the faucet squeak. The sound of rushing water stopped. Gradually, the steam dissipated, enough for her to see the reflection of her grandfather staring at her. Catching an errant ray of sunlight, his eyes flashed gold. He smiled.

The mirror shattered into a million pieces, and, behind it, a vacuum sucked him into the blackness.

Alina screamed, and she ran to the sink. It was so tall, her five-year-old arms could hardly reach—but, somehow, her little fingers managed to grab hold and pull her body up onto the porcelain lip.

On wobbling knees, she stared into the darkness, and she jumped in after him.

And she saw, flapping beneath her, the form of her grandfather, swaddled in a great black cloak, its fraying ends extended like wings or arms, extending upward as if to embrace her. He smiled at her. She reached for him, grabbing at the cloak, as they both tumbled and spun, the rush of air deafening them. Her fingers almost brushed his clean-shaven cheeks, his chin.

Then he struck the abyssal floor, and that smile was locked on his lips forevermore.

Staring into his white, unmoving eyes, she saw him now as she hadn't wanted to imagine him: shrunken, gnarled, like a desiccated tree fighting a losing battle against the unyielding pull of gravity, his face bearing the marks of an uncountable slew of tragic stories, the purpled flesh around his eyes like putty across which a family of crows had hopped.

They'd held a funeral for him. An open empty casket. His body had never been recovered, but a year was a long time for an old family man to wander. The fact that he hadn't returned made it all but certain that he'd died somewhere, alone, confused, unable to get home.

For months, she'd thought not *knowing was worse than the truth. Now she wasn't so sure. Even the thought of him really being dead and gone was—*

In this unreality, this dreamlike non-world, Alina stood over Tahtoh's imagined body, weeping, beating her fists against his unmoving chest. Finally, she touched a tear-smeared palm to his sallow cheek.

He began to quiver, convulse, jerk like a puppet yanked by its strings.

She leapt backward.

He froze, jaw hanging limp, tongue lolling. One of his eyes popped out of its socket. Wriggling out from his skull was a blood-drenched crow.

It cawed at Alina—

—and she opened her eyes, fell from the bed with a thud.

In the tranquil darkness of her motel room, her face a salty canvas of tears and sweat, she whispered, *"Talaganbubăk."*

28

ON NIGHTS WHEN HE had himself a tall glass of dark beer—one of his few and rare indulgences—Tahtoh would sit with Alina in front of the hearth and tell her ghost stories. That's not what he called them, but that's what they were.

More than all of Alina's late-night readings and memorizing flashcards of Aelf abilities, weaknesses, strengths, and locations, it was Tahtoh's midnight verbal wanderings that had most profoundly shaped her understanding of "the Others," the Aelf.

He'd stare into the flames, licking his lower lip, scratching the scruff on his chin. Every now and again, he'd pause, swirling the frothy liquid in its short stout glass.

One midwinter, when the white frost crawled up the windows, Tahtoh spoke in little more than a whisper, as the embers in the hearth burned low. He'd usually start as if in the middle of the tale: "As you know, there are some Others who lumber as beasts of the earth do, with no more intelligence than a squirrel."

Little Alina had chimed in, "Like the Quixiil."

"Just so. And you know, too, that there are those who have all the cunning of men. Sometimes more."

"Changelings! I learned about them today."

"Very good. Very good, Cabbage. But, have you learned yet of the third kind?"

"Another kind of Aelf? What's between 'sen-teent' and 'non-sen-teent?'"

"'Sentient,'" Tahtoh corrected softly, turning his pointer finger in slow circles. "And not between, *Alina, but* above. *Beings of poise and power."*

"'Poison power?'" said Alina. "Wow."

"No, 'poise' and *'power.' Grace, speed, agility. And a fierce and cold intelligence. Older than humankind, filled with anger and sorrow."*

"Oh! You're talking about dragons."

"A very good guess, but I am thinking of a different creature entirely. He of whom I speak is one of the Demidivine*—apart, above, and* beyond *the dragons. And he is a familiar shadow in Truct, roaming the regions surrounding our Torvir province. Some call him 'the Mireman,' and some 'Kinderlokker.' In the Sfenian tongue, he is 'Talaganbubăk'—The Old Man of Long Candles. He is a fickle one, never overly fond of any one form. Those who look upon him usually see only animal-like shadows. Their minds cannot grasp what he really is—a gaunt, tall fellow, often wearing a long cloak and a red mask with a hooked, beaklike nose."*

"Why?"

"The cloak is for hiding his wings."

"Wings?"

"Feathers of midnight, or the mud of the marshes. The hood and mask he wears, always, as none must know what he really looks like. Some believe he's shy, others that he's hideously disfigured."

"Which one is true?"

"Which do you believe?"

"I think he's protecting a secret identity. Like a superhero."

He looked sternly at her through his small, round spectacles. "Have you been on that blasted, mindless Watchbox again?" He scoffed. "Superheroes…"

"No, no. I promise, Tahtoh. I haven't."

"Well. Where was I? Oh, yes. They say that on clear cold nights—much like this one—he walks about. Seeking children."

"Children?" Alina scooted a little closer to him and to the fire. She glanced over her shoulder toward the windows and the darkness beyond.

"Children who are unhappy, who run away. Children who are cruel or thoughtless." He smiled slyly at his granddaughter. "And especially children who do not listen to their elders. They are his favorites."

"Will the—" she gulped—"Talaganbubăk come to get me?*"*

"Not if you always do as I say."

She had run over to him, then, hugged his leg.

He'd stroked her long black hair. She'd stopped shivering.

Lying down in front of the fire, she'd fallen asleep at last.

When she'd awoken, her grandfather wasn't there, and the fire was out. The night had lightened ever so slightly—or, at least, the darkness had weakened.

She saw a shadow against the windowpanes. Rooted to the spot, her palms and scalp tingling, she watched it take on many shapes—a cat with its back arched, a squid with whipping tentacles and a champing beak, a crow with a ridge of spikes running along its spine. She screamed, and the shadow recoiled and then retracted, leaving only moonlight in its wake.

Tahtoh came rushing out of his bedroom, out of breath. "Cabbage. Cabbage." He held her close. "What is the matter?"

Through the tears, she blubbered, "It's the Talaganbubăk. He's after me. I saw him in the window." She pointed with a shaky hand.

He followed her finger. "Now, now. There's nothing to be afraid of. No one's seen Old Longcandles in a very *long time."*

"I saw him, though. He moved in the shadows, and he—he changed a bunch. Just like you said."

"It was a trick of the light, Alina. Tree branches in the moonlight. You are safe. I am here."

"But how do you know *we're safe?"*

"Because I destroyed the Talaganbubăk many years ago."

"You're telling the truth?"

He nodded.

"You'll keep me safe?"

He placed a cold hand on her forehead.

29

THE MACHINE IS A crutch and one of the cardinal sins of Man," Tolomond recited as he applied his heavy foot to the accelerator pedal of the hovercar he'd just stolen.

Through the shattered driver-side window, frigid winds whipped his face. Between his legs, against his right knee, rested his greatsword. Glass crunched under the heel of his boot. He gripped the steering console as if it were the vessel that contained his very soul.

Author forgive him, but he loathed driving. He'd only ever had to do it twice before, both occasions ending in death. Once, nearly his own. But, the Divine Hand had preserved his life on that day so that he might live to erase more infidels from Creation.

There were those in The Sanctum who saw things differently, but to Tolomond technology was just another form of magic—a puss-filled boil on the heart of humanity, one in dire need of a lancing.

Flying cars. Talking, moving images. Body modifications. These were affronts to The Author, who wrote into existence all that was good. With every supposed "advancement," Man took another step away from the light.

However, there were times when one must fight fire with fire. To that end, Tolomond sped—down the wrong side of the highway through the center of New El—toward the Dyrex District. Where lived Ordin Ivoir.

The Authority's agents—worms in service of a false idol—were nowhere to be seen. They must have been distracted. Again, The Author stooped to secure his humble servant Tolomond a victory. Tolomond felt his heart might burst with rapture. But not yet. First, the work. Then penance. Then, if he deserved it, rest.

Tarus had done everything he could to sway Tolomond from the righteous path. Tarus could not be trusted; he had lied about the Hierophant—lied about everything.

Tolomond would show them all the strength of true faith.

Hover vehicles darting out of his way, horns blaring, curses flung at him like so many darts, he drove for half an hour. He searched the club parking lots, airways, and upscale restaurants for both the stretch limousine and silvery sports car that were registered in Ivoir's name. He'd learned much about the young heretic's life and habits through that briefing given to him by a servant of the Walazzin Family.

He made a mental note to later mortify his flesh in penance for the crime of colluding with evil. However, he must admit, using the tools of one Family to destroy another—there was some beauty in this tactic.

They thought they were so deviously clever, all of them. Yet, their sins would be redeemed; none could escape judgment.

"My wrath is The Author's," Tolomond repeated under his breath, as he circled the blocks surrounding Ivoir's home. "I know you'll show yourself. I am patient. With gratitude do I accept my charge; my soul is lifted above all earthly doom. I am lighthearted in the face of death."

There. His fingers wrung the steering column as if it were a wet washcloth. *There he is.*

Up ahead, idling at a stoplight, was the limo. Flanking it, two hovercycles ridden by armed bodyguards.

"The Author is my armor and my shield," Tolomond said, weaving between stationary vehicles. Horns sounded all around him, and onlookers from shopping center overlooks pointed and shouted, but these noises faded to the extremities of his perception. He had eyes only for the limo and its guardians.

The commotion caused the bodyguards to look around them. Even had any one of them noticed Tolomond, they would have been powerless to stop him. The limo was trapped between vehicles on all sides.

Tolomond crashed his vehicle into the left-hand hovercycle, sending its driver hurtling through the air, over a balcony, and screaming all the way to the ground, three hundred feet below. Jamming his thumb into the altitude-control button, he raised the craft up by twelve feet or so, jerked the steering column to the left, and then cut the engine. The second hovercyclist glanced upward just in time to be crushed by two tons of solid steel.

As he switched off his vehicle's engine, Tolomond scrabbled over to the passenger's side, kicked open the door, and leapt onto the roof of the limo. The car bobbed as he landed.

The vehicle lurched forward, turbulence causing it to buck like a wild horse agitated by a flash of lightning.

Tolomond thrust his sword through the limo's roof, clinging to the hilt as he was thrown off his feet by the sudden burst of speed. Bouncing, he half-rolled, half-kicked himself in a semi-circle, just barely dodging five or six shots fired from within the vehicle.

Checking ahead to anticipate the limo driver's path, accounting for wind resistance, he swung his weight forward and to the left. Tumbling, he kicked, heels first, straight as a fire poker, back toward the car, shattering one of its windows. Now inside the vehicle, he could feel it losing speed; the driver began to pull over.

There were two men in the back. One of them happened to be the blue-suited fool from the other night; the other, Ivoir himself.

The Plastick, caught in the middle of reloading his handgun, hesitated.

Cutting into the cramped space between them was the blade of the greatsword, still lodged in the car's roof. Tolomond grabbed the Plastick by the neck and thrust his face into Rhetoric's edge. The man in the blue suit screamed, but only briefly, and then he went limp.

The limo came to a stop. Tolomond watched the driver fumble with his seatbelt, open the door, fall out of the vehicle, and run off.

Turning back to Ivoir, Tolomond smiled, scratching his stubble with bloody fingernails. "All that money, but you'll never know real loyalty."

Something was wrong, though: Ivoir showed suspiciously little fear in the face of certain damnation.

"Beg for The Author's mercy and perhaps He will take pity on your apostate soul," said Tolomond.

Ivoir looked at his would-be killer. "My creator claims I have no soul." He cocked his head. "Regardless, I do not think I want to die. Why do you suppose that is?"

Tolomond's smile twisted into a grimace. "What are you saying?"

Ivoir reached out with eerily steady hands. "No, I do not wish to know what death is." Curiously: "Who are you? Are you going to save me?"

"Yes." Tolomond grabbed Ivoir by his scrawny chicken-neck and yanked, screaming, "Finally, enough of you."

He tore Ivoir's head clean off his shoulders.

As the body slumped on the black leather seat, he stared in disbelief at the blinking lights and sparking, severed wires protruding from Ivoir's throat.

He gazed into the head's eyes. Ivoir winked, smacking his lips, inviting Tolomond to kiss them.

"An android?" said Tolomond. "An impostor!" He screamed again, slamming the head against the floor, the roof, the jagged glass edges of the broken window.

When he regained control of himself, the head was a mangled mess of wires and cracked-porcelain skin. Clumps of its hair had fallen off, some tufts wedged deep in its skull.

Knowing the real Ivoir must be watching, laughing at him, Tolomond locked eyes with the android's. He said, "I'm coming for you. You can hire all the fighters in New El, build yourself a thousand decoys—it will never be enough."

He flung the head over his shoulder and out the window.

Clambering into the driver's seat, he heard them, in the distance. Sirens.

The Authority was coming at last.

He remembered that his sword was still jammed in the roof. He climbed up and removed it, tossing it onto the front passenger seat.

The sirens grew louder by the second.

They mustn't prevail.

"Who said that?" Tolomond spun around and around. "Who's there?"

The voice came from everywhere—*You must finish your chapter of the Great Work*—and nowhere.

"My—my Lord?"

Be not discouraged. The devil's wiles are many, but you are stronger. The voice was as a campfire, gently crackling in the long, cold night. *Finish your chapter.*

"Is it truly You?"

My son. Filled with light. *Do not lose focus.*

"What must I do, Lord?"

You know the true enemy.

"I do. I do."

And you know what you must do to lure him out.

A vision of *her* danced before his waking eyes—the girl, Ordin's new toy.

Use her, said The Author. *She is my Instrument, to be wielded by my one true son.*

"I don't deserve this honor."

You are the only one who does. Now go.

Make me proud.

30

AFTER THE LORESTONE VISION, Alina might have blamed her inability to fall asleep on a sense of excitement, but the real culprit was the flareup of agony in her arms. Her skin was being cooked from the inside out, and a thousand red-hot needles pierced her every pore. Actually, it felt more like an acid shower, scalding her from skull to toenail.

In that moment, she could think of no explanation for her misery other than *the curse.* She'd tried to ignore it; for so long, she'd tried. She'd walked it off, dismissing what was happening to her as a weird skin condition, something that would go away with enough moisturizer. But the pain was unbearable now. It stomped across her fingers, wrists, and forearms, along her elbows and up to her shoulders.

Along with the pain, doubt kicked through the attic of her mind, knocking over file cabinets and stacks of papers, less searching for answers and more raging over the lack of them.

Somewhere down the line, she had to have been cursed. With no idea where she might have been infected by such evil magic, she nevertheless had to acknowledge her months-long fears.

The flesh on her arms had been… decaying. There was no other word for what was happening.

Graying, turning scaly. Flaking and itching and bleeding… black pus.

A back-alley doctor had told her it was unlike any disease he'd ever seen. He'd spoken a prayer over her, for he could think of nothing else. Hadn't had the heart to charge her for such a bleak diagnosis.

Alina had pored over old medical and arcane encyclopedias at the Truct public library, searching for any connections, no matter how slim. There were hundreds of degenerative diseases and several enfeebling spells, but none of them fit what she'd been experiencing. Nothing but dead ends. No credible scholar, doctor, historian, or mage, historical or contemporary, had ever written about a condition like hers.

She'd gone home, emptyhanded and void of hope. The best she'd been able to do for herself was keep her bandages (relatively) fresh. Whether the ointments she'd used had even slowed the flesh-eating was hard to tell because she hardly ever could summon the nerve to check, but it certainly hadn't cured her.

The curse had been manageable for half a year. The migraines and joint aches were only occasionally troubling. But she'd been kidding herself, thinking her situation hadn't been worsening.

To her, out of sight hadn't meant out of mind, but, for all her research and reasoning, she couldn't decide what to do.

And then the bills had piled up, and everything had fallen apart.

And *now* she felt so nauseous that she couldn't stand or even keep her eyes open.

Finally, she was able to waddle, bent at the waist, to the bathroom and drink some tap water. Abs sore, arms quaking, she crashed into bed.

Then she did sleep for a little while.

Restlessly.

Alina dreamed the same dream on repeat all night: Tahtoh, shaving over that small, white porcelain sink, shearing the sharp black bristles from his leathery cheeks and bony chin.

Again and again, she watched him, the process unfolding in exactly the same way each time. They didn't speak, and he did not acknowledge her.

Her fever painted the room in strange colors, cast strange shadows on the walls, made strange faces peer at her from the steam rising from the sink.

Small hands grabbing her by the collar, shaking her.

Alina opened her eyes to see Cho above her. Her arm-pain remained, but it lingered in the background now, tolerable.

"You didn't hear that?" Cho flicked her head toward the door. "Someone's knocking."

Alina slid off the bed, pulled her pants up a bit higher on her waist, and opened the door.

The motel manager scowled at her, sniffing. "Busy night?" A muffin crumb fell from his soul patch.

Alina's jaw cracked as she yawned, her nerves flooding her cheek with heat. "You could say that."

He tried to peer into the room, but Alina, being taller and broader than he, blocked his view. "No guests allowed," he said.

Alina coughed. "Guests?"

"Don't play dumb, chicky. I heard voices. More than just you. Don't think that the price stays the same with more people in here. You have to clear that we me, and extra costs extra."

"That doesn't make sense."

"Oh, but it does. Damages and all. You have to clear all newly arrived guests with me. They've got to check in. It's the law."

"Feel free to check, then," Alina bluffed, throwing the door open. (Cho had managed to hide somewhere in the past several seconds.) "No one's here but me."

The manager poked his head in, sniffed a few more times. "Got my eye on you." Squinting out one eye at her, he stroked the coarse hairs below his lip. "*Anyway*, I'm here to inform you that the rate's gone up."

"What? Why?"

"You're kidding, right? Don't you ever watch the news?" He barged into the room, snatched the remote from the unmade bed, and switched on the Watchbox, muttering to himself, "This is why men run everything."

A reporter with long dark hair, and wearing a high-collared yellow and black latex jumpsuit, was saying, "… reports coming in from Authority Enforcers on the ground indicate that the Bane of New El has struck again. The most recent victim, according to our sources, is Antonynus Xaveyr, firstborn son of Consul Kellestro Xaveyr. We can confirm that the victim's entourage and associated security personnel were slain as well, bringing the fatalities up to twenty." Staring directly into the camera: "Assets, this represents by far the direst threat to our national security in recent memory. Detective Ding, the officer in charge of the task force dedicated to destroying the Bane, in an official statement this morning, urged everyone to stay inside their homes and offices until further notice."

The program cut to Detective Ding standing in front of some steps, leaning on a podium. "I want to assure all of you, my fellow Elementals, that The Authority has the situation well under control. Even now, we are closing in on the target. We anticipate that, within forty-eight hours, we will have brought this situation to a just resolution. We express our sympathies and continued unwavering loyalty to the Consul." For a moment, it seemed like he was done. He cleared his throat, though, and added, a bit gruffly, "And it is clear now that the Aelfravers from the Terrestrial provinces have done far more to encumber our investigation than they have contributed to it. It is for this reason that we advised the Consul to issue an emergency declaration to evict all the tourist Aelfravers, effective in T-minus twenty-four hours." He held up a little black device, pressed a button, and a holograph popped up displaying a document in minuscule print, bearing a fancy seal and swirly signature. "The Consul personally instructed me to advise all Landsider Aelfravers that, should they fail to comply with this order and depart from our city within the timeframe given, The Authority will enforce the decree to the fullest extent of our granted powers." Reporters were shouting. Camera drones buzzed around Ding's head like fat houseflies. Dozens of rapid-fire indigo camera flashes. "No questions at this time, thank you. My colleagues and I have an Aelf to smoke out."

The motel manager muted the Watchbox.

Alina didn't know what to say.

Dabbing at his thinning hairline with a handkerchief, the manager quickly said, "Seeing as you're now persona non grata in town, we need to renegotiate. Here's the deal. I'm nice guy, and I'm not one to turn out of my establishment a damsel in distress. But I've got my business to think of. And company policy. My hands are tied, I'm afraid."

"'Company policy?' You're the only employed here."

"Be that as it may, be that as it may, I need to think about our relative statuses. As you just saw, you're not welcome around here anymore. Again, I'm a decent man, a kind soul. Best be thankful I'm saying you can stay out the nights you've paid for. But the room fee for those nights has just doubled."

"Doubled?" Alina shouted. "But you heard the detective—Ravers won't be booted out of town for another day!"

"Look, girl, I don't make the rules."

"Yes, you *do*."

"Okay, you're right," he said, stumbling over the words. He puffed up his bony chest. "I make the rules, I do. And *I'm* telling you the rate's just gone up."

Glaring at him, Alina drew herself up and out of her habitual slouch. Now standing several inches taller than he did, she said, "If that's how it's gonna be, then I'm out of here. I can sleep in the streets for one night. I've done it before."

"Spoken like the Terrie you are," the manager said with a sneer.

"Rather die a Terrie than a useless money-gouging blob."

"I'm not useless! I'm a businessman."

"What's the difference?"

"*Oooh!*" He shook his copy of *Basic Economics* in her face (she didn't flinch). "You'd better be out of here in one hour."

"Cool. There's no way I'd stay here any longer than that anyway. Now, back off and get out."

"This is my establishment. I'll leave when I—"

"Out," she screamed, throwing her hand up, fingers twitching.

The manager was flung backward, and the door slammed shut after him. She could hear him groaning in the hallway, picking himself up, calling her several unflattering names.

Locking the door, Alina muttered, "You can come out now." And, as Cho and Mezami crept out of the tiny closet and from behind the toilet, respectively, Alina began cramming her few personal belongings into her bag.

She was just about to turn the Watchbox off when Mezami buzzed in front of her face, saying, "Wait: you." The Pyct flew close enough to lick the screen. "Slaughterer: him. Evil: *him*."

Midway through thrusting her arms into her jacket's sleeves, Alina paused and checked the Watchbox.

She gasped.

The news broadcast now displayed the image of a man—close-shaven head; scars on his lip, forehead, scalp, and neck; a gray wool tunic billowing around his muscular body; a sword clutched in two hands. Below the slightly grainy still-image, most likely captured by a street camera, was the caption: "Man-hunt: Tolomond Stayd. Armed and extremely dangerous."

Lunging for the remote on the bed, Alina turned up the volume.

The woman providing the voiceover was saying, "… suspect is wanted in connection with numerous offenses, including aggravated assault, destruction of private property, resisting arrest, and mass-murder. This just in: among Stayd's victims is renowned Master Gildsman Ugarda Pankrish. It has also been confirmed that Stayd is a Sanctumite. The Hierophant of The Sanctum, Pontifex Ridect, has declined to comment. Stayd was last seen in the Dyrex District. Extraordinary caution is advised. More on this story as it develops. Back to you, Hilace."

Alina tuned out the rest.

So, that Tolomond guy was a killer after all. And he went for *the* Ugarda Pankrish and *won*. Alina didn't linger too long on how amazing a feat that was. All she could think about was how decent and down-to-earth Pankrish had been, how he'd known her and her Tahtoh, how she'd always respected and admired him. And now he was gone.

Gone.

The bastard had *killed* Ugarda Pankrish. Murdered him.

Collapsing onto the bed, Alina covered her face with her hands.

Something else struck her, then. The Dyrex District—that was between here and Ordin's place. Tolomond had previously gone after Ordin (and her). What if he tried it again?

What if he did so *today*?

Between the eviction order and the murderer on the loose, the gods apparently had plans for Alina that did not involve staying cooped up in this motel room. In fact, they'd given her three compelling reasons to leave: the scheming manager looking to make a quick gelder off her misery; the new twenty-four-hour time limit on her stay in The Capital; and the potential threat to Ordin's life. Four if you counted her need to tell Ordin what she'd learned about the identity of the Bane of New El—that it wasn't an Ushum at all, but something even more threatening.

So, in summary, she had less than one day to find *and* defeat a mysterious Demidivine Aelf and make off with the money. Meanwhile, a deranged, sword-swinging lunatic was out there, somewhere, angling for her. And, of course, at some point during all the hubbub, she maybe should carve out a half-hour to actually plan for the fight itself—but, hey, that couldn't be too important, right?

Her eyes darted around the room, seeing nothing. She began to hyperventilate.

After a few moments, she realized Mezami had been tapping her shoulder and talking to her.

"Help: me, you," he was saying.

Alina bit her lip. "Look, I *know* what I told you. But what do you want me to do? Did you just hear all that other stuff? If I'm not out of here, I'll be arrested—or I'll just get offed in the chaos. Some stray Authority bullet will snag me right between the eyes. The guy you're after is the same one whose gunning for me. You get that, don't you, Mezami? It was one thing when I thought I'd be helping you track down a couple of newbie Gild students. But, this… Here's the thing, Stayd *murdered* my idol."

"Clan: mine. Murdered: he."

"Yeah, I *know*." She wrung her hands in front of her face. "Even more of a reason to avoid him. Look, what do you want from me?"

A shudder of fury rippled through Mezami. "Him: fight."

"I can't! I'm telling you, it's done. He's too strong, and I've got *so little time*. If I don't get to my target in less than a *day*, I lose everything. You get me? Everything I did, it'll all be for nothing. Nothing! And you know I have to complete this contract, guys. Have to. Or my life is officially over. I'll be living in the streets."

"I already am," said Cho from the corner.

Without facing her, Alina snapped, "Don't do that. You know what I mean."

"Promised: you."

Alina growled and threw a pillow across the room. "I know. I know I promised, damn it." She jabbed a finger at Mezami, who zipped backwards, fairy wings humming angrily. "What are you gonna do against someone like Stayd? He already got the best of Ugarda freakin' Pankrish. And you're just a Pyct. One Pyct. By yourself. You weigh like two ounces. He's a monster. He'd have a tougher time fighting a paperclip!"

"Alina, stop it," Cho shouted.

Alina bore down on her. "Keep your voice down. I don't need any more trouble on your account. Chasing after you almost cost me everything. And it might still."

Cho gritted her teeth. "Oh, yeah? Without me, you wouldn't even have your stupid stone. Don't pretend like you would've come after me if you weren't so worried about that thing. You only care about yourself." She tried to shove Alina but only ended up pushing herself backwards. "Take back what you said about Mezami. You can't treat him like that."

"He should hear the truth," said Alina, narrowing her eyes. "Might just save his life." Turning her back on Cho, she shouldered her bag. "I could've left you in there, you know. Could've snuck around until I found the Lorestone. It would have made things so much easier. But I looked for you, and—" She shook her head. "I don't have to explain myself to you, Cho. I don't care if you're technically a Torvir. You're just some kid, really."

Cho's face went pink and hot, tears pooling in her eyes.

She ran from the room.

Mezami stared at Alina, stared down his long rodent-like snout.

"What are you looking at?" said Alina. "Any other Raver would've snapped you in half by now. Get outta my face. You're nothing but a burden."

Without a word, Mezami went to the window, cracked it enough for him to squeeze through the gap, and zoomed out of the building, into the sky.

Feeling faint, Alina dashed into the bathroom, threw the toilet seat up, and emptied what was left of the contents of her stomach. After a few seconds, she lifted her head.

The contents in the bowl were gray. Gray with *fuzzy* black lumps.

"What's happening to me?" she moaned.

The skin on her arms burned more fiercely than ever. Tugging up her sleeves, unraveling the crusty bandages, she saw that the flesh had putrefied, it seemed. But, no, that wasn't quite right. Her arms weren't goopy and didn't smell like they were rotting. They were just gray in color, rough of texture, like a cat's tongue but pricklier. Vision swimming, Alina blinked until she could make out the little black spikes jutting sporadically from her skin. The largest concentration of them was near her elbow, but a snaking trail of the spikes (or quills?) ran all the way from her shoulder to her wrist.

She brushed her fingertip up against one. It was sharp enough to draw a dot of blood.

Leaning against the shower stall, sweating, shaking, she unblocked Calthin's number. She tried to call him. Five or six times.

He wouldn't pick up.

Her first two messages were about how sorry she was, how she'd never do it again, how she just wanted to talk to him. Her third message demanded that he pick up because she really needed a friend right now. The last two were mostly strings of expletives and some stifled sobs.

She threw the phone across the motel room.

When she'd calmed down, she used cotton swabs and rubbing alcohol to clean the ooze from her forearms and elbows. Scowling at her reflection in the grimy mirror, she applied fresh bandages, courtesy of Ordin.

Ordin.

Now that everyone else had moved on, he was the only one she could turn to.

She had to make sure he didn't share Ugarda Pankrish's fate. And maybe, between the two of them, they'd be able to find her a way out of this giant *iurk'et* pile.

31

THE RHYTHM OF LIFE on New El—its unique music—had always been dictated by the concept of limited space. As frantic and chaotic as The Capital sounded at first, underneath the competing synthesizers and improvised high and low notes, there was a steady, deliberate bassline. The slow thumping of this rhythm could best be noticed in the grids of buildings, parallel streets, subterranean utility lines: each of these had been planned by committee, and extreme care had been taken at every turn to maximize their efficiency. Any and all additions or changes to the city's framework had always been implemented with extreme conservatism over the course of decades and centuries. Ever since the last free acre of land on the planetoid had finally been zoned for retail use, the only way for new construction to be approved was for an old structure to be torn down and replaced. This process required countless meetings, blueprints, revisions, arguments, and—as always—the continuous attentions of cautious minds, their thoughts pulsing firmly in time with a guiding beat. A slow, steady rhythm.

In the Dyrex District, four blocks south of Mycul's Copse, snugly nestled among the glinting high rises, there was a three-hundred-year-old museum. A squat, two-story construction with a roof like an unevenly folded sheet of paper—thin and angular and unsettlingly off-kilter—built during the Reinvintage era of architecture. A gaudy throwback to the Elementals' favorite style at the beginning of the fourth millennium, the museum had once been stuffed to the brim with a random assortment of colonial puffery. The place was a standing monument to self-praise and the short attention spans of the empires of men.

Many decades after this pet project of some unimportant son of whatever nobleman had been erected, a series of lawsuits—claiming the property within had been stolen—finally shut it down. Still more years had to pass before the place was acquired by one of the Plutocrats and summarily condemned.

This half-collapsed, abandoned heap happened to be scheduled for demolition early next week. It had been stripped down to its nuts and bolts. All the paintings and sculptures and other archaic trophies—rather than being returned to their original creators and owners in distant lands—had been hastily acquired by anonymous buyers. Even the marble and other valuable building materials had been pulled from the walls and pillars, to be recycled or reused elsewhere. What remained was mostly rotten wood and crumbling concrete and some odd bits of junk, too moldy or unsightly to be of interest to anyone.

Except for the rats and the roaches, no one had set foot inside in years, not even stereotypically adventurous teenagers. Warnings of structural damage and high risk of collapse had kept everyone out.

Thus, all had been quiet for a long, long time. Until Tolomond Stayd rammed a limousine through the "caution" tape covering the rusty front doors.

Clouds of dust blew off the pillars and busted furniture. Air whistled along the naked metal window panes. The hovercraft screeched to a halt inside the dilapidated lobby, its crumpled front end beginning to smoke. Its engine sputtering, it remained in neutral. Tolomond climbed out, covering his mouth with his sweat-slick arm.

He sprinted up the open staircase that occupied half the lobby. Sword resting on his shoulder, he hung a right at the top of the stairs and flung open the nearest door. With a pained groan, it gave way, and he rushed inside.

The room was empty except for rolls of plastic sheets and a cluster of forgotten, rain-scarred, rusty tools. A red-brick fireplace covered most of the right-side wall; the others were white and spotted with black mold.

Tolomond walked to the windows on the left.

Outside, in the visitor parking section, three hovercycles and one armored vehicle touched down. From the latter, a team of six officers stepped onto the asphalt. Their uniforms were the lavender and midnight blue of the Xaveyr, advertising their status as lapdogs of the Consul of El himself. The ones on the cycles were garbed in silver and white—Ivoir's bought-and-paid-for henchmen.

For a moment, Tolomond struggled with himself. Must he kill these poor, deluded fools, too?

Then he was reminded of the sinfulness of The Authority. Though they claimed to govern and protect the people of this nation, in reality, they were nothing but a collective of gelder-grubbing clowns in expensive costumes—far less unified than their name would suggest.

Take their commanders, for example: Elementals handpicked from among the bannermen of each of the Twelve Families, who enjoyed long, rich lives spent barking orders from behind their desks. They owed their comforts to the nepotism and favoritism of those who worshipped at the altars of wealth and prestige.

By contrast, the Enforcers were mere guns for hire. Plucked from the rank-and-file, these were usually Terries simply seeking a leg-up in life. They literally looked to the skies for salvation without once searching within themselves, and so they ignored the corruption that grew like cancer within their very hearts. They allowed their masters to twist them into foot-soldiers, blind to the injustices of the hellish world they fought to preserve.

What were the wages of sin, then? What were these people promised in return for their souls?

Material comforts.

Every ten years, a new Consul was elected from among the patriarchs of the Families (by the Plutocrats themselves). This process was important to the Enforcers because the Consul's personal forces received special privileges, such as better food, higher wages, and much more leeway in how they administered their "justice." The promise of such rewards naturally caused the Plutocrats' men to fight for their own master's promotion to the position of commander-in-chief.

Thus, the mobs of Enforcers were certainly no strangers to politics. The machinery of government, after all, kept them fed, drunk, and carnally spent. They catered only to their animal instincts. They were dogs—vicious mutts, rabid and wracked with mange—and therefore they must be put down. Like dogs.

It would be a mercy.

Pressed against the wall, Tolomond counted the Enforcers as they mobilized below.

They were coming for him. Why? Because he'd killed Ugarda Pankrish? Because he'd cut down a handful of Ivoir's henchmen? Madness! He'd done nothing wrong, but they were coming for him anyway. It was all they could do, for well-fed dogs do not disobey.

These wretches were broken beyond repair, only when they were dead—every last one of them—would the world be clean.

Abandoning all doubt, reciting a prayer, he closed his eyes. "Author, give me strength. Write me into Your Story. I ask only for the span of a footnote. But let me live well and, when I depart from this mortal coil, grant me dignity in death and let me rest in bliss, by your side in Nehalennia."

But not yet. Tolomond would not be among the dead that day.

From downstairs, he heard the tinkling of shards of glass on concrete followed by metal clanks and rolling. A trio of thunderclaps.

Not knowing that Tolomond had already headed upstairs, the Enforcers had just expended their flashbangs. They were about to breach.

Tolomond watched the lobby from above, leaning against the warped wrought-iron railing.

A shout came from outside, and the doors burst open, six Enforcers rushing inside, fanning out, covering all angles. The beams of their rifle-mounted flashlights scythed the dimness.

It was a common joke that each Sanctumite was allowed not even one personal possession. This was false. Each sworn brother or sister was outfitted with robes, the iron quill pendant representing The Author's Living Works, and (in the case of Instruments like Tolomond) a weapon. These were the standard items presented to the faithful by The Sanctum leadership. Each item could be replaced at a moment's notice with an identical replica. However, to maintain the "Essential Minimum," the standard of living that molds the mind and body into the perfect tool for The Author's use, all practitioners of the one true religion were granted the right to exactly *one* personal belonging of his or her choosing.

Tolomond had chosen a box of matches as his keepsake. His earliest memory was of a fire—perhaps the one that had taken the home into which he'd been born, where he'd lived the first five years of his life, where his mother had burned, before he'd been inducted into the mysteries of The Sanctum.

Fire was steady, reliable, knowable: a touch would hurt; a lingering embrace would kill. When all appeared hopeless, Tolomond would watch the candleflames dance upon the stone altars in his room at The Sanctum and take comfort in knowing that—on one fine red day, soon enough—the material world would die in a great cleansing fire.

As he held the box of matches in his hand, he smiled at the thought that he might just be beginning that fire. Right here and now. Author-willing.

He pulled out one of the matches, striking it against his stubbled cheek. The flame caught. He tucked the match back into the box with the others.

After disembarking, Tolomond had nicked the limo's fuel tank. Hydrogen gas had been spilling into the lobby for two minutes by this point. Even at room temperature, hydrogen gas was about as flammable as can be.

He flung his box of matches downstairs toward the limousine he'd parked in the middle of the museum lobby. The vehicle exploded—a plume of blue and white flame that ripped through two of the officers, blasting their uniforms and flesh. They went down in clouds of smoke and cinders and screams. Another two were thrown forward onto their bellies to crawl like the worms they were.

The pair that remained standing fired a few bursts up at Tolomond, who ducked out of the way.

One of them shouted, "Sound off if you're still alive."

In turn, three other voices, one man, two women, replied: "Vanguard 1, not dead yet."

"Vanguard 2, still breathing."

"Vanguard 4, by Plutonia, everything hurts, but I'm more than ready to hit back."

Their squad leader said, "Get on the horn, Raggel. We need backup."

"Who the hells is this guy?"

"Uppity Terrie Raver trash by the look of him."

Tolomond hissed under his breath. Ignorance. *"Lord,"* he prayed, *"let me end these men."*

He heard the crackle of static as the one called Raggel shouted a request for support into his shoulder-mounted personal communicator. The others dragged the two wounded (and probably dead) officers behind an overturned table.

The leader said, "Listen up, fugitive. That was some move you just pulled, offing two of my men. Well, now it's our turn. And when we're done, it's gonna take forensics a whole week to scoop a thimble's worth of you. Consider this your official notice that the negotiation window has closed."

As he yelled the word "closed," rapid pulse-cannon fire rattled off from three sides, triangulating on Tolomond's position. The holes punched in the wall were fist-sized; the blasts pulverized the brick, and any part that didn't totally disintegrate was either scarred black or smoldering around the edges.

The pulses were focused, coordinated. Whenever one Enforcer stooped to switch out his rifle's battery pack, another would pick up where he left off. Tolomond was effectively pinned by continuous flashes of indigo just above his skull.

Then three hovercycles crashed onto the second floor through the pockmarked, structurally weakened wall.

In that instant, he tensed, and his mind sparked, ablaze with a thousand tactics, a thousand options. Limbs sizzling with a fresh rush of adrenaline, he determined his best chance was to surround himself with bodies the hovercycle pilots wouldn't dare target.

Tolomond leapt over the railing—air roaring in his ears—and into the middle of the four officers on the ground floor.

They hadn't been expecting his jump.

Capitalizing on the confusion, he swept Rhetoric in a rising, spinning arc—tearing through an ankle, the meat of an arm, a torso, and a neck. Two officers went down. One of the others popped off a few rounds, but they were conventional bullets—not pulse rounds—which was fortunate for Tolomond because he was able to bring his blade up, using it as a shield. The bullets ricocheted, embedding themselves in the ground and wall. Before the Enforcer could squeeze off a second burst, Tolomond kicked his heel into the side of the man's knee. As he went down, Tolomond delivered an elbow to his chin. A crack.

With that Enforcer prone and groaning, Tolomond advanced on the last one, the mouthy leader. He whipped up his rifle, its barrel smoking, its red-dot sight obscuring his right eye. Tolomond sidestepped and swung, his blade cleaving the gun in half. The Enforcer gasped and leapt backward, the hunks of now-useless plastic spilling from his hands. With his primary out of commission, he unsheathed a combat knife, which Tolomond dealt with by lopping off his hand.

Tolomond dragged the wailing, stump-clutching officer by the collar, walking him over to the service elevator, making sure to keep his hostage between himself and the heavy guns of those three cycle pilots.

They were shouting at each other, circling like vultures.

Tolomond marched right up to the open elevator doors. The lift itself rested two floors down. Without power, he had no way of summoning it, but he wasn't planning to.

The squad leader turned and looked down into the darkness. "Just give up," he croaked. "You'll never ma—"

Tolomond shoved the back of the man's head, pitching him down the shaft. By the time the scream cut off with a sickening crunch, Tolomond had leapt in after him. A lurch of the stomach and a rush of stale air. Then he collided with the presumably dead officer's back and rolled to dissipate some of the impact of the fall.

It still hurt like hell, but not half bad as the rituals to which he subjected himself almost every day.

A purified soul guarantees a vigorous body.

He took a deep breath of basement dust and murk.

It would be several minutes at least before the hovercyclists could safely catch up with him. Their vehicles would be too bulky to fit down the shaft, and the stairwell had been sealed.

Several minutes was more time than he'd need.

In the middle of this underground parking deck were four central concrete pillars—the main supports for the entire building. Packed tightly around these pillars were enough pounds of plastic explosives to get the job done.

Tolomond smiled—

Hellfire.

—and got to work.

Within five minutes of Tolomond's destructive entrance into the condemned museum's basement, two more armored truckloads of Authority Enforcers arrived on scene, sirens blaring.

From his vantage point on a nearby balcony, a sweaty, panting Tolomond noted that they approached more cautiously than the previous group had. These officers sent in a pair of Situational De-escalation Drones (which the dregs of society called "Sads") ahead of them, rather than charge in brazenly. A wise show of restraint.

When the drones scanned the first and second floors and determined them clear, they were deployed to the basements. The Enforcers—all twelve of them—entered the lobby.

Tolomond wondered at the motivations of these mercenaries. They must have known the museum had been condemned. Why did they go inside? Loyalty to their fallen comrades? A craving for revenge?

He spoke a prayer over the detonator held in his hand. "I commit your souls to The Author," he said.

His thumb crushed the button.

32

IN THE CAPITAL, THE wealthiest traveled via magically generated, personal bubble-shuttles (or, as Alina now called them, "bubshas"); the average Elemental (still much richer than the richest Terrie she'd ever met) made use of more conventional trains, buses, and hovercabs. Up until this point, Alina had walked or taken the subway everywhere, the latter option being free to Gildsmen for the duration of the Rave. However, since Terrie Aelfravers had received a black mark from The Authority, traveling among large groups of Elementals seemed a significant risk. Also, Alina was in a hurry. Therefore, she could justify spending some of Baraam's cash.

As she handed the cabbie a wad of gelders, she felt a little pang of guilt, thinking about where the money had come from. Without Cho, who'd lifted Baraam's credit card, Alina wouldn't have had a penny to her name by now. She shook the feeling off, reminding herself that Cho simply couldn't be a priority right now.

No one was going to help Alina. No one but herself. There was nothing for it. Cho and Mezami—well, they'd just have to understand.

She demanded the cabbie step on it as she brought up her contacts list on her phone and tapped the entry that read "The Most Charming Ordin Ivoir."

"Come on, pick up." With her thumb, Alina jabbed the call icon again.

Ringing. Ringing. Voicemail. Same as before.

Testament to how desperate she was: she'd left three messages. Yes, she'd become *that* person. Twitching. Soaked in her own pit-sweat.

This was the fourth one, now. "Ordin, it's me again. I'm not flipping out or anything, okay? I just really need to talk to you. It's about the, uh—the job. The one we talked about." She considered how her tone must sound not-at-all-suspicious to anyone listening. Deep breaths, she reminded herself. She had to calm down. The Authority's AIs would be primarily focused on keywords or abnormal phrasings that sounded like coded messages. As long as she kept it vague, she'd be fine. Probably. "Anyway, need your opinion ASAP. Call me as soon as you get this. Hope you're alright. Um, bye."

Her forehead thumped against the back of the driver's seat as the cabbie took another ninety-degree, forty mile-per-hour left turn.

Ears ringing, she thought she heard distant sirens. She might have imagined them, though.

"You should try to giving him some space, hey?" said the cabbie in a heavy Heran accent. In the rearview, the reflection of his eyes met hers. "Your boyfriend you call. Why not instead coming to party tonight with this guy? Heh, heh!" Stiff-wristed, he pointed at himself. "Have good time."

"Watch the road," shouted Alina.

The cabbie slammed on the brakes just in time to avoid rear-ending the vehicle idling in front of him.

Fully-stopped, he threw his hands up in frustration, slapping the steering column. "Traffic jam? So not very cool."

Alina lowered her window, poking her head out into the crisp, gold-lit morning air to scan the long line of vehicles ahead. No sign of movement as far as she could see. Even the lanes dozens of feet above and below were crammed with cars.

She cursed under her breath. The whole point of taking a cab to Ordin's had been to save time.

Two minutes passed. And another two. Every time Alina checked her phone, there it was—the cold, hard fact that two whole minutes had slipped away. With each second, she nibbled her fingertips and her nails closer to the quick. She didn't have time for this.

Finally, the vehicles did begin to inch forward. And she squirmed in her seat, raking the fake leather with her fingernails.

Stillness should have come easily to her, what with how often she'd suffered through boredom and forced silence as a child. Half of Tahtoh's lessons seemed to involve "patience," his justification for having Alina stand perfectly still in a stream in the forest, sit in an empty room with gray walls, or meditate through sunny days when she'd rather have been out playing or something. (Not that many kids had wanted to play with the lanky weirdo who lived with the crazy old martial arts instructor—the one who could set household objects on fire with a word or uproot a plant without touching it.)

Many of her childhood days had been spent this way, learning to hear her own thoughts as sharply as the call of a hawk or the rustle of a squirrel's skittering through the brush.

Then there'd been the endless drills. Punch-kick combo number one. Disarming grab. Escape grapple. Again. Again. *Again.* Those had only gotten interesting when she'd squared off against real live opponents. But in the first several years, it had been just her, solo, going through the motions. Hungry, tired, sweating into her eyes, her Tahtoh watching, clicking his tongue, nudging her elbow a fraction of an inch to the left, her heel one degree inward.

He'd finished every lesson with the comment, "Well, there's always tomorrow." Somehow, Alina's form, her energy, her Niima-channeling were never quite good enough. And they never would be: her grandfather had disappeared the morning after his final "Well, there's always tomorrow." His last words to her.

She'd never know if there would ever have come a "Perfect," a "Well done," or even just an "Eh, s'alright." She'd never find out.

And *why* had he left? Had he lost his patience with her, finally?

Maybe that's why sitting around and doing nothing *killed*: some part of her mind was always pushing *what's next.* All that repetition had only taught her to long for the end.

She had internalized Tahtoh's lack of satisfaction, after all.

"Isn't there some other route we could take?" she asked the cabbie as traffic grinded to a halt again.

"What you want me to do? Cars behind me and cars ahead. I have to staying in my lane. Sorry. Can't control Authority business. Hope you still rate good stars."

"What? Yeah, I'm not gonna give you a bad review. I wouldn't do that," she said absentmindedly, thinking about how ridiculous this situation was and how she had to get out of here *now*.

Clock tower bells tolled the hour of noon, an alarm to remind Alina that she'd been sitting in this cab for a little under an hour.

Just when she thought she might die of frustration, however, there was a blinding white flare followed by a deafening boom, and a hail of small chunks of rock. A roiling cloud of dust spilled over the lanes of gently swaying hovercraft.

The cabbie quickly rolled up the automatic windows, not quite in time to avoid a lung-full of the gusts of dirt and powder. His cough was so violent that he doubled over, bumping the horn with his pasty forehead and straw-like hair. "Lord save me," he exclaimed. "What's happen?"

Alina saw flashing purple lights up ahead, the telltale sign of an Authority blockade. "Maybe it has something to do with the checkpoint up ahead."

"Checkpoint?" All color drained from the cabbie's face. "My license is three days expired, man."

"Buthmertha help me," she murmured. Switching sides, she stared out the right rear passenger window, saying, "They might write you up for that, but I highly doubt you're the type they're looking for."

Fidgeting with the center-console touchscreen, the cabbie said, "I play some music. What you like? Tribalectronica? Gospel-Pop?"

"Got any Alternative?"

"Alternative?" He made a face. "To what? You mean, maybe, DJ Alt-Hurt-N4ybor? How about Sanzynna?"

"Who's that?"

The cabbie did a double-take. Her ignorance seemed to have completely distracted him from his momentary panic. "Sanzynna?" Trying to hit notes way above his range, he sang, "'Ooh, baby, come meet your Maker, yeah,

yeah'? You don't know? 'He loves His faithful, oh-woh-oh?' You never hear of Sanzynna, big, big talent?"

"Name sounds familiar, but she's probably not my cup of krunk."

"You don't like catchy tunes with good message?"

"I do. It's okay if you like her, I wasn't trying—"

"Don't you believe The Author? God?"

"I believe in the gods, yeah, but—"

He interrupted her again and tried to educate her about music and religion some more, but then he had to stop because they'd arrived at the front of the line and a black-clad Authority Enforcer tapped on the driver-side window.

Grateful the one-sided convo was over, this was the first time Alina could remember feeling legitimately relieved by The Authority's presence, if only for a moment. After two seconds, she shifted back to nervousness.

The Enforcer, a man standing on a four-by-four flying platform held a flashlight in one hand and a holopad in the other. When the cabbie lowered the window, the officer said, "Papers, please."

The cabbie reached into the glove compartment, fishing for his paperwork. "Here's the thing, officer, I—"

The flashlight's beam passed over Alina's face. "Her, too."

Alina frowned. "Excuse me. I'm not driving, so why do I have to show you anything?"

"Are you being belligerent with me, ma'am?"

"No, *sir*, I just don't see why you're—"

"I'm not asking for your driver's license, ma'am. I'm *telling* you to show me your PAC."

"My what?"

"Your Proof of Assetship Card. Now."

The cabbie said, "Just, please, lady, give the nice gentleman what he want."

"I'm not—I don't—I have a work permit."

"No PAC? You from the mainland?"

"Yeah," she said hesitantly.

"Purpose of visit?"

"Business."

"Profession?"

"I'm a, uh, I'm an Aelfraver."

He finally glanced up from his holopad's display and looked her in the eye. "You're aware of the executive order for your removal, I assume."

She checked her phone. "Still got, like, fifteen hours, don't I?"

"Just make certain you get yourself to Mercy's Approach with time to spare. Unless you love The Capital so much you want to live here on a… much more permanent basis."

"Thank you, I'll be sure to do that."

"In the dungeons," the Enforcer added with a sneer.

Alina muttered, "Yup, got that."

"Did you say something, ma'am?"

"Here's my Raver-X license," she said loudly, passing him the card through her window. To keep her teeth from chattering, she cradled her chin in the crook of her arm.

The Enforcer leaned forward, but never got a chance to finish his inspection.

Craning his neck, he squinted over the roof of the cab. Then his eyes widened and he reached for his sidearm.

Alina's head whipped around. She saw what the Enforcer was reacting to, then, and shouted at the cabbie, "Oh my gods, look right!" But it was too late.

It took a second or two for the cabbie to interpret her words and obey her command, a delay that removed all possibility of dodging the armored car barreling toward them.

The vehicle—an Authority special personnel transport vehicle (SPTV)—t-boned the cab at about thirty miles per hour. The collision caused the cab's rear-end to swing in an arc, slamming into the Enforcer on his four-by-four platform. The man was pitched off his footing and, with a scream, fell hundreds of feet down to street-level.

The cab continued to spin, its driver howling in terror. He slammed his foot onto the accelerator. The vehicle's engine revved, and it zoomed forward. Directly into the side of a skyscraper.

Alina's head bounced off the hard plastic of the passenger door, and she was out.

First, there was only rocking. A wave-tossed boat. Then, a single candle. Otherwise, darkness.

Water dripping, somewhere, not too far away. Dripping onto a metal grate. *Tonk. Tonk.*

Tonk.

As time undulated around her, slipping away like noodles escaping through the holes in a colander, no part of Alina felt alright. Her headache radiated outward from the center of her brain, pinching her eyes and melding with the ache in her neck, shoulders, lower spine.

She opened her eyes.

The radius of what she could see, by dim candlelight, was roughly six feet. She felt firstly, and saw secondly, that her wrists and ankles had been tightly tied to a wicker chair. Her jacket hung on an identical chair five feet in front of her; she could just make out the dirt-flecked edges of its familiar sleeve.

So thirsty. Her dry tongue scraped across her chapped lips.

"You're awake. Say something. Though, I warn you, witch, if you try to cast a spell, I will cut you down without hesitation. Do you understand?" It was a man's voice—grating, strained, caught in the throat, as if he were forcing out unwilling syllables. "Say 'yes' if you understand."

"Yes," Alina said hoarsely. "Where am I?"

"I ask the questions here, heretic. What is your name?"

"Stitcher."

"You lie. Once more, and I'll take a finger. What is your name?"

She couldn't see him, but she could tell by his voice that he was standing less than ten feet away from her, just outside the circle of low light.

Her lip quivering, she tried to come up with a way out of this, but her mind had gone blank. Her throat was so dry. She croaked, "My name is Alina."

"Are you ready to accept the merciful embrace of The Author, Alina?"

"That depends."

A hulking man in a gray tunic lumbered forward, raised his arm, and back-handed her across the face.

Reeling from the force of the blow, her head lolled. She spat a few drops of blood. Her tongue was bleeding, cut on her teeth.

Dizzily, she gazed at the scarred face of Tolomond Stayd, who growled, "Never make a mockery of the Lord's mercy, Alina. You have but one more chance. Your next offense will be your last."

"What do you even want from me, man?" she said, tongue swelling, tears tumbling from her eyes. "I don't have any money, believe me."

"How *dare* you imply that this—any of this—has anything to do with so base a concern as coin?" His hand went up again and hung in the air. He lowered it, reconsidering. "I am on a mission, witch. A divine mission to eradicate the enemies of God. And you can help me. You can serve the light. For once in your miserable, sinful, awful existence, you can earn yourself a chance at redemption. You need only renounce your false gods, sever yourself from all your magical vices, and do exactly as I say from here on out. Until we both meet our Maker."

Alina *almost* said, "*Oh, is that all?*" But, just as the words were about to slip out, she caught them. She coughed to cover her verbal tracks. Then, "How could I possibly help your God?"

"*Our* God," Tolomond corrected. "*The* Lord. And, finally, you ask the right question: how *can* you serve the One? Thankfully, the answer is simple. All you have to do, for now, is call Ordin Ivoir."

She forced herself to suck in sharp shallow breaths, tried to think clearly.

She considered the man leaning over her, his glistening and ash-streaked forehead, furnace-blasted breaths, muscles as tough as braided ropes. Beside him, against the slimy wall, leaned a huge sword. And it struck her, again, how absolutely alone they were.

Considering all these details, she could only conclude that she wasn't supposed to make it out of here alive. No version of this story could end with both her and this bug-eyed bear-man leaving this dungeon together, laughing and chatting and giving each other pats on the back.

Wherever she'd been taken, she was going to die down here, she knew. Unless she acted.

She said, "What's Ordin done to you?"

"His sin—its reek pervades Creation. He is rot personified. He, and all like him, must be purged."

"And what about me?"

"Through The Author's benevolence, you may still be saved. But you must obey my commands, all of them, and you must follow me, your guide who will lead you into the light."

"Okay," she said. "Just don't hurt me again."

"Often, pain is the only thing that can cleanse corruption. I feel no remorse for striking you. You needed it. Now you see a little clearer."

"Yeah, I see." She twisted her wrists, judging if her restraints had any give in them. "I see." They didn't.

"Good." He grinned, revealing a gap where his right canine tooth should have been. "Very good. Yes! We will walk a long road together. One day, you may stand with us, sanctified. But, first, begin your path. Take your first step. Show me a token of your good faith."

"I—I'll give you what you want." She had no choice. There was only one way forward. One possible way out of this. "I'll contact him."

"No magic," said Tolomond, looming over her, his chest heaving with every breath. "No tricks."

"No," said Alina, shrinking. "A phone call. I promise. Just a phone call."

He took a step back, nostrils flaring. "Very well." Rummaging through her jacket pockets, he found her phone.

"I'll need one hand free," she stammered.

"No. I will do it for you."

"Okay. Just—my code is 3462. Yeah. Hit the white speaker symbol." Alina silently prayed to Buthmertha that Tolomond was as technologically illiterate as his style of dress, choice of weapon, and medieval demeanor suggested. "Tap it. No, don't hold. Tap. See, now you've opened the options menu."

He glared at her, face reddening, veins bulging.

"I'm sorry," she muttered. "I'm sorry. Just—I—"

"You do it, then," he spat. His fingers tore at the knot on the ropes tying her left hand to the armrest.

She could barely hold the phone, she was shaking so violently, but she managed to navigate the icons, swipe left, left again. There it was, the app she wanted. Her thumb hovered above the icon.

For the briefest instant, she'd considered calling Ordin. Maybe he'd have been able to pull something together, get the cavalry, charge in and neutralize Tolomond.

But then she remembered. She wasn't the type of girl who needed saving.

She'd skipped right past the call button and tapped the white envelope icon, opening her digimail app. From the dropdown menu, she selected the "sent" folder and saw it—the last digimail she'd put out.

The text field was empty. There was only one attachment, and a surprisingly small file at that. Sent to "ThimbleBoy@TownshipMail.mag," the subject line read: "Hubris Demon DO NOT OPEN – K Thanks."

She thumbed the paper-clip image, opening the attachment.

"Is it going to go through?" said Tolomond, crossing his arms. "The call?"

"I think so," said Alina, breathlessly. She began to chuckle, then laugh outright. A from-down-deep, can't-contain-it, bubbling-to-the-surface explosion of a laughing fit.

"What's happening? Give me that." He ripped the phone from her hands and put it to his ear. "Ivoir, I have the girl. If you wish to—" That's as far as he got before the device released an ear-piercing screech that bounced off the dank, dark cell's thick, stone walls.

Rocking her chair, trying to tip it sideways, Alina watched as Tolomond held the phone at arm's length—and it began to froth, shiny blue-black bubbles emanating from the mic and speaker. The device itself glowed red-hot now, and Tolomond dropped it. It didn't merely break when it hit the damp stone floor—it burst into a thousand razor-shards, all of which shot toward him. They pierced the arm he'd raised to shield himself, some of the pieces nicking his chest.

"Treachery," he shouted.

Alina managed to knock her chair over, the force of the impact with the floor cracking the armrests and one of the legs. She wiggled her restraints towards the fracture.

As she struggled, from the corner of her eye, she saw the glowing phone-shards coalesce and grow. Within seconds, the liquid metal and plastic had taken the shape of a slender, headless man wearing a suit. A long red tie sprouted from the cavity in his neck, out of which popped his grinning face. Two sinewy arms grappled with Tolomond even as a second pair—made of shadow—with long, clawed fingers slicked back his golden hair.

"Hubris," said the demon in a voice older than the oldest civilization. Before the first village—before the first tribe, *it* had been there, waiting, watching, judging. When there'd been no men, only apes, swinging from branches and cowering in caves, killing one another over territory, pride, or mates, it *had* been there. It was a voice that carried all the weight of the ages between present day and that dark moment when a caveman first stole another's pile of rocks. With those two syllables, "Hubris," it breathed life into all the petty and selfish ambitions of humanity, relishing their flavor while simultaneously expressing absolute contempt for their pettiness. Again, it said, "Hubris."

Osesoc'ex-calea, the Greed Demon, formed its shadowed second set of arms into spears and thrust these at Tolomond. Pinned to the wall, legs flailing, the man screamed.

He flung out his arms, and from his left wrist there burned a white light. The flesh exploded, searing, instantly filling the cramped space with a stink like charred pork. A gleaming chain unfurled from the hole, the hooked silver blade at its end dropping like an anchor. Tolomond jerked his body and the blade flashed out, slashing the demon across its throat.

The wound shone from within, a blazing orange, emanating an audible hiss as it steamed. The demon screeched, backing away, dropping Tolomond. It back-flipped into the shadows.

Tolomond grabbed his sword and readied himself, his three-pronged hook blade hanging from the chain clasped in his blood-drenched left hand. The hook blade had been forged to bear a sculpted resemblance to roaring flame, but something about its shimmer brought to mind alchemy, smoky mysticism—as if it were less tangible metal and more genuine flame in a silver cage.

Osesoc'ex-calea burst from its hiding place, a blur, but much larger than it had been a moment ago—a spiraling bundle of whipping, limber ligaments and spiky, bony, blade-like protrusions. It collided with Tolomond, smashing him through a solid stone wall.

The candle fell from the ledge on which it had been set. As soon as it struck the floor, the flame was snuffed and Alina was engulfed in darkness.

She'd snapped the wicker armrest, freeing her right arm. Now she busied herself tearing at the knots around her ankles. Hard work when the only light source was intermittent: the clash of steel against demonic tooth and claw, and the sparkle of Tolomond's strange chain-weapon.

Alina had to hurry: no matter who won the fight, the victor would want her dead.

Head ringing from Tolomond's beatings, she could hardly stand for the pins and needles in her legs. The stinging graduated to legitimate pain as the blood rushed back into her appendages.

How long had she been kept down here?

And where *was* here?

Blind, she fished for the overturned candle. When her fingers brushed against the wax, she muttered a few words and the wick sprouted a new flame.

Holding it up, she used the dim light to guide her way forward, forcing herself to take care. Who knew what kind of pitfalls or dangers might lie ahead if this was Tolomond's basement or something? She wouldn't put anything past the likes of him.

After a few minutes of hurrying away from the deathmatch, she could only faintly hear the screams, thumps, and crashes.

Her ears pricked at the gurgling of water nearby. The candlelight revealed a gutter on the right side of this passageway.

With no better plan springing to mind, she decided to follow the flow. Eventually it would have to lead her out of this place and, hopefully, to a sewer grate.

Her soft orange light drifted over slime-slick bricks. At regular intervals, there were white bricks among the red, the white ones bearing strange markings. They were not words in any language she knew or recognized, but clearly these symbols had deliberately been carved as some sort of marker.

When Alina's boot crushed something slim and brittle, she looked down to find a bone split by her heel. A human bone.

"A mausoleum," she whispered, seeing now that, a few inches higher than she'd been looking, there were row after row of skulls set into the wall. Recalling what few facts she knew of Tolomond, she assumed she must be inside The Sanctum's Undercroft, where they buried their saints and martyrs.

Some of the skulls were missing teeth, or had been cracked or caved-in. A few had been charred or warped—possibly by a magically concussive blast (Alina had seen a special about thaumaturgical force trauma on the Watchbox once).

If she was in the Undercroft, then that meant that above her was The Sanctum proper. And all of Tolomond's buddies. Seeing as she most definitely was not anxious to meet anyone *else* like Tolomond, going up for sure was not an option.

Follow the water. Down and out.

There were too many parallel paths and intersections to choose from; the place was a maze that put all others to shame, a web of carved tunnels to house the faithful dead; an inverted monument in memory of the nameless thousands who'd pledged their bodies and souls to The Author. Each of the countless marker-stones had been lovingly and attentively etched with complex and, to Alina, gibberish symbols. Clearly, every inch of this underground labyrinth had been designed with patience and devotion.

Each potential new path was identical to the last, Alina began to despair that she'd never get out. As much as she could, she ignored these doubts, batted away the inner monologue telling her she'd made a mistake, that the gutter would only lead her deeper into oblivion.

She kept on walking.

Maybe it was the exhaustion, the dehydration, but she could've sworn that she saw a cat up ahead. There it was, scampering at the edge of the shadows cast by her candle's flame. Whether the playful flick of its tail was real or an inside joke between her tired eyes and mind, she couldn't be sure. Nor did she know how long she walked. It felt like hours.

Yet, her candle hadn't burned much lower by the time she saw a glimmer up ahead. Like light reflected by water.

Stifling her impulse to make a mad dash for the light, she still picked up her pace.

There was indeed a pool up ahead, and the sound of rushing water was much louder down here. Maybe that was a good sign. (She wasn't a sanitation expert, so she could only guess.)

On the way, something sticky and furry bashed into her shin and squeaked. Thinking she'd stepped on the cat, her immediate response was to feel awful. But there almost certainly was no cat down here. Then her overheated brain recognized the agitated squeak for what it really was.

Under normal circumstances, she actually liked rats a lot, but literally bumping into a wild one—alone, in near-total darkness—after everything she'd gone through? Too much.

She spun around, slipping as she did, and skidded into the gutter on her right. The slope was much steeper here than she'd thought; the force of the current pulled her down into the swirling pool and sucked her under.

Worst water park ever.

She tried to escape the flow but was dragged headfirst down a long chute. Falling, rolling. Water in her ears, her nose. Her eyes stung, her lungs burned, and she continued to accelerate, sliding, sliding, until she hit an incline.

Blinded by her sudden immersion in sunlight, water drops all around her blazing like tiny suns, she flipped over a ledge and was flung into the air. She spun like a top down another waterfall, yelling as she fell those last ten feet.

With a teeth-cracking splash, she landed in a pool. Kicking and sputtering, she touched the bottom with her heels and pushed off. Cresting the surface, she gasped for air.

And she found herself staring down the length of a high-powered pulse rifle's ominously humming barrel. The Authority Enforcer on its other end glared at her.

Coughing, she slowly raised her hands.

33

JUST HER LUCK. HAVING escaped one interrogation just to fall face-first into another, Alina listened to the rhythmic beeping of the heart monitor. One of the nearby machines was emitting a Niima-nullifying pulse; she could feel its effects like a physical force, a weight dropped on her chest.

She'd been handcuffed to the metal siderail of a hospital bed, a flimsy, threadbare sheet rumpled over her legs. One of her eyelids was swollen, sore, and twitching. A cut on her lip had scabbed over. Bruises on her back, wrists, and ankles—the results of being tied up, running, falling, and all the other traumas of the past few days.

During the entire admission process, she'd been cuffed and under heavily armed guard. The nurse examining her hadn't bothered to hide the look of horror on his face as he tore up cotton balls and sponges in the attempt to clean her graying, spiky arms. Finally, he gave up and simply bandaged them, sighing with relief as he left.

They'd drugged her; the sedatives made it hard to think. Counting the minutes as they crept by, she'd spent a long time alone.

Her thoughts had refocused eventually, her perception sharpening. But her body had remained weak, putting her totally at the mercy of the man who'd entered and seated himself beside her bed, between the devices measuring her vitals.

Detective Ding sucked on his teeth, flicking a holographic pen against the holographic display of a rap sheet. The holopen left little holo-dots on the projection.

From Alina's perspective, all the letters on the rap sheet were backwards, but she could see clearly enough the picture at the center of all the information—her mirrored face, scowling at the camera.

Having no desire to discuss any of her business with this pinkojack, Alina said, slurring her words a little, "You've taken all these precautions to keep me here. Did you at least get the guy who kidnapped me?"

"And who would that be?" said the detective.

"Tolomond Stayd. Big dude with a bigger sword? Crisscrossing scars like he got in an argument with a woodchipper? Rage issues? He's a Sanctumite. I was running from him when your pals caught me and brought me here."

"We're not here to talk about who you may or may not have been fraternizing with."

"Fraternizing?" Alina said, wrist straining against the handcuffs.

"Keep yourself in check, there. I have the power to make you much less comfortable."

Alina took a breath.

"That's better. So," said the detective, leaning back. "Alina Z. K'vich. Resident of Truct, Torvir Province. Age seventeen. 5'11", only child, high school drop-out—excuse *me*—middle school drop-out." He looked up at her. "Care to comment?"

"No. So far you're doing a fine job, officer."

He clicked his tongue. "That's *detective*." Inspecting the file again, he continued, "No social media presence. No friends to speak of. No credit cards. One bank account, local, and in good standing until recently. And no criminal record. Not one fight or childish prank. No hijinks whatsoever."

"I've tried my utmost to avoid jinking any hi's."

"Glad to hear it. And, on paper, you're almost the model Asset, really. Except, your behavior over the past week has been a bit, shall we say, suspicious."

"How so?"

"I'm glad you asked." His finger flicked across the projection, enlarging the image of her local branch of Geldwerp Community Bank. "Closing out your checking account." He tapped another box and a picture of her at a kiosk at Gladjaw Junction popped up. "Buying a one-way ticket to The Capital." Then, again, a high definition shot of her face. He zoomed in until you could see every pore, focusing on her eyes. "The fact that you claim to be an Aelfraver, but you have no discernible ties to anyone other than your grandfather—who's in the wind, by the way, completely unreachable. Well, maybe you're beginning to understand why I'm somewhat perplexed."

"I can explain all that. Like, pretty easily."

"Please." His lips smiled, but his eyes flared with smoldering disgust. "Please, do tell."

"When Dimas, my grandfather, was declared legally dead, I was left with nothing but bills. I emptied my account when I heard about the open contract on the Bane of New El. Figured the Rave was my last chance. That one-way ticket was all I could afford, *detective*. And I don't 'claim' to be an Aelfraver—I am one. Like my Tahtoh before me."

"Except you aren't." He held between two fingers a pair of ID cards, which he flicked at her. "You'll recognize that first one as the forgery you paid to have made. It's a pretty good one, I must admit. There can't be *too* many individuals in a backwater hole like Truct who could have accomplished that job. Don't worry, we'll be making inquiries." He cleared his throat, picked up a glass of water from the counter behind him, drank. "As for that second card, unless you and Baraam bol-Talanai are secretly the same person, I'm going to go out on a limb and guess you stole that Raver-S license off him. The one he reported missing a couple of days ago. Am I right so far?"

"Lawyer."

"What?"

"I want to speak to a lawyer."

"How cute. Firstly, you couldn't afford one. Secondly, you *actually* think you get a lawyer? You, a seditionist?"

"What?"

"Oh, cut the crap, Alina. I know about your parents. It's a matter of record. We have a file on them going back to the '70s, when they were a pair of dopey, naïve teenagers. They had direct ties to anarchist groups throughout El, and indirect connections with foreign governments. Including Ozar. You mean to tell me you had no idea?"

Alina was speechless. She curled a strand of her hair behind her ear, her knuckles brushing up against the lobe. She noticed her earrings and studs had been removed.

Ding shook his head. "A criminal like you thought you could escape our notice, as brazen as you are? You're just as shortsighted as good old mama Zatalena and papa… Yurgi—Yorgoosh."

Alina snapped, "It's Yurgeius. 'Yoor-gey-oosh.'"

"Yeah, yeah," said Ding. "So, what made you do it? Forge the Raver-X license, steal from the number-one-rated Raver in the country? Why, Plutonia help me, did you think you could get away with it, huh?"

"I told you already. Were you not paying attention?"

"Watch your tone, young lady." He waggled his finger. "I say the word, you go into a holding cell until we decide what to do with you. If there's a trial—if—it could be a long time coming. One guy we've had locked up for so long I honestly can't remember what he even did."

"That's cool. No wonder everyone loves The Authority so much."

Grinning, Ding rubbed his hands together. "There's that little anarchist I knew was in you. We've made so much progress already. Let's keep this wonderful momentum going by you telling me who your accomplices are."

Scrunching up her face, Alina pretended to think for a moment. "Baraam bol-Talanai."

Ding glowered at her.

"I'm serious. It's all an elaborate front. He hired me to throw you off his trail. He's trying to take down the government. The man's crazy. Used to run his mouth all the time about how he hated The Authority and the Consul and everything that had anything to do with New El."

Stowing his tablet inside a black leather case, Ding said, "I can see you aren't ready to fully cooperate, so I'll be recommending you for our *enhanced* interrogation program. As soon as you're well enough to be discharged from this hospital, you belong to me. And I'm betting that, if you give me a day or two, I'll have you singing all sorts of interesting names." Grinning now, he added, "And, rest assured, we *have* made a note of the bizarre infection eating away at your arms."

Alina gritted her teeth.

"When the lab gets back to us with the test results, we'll know exactly what we're dealing with—what messed up disease you brought into our fair city." He clicked his tongue. "I must say, it's not often that one twerpy little Terrie represents so many risks to the public all at once." He ticked off his fingers as he said, "Fugitive. Forger. Anarchist. Dissident. Biohazard. What more will we uncover by digging through that thick head of yours? I, personally, can hardly wait to find out. In the meantime, we'll keep you where you belong—quarantined." He got up. "For your own sake, consider being more forthright when I come back. The associates I'll be bringing in are far less compassionate than me."

As he exited the room, Alina asked, "Do I at least get a phone call?"

He laughed his way out.

Handcuffed as she was, and probably being watched by The Authority even then, Alina carefully thought about her next move. The clock on the wall told her it was only 9:30 at night. Even with all that had happened, it had only been a few hours since Tolomond had abducted her.

Which meant she had, give or take, twelve hours before all Terrie Aelfravers would be required to leave The Capital. Merely half a day to catch up with Ordin, come up with a plan to deal with the Bane of New El, and execute said plan.

First of all, though, she'd have to escape this hospital.

She had one thing going for her: The Authority, obnoxious as they were, were fundamentally lazy. It was a byproduct of their corruption. They cared most of all about making problems go away. That's what all the hoods and punks always talked about on the Aetherthreads: the Enforcers only bothered about you if you were the one causing their headache. So, one way to get out of hot water was to erase a problem bigger than you were. In other words, if Alina could somehow deal with the Bane, maybe they'd drop the charges against her.

Hah. Maybe.

One thing was for certain: Baraam would never help her out of this. He was probably just outside right now, making sure Ding's people kept her in custody. If he even knew or cared where she was.

She'd messed up by telling Detective Ding that this had all been Baraam's idea—an unbelievable lie. If she'd played that game a bit more cleverly, she might've been able to fake her way into some kind of plea deal. But that option was out the window.

Too bad *she* couldn't leave that way. Even from her vantage point, she could see that they'd put her on the third or fourth floor.

Completely at a loss, she just sat there for way too long.

What could she do—she, by herself, exhausted, low on Niima—against a squad of Authority goons with guns and way too much time on their hands? Besides, the cuffs binding her to the hospital bed were of the Niima-suppressing variety. And there was also that Niima-nullifier module installed in one of the devices in the room. Until she got out of there, she would effectively be paralyzed, and she would be paralyzed until she got out.

Stuck.

Even if she did escape, there'd be some fanatic sword-swinger waiting for her. And, even if she survived *that*, she'd have to contend with the Bane of New El.

Hells, she'd almost died today. Maybe she should accept defeat. Go home, hand her keys over to the Mrs. Qamasque, and watch Baraam waltz in and destroy The School.

Tears in her eyes again, the acid boiling up from the pit of her stomach, she screamed. Wordless. Long. Loud.

She'd tried and tried and tried, given it everything. She'd spent all her might fighting.

Had she really come all this way just to fail?

She screamed again, jaw taut and aching, shoulders twisting, wrist pulling at the cuffs.

An officer (not Ding) threw open the door, looking half-worried and half-enraged, and told her to shut her mouth. But his words were drowned out by a *third* scream, a much, much louder one than any Alina could have produced—a keening roar that rattled the floor and walls of the whole building. It sounded like the recording of a freight-train's klaxon but sped up and warped.

All the machines attached to Alina suddenly switched off, as did the fluorescents. The only light now came from the street lamps outside.

The Enforcer looked to the dark-screen monitors, to the shaking walls, to Alina. He shouted at her, shouted at the top of his lungs and still was barely heard, "Are you doing this?"

Alina clamped her lips shut, shaking her head.

When the noise stopped, her ears ringing, Alina reminded him, "You have a magic dampener on me."

He held his wrist-watch-looking communicator up to his mouth and said, "Sir, lights are out. You having the same trouble? Sir?"

There was no response. He ogled the device with disgust. His eyes darted back and forth from Alina to the door.

"Stay here," he said.

He was halfway down the hall before Alina could retort, "Where would I even go?"

Over the next few minutes, Alina craned her neck this way and that, trying to see anything at all of what was happening outside.

Someone cleared her throat.

Alina's neck snapped around just in time to catch the de-cloaking of a small, barefooted figure; starting with her toes and ending with the top of her capped head, in a wave of pixelated blue light, she appeared at the foot of the bed. Where there had been nothing but air, now there stood Cho.

"Invisibility, huh?" said Alina. "What can't you do?"

Cho shrugged. She gestured at the room. "Nice work."

"What?"

"I leave you alone for five seconds and, boom, you're arrested. Dunno if you noticed, but there are, like, a ton of jacks out there."

"What? All for little old me?"

"No. There's a riot happening. Pretty close by, too. Were you asleep or something?"

"Yeah—well, more like knocked out. I got punked by that chump Tolomond. Speaking of, where's Mezami?"

Cho flicked her head back toward the hall. "Getting me a soda."

The Pyct flew in, then, hauling a pair of cans larger than he was, one in each hand. "Favorite, yours: Not know, I. Chose prettiest color: I."

Holding out a hand to accept the red can, Cho said, "Thanks, Mezzy." She opened it with a pop and guzzled it dry. Tossing the can over her shoulder, she burped a warbling burp for three whole seconds before telling Alina, "You said some really stupid stuff, you know that, right?"

Cheeks burning, Alina nodded. "I know. I'm sorry. I didn't mean any of it. I was a real pile of garbage. And I don't even have anything to show for it."

"What do you mean?"

"Just look at me. Chained to a bed, bloody. I'm probably gonna end up in prison, or a Zinoklese labor camp. It's over, Cho. I really, really screwed up."

"Ain't that the truth." She plucked the other soda Mezami had brought in, cracked it open, and sipped, grunting with satisfaction. "But you're not done for yet. Mezzy?"

Mezami landed next to Alina's left wrist and grabbed the handcuffs. He bit into the metal chain, snapping it as easily as a potato chip.

Freed, Alina lifted her hand, flexed her fingers. "I thought you hated me."

"You still majorly suck in my book, but—being the gracious dame that I am—I'm willing to give you another chance. Under one condition. Well, two conditions."

"Okay…"

"Number one: you go get that monster you're after. And, two: I get fifty percent."

Unable to keep a straight face, Alina burst out laughing. "Fifty?"

"Hey, that's the deal. Take it or leave it. Mezzy can find another a pair of cuffs, put you right back where we found you."

Shaking her head, Alina said, "Oh my gods. Fine. Fifty it is. Really milking my gratitude for all it's worth."

"Oh, I haven't gotten to 'all it's worth,' but that'll have to wait. You got a Rave to get to."

"Have to find the Bane first."

"Didn't you see?" Cho pointed out the window. "It's right out there, in the sky. Not hiding at all anymore."

"Are you kidding me?" Alina flipped off the bed, pinching the rear flaps of her hospital gown together.

"No joke," said Cho.

"Giant crow: it," said Mezami, fluttering at ear-level between them.

"A giant crow? That's—" Alina's eyes went wide. The Talaganbubăk was known to take the form of a black-winged, titanic bird—Master of Dark Wings. She smiled despite herself, despite everything. "I was right. I figured out what that thing is."

"Great. Now what are you gonna do about it?" said Cho.

"Gotta get to Ordin's. I could use his help." She cleared her throat. "And I could use yours, too."

"Oh, yeah, we're so coming with you."

"You are?" said Alina, searching Cho's eyes. "Even after everything?"

"Of course, because that's the third part of the deal: we're busting you out of here so that you can chase your dream. And, with that crazy murderer after you, Mezami's sure to get a stab at revenge."

"Wait a sec. I'm bait? You're making me bait?"

Cho shook her head and looked away quickly. She was smirking.

"Eh, sure, why not? He's gonna come at me anyway. Backup might be nice for a change." Alina locked eyes with the Pyct. "I'm sorry," she said. "I made you a promise. And I'm ready to keep it."

"Help me: you," he said, offering his tiny paw. "Help you: I."

Alina enveloped his paw, wrist, and part of his forearm with her thumb and index finger, and they shook on it.

She turned to Cho. "Got any money for a cab?"

Cho snorted. "I'm always ready for a quick getaway." She tossed a plastic bag at Alina. "That's your stuff. Sorry I couldn't find your pack."

Catching the bag, Alina smiled. "Cho, you're amazing."

"I know." She smiled back. Sliding onto the edge of the bed, she pulled on a pair of bright orange shoes.

Alina threw on her clothes—which really, really obviously needed a wash by this point.

Then Cho said "You ready?"

Alina nodded.

"I'll go first."

Starting at the soles of Cho's new-new footwear and working its way up, the electric blue, pixelated wave passed over her, leaving her invisible to the naked eye.

Mezami flew up to the ceiling and began to crawl along it.

Alina followed. "How did you find me?"

"The patch you sewed into my jacket." Cho's voice floated through the hall. "Did you think I wouldn't notice? Mezami could smell you off it. Tracked the trail all the way here. He's so good at that." Pause. "This way."

Alina followed her voice as she continued, "You disappeared in that mountain-church-building with all the gray weirdos in it. I thought you were dead for sure. But we stuck around just in case. Then the jacks got there, pulled someone outta the water. Knew it had to be you. So, we followed. And here we are."

"Yeah," Alina said quietly to herself. "Here you are."

"Before you get all gushy on me, we didn't come back for you because we care about you or anything. We just figured you could use a hand. And looking at you and how badly you got your ass kicked without us, we were right."

Ever since she could remember, Alina had had to do everything for herself. For about ten years, she'd had her grandfather to guide her, true. But, often, he would leave, and he'd stay gone for a long time. And she'd cook, clean, stare at the walls, stand on one leg, train, run laps—do whatever she could to keep her mind and body occupied. Because it was just her, at The School, left to entertain herself.

Calthin would come by occasionally and pull her out of her silent sanctuary, have her join him on some ridiculous make-believe adventure. But then he'd go back to his family. His brother, his parents. And, as he got older, he spent more and more time minding the shop.

Though there were distractions from the stillness, in the end, Alina always returned to herself. Alone. At The School.

She had had plenty of time to teach herself the fundamentals of alchemy, the beginning-to-mid-level forms of various martial arts, the names, statistics, and habitats of a large number of Aelf species.

Whenever Tahtoh returned, he would bring a gang of new students, and they would come and go as they pleased, as would he. Sometimes she would train them in what she knew—if Tahtoh asked, and if they didn't balk at the idea of being taught by a teenaged girl (which, sometimes, they did).

Over time, Tahtoh's absences got longer and longer, and even when he was around, he wasn't quite all there. Then, one day, he simply didn't come back. And that was when Alina's life-long fear was fully realized: she had never really had a friend or family member she could rely on.

Her parents—dead.

Her grandfather—disappeared and dead.

Calthin Amming—living his own interesting life, leaving her behind.

All Tahtoh's students—gone.

Baraam, whom she'd known since she was six or seven years old—even he wanted nothing to do with her. To him, she was an impossible screwup.

And, when Dimas K'vich hadn't returned, Alina knew Baraam must have been right about her. They'd all been right to leave because she was nothing but an abnormal, shadow-clinging geek. A curiosity. Good for the occasional visit. But not enough to be anyone's friend.

They didn't need her, so she didn't want them.

But Cho had come back. Mezami, too. They'd followed her. And no matter what callous words Cho draped over that action, Alina would always know that two people had *cared* enough to find her, to see her again. Even though it was hard. Even though she'd treated them like trash.

They'd come back.

Trailing behind invisible Cho, with Mezami scuttling overhead like a beetle, Alina kept a keen eye out for any signs of trouble. They passed by closed doors to private rooms, nurse stations, coffee dispensers, bathrooms, elevators. People were whispering or weeping inside, but no one tried to stop them. She was merely a blurry shape sneaking awkwardly through the darkness.

The lights never did switch on or even flicker. And it seemed The Authority had mobilized elsewhere, probably to investigate and deal with the cause of the commotion.

The giant crow. Alina shuddered. They had no idea what they were up against. The creature's disguise masked its true danger: although no one had noticed, it was the Bane that had been in control from the very beginning. It appeared only when, where, and how it wanted to. The fact that it had chosen to reveal itself now…

The Authority would think it some mindless beast, just another target to shoot down. The Talaganbubăk, however, had been living among the Elementals for some time now; it would know how they responded to a crisis.

It could anticipate their counterattacks.

Alina was quite familiar with the folk legends surrounding the Talaganbubăk's cunning. Before she was born, the creature had terrorized her home province. It was the bogeyman, the ghost story you told around a campfire as the witching hour neared. If you were wicked, lost, or afraid, the Talaganbubăk would come for you.

Night-wing. Corpse-eater. Child-stealer.

For generations, none of the inhabitants of the neighboring villages and towns—no matter how many pitchforks and torches and rifles and tracker dogs they had with them—had ever caught their monster off-guard. Until, that is, a young Dimas K'vich had hunted it down and destroyed it. That was the Rave that had made him famous throughout the nation.

But now, somehow, the Talaganbubăk had returned. The creature must have tricked Tahtoh, as it had all those who'd come before. Or, perhaps Tahtoh had only wounded it, driven it into sleeplike state—a coma—rather than kill it. However it had happened, after decades of slumber, the creature had awoken. And, by the sound of that terrible cry from earlier, it was enraged.

"I'm going to finish this. In the name of my grandfather," Alina muttered. And she silently swore that the world would remember her for it, for what she would accomplish tonight.

Cho opened and held the door to the stairwell. Her and Alina's footsteps echoed as they descended.

On the way down, Alina paused, remembered something important, and, with her pinky, tapped Mezami lightly on the shoulder.

"I owe you something, my friend." She pulled a squat glass vial from one of her secret inner jacket pockets. The purple liquid glistened, the flecks of gold floating within it sparkling in the fluorescent light. "*Chymaeric fortissimio*, commonly called 'Bull's Blood,' or just 'Bull.'"

Mezami crawled onto her shoulder, his glinting black eyes fixed upon the concoction.

"Down this now."

"Safe: it?"

"Safe?" Alina shook her head. "Oh, no, not in the slightest. But it'll blow the lid off your limits. More power'll rush through your veins than you'll know what to do with. Lasts a full day, too. You'll just have to sleep for a week after."

"Not need: you?"

"Not gonna lie, I'd been saving this for a rainy day. Like today. But—" She trailed off, beginning to reconsider her offer, so she quickly added, "Just take the stuff before I change my mind. Call it my way of apologizing—equalizing us again." She hesitated, but the words spilled out anyway, before she could catch them: "The guy you're going up against—you're gonna need some extra pip in your pop."

"Kingly gift: this."

"Don't mention it." She passed him the vial. "No, really, don't. I'll cry."

He drank up the Niima-charged liquid.

Before she could do anything more than flinch, she watched the Pyct twitch and spasm and drop the empty vial. The expensive, magically treated glass container shattered into a thousand pieces.

Mezami rolled around on her shoulder, nestled against her neck, as his body temperature spiked.

He'd be alright, but the process was going to suck. Poor guy.

With that, Alina had just one more Auggie at her disposal. The last of her grandfather's supernatural potions. She hoped it would be enough.

And she hoped what she'd given Mezami would be, too. Going up against Tolomond Stayd might just be a death sentence no matter how juiced the tiny Aelf was.

Exiting the stairwell, Cho and Alina peeked into the lobby—abandoned wheelchairs, papers and folders scattered everywhere, but no sign of people. Everyone must have left in a hurry.

Raised voices coming from a reinforced door opposite the stairwell gave Alina pause. So, that's where all the docs and nurses and important patients were. A bunker of some sort. Alina scoffed. They were all just chilling in there while she and the other dead weight had been left to their fates.

The Enforcer tasked with guarding her was nowhere to be found, either. Maybe he'd skipped into the bunker, too.

Well, as troubling as it was to think about all those who might have been abandoned on the upper floors, it certainly worked in Alina's favor that she and Cho encountered no resistance. Also helpful: likely because of an emergency failsafe to prevent anyone from being locked in the building during an earthquake or fire, the automatic doors to the outside had jammed in their open position.

The two young women (with the Pyct riding on Alina's palm) left the hospital.

A shadow passed over the moon as Alina looked to the sky. At first, she thought it might be the crow, but it was a stormfront. An angry, swollen, dark mass of cloud that—with a flash of lightning—opened.

It began to rain as if, after three-and-a-half thousand years, the heavens had determined to flood New El and, at last, drag it back down to earth.

A few minutes later, they were outside, circling the building. Alina felt either nauseous or hungry, hard to tell which. She shrugged the feeling off, scratching at the bandages on her arms

A chunk of the hospital's façade was being renovated; there were yellow cones everywhere, flashing yellow lights atop them; holographic messages snaked sharply through the air between them, reading, "CAUTION – STAND CLEAR – NO ENTRY BEYOND THIS POINT." From high above, two spotlights weaved across the streets, passing over rooftops and terraces, cutting through alleys and playgrounds.

A rumbling metallic cry rattled the windows behind Alina, and she looked up to behold H'ranajaan, The Authority's "dragon," soaring through the skies on a search-and-destroy mission. Deployed to annihilate the threat against New El.

That was one fight that Alina wanted to be *nowhere near* once it got underway. The outcome was anything but certain, yet one thing she knew for sure was that those two behemoths battling it out would cause a whole lot of collateral damage. And she had no plans to become just another statistic.

After moving to the right side of the hospital, she and Cho jaywalked across the street. Alina's first concern was putting distance between themselves and Detective Ding and all those Authority boots.

Alina, however, was experiencing some problems: her mind had slowed, her thoughts grinding their way through her brain; and there was this persistent itch at the base of her skull and in the meat of her forearms and under her shoulder blades.

She began to shiver. At first, she thought she was only cold because of the rain. But then she got dizzy, and Cho grabbed her sleeve and gave it a tug.

"Alina, your face is—" Cho was clearly frightened. "It's really red. Like, purple-red."

Through chattering teeth, Alina told her, "I'm f-fine." Clenching her fist, with her other hand she touched her forehead. Scalding hot.

Mezami poked his head up and said, "Burning: skin, yours." Cho moved him to her own shoulder.

Cho's jaw dropped. "The rain! It's evaporating." She squinted at Alina, leaning in. "Before it's even touching you."

Cho was saying something else, but Alina missed whatever it was as she spun on her heels, slapped her palm against the nearest wall, and proceeded to be sick all over the sidewalk.

What came out, it was black again.

"Ugh, are you sure you—"

The rain washed away the mess. Alina held her face up to the deluge. Closed her eyes a moment.

She teetered on her feet, but said, "Just allergic to one of the meds they gave me, I think." She leaned against a lamppost, half saying, half groaning, "Say, d'you think you could call a cab?"

Looking really worried, Cho shook her head. "The news said only The Authority would be allowed to drive now. Until the monster's killed."

"No cabs? No cars?"

"Right. I'm sorry. Maybe we—"

"Then what's that coming towards us?" Alina raised a limp finger.

Cho turned and shouted as a silver hovercraft sped straight toward them, thrusters kicking in at the last possible second to spin the vehicle sideways. The gleaming bullet-shaped car swerved around them, narrowly missing Cho, and came to a full stop.

Its vanity plate read, "MAG!CM4N."

The passenger-side door, which was closest to them, popped open, gliding upward with a mechanical fizzle. The driver leaned over, reaching out to them.

"Get in," said Ordin.

34

IN THEIR DECADES AND centuries of fitful sleep, the stacks and stacks of bodies buried and bricked-in beneath The Sanctum were accustomed to darkness. They were used to silence, too. The twin calms of quiet and sightlessness were interrupted, however, by the life-or-death struggle underway.

The walls had been scarred by sword-strike and claw-drag, markings etched like arrows, pointing the way to a pair of figures, one of whom was a man—a small thing compared to the heaving, screeching, sweating, fleshy bulk that snapped and swiped at him. With each clash of bone and blade, a spark speared the sweet and soothing mist of death that had settled like dust upon fungus-blotched stones.

Pinned down by six of the demon's barbed and segmented pincers, Tolomond dug his heels into its triangular maw, along whose oozing folds ran rows of squat, ridged fangs. Its long red tongue lashed at him, and every time the muscle raked across his flesh, the cuts it left behind burned.

His sword was buried in the fleshy underbelly of this spider-crab-worm-like monstrosity. It did not seem too bothered by this fact.

"Back to hell," Tolomond shouted, kicking it in the forehead, the fang, the shoulder joint.

“Hell is a mindset,” said a mocking voice, far too calm and jovial to reasonably have belonged to this freakish thing. But, all the same, it had to have been the demon who’d telepathically communicated the comeback: there was no one else down here. No one but the innumerable departed saints and martyrs of The Sanctum.

Tolomond could feel their unseeing eyes upon him, boring into him from beyond the grave, from the blissful plains of Nehalennia. Watching. Judging him.

Rage coursed through him—rage that such an abomination had been allowed to desecrate this holy tomb. The girl, Alina, had summoned this evil, true, but it was he, Tolomond, who had suffered it to pass into these halls. It was he who must atone.

With blood, he would purify the souls of Ordin and Alina both, but first he must defeat this abomination. And, for that to happen, a sacrifice was necessary.

He released one of the spiky shoulders he’d been pushing against, allowing the attached pincer to pierce his hip. But, in doing so, the long red tongue flitted forward, exposed. Tolomond grabbed onto its slippery, sinewy length and twisted and pulled with every ounce of strength left in him.

As he tore at it, he heard a hissing sound, like rice falling from a plastic bag but much louder. Then, a crackle, like bones crunching or wood splintering. Finally, a pop—and the tongue came free.

Drenched in black and gray fluids, Tolomond tossed the organ aside and roared. The demon spasmed and screeched, releasing him, retreating.

Tolomond did not let up, not even for an instant. He grasped the chain fused to his arm bone, the glowing flame-shaped hook-blade at its end scraping along the stone floor. Spinning it at his side, he spoke a quick prayer to The Author. Then he threw his hand forward, and the blade shot out, straight and true, embedding itself in the demon’s flesh. He thrust the hook upward, carving the fiend from the inside out.

As it fell to the ground, Tolomond ran up, his clenched fist radiating silver light, and pressed his palm and the hook-blade into the creature’s maw.

It shrieked, sputtering, spitting, hacking up black goop. The hideous cry was cut short.

It lay still.

The radiant light grew in intensity, engulfing the demon, whose flesh incinerated before Tolomond's widening eyes.

The thing burned away, the searing, white-hot light slowly fading to a dull red. Black flakes of charred flesh wafted down the sewer tunnels until there remained no evidence that the demon had ever existed at all.

"As it was Written," said Tolomond solemnly.

He fell to his knees, partly from exhaustion, partly from rapture.

Truly, by the will of The Author, nothing was impossible.

He prayed, there, alone, in the Undercroft.

After an unknowable length of time, he heard voices coming from behind him. He opened his eyes, stood, and turned to face the new arrivals. Seven men, six of them carrying torches.

He fell to his knees again just as soon as he saw who headed the group.

"My Lord Hierophant," said Tolomond, averting his gaze.

"Get up," said The Living Voice of The Author. "Look at me."

Six Sanctumites flanked Hierophant Pontifex Ridect—a man in his fifties, tall, thin, sickle-nosed, balding, but whose upright posture emanated righteous strength. The others were initiates, in their gray tunics. Among them was Tarus, who grinned to himself.

"Whatever are we going to do with you, Tolomond Stayd?" said Ridect, speaking the name with obvious distaste.

Tolomond's stomach dropped at the sight of how furious this great shepherd was with him. "Lord, what have I done to anger you?"

"Damn my eyes for gazing upon you, where even to begin? You murder and instigate wantonly, charging into danger and intrigue like a babe, blind to all peril. You're far more beast than man, you fool." The Hierophant glowered down the length of his hooked nose. "Worse than your having embarrassed us is your jeopardizing our mission, our holiest work. And you have done so for the very last time. We set out to reshape the world in The Author's beauteous image, and we can afford no more missteps from the likes of *you*." Ridect sighed a practiced, cutting sigh, one he'd let slip many times before. It had been his primary method of communicating with Tolomond, ever since Tolomond could remember. "It is only through our connections with the Walazzin and the Xaveyr Families that we have, thus far, managed to keep you out of the hands of The Authority. Even now, the agents of the worldly powers swarm our Sanctum like plague-flies, buzzing ceaselessly. They want you, Tolomond Stayd. But we cannot afford to let you fall into their hands. Not knowing what you know, or having acted as you have."

"All I did, I did in service to The Author," Tolomond protested, voice cracking a little. He winced; at least one of his ribs was broken. "Under your guidance. By your directive."

"It is not what you've done," said Tarus, stepping forward, arms crossed and hidden in the folds of his gray cloak. "What offends is the manner in which you've acted."

Ridect's jaw muscle spasmed. "Tarus speaks truth. You were a wastrel when we found you; you are a wastrel still. You act as a dog, with no mind of your own. This served our purposes for a time—we would point, and you would attack, like the servile hound you are. But, now, it seems you've gone rabid. Your public displays of violence against the heretics Ugarda Pankrish and Ordin Ivoir, not to mention the K'vich girl—You have made an impossible mess of things, my child. And we have never been more disappointed in anyone."

"But Pankrish is dead," Tolomond shouted, tasting blood on his tongue.

"That's all well and good," said Tarus, matching his volume. "But now you've drawn The Authority's eye to the Sanctum. A sacrifice is necessary to preserve the secrecy of our designs."

"I am speaking to the Hierophant, not to you, Tarus," snapped Tolomond.

"Tarus has served us far more consistently and reliably than you, errant boy. It was he who brought your slipping faculties to our attention. Oh, how far you have fallen. The spectacular manner in which you failed to end the lives of the Ivoir scion and the Dreamer Witch is but the latest piece of evidence that has shown me, beyond the shadow of a doubt, that you have outlasted your usefulness. Our God does not reward halfwits capable only of half-measures." The Hierophant grasped Tolomond by the shoulders, pausing for the span of a breath. Then, to his entourage, he said, "Take him to the Pit. One hundred weeks of Penitence and Reflection will do his soul good. In the Year of our Lord 3504, we will reassess his case. So be it."

"So be it," said Tarus.

"So be it," echoed the others.

"Father," said Tolomond, tremblingly reaching for the skirts of Ridect's robes. "Father, *please*."

The Hierophant leaned in, whispering in his ear, "No son of mine could be so unworthy." And he, with three of the initiates, left the way they'd come.

Tolomond stared in disbelief as the Hierophant, haloed by torchlight, disappeared from his sight.

Tarus and two others stood over him. Roughly, they lifted him. Tarus's soft hands pushed him between the shoulder blades. Away from Pontifex Ridect.

Tears falling from his unblinking eyes, Tolomond allowed himself to be led deeper into the sewers, to the secret door that opened into the Pit. Perhaps that was where he belonged, after all—a dank cell where men went to starve, whip, and shame themselves into humility. Some happy few were remade, the stories of their lives rewritten in solitude and darkness. Most merely went mad and took their own lives.

He'd failed his father. He deserved this.

But then Tarus said something that shook him from his stupor: "I always knew this day would come."

"Always… knew…?" Tolomond repeated dumbly. His arms that had hung limp at his sides now twitched. He began to long for the grip of Rhetoric. *No,* he thought. *I must abstain. Violence is what brought me here.*

You are wrong, my child, said the voice.

That voice…

"Who are you?" Tolomond demanded.

You know. You have always known. Yet, if you must hear the Word in order to believe, then listen well: I am He Who Wrote the First and Final Words. I am Creator and Destroyer. You and all the world are merely a song, a clipping of poetry I whispered to Myself in passing. I am The Lord, Thy God. Do you dare disbelieve?

"I believe," Tolomond shouted into the dark. "I have always believed. I am Yours."

The pair of initiates gripping him tensed. "What's wrong with him, Tarus?"

"He's gone completely, utterly, stark-raving mad. Just as I'd suspected he one day would."

Tolomond Stayd.

"Yes, Lord?" said Tolomond.

I have a new charge for you. You, who burn so brightly, have been deceived. You beautiful thing, you have unknowingly served a great evil these many long years.

"Tell me its name and I will end it."

Not 'it,' Tolomond. 'Who.' It is your false Brother Tarus you must destroy. He is in league with the Silent Enemy, a liar and a demon wearing the skin of a man. End his life and be free. Serve your true purpose. Embrace Me, for I am your destiny.

"Stayd," said Tarus, shoving Tolomond by the chest.

Jostled, Tolomond stumbled backward a few steps. The initiates inched away from him.

"Tolomond!' Tarus threw a punch.

Tolomond's hand snapped up. He caught Tarus's fist and twisted, shattering multiple bones in his wrist.

Howling in pain, Tarus leapt backward. The other two initiates advanced.

Rearing back, pushing off his heels and utilizing all his bodyweight, Tolomond slapped the first one right on the chin, dropping him like a bundle of socks. The second one, Tolomond grabbed by his inseam and neck, swinging him horizontally overhead, slamming him against the wall. He, too, fell to the ground and lay still.

Tarus clutched his destroyed hand to his chest, holding the other out. "Stay back. Unclean. Blasphemer. The Author will protect me, for I have always been His most faithful servant."

Grabbing him by the face and squeezing, Tolomond said, "It was The Author who told me what you really are."

He left Tarus a ruined husk leaning against a mound of broken bricks.

From one of the other two dead men, he retrieved Rhetoric, his holy weapon.

Tolomond, said The Author, the soundless words rattling the man's breastbone.

"Yes, Lord?"

I have one more task for you. The one you were given but have yet to complete.

"I am Yours to command, now and forever."

The Hierophant was deceived, as you were, by the wretch Tarus. Tarus is dead, and this is a very good thing. But to reclaim your father's trust, you must prove yourself. Three more lives remain for the taking.

"The witch."

Yes. And?

"The girl."

And first of all?

"Ordin Ivoir."

35

FOR EIGHTEEN LONG MINUTES, they rode in silence. Ordin gripped the steering column with both hands, occasionally manhandling the manual gearshift, but never taking his eyes off the road.

Every so often, he'd open his mouth, hesitate, say nothing.

He'd switched his AI copilot off, doing eighty miles per hour in a forty-five zone. As they flashed past, beams of amber streetlamp light illuminated his grim expression. Tonight, he had no product in his wavy hair, which was parted at the middle and hung down to his chin.

As the nausea finally began to lessen, Alina broke the silence. "How did you find me?"

"I slipped a tracker onto the base of the bottle of antiseptic I gave you."

"Oh. Didn't trust me?" she laughed weakly.

"Hah," said Ordin. Glancing at the rearview mirror, he added, "You can come out, whoever or whatever you are. My car's equipped with a biometric scanner. I only see three lifeforms in here, but I know there are four."

Cho pointed at herself, pretending to be confused. "Me?"

With a sigh, Ordin raised his black-leather-gloved hand and a few indigo sparks flared from his fingers. "I don't have to see you to paralyze you. This is your final warning."

Mezami hopped out of Cho's jacket pocket, his hands up. "Me shoot: not, you."

To Alina, Ordin said, "Please tell me you didn't know about that thing."

She didn't answer.

"I can't *believe* you. What are you doing with a Pyct in your care? And, look at you. You look horrible."

"Thanks for that," said Alina.

"That is *not* how I—You know what I meant, damn it. Stitcher, tell me what's happening."

She pulled the Lorestone out of her bag at her feet. Holding it up, she said, "I know what we're hunting."

"Where the blazes did you get that?"

"No time to explain. There's only a few hours left before all the Ravers get kicked out of town."

"Only the Landsider ones," Ordin corrected.

"Yeah, and I can't afford that," snapped Alina.

Ordin vigorously shook his head, his leather gloves squeaking as he strangled the steering column. "It's over. The Bane of New El is in the skies for all to see. This is far beyond us and The Gild now. The Authority will handle it."

"You honestly think they *can*? Really?"

"With all the firepower at their disposal? Yes, I do. It's unfortunate, sure. They'll level a few city blocks in the process, maybe, but no Aelf can withstand what's coming."

"An Ushum could."

Ordin smirked. "And that's what you think we are up against? A Dragon?"

"Not a Dragon, no. Something worse, though? *Yes.* I'm telling you, we're dealing with a creature as ancient as the Dragons, and probably more cunning. I think the Bane is a Demidivine."

"How perfectly ominous." Ordin snorted. "You forget that the Demidivines—if there are any left—have been pushed to the farthest, darkest corners of the world."

"What if the Bane's been biding its time for years—hells, maybe even centuries, I don't know. Think about it. Why is it back *now*? Why kill these *specific* people? We've been assuming it's like a wild animal. Hunting and hiding in panic, acting on instinct. But the Bane can *plot.* You have to have noticed that by now. It has a plan, and it didn't show itself until it was ready. Add to that its strange abilities, and—"

"Alright. Let's say I believe you. Enlighten me, then. What are *you* going to do about it that The Authority can't?"

"I don't think I appreciate your attitude, Ordin."

"That's all well and good, Stitcher—"

She tried to interrupt: "For the record, I know *exactly* what the Bane—"

"—but I don't believe I care," he said loudly. "You have consistently disregarded every piece of advice I've given you. You brought a mountain of trouble down on my head and my House. I hardly understand why I even came to collect you."

Alina crossed her arms, stomach acid boiling. She couldn't tell if she was sick or furious. Probably both. "Figured it was 'cause we're partners in this."

Laughing outright, Ordin said, "Oh, because you've certainly treated *me* like one."

"Yeah, okay, well what about that phony assignment you gave me? 'Hey, why don't you rifle through this box of old court dockets that have nothing to do with anything just so I can pretend I'm letting you be useful?' What was that all about, huh, Ordin? Wanna tell me, finally?"

"What are you implying?"

"You put me in a corner from the beginning. You never needed my help. The dinner, the Darkthreads, burying me in pointless paperwork—it was all to keep me tucked away. My question is 'why?' What were you getting out of it? What could you possibly have wanted with me?"

He fumed silently for a minute. Through his teeth: "You have no notion of what you're talking about."

"H-he's lying," Cho interjected. "His heartrate just shot way up."

Ordin glared over his shoulder at her. "And just who are *you*, eh?" He paused, looking her up and down, his eyes flashing ghostly white, and then he smirked. "Oh, that *is* interesting. A quick scan of the serial numbers on all those cybernetics of yours tells me you're no mere tramp. I misjudged you. Tell me, what's your name, little girl?"

Cho clamped her lips shut.

"Have it your way. I'm running the serials right now. I'll have my answer in about five minutes."

"Where are we going?" said Alina.

"My place. Where we'll stay until this storm has passed."

Alina stowed the Lorestone back in her pack. "No." She thumped the console in front of her, jostling the screen that showed the weather forecast. "Stop the car. Let us out. Now."

"Why don't you take a good look at yourself, there, Stitcher? You can barely hold your head up. Your eyes are dilated. Discolored skin, clammy to the touch. I'd guess you were concussed, but that doesn't explain the necrotic fluid oozing from your arms."

Alina glared at him. Gone was the by-turns charming and disarmingly awkward guy who'd given her glimpses of luxury and made larger-than-life promises; he'd been replaced by this rain-soaked, coldly furious, calculating, pale-faced Elemental. He'd become someone she couldn't recognize and didn't want to know.

"I don't know what you're talking about," she said.

"Enough." He tapped his brow. "These eyes can do a lot more than the ones I was born with. Infrared light, far-distance, the most microscopic facial tics—I can see everything. That's how I know there is something very wrong with your body, but I haven't been able to discern what it might be. So, what—were you cursed?"

"I—" Alina's growl faded to a low murmur. "I don't know. It started a few months ago. These weird little bumps. They looked like nothing. Then they started growing. Spreading. And—" She got angry again. "You don't really care. I'm just—what—a weird little pet to you, or something? You only wanna know because you're so arrogant you have to know everything."

"After all I've done for you." He grinded out a slow, humorless chuckle. "That's what you think of me."

"Stop the car, Ordin."

Looking straight ahead, dead-eyed, he said, "Or what? No, Stitcher, the only way you're leaving this car tonight is if you're entering my family's home."

"You're abducting me? And Cho and Mezami?"

"I am *trying* to keep you alive," he shouted, slapping the steering column. Taking a breath, he added, "Call it what you will."

"Ordin," said Alina, feeling the Niima flowing like a flood-fed river from her heart to her hands, "I'm warning you. Don't make me do something we'll both regret."

Holding the steering column with his knees, he peeled—finger by finger—the glove from his right hand. He reached for Alina's cheek with a tender deliberation. The gesture caught her off-guard, and before she could decide whether to lean into or shrink from it, his hand struck her like a pale five-headed snake. His digits latched onto her cheek, chin, and the tip of her nose almost magnetically.

She struggled to stay conscious, but the urge to close her eyes was overwhelming.

36

TOLOMOND WRENCHED THE PULSE rifle from the crying Authority agent lying prone next to his hovercycle. He checked the power cells on both weapon and bike. Each was half-full.

Plenty.

He kicked the Enforcer in the head. Then he straddled the hovercycle, hitting the ignition button, revving the engine.

And he peeled off into the night, just as it began to rain.

A cleansing downpour to wash away the night's sins.

37

ONCE AGAIN, ALINA STOOD before that familiar bathroom mirror, gray morning light filtering in through the half-drawn cheap plastic blinds on the window above the small tub. Steaming water ran down the grungy drain of the white porcelain sink. She seemed to be alone.

The mirror was fogged over. Pulling her sleeve over her palm-heel, she wiped the glass.

The face that stared back at her was her grandfather's. Tahtoh smiled, putting a finger to his lips. His eyes flashed gold.

It was her own face, then, gazing back at her. Those golden eyes, flecked with abyssal black.

The mirror's image changed again, revealing now the lighthouse in Ordin's corner of the Darkthreads—the Ordin Airy. Alina cocked her head, reached into the glass and *through it*, first with one arm and then the other. Her fingers clung to something on the other side. Pipes or rebar, it didn't matter. She gripped these and hauled herself through the mirror.

The touch of the glass was like ice, and it raked her flesh, each scrape oozing viscous, cloudy, gray fluid.

She crawled through a long dark tunnel, at the end of which was a light—the lighthouse's flame set behind a grille of black iron.

When she reached it, she clambered out of the hole and touched down onto the lighthouse's balcony.

His long cloak batted by the wind, Ordin was standing on the metal railing, balancing precariously, staring at her.

"Where is Cho? And Mezami?" said Alina.

"I won't hurt them. I'm not evil, despite what you've made yourself believe."

"Um." Alina spread her arms, spinning in a circle to indicate their surroundings. "You've trapped me here. Pretty sure you didn't pull that move from the Stand-up Guy's playbook."

"A necessary measure. I couldn't have you running off to face the Bane."

Alina kicked the railing, the metallic thrum reverberating. "Why?"

Knocked off-kilter by the vibrations, Ordin flailed his arms to steady himself. "Because I l—" He hopped off the railing. "Because I don't want to see you hurt."

"What you want out of this situation doesn't matter," she snapped. "If I don't clear this Rave, I'll lose everything. I need this."

As he spoke, Ordin drew nearer and nearer until his and Alina's faces were only a hand's width apart. "Is it the money? Well, then, you don't have to worry anymore. Stay here, in New El. With me."

She exhaled, closing her eyes.

"Of course, we'd have to put you to work as a servant. But only until my father passes away. Then I'll be the man of the house, and—"

Alina grimaced, pushing him away. "As much fun as that sounds, it's not about the *money*. If it was, I could've figured something out, lived in some other dumpy part of Truct. But, no, it was always about The School. I'm not ready to let it go, and I probably never will be. And I'm not going to let you or Baraam or even the Bane of New El stand in my way."

"But money would solve *all* your troubles! You could pay off your debts, refurbish." He threw his hands up. "Hells, I could help you *buy* Truct. It'd be no issue for me. If it's your school you want, I'll *give it* to you. I cannot understand why you won't accept my offer."

"I know you can't." She thumped her fist against his chest. "Try to hear me now: I don't want live my life in your debt because—well—it wouldn't be *my* life anymore. You'd always have this on me, always hold it over my head, even if you didn't think you were. And we'd both feel it. It would change who we are to each other."

"Would *I* really be such a bad creditor to have? I thought we—I just thought—"

"It's my business. My family. My mess to fix. A little help is fine, something I can accept. But—please get this through your head—I don't need to be saved or whatever. Not by you, not by anyone. You're not going to make me into a polished, shiny version of me you can approve of, no matter how hard you try. I've always done things my way, and I'm going to see this through. The School is all I have left. Don't make me *owe* it to you."

Ordin's nostril's flared. He wiped his reddish eyes with the back of his gloveless hand. Clearing his throat, he said, "The name on the deed isn't all-important, though. Even if you fail, and Baraam buys the property, he would let you visit any time you'd like. He's not interested in destroying you, Stitcher. The opposite, in fact."

Her wrists went numb, her stomach knotting. "Why are you saying this? How could you possibly know?"

A long silence.

"I'll tell you—everything there is to tell. But you have to promise that you will listen. Hear me out until the end. And, then, if you want nothing to do with me, I'll understand completely. Only, give me the chance."

Alina held her breath.

Ordin turned away, facing the artificial sun as it descended into the almost still waves. "I told you about my heart's oldest desire, to find the island. To see my friends again, or to confirm that I was simply out of my mind. One way or another, I have to know."

Jaw jutting, Alina said, slowly, "What does that have to do with me?"

"Two years ago, I theorized that maybe the island exists predominantly in my own mind. Or, at least, that its location can only be unlocked with a certain mind-state. A unique mental signature, if you will. That's why I have never been able to return—it was a boy who entered, and that boy lived and died on that island. He was part of me, and the loss of that love within himself destroyed him—destroyed a part of me. The part I *need.* The 'real' Ordin is a collection of so many shades of personality—"

"Yeah, you're a magical and special little boy, I get it."

"We're all that way, I realized. And it is this conclusion that led me to study a wholly unique branch of magic. It's similar, I think, to the power that originally unlocked the Darkthreads, but it differs in that it relies less on *physical* sub-universes than it does *metaphysical* ones."

"Fascinating as this is, could you summarize, maybe?"

"Even I can't yet understand what I've touched upon. But I know that the key to it all lies on that island that is simultaneously within and outside *me.* If I find it again, I'll be pioneering an entirely new field of the arcane."

"So," said Alina, crossing her arms, leaning back at the waist. "Let me see if I got it: the innocent, messed up, but still endearing story you told me, that's all out the window now. *Now* you only want to find this lost place—if it even exists—because it'll make you more powerful? Richer? Wrap another bimbo around your arm?"

He flinched. "When you put it that way… It's true, my original intentions were somewhat more innocent. But I'm not pursuing this only for personal gain. What I do, I do for my family and country."

"Oh, sure. Yeah, I get that. And if you get five hundred interviews and your face on all the billboards in the process, that's just a nice bonus, right?"

"Anything to help me one day be elected Consul."

"Hah!" Alina shouted. "There it is. But I still don't see how this—any of it—has anything to do with me and hunting down the Bane of New El? Newsflash: your city's gonna burn if you don't let me take a crack at it."

Ordin laughed. "And you accuse *me* of arrogance. You have an awfully favorable opinion of yourself. I would say look in a mirror, but you've already done so." He squinted at her, lips pursed. "Why is it that you keep going back to that moment, Alina K'vich? What happened there? Who hurt you?"

She charged forward, palms out, arms stiff, and shoved Ordin backward. He struck the railing and made a show of tumbling over it.

Alina rushed forward, yelling his name. He floated upward, grinning.

"So, you are capable of violence. Noted. But you forget: nothing can hurt me in this place, Alina."

"You don't get to call me that." She lunged for his neck, but he drifted backward, cackling. "Let me out of here!"

"I can't do that. Because, for my plans to come to fruition, I need access to the innermost vault of the Crystallarium. I need just *five minutes* alone with the Librarian's private collection."

Alina thought of her enigmatic exchange with the tall blue-skinned, fire-haired Iorian.

Clenching his fists, Ordin continued, "That type of clearance is a privilege granted only to a select few, including the Top Ten Aelfravers in the country. And I'll never get there with men like Baraam bol-Talanai standing in my way." Ordin spread his arms, and a dozen lightning bolts struck the sea, electricity fizzling along its surface.

"Not with that attitude, you won't." She jabbed a finger up at him. "You're making him out to be a demigod or something. He's just some dude with a superiority complex."

"Maybe. But it doesn't matter anymore. I found a shortcut to my dream. Instead of climbing over Baraam—a modern-day legend, a Bryndtian hero—I played my cards right, had him *offer* me a helping hand. In exchange for one small favor, he will grant me the access I so desperately crave."

The rumble of distant thunder, the crashing of the waves hundreds of feet below, these nearly drowned out Alina's words: "What was the favor?"

She didn't really need to hear the answer. She knew what he would say.

Ordin glided down, closer to her. "It started off as just a job. I was supposed to keep you away from the action. Baraam knew you weren't ready for this."

"He… told you that."

Now floating below Alina, looking up at her, Ordin said, "When I met you, that's when everything changed for me. You were so different from anyone I'd ever met—Terrie or Elemental. You are fundamentally you—you're a force, a soothing shadow in a world of garish neon. A burst of clean air in a smog-choked sky."

"You lied to me. From the start."

"I did. It was just a job. It was my chance to achieve everything I'd ever wanted. But, when we met, I started to want something else."

Alina shook her head. "You think I'm going to forgive you. You *actually* do! You think your ten-minute speech is all it'll take to win me over. Well, I don't really know how you Elementals do things up here, but, where I come from, you can't lie to someone's face for days, lock them in a digital prison, sign them over to their enemy, and get out of all responsibility by claiming you—what? Developed a crush on me? Is that what you're saying?"

"Baraam's not your enemy, Alina. And neither am I."

She was shaking. She had no idea what to do. She knew what she *wanted* to do—take Ordin's head in her hands and crush it like a soda can.

"I kinda liked you, too," she said, feeling a tear run from her eye to her lip. "Ya jackass." She licked the tear, tasting the salt. "But you ruined it. You're just like all the others."

A crow landed on her shoulder. It cawed at Ordin.

He stared at the bird. "What—that—that's not supposed to be—"

He looked to sky. So did Alina.

There were hundreds of crows, up there, circling. A thousand dark wings dramatically backlit by flashes of purple lightning.

On reflex, Alina raised her arms to shield her face, and what she saw confused her senses: though attached to her body, her arms and hands were no longer *hers*. They had become unrecognizable—gray and rough, dotted with dark flecks, the knuckles ridged with black callouses. The thick gray skin went all the way up to her shoulders, and from her elbows and underarms hung long black feathers bearing a waxy sheen. They looked like crow's feathers, but they were as sharp as blades.

As Alina gaped at them, they flexed, the whole row of them undulating, quivering like cat tails.

"How are you doing that?" Ordin shouted, rising high into the sky. "How are you changing things?"

"I don't know," Alina admitted, shrugging. She focused her glare on Ordin. "But I'm gonna roll with it."

The circle of crows dive-bombed, striking him in wave after wave, knocking him this way and that. Steadying himself, he flung out his hand, and the crows disappeared as if erased by a photo-editing tool. But there were more crows; they were spilling forth, in ever greater numbers, from a black tear in the sky.

Ordin couldn't wave his hands fast enough. He couldn't control the virus, the glitch, whatever it was that was happening to his perfect little illusionary world. The crows pelted him, digging with their gray talons and beaks, screaming at him as they swung around for another swipe, and another. They didn't let up. He had no time to breathe.

"Stop!" he cried, and everything did.

The crows locked mid-wingbeat, the lightning halted mid-strike, and the paralyzed seafoam looked like frosting. All noise ceased. Alina heard only her own heartbeat and Ordin's ragged breathing.

He dragged a hand over his torn-up and bloodied face, and his avatar was restored to its default state. Despite appearing healthy and whole again, he clearly remained off-balance, shaken.

Alina felt something powerful stir inside of herself. Before she could understand what was happening, that force blasted from her body, burying itself in the lighthouse walls. The stones beneath her feet quaked.

"What are you?" said Ordin.

She said, "Guess we'll see."

Time barreled forward. The crows, storm, and waves were released from their stasis. And the Ordin Airy exploded, stones flying in all directions in a burst of shadow and flame.

Just before they could slam into him, Ordin raised his arms and blocked the rain of car-sized stones. The strain immobilized him.

From the hole in the earth caused by the destruction of the lighthouse, a colossal arm emerged—a muscular gray appendage capped with claws that were each as large as Alina herself. The massive hand closed around Ordin's form. And squeezed.

Alina could hear him screaming, but she did nothing to stop what was happening. She wasn't quite sure she could have, even had she wanted to.

Then, a sound as loud as Alina's own frantic thoughts: Ordin snapped his fingers—

Alina woke to reality, finding herself in Ordin's parked car, leaning over the gearshift. Her fingers—long and clawed and gray—throttled his throat.

He was gasping for air, struggling against her grip, weakening.

With a shout of alarm, she released him.

He opened the driver-side door and fell backward out of the vehicle. Alina dragged herself out after him.

Lit only by the glow of the headlights, she stood over Ordin, the rain drenching them both. He scooted across the slimy street, away from her. She advanced, flexing her claws.

"Alina," said Cho, sliding off the back seat and into the open. Mezami fluttered after her.

Ordin couldn't take his eyes off Alina's arms. "They're real," he kept saying, "They're real."

"Alina, what happened?" said Cho. "It was so dark. Where were we just now?"

"He," she pointed down at Ordin, "tried to trap us. He's a liar."

"I wasn't lying," he protested.

"Shut up." Alina lunged at him, grabbing him by the collar with one hand, raising the other, claws extending. "You used me. All you care about is yourself."

Something crashed into her, then, and she hit the ground. Gutter water ran along her neck, her scalp.

Coughing, sputtering, she rolled over and saw Cho's sniffling face. "Don't do this," the girl said. "You beat him. He can't hurt you anymore, can he?"

Posted on her elbows, Alina said, "Him? He might try."

"But, if you kill him, you'll be just as bad as all the people who think they *should* kill just because they *can*. You're not like them, though. You're better."

"You don't know that. You don't know me."

"Yes, I do. You helped me when I needed help. You're my friend."

Staring at Ordin's pathetic face, tears running down her own, Alina got to her feet and said, "He needs to suffer, or he won't learn."

Cho said, "Look at him, though. He's crawling on the ground like a worm. You showed him. It's done."

Making a fist, Alina stood over the man who'd betrayed her. Grungy water running down her mutated, slightly elongated arms, she finally shook her head.

Over the rush and hiss of the rainstorm, she said, "She's right, Ordin. I don't need to do anything else to you. After all, you're just Baraam's stooge." Turning her back on him, she added, "I never want to see or hear from you again."

She left him there. He sputtered a few half-words.

She stomped over to the car, got in the driver's seat. "Get in," she told Cho and Mezami.

Ordin made no moves to stop them.

"Where we going now?" said Cho, climbing in through the front passenger's door.

"Away from here," Alina said.

With all the doors closed, she hit the ignition button, slammed her foot on the accelerator, and sped off.

Through the rearview mirror, she watched the water-blurred, red-lit outline of Ordin grow smaller and smaller. Then she turned a corner.

Her own eyes, reflected back at her, glowed golden for a moment, and then faded back to their natural green.

38

HUNCHED OVER, HEAD DOWN, Cho fidgeted in her seat, saying, "Aren't you worried the pinkojacks are going to come after us? This is a stolen ride. And the bro you stole it from looked pretty rich and important."

"Of course I'm worried," said Alina, fumbling her way through remembering how to drive a car. (Remembering wasn't quite the right word. "Learning" might have been more appropriate. The most she could say about her past driving experience was that Tahtoh had once let her take a tractor for a spin in the middle of an empty field. Maneuvering Ordin's sporty silver hovercar through the multi-level traffic lanes of New El was proving to be just a little bit more complicated.)

When they'd fled the area surrounding the hospital, Ordin had weaved in and out of lanes, dodging the speed-limit-abiding hovercars. Alina had no such luck; five minutes after ditching Ordin, cursing, she came to a slow-gliding stop at the end of a long, long line of vehicles.

The purple lights ahead indicated that they were approaching an Authority checkpoint.

"What in the hells are these idiots doing out here? I thought there was a curfew. They should be at home."

"Maybe we should head back to the motel," said Cho. "Wait for all this to blow over."

"Two problems with that." Alina held up one finger. "It's not going to 'blow over.' I don't know what the Talaganbubăk wants, but it won't be leaving until it's satisfied." She added a second finger. "And The Authority might have someone watching the *Peacock*, in case I come back."

"How do you know?"

"It'll be dawn soon. I'm a Terrie Aelfraver. In less than an hour, they're gonna round us all up and shove us onto the first train off New El. If we're lucky, they'll only crack a few skulls. But now that I know Ordin betrayed me, there's no telling what he'll do. The Authority's just the private army of the Twelve Families. They'll do anything an Ivoir tells them to."

"He probably already reported this car stolen."

"Yeah. No kidding."

A moment of silence. Cho was thinking.

She said, "I thought The Authority and the Families were the ones who were supposed to pay you when the job's done?"

"That's right."

"So, like, if they're really out to get you, even if you stop the Aelf, you'll never get a gelder of that money. Right?"

"Look, Cho, you're almost certainly correct, okay? What do you want me to say?"

"Tell me *why* you're still going to try, even though this can't end the way you want."

"Because I've come too far to stop now. K'viches always finish what we start."

"Even if it's a choice between stopping and dying?"

More silence.

Cho grumbled for a few moments. Then: "That purple-haired pale guy… Were you like boyfriend-girlfriend or something?"

Breaking into a cold sweat, Alina didn't really hear the question. She couldn't figure out why she was panicking at first. Then she said, "Mezami?" She twisted the rearview mirror to get a better look. "Mezami?"

Cho stood in her seat, checking out the back section of the sleek car. "Where is he?" She looked to Alina. "Where *is* he?"

"Did he not get in the car? What do we do?"

"How should I know? You're the adult."

"And you're the street-wise scrapper with a tech catalog's worth of cyber-parts in you." The line of hover vehicles simply wasn't moving. Alina bonked her head against the steering column and said, "Screw this, I'm pulling over."

Performing a sloppy five-point turn, really irritating both the driver ahead and the one behind, she cut across several lanes and parked Ordin's car in front of an ice cream shop. "I don't know about you," she told Cho, "but I'm hungry."

"Ice cream?" Cho made a face. "Really? How can you be thinking about *dessert* when your friend's in trouble?"

"He's a fully grown Pyct. If he chose to leave us without saying anything, that's his business."

"We should be trying to find him, though."

"How? How, Cho? Tell me that, and I'll totally be glad to make it happen." She drummed her fingers on the steering column in time with the rain pattering against the windshield. "If you're expecting me to make responsible decisions right now, you picked the wrong car." She unclipped her seatbelt. "Here's something you should know about me: I make *bad* decisions. I lied to get ahead. I cheated and gambled when I should have scrimped and saved. I could tell you I did it all out of desperation, and that would be true. Mostly. I could say the whole system's hardwired against me and people like me, and that's no lie, either. But, truth is, it doesn't matter—nothing I did *really* mattered. Every step of my choose-your-own-adventure of a life was always going to have the same result." Quietly, to herself, "I was always going to end up here." She glanced at Cho. "No matter what happens today, my old life is over. So, I deserve a frozen treat. With toffee, damn it."

"Your life doesn't have to be over."

In answer, Alina held up her spiky, gray, long-clawed hands.

Frowning, Cho said, "You don't know what that is."

"Exactly. That's the problem. But, whatever's happening, as soon as anyone sees me like this, I'm finished."

"How were you planning to get ice cream, then?" said Cho.

Alina opened her mouth. Closed it. "Okay, you got me. Would you be a doll and help me out one last time?"

"What's in it for me?"

"This car."

Cho rolled her eyes. "No good. Too hot. How about this: after you're arrested, can I keep your jacket?"

"Get me rainbow sprinkles on my two scoops and you have a deal."

Cho got out of the car, sauntered over to the ice cream parlor, and went inside.

Alina slumped in her seat.

Maybe the news channel would have a lead on the Bane. Or even Mezami. Biting her cuticles, she turned on the radio.

She shouted as the speakers exploded with a stereo-bursting amount of bass; her hand shot out in an attempt to turn the volume down to a humanly tolerable level. Instead, her claws pierced the console, sending sparks flying.

The radio rambled a few low, warbling measures, then died.

Well, at least that put a stop to the music.

Holding her trembling palm up to the streetlamp light, she made a fist.

And she began to laugh.

Tahtoh.

And laugh.

Ordin.

Tears flowed from her eyes down her cheeks, rounding her chin.

Baraam.

Still she laughed.

When Cho reentered the car, Alina stifled the last of her involuntary spasms of laughter. She accepted the ice cream cone, noting the abundance of rainbow sprinkles.

"Three scoops," Alina noticed.

Cho shrugged. "You crying?"

"It's nothing. Thanks, Cho. I'm really sorry about Mezami. I'm sure he'll turn up, though. He has to."

"Do you think he went after that guy, the one with the big sword?"

"Maybe." A shiver ran down Alina's spine. "Maybe he saw him in the street?"

"I heard the jacks are still looking for that creep. The news was talking about it."

Licking at her toffee-flavored ice cream, Alina said, "Oh, yeah? Any specifics?"

"Nah. But they mentioned riots happening in front of City Hall." Cho gaped at the slashed-up console. "Whoa, what did that radio ever do to you?"

"I've never liked pop," Alina said dryly. "What's that about riots, though?"

"The Ravers are out there, yelling at The Authority. They don't wanna leave. I didn't listen to the whole thing, but the ones they interviewed were screaming about getting paid."

"I can sympathize. So, what, are they gonna fight or something?"

Cho shrugged again. "What do I look like, someone who knows stuff about Ravers? You're the first one I met that didn't completely ignore me." She attacked her own cone, her nose dotted white with vanilla.

Alina cleared her throat. "By the way, thanks for stopping me. Earlier. With Ordin."

"You just needed to be reminded."

Alina gripped the steering column with one hand, the cone in the other. "You are a little too insightful sometimes, my friend."

Cho slurped up a chunk of cookie.

"For what it's worth, I'm glad I met you, Cho. No matter what happens."

Mouth full, Cho snapped, "Stop talking like you're dead! You'll be fine as long as you don't go to where the Ravers are."

Alina chuckled weakly.

"Oh, no," said Cho. "No. You don't have to. Let's just go find Mezami. We could leave on the next train out. You promised me." She locked eyes with Alina.

Alina said, "If I'm alive by the end of today, I swear by my grandfather Dimas K'vich, and by Holy Buthmerta, I *will* get you out of New El. You can come live with me. I promise. But first I have to finish what I started. I have to."

"You don't even know where to go, though! It's a huge mess everywhere." She pointed to the traffic jam they'd just left. "And it's only gonna get worse the closer you get to downtown."

"You're right. Everyone's panicking. The people. The Gildsmen. The Authority." Thinking fast, Alina mumbled, "Whenever there's trouble, you protect your most important resources. And, in The Capital, nothing's more important than money. So, the banks. And the biggest bank of them all is… City Hall!" To Cho: "Oh my gods, it's like you said—riots at City Hall. That's where The Authority will be. So, that's where *it* will be."

"What?"

Alina smirked. "The Bane's attacks haven't been random; each victim's been a high-and-mighty member of New El's elite. The last one was the *son* of the Consul himself. The killings all happened in the rich parts of town, within a few miles of The Gild. Clearly, this Aelf is not afraid of Aelfravers. So, we know it's confident *and* intelligent. It's sending a message."

"To who, though?"

"The Elementals? All of us? I don't know. But, when it didn't want to be caught, it moved in secret and attacked at night—leaving no witnesses. No reliable ones, anyway. And now, suddenly, it appears in the skies for everyone to see? Seems obvious to me that panic is the reaction it wanted."

"And now the jacks and Ravers are getting ready to fight each other."

"Yeah, everyone's distracted and at each other's throats. So, what next? If you're an ancient Aelf, how do you make sure everyone knows you're playing for keeps? What's the one factor keeping the Elementals from fleeing their homes all at once?"

"Laziness?" said Cho.

"The city's defenders. The Aelfravers. The Enforcers. You heard Ordin. Even he was completely convinced that this Aelf stands no chance against The Authority. Well, based on the Bane's past behavior, I don't think *it* is worried." Alina bit down on her ice cream cone. "It's got everyone riled up and gathered in one place, and now it's coming for a target no one in their right mind would ever expect."

"You mean the Ravers?"

Alina nodded. "And The Authority's forces, too. Two birds, one stone. Or, well—two stones, one *bird*." Finishing the cone, she thought twice about licking her fingers. "You ever hear about the Talaganbubăk?"

Cho shook her head.

"According to legend, it feeds on fear. The more complete the fear, the more energy it gets out of the bargain. The Elementals up here have gotten too comfortable with their supposedly Aelf-free lives. When they realize they're just as unsafe as us Terries—well, I bet the Talaganbubăk's going to get fat off this buffet. If enough people are terrified of it, it'll become too strong to stop."

"But if the Authority and all the Ravers don't stand a chance—"

"They stand a chance, don't get me wrong. Just not a very good one. Because they don't know what they're up against. But I do."

"What are you gonna do?"

"Make sure I'm the one who finishes this. Not Baraam or any other Raver. Me."

39

STANDING IN THE COURTYARD outside his own home, Ordin Ivoir seemed confused by the two Authority hovercycles parked in his driveway.

Rather than arriving in his limousine or sports car, he seemed to have walked all the way here; he was drenched from head to toe, and his steps were stiff and unsteady.

He'd paused once he'd noticed the hovercycles, and his eyes searched the circular driveway, the open front doors, the bronze statue of a scholar holding aloft its book of blasphemies.

"Hello?" he called. Then his gaze fell upon the shadowed balcony, and Tolomond knew that he'd been revealed.

Leaping from the darkness, sword in his right hand, Tolomond flung his hook-blade around the stone beak of a phoenix-shaped gargoyle and swung down toward his prey.

Despite his limp, Ivoir remained quick on his feet; he leapt backward just in time to watch the greatsword crack the pavement upon which he'd been standing a split-second ago.

"Tolomond Stayd," he said, hands in his pockets, his gaudy effervescent hair matted over his right eye. "I'm having a bit of a night. Could we maybe take a rain check?" He looked up, closed his eyes to the downpour. "Oh, wait. Never mind." Staring daggers at Tolomond, he said, "I assume you've executed the Enforcers to whom these bikes belonged. And my servants."

"Only the guilty ones," shouted Tolomond, hefting Rhetoric. "Those who resisted."

"How convenient that anyone resisting a home invasion is guilty. It must be comforting, having such a simple world-view. So, what do you want with me?"

"*From* you. Your head."

"That's problematic: I'm sort of using it at the moment."

"You're an ass."

"And you're a blunt tool, Tolly-boy. Nothing more." Glowing bright indigo, his hands shot out of his pockets, fingers taut and twisted as if bound by marionette strings.

Tolomond heard a hydrogen engine whir to life behind him, and the sound of a minigun barrel beginning to spin. He somersaulted aside as the hovercycle—without a pilot—swung in an arc and fired its guns at him. The bullets buried themselves in the concrete base on which the bronze statue of the scholar had been set.

With short bursts of fire, one vehicle kept Tolomond pinned behind cover. The other zoomed over to Ivoir, who climbed onto the bike and sped off.

After a few moments, the first cycle ceased auto-firing. Ivoir must have left the functional range of his ability. Or the gun's ammunition had been depleted.

Tolomond stood up, swiped the shards of concrete off his shoulders, nose, and chest, and sprinted toward the bike. Swinging his leg up, he mounted the vehicle, hit the ignition, and began the chase.

40

THE HISTORIC DIVITIA DISTRICT bristled with stately alabaster edifices and the statues of millennia-dead heroes and founders of New El.

In the northern section of Pluto Plaza, the gold-handed clocktower perched atop City Hall—home to the Elemental Bank, the largest in the world—was illuminated by a million or more white bulbs running up the tower's edges and rimming the clockface. The time was 5:11 AM.

The expansive sky lightened to a sheet of lavender—the first sign of dawn—and this color blended with the uniforms of some five hundred Authority Enforcers standing in a long line, two men deep. Their backs to City Hall, they surrounded its ornate entrances set behind columns of white and pink marble.

Opposite them stood a motley army of, give or take, two hundred Terrestrial Aelfravers. Besides their profession, the Terries seemed to have little in common: some wore jeans and torn jackets, others sported full suits of top-of-the-line nanocomposite body armor; some were decked out with weapons, others cracked their bare knuckles; some stood perfectly still while others tensed, the full light-spectrum of Niima auras billowing from them. A mouthy few slung insults at the mostly stoic Enforcers. The majority, however, waited quietly.

The rainstorm had passed. The twenty feet between the two opposing sides was dotted with puddles. Sloshing into gutters, runoff rushed in front of the steps atop which waited The Authority.

Contrasting with the Terries, the Enforcers were a real army. Outfitted in standard issue riot gear and bullet-proof vests, they cradled stun batons and pulse rifles. At their hips rested pouches stuffed with tear gas canisters and concussive grenades. This military force defending Pluto Plaza was predominantly composed of the lavender- and black-on-silver-uniforms of the Ivoirs and Xaveyrs. However, the wide array of colors and sigils—gold and red, white and blue, green and gray, and more—revealed that all the Families were represented here, today.

For now, both forces seemed content to wait—or, unwilling to make the first move.

On the opposite end of the plaza, Alina and Cho were among the crowd of Elementals and their servants who'd gathered to see what all the commotion was about.

Despite there being a curfew in full effect, this incident had the chance to become the fight of the century: the "trashy" Terrie Aelfravers versus The Authority, "the guardians of New El." More importantly, for many of the people present, it was a matter of supremacy—an army of uppity Terries couldn't be allowed to cross the protectors of the Elementals. Not without suffering the consequences, at least.

A man in a salmon-colored sweater and brown loafers standing near Alina muttered something along the lines of, "Those mud-dwellers need to be reminded of their place."

And because any good show would be incomplete without snacks, food vendors had opened early to seize the opportunity presented by this spontaneously appearing, massive audience. Carts were pushed through, men and women advertised their offerings—wraps, hot buns, pretzels. Yawning, pajama-clad onlookers pressed their wrists to the vendors' tablets, scanning their built-in credit chips to instantaneously transfer funds in exchange for steaming hot snacks.

Paying with cash, Cho grabbed Alina and herself each a vegan falafel, a Kadician specialty. They munched on the wraps, Alina savoring the bites of fresh cucumber and tomato, and the yogurt-based sauce. Satisfied, she tossed her trash in the nearby bin, and she tugged the fresh bandages on her arms just a little tighter.

She'd used the last of Ordin's first aid supplies to hide her disfigurement. The wrappings wouldn't survive long; the spiky black protrusions and saw-like feathers on her arms were already ripping the strips of latex.

"What are we doing here, Alina?" Cho finally asked.

"Waiting."

There was one Raver who was most conspicuous for his absence; Baraam was nowhere to be found.

For a moment, Alina doubted her intuition. Had she been wrong in her guess that the Bane would strike here next? Had Baraam determined its real target? Was he about to outdo her again? These questions plagued her, even as she held her breath, watching the two armies from afar.

Any second now, the fireworks were set to kick off, and she might have bet on the wrong place.

The suspense was a stinging nettle in her gut.

Then, just over the brightening horizon, there erupted in the sky a deep, rumbling call—a cry that could only be likened to that of a bird of prey hitched up to ten thousand amplifiers. The noise rattled the very ground on which the bystanders, Aelfravers, and Enforcers stood, and a few windows nearby cracked from the sheer force.

The beast itself came into view, a great black mass, impossibly colossal—it must have measured a hundred feet, wingtip to wingtip.

It cried again, and many of the people around Alina ducked, covered their ears, screamed, threw themselves onto their bellies, onto the ground. Some ran, others were paralyzed, as the great crow-like creature drew nearer and nearer. With each flap of its night-feathered wings, awnings were blown away, windows shattered, satellite dishes snapped off their moorings to soar through the air.

Alina gaped at the thing. What was left of Cho's falafel slipped from her fingers.

Most of the assembled Assets of New El came to their senses, then, and scattered, sprinting in all directions. Some carried squalling children over their shoulders or in their arms; a few abandoned their kids in the middle of the chaos.

The monstrous form of the Talaganbubăk ascended to the top of City Hall and perched on the shining clocktower. From there, it let out a third and final cry—the minute hand of the clock shook ominously but did not drop.

That creature ripped straight out of song or myth made not another sound.

As one, the heads of the Aelfravers and Enforcers swiveled upward.

A scream of a different kind tore through the skies, followed by another three identical ones. Alina searched for the source of the noise, but, before she could see what had happened, a cluster of explosions rocked the crow. Four destroyer drones—silvery, triangular blurs—flashed past, circled around the Bane of New El, and immediately released a second payload of explosives. The projectiles burst as they struck the head and torso of the huge beast, and a whirlwind of flame engulfed its entire body.

The drones flew over Alina's head, and she heard the echoes of the *pop* as they simultaneously broke the sound barrier.

She looked toward the creature, expectantly. The fire cleared, and the white smoke dissipated.

The Talaganbubăk rested calmly atop City Hall. Unfazed and unimpressed.

From the surrounding rooftops, armored hovercraft revealed themselves. Alina hadn't noticed any of these earlier; they must have been rendered invisible by light-bending tarps. The camouflage was now thrown aside as cannons were raised. Blast after blast sounded, reverberating throughout the plaza. Bundles of flickering amber light arced through the air, expanding into electrified and magically charged netting that ensnared the great crow.

A voice crackled from a loudspeaker hidden in a patch of flowers and greenery near Alina: "All Assets are to evacuate the area immediately. For your own safety, return to your homes and await further instructions."

Net after net fell upon the Bane, entangling it, pinning it to the tower's roof spire. Shingles cracked, slid off, and fell to street-level. The creature's molten-gold gaze shifted—not toward the net-throwers but toward Alina. Her breath caught in her throat, and she stumbled backward, but then she realized that it wasn't looking *at* her but *behind* and *above* her.

She spun around just in time to catch sight of the tail end of the artificial dragon H'ranajaan, the armored plates of its segmented body gleaming by the emerald lights of its eyes. It opened its wire-lined maw—a tangle of green, red, and yellow behind diamond fangs—and its roar was like a destroyer's steam siren.

Its tail flailing, H'ranajaan beat its dark blue, solar-paneled, bat-like wings and climbed toward the Talaganbubăk.

Not wanting to witness the titanic struggle from *too* close, both armies—Enforcers and Aelfravers—in silent agreement, backed away from City Hall.

General cries of joy and relief could be heard.

These were premature.

Each of its joints grinding and screeching like the brakes on an antique train, H'ranajaan furiously beat its wings, shaking the plaza with its titanic voice of fiberglass and steel. It dived straight for the immobilized Bane of New El.

The first blow was set to be a decisive one, it seemed, until H'ranajaan's huge head jerked to the right—as if listening—and it pulled up. Changing course at the last possible instant, it missed colliding with the Bane of New El by a mere few dozen feet.

The artificial dragon flew northeastward, away from City Hall and the biggest threat The Capital had faced since its founding.

The Aelfravers were the first to shout in protest and disbelief. Alina couldn't hear what they were saying, but she could imagine the taunts, the mockery, the pleas to let *them* have a go at the monster.

The Authority closed ranks again as the Ravers pressed forward.

Then the crow shrieked, extending its wings, and the light-nets were shredded by its blade-like feathers. The tower's golden minute hand wobbled again, and this time it snapped clean off the clock-face. Like a slab of mountain shorn by a quake, the minute hand fell.

Alina shouted, "Watch out!" But, if there were any Ravers or Enforcers who'd noticed the danger, they could do nothing about it: the press of bodies behind them pushed them ever closer to City Hall.

The ship-sized minute hand plunged downward, only milliseconds away from crushing dozens of people.

A bolt of lightning struck that spear of death, then, and slammed it sidelong into the tower, which quivered from the force of the blow. A ring of dust spread outward from the point of impact, and when that dust cleared, the cyan-glowing form of Baraam bol-Talanai could be seen. Glaring, crackling with electricity, he clung to the twisted golden hand of the now-broken clock that he'd embedded in the stone wall of the clocktower.

Almost as one, the Ravers looked up. And, regardless of whether he'd intended his arrival to have this effect, Baraam became a beacon to his colleagues. They threw their fists up, let sound their horns and battle cries, and brandished their spears, swords, flails, bows, brass knuckles, guns, and shields.

Forever afterward, everyone—from the nobility to historians to elementary school-aged children—would viciously argue over who'd fired the first shot on that fateful morning. Whether begun by Authority gauss-rifle or Aelfraver Niima-blast, however, one detail was beyond dispute: the Battle of City Hall was a disaster whose aftershocks would, one day, lead to the end of the Nation of El.

Trying to keep her falafel down, Alina unwound the bandages from her arms. The latex was too constricting to her range of motion, and there was no point in keeping up the weak disguise now.

As the faintest rays of dawn rounded the corners and crept up the balconies of the nearby shops and apartment buildings, she pulled her last Auggie out of her jacket pocket and chugged it.

Though she always tried to recycle the bottles, this one fell from her grasp as she struggled to breathe. Her chest heaved, veins in her neck and arms bulging, eyes rolling into the back of her skull.

"Alina?" said Cho, poking her in the ribs. "Hey!"

Alina inhaled deeply and evenly, steam spilling from her nostrils.

"Um, what did you just take?"

"Fyrevein." Every inch of her quivered as she tried to contain herself. "It's time, Cho. Gotta face the music."

Cho threw her arms around Alina, saying, "You promised." She broke the hug to punch Alina in the thigh.

"Yowch." Alina staggered back a step.

Holding her fist up between them, Cho said, "The bruise is so you'll remember."

Alina's smile faded quickly as it'd come. "If I don't come back—"

"*Stop.*"

"*If* I don't come back, take what's left of the money and get yourself a ticket to Truct. Go to 'Amming & Sons,' in town. Ask for Calthin. He's a friend. He'll help you."

Cho shook her head. However briefly, she finally did look her age—a girl in an overly large hoodie and ratty, baggy sweatpants. Hunched. Scared. "You promised."

"I did. And, whatever comes next, you're getting out of this city." She gritted her teeth. "I can feel—It's taking effect now." She turned around. "This is it."

"Alina!"

"Cho." Alina dug her nails into her own palms. "Thanks." And she dashed toward the chaos ahead.

A few dozen feet of open space stretched before her. Her boots slapped the ground in long strides, puddle water splashing against her legs, the tail of her coat unfurling like a flag behind.

All thoughts were banished from her mind as multicolored beams of magic split the vanishing twilight, arrows and bullets and pulse-rounds flew in all directions, shafts of dawn-light gleamed off bladed weapons.

The world around her exploded, ripped apart by screams and the patter of machinegun fire against forcefields, the clang of swords against riot shields.

And Alina ran toward that storm of screaming and whirling, shooting, stabbing, burning death. She felt—not calm, but still and alert. Ready. The

Fyrevein had emptied her mind of anything that might have come between her muscles and pure, animal reflex.

A twist of her heels, a duck, hop, a spring-heeled leap forward—her enhanced instincts guided her through, under, and between the combatants in the free-for-all. Twirling, she dodged an Authority truncheon, then a Raver knife. Neither attack had been meant for her, but the fighters were swinging and firing blindly by now.

Thrown five feet to the side by a sonic boom, she steadied herself with her clawed hand, glancing upward in the nick of time. The muzzle of a pistol aimed at her face flashed. The clump of tiles and rock she flung in front of herself saved her life.

Thrusting her hand out, she slammed the rock into the Enforcer's helmeted head, knocking him onto his back.

She wasn't the only Geomancer on the battlefield. A trio of them had raised a defensive wall around a group of twelve other Ravers—some of whom were slouched, wounded—as they regrouped. Alina took advantage of the cover, running behind it as a spray of pulse rounds bored into it.

Fighters were closing the distance between her and them. She ran. Just before she crashed into a line of stabbing weapons and electrified batons, she released a jet of Niima beneath her, leaping into the air even as a column of stone burst forth, pushing her, and she soared—legs kicking—higher and higher.

Her fingers latched onto the second-floor ledge of City Hall, and she looped her elbows over the edge and hauled herself up.

Now firmly on the balcony, she kicked the heel of her boot squarely against the tall window frame directly in front of her. The lock broke, and the window swung inward.

Inside, near-total darkness. The blinds were drawn, the doors sealed, the computers all powered down. City Hall still slept, but it was about to get one hell of a wakeup call.

A stray pulse round embedded itself in the wall beside her head. She ducked low, hustling inside.

41

THOUGH HE DESPISED ALL modern weaponry—barbaric, inelegant, children's toys—desperate times called for desperate measures: Tolomond squeezed the trigger of the pistol he gripped in his right hand, maneuvering his hovercycle with his left. Aiming down the sights, he jerked to the left just in time to avoid a sanitation drone that had swung unexpectedly in front of him from a side street.

He'd managed to close most of the distance between himself and Ivoir, despite the heretic's head-start. For his part, the coward did everything he could to throw Tolomond off: Ivoir would raise his hand, there'd come a flash of cyan, and another of the city's mechanized abominations would attack, block, or otherwise hinder Tolomond.

But Tolomond was guided by the Hand of The Author; his course stayed true, and he dodged every maintenance drone and malfunctioning hovercar. He chased Ivoir between the high-rises, all the way down into the underbelly of the city. As metal pipes hissed and clanked, whizzing by, Tolomond took aim again.

A metal door was flung open.

He swerved, nearly colliding with a garbage disposal unit.

Bright orange and amber lights, the whirr of massive fan blades, and the squeal of self-regulating pressure valves informed Tolomond that they'd entered the Tilitatem District of New El, where was generated the energy needed to power the entire city, where occurred all the meatpacking, water purification, and other vital industrial activities. Columns of exhaust rose from field-sized vents, gymnasium-length filtration facilities processing and recycling the city's water and air. Tolomond serpentined around these grilles, the steam preventing him from lining up a shot.

Armies of fist-sized drones swirled like schools of fish through the air, scuttling over the walls, monitoring, welding, as if directed by an invisible hand. Another flash of cyan from Ivoir, and, in unison, every one of the hundreds of luminescent orange lenses fixated on Tolomond and converged on his position.

Kicking his hovercycle's engine into overdrive, he shot forward, weaving up and down between caution signs and switchboards. The drones weren't sophisticated or agile enough to keep pace. Many crashed into poles and walls, crumpling into scrap.

Piercing a veil of steam like a pencil puncturing a sheet of paper, Tolomond raised the pistol, preparing to unload another series of rounds, but he shouted and jerked the handlebars, then, narrowly escaping a collision with the bear-sized, ghostly, blue-tinged image of a wolf-like demon. The creature snapped its bear-trap jaws—Tolomond ducking his head—and it gnashed its fangs with a distorted, synthesized sound.

The creature's form vibrated, strings of runes and digitized code splitting from its shifting, writhing mass. It took another bite at Tolomond's bike, missing by inches, before tearing off after him.

Peering over his shoulder, Tolomond let fly a pair of shots. The rounds phased through the translucent beast, having no effect.

The summoned monster's jaws flapped, and from its incorporeal throat came Ivoir's mocking voice: "How d'you like my Exxy, eh? A projection from the Darkthreads given substance on our material plane—why, I sometimes amaze even myself."

"Shut up!" Tolomond bellowed.

"There's no use in fighting it, by the way. No tangible weapon can hurt it, but it can hurt *you.* The benefit of its bite being imbued with Niima. Rather nifty, no?"

Neither tiring nor slowing, the beast kept pace with Tolomond's vehicle, yet he felt no fear. Only irritation. It was merely another obstacle to overcome. Another challenge. This conjuration was bound to Ivoir, which made the solution simple enough: if he destroyed the caster, he'd dispel the magic.

Maintain the pressure, commanded The Author. *Do not disappoint me.*

Tolomond rounded the base of a rusting steel silo, oily runoff seeping from between its plates, and he saw Ivoir before him, only fifteen feet ahead.

Firing wildly, Tolomond screamed at Ivoir, willing him to fall and die.

Ivoir weaved, narrowly dodging the blasts. Hair whipping around his head, he risked a backward glance—naked terror splashed like water across his features—facing front just an instant too late to avoid the steel pole in his path.

His hovercyle compressed from the impact, which sent his frail body spinning through the air. He crashed somewhere out of sight, just beyond a stack of compacted garbage cubes.

Tolomond swung his own vehicle around, not bothering to come to a complete stop before leaping off. The hovercycle flipped over, grinding into the ground in a shower of sparks.

The blueish beastly apparition leapt forth, its guttural roar distorted and clipped. Fangs gnashing, spear-like claws extended, it soared toward Tolomond, who turned and raised Rhetoric to meet its maw.

With a burst of light, and a noise like a low-quality recording of a thunder boom blasted from a blown-out speaker, the creature exploded into disparate fragments of code, which disintegrated with a faint hiss.

Ivoir must have lost concentration on his spell.

Perhaps the fall had killed him. Perhaps he was simply unconscious. Beyond a doubt, however, he must have been in dire straits to have suffered the disappearance of his last line of defense.

Pistol at the ready, sword at his side, Tolomond advanced, step by step, shimmying between the plastic and metallic reds and blues and silvers of crushed trash cubes.

He found Ivoir lying there, slumped against a jagged pile of junk and ruptured plastic bags filled with slimy offal.

Ivoir held up his hand, groaning. "Why? Why do you want me dead?"

He'd been wounded. The clothes and skin on his right arm and part of his chest had been scraped away. But his blood was the wrong color—it shone like quicksilver. The fluid poured from his torn pale skin, under which buzzed and whirred and clicked a latticework of tubes and wires and sheets of metal.

"Another android?" Tolomond yelled.

Ordin's throat, along with the speaker inside it, had been damaged, so his voice sounded hollow and tinny. All the same, he pushed out the words: "No, I assure you, I am Ordin Ivoir. End me, and you'll have yet another murder on your conscience."

Tolomond knew it to be true: the enemy at his feet was no mimic. This was his chance. He said, "To kill an infidel is not murder. It is the path to Nehalennia. My conscience is clear."

"Is it really so effortless for you, to snuff a fellow human being? I have a name, a life—family, dreams."

"You're a *mistake*. Look at you, a product of Man's great folly and arrogance. Wires in place of veins, steel in place of bones—we don't even *bleed* the same color, you and I." Tolomond gagged at the thought. "We are nothing alike. You are a single withered branch on an old, sick tree, and I am a great fire come to scorch the forest. Can a dead branch claim kinship with fire? No, you who have done all you can to run from your humanity, The Lord has judged you. You are aberrant in His eyes. And you will burn for it."

"You don't speak for the gods."

"I am *the* Instrument of *the* God. The one and only. And He has willed that you die by my sword."

Ivoir wheezed. "You won't kill me, Tolly." And he laughed, the tones switching erratically from high to low, as if he'd been poorly autotuned.

"You don't believe I can? I, the very Hand of The Author?"

"Oh, not at all. Clearly, you're more than capable…" Ivoir hacked up a lungful of his silvery blood. "But you won't get the chance."

"I have you at my mercy. All the elements have aligned. Even were you able to, you'd have nowhere left to run. What could *possibly* stop me now?"

Weakly, Ivoir lifted a shattered, sparking finger. "That."

A vibrating, metallic, echoing roar came from above.

A shadow fell upon Tolomond's face as he turned, and he beheld the shining breastplate and massive wings of H'ranajaan, ace in the hole of The Authority, dragon defender of New El.

Having acquired its target, it dived.

"You're bluffing," Tolomond shouted. But the mechanical dragon landed on the rooftop of the processing plant just in front of him. The lenses of its eyes shone like back-lit stained glass. It opened its mouth, revealing red and yellow cables, diamond-dusted, saw-like teeth, and a glow emanating from its core.

H'ranajaan was so gargantuan that it couldn't stand at street-level, here, where the powerplants and storage facilities were packed so tightly. The dragon, however, did not need to come closer: it flicked its slatted, spiked tail, punting Tolomond backward; with a resounding clang, like the sounding of a gong, he bounced off the metal cylindrical structure near where he'd discarded his hovercycle moments ago.

He didn't have enough time to breathe, let alone stand, before H'ranajaan followed up with a second attack—a finisher. Its jaw unhinged like a snake's, the blue-green light from its core now radiating from its maw. Rearing back, from its body came a series of whirring and grinding sounds—like the air-chopping of a helicopter's blades mixed with the revving of a truck's engine, but much, much louder. Aiming its wide-open mouth at Tolomond, it unleashed a blue-tinged barrage of energy, bludgeoning him, and he was blasted backward and ten feet up; the metal structure behind him bent, groaned, and folded—with him pressed up against it.

Gritting his teeth to their cracking point, his every muscle strained as the force bent the rusty steel plates against which he was being crushed. His body had been reduced to a fleshy hammer, his bones creaking as the metal groaned.

When it finally ended, he fell onto the ground. He coughed up a mouthful of blood. Every joint, every bone abused. Multiple contusions and fractures, guaranteed.

The inhuman power of that breath-weapon attack should have killed him. Had he been a lesser man—any other man—anyone not chosen by The Author to perform His Sacred Work, he would have been dead.

Muscles quivering, wiping the blood from his lips with the back of his hand, Tolomond leaned on Rhetoric. And he stood up.

"How are you still alive?" said Ivoir, his voice modulator making him sound years younger.

The dragon's tail whipped towards Tolomond, who threw himself behind the nearest pile of junk. The spear-like tip of the tail sheared clean through half the cubes. Before it could strike again, Tolomond grabbed ahold of it. Though he nicked his fingers on the jagged protrusions jutting from the metal, he clung to it, and was therefore carried through the air and behind H'ranajaan's body. Before the automaton realized his new position, he began to scale its tail, cutting his hands and arms, knees and shins over and over. But Tolomond Stayd was used to pain; he ate it with his daily bread; he drank it like life's water. Pain had never before deterred him, and it would not slow him now.

As H'ranajaan sweeped its tail back and forth, attempting to throw off its unwelcome passenger, Tolomond pulled free the chain fused to his wrist and bit down on its hook blade. Slowly, his arms burning, sweat pouring from his torn and tattered gray tunic, he climbed the dragon's body.

Before he reached its wings, it flapped them, nearly tossing him down to earth. H'ranajaan lifted off, and Tolomond buried Rhetoric in between two of its titanium plates. Clinging to the hilt of his sword, he watched as he rose above first the streets and then the rooftops. H'ranajaan continued to ascend, higher and higher, and Tolomond knew that, if he didn't disable this leviathan now, he was done for.

Clasping Rhetoric's pommel and handle, he looped his feet under a tangled mess of gold-plated cables, and he dug in with his heels. At the same time, he yanked backward with his arms, using his blade as leverage—pulling, tearing, twisting, and pulling again.

By now, H'ranajaan soared hundreds of feet above New El, the city's dayshift Assets and their stores just beginning to awaken as the sun rose to greet them. The golden glow of dawn hit Tolomond full in the face as he heaved, rested for a breath, and heaved again.

The dragon barrel-rolled, and Tolomond's stomach lurched. He momentarily lost his grip on Rhetoric, but his entangled feet saved him. Grabbing hold again, he returned to his task, noticing that the plate he'd been attempting to pry off now hung loose and rattled with every beat of H'ranajaan's great wings.

With one final effort, Tolomond screamed his defiance, and *pulled*—and the plate was dislodged, the bolts holding it in place screeching as they were bent out of shape and snapping in two. Latching onto the plate with his bleeding fingers, he tore it clean off, and it whooshed past his ear.

There was now exposed a short and narrow tunnel leading into the dragon's innards, at the end of which lay the source of the emerald light emanating from its core.

The chain still between his teeth, Tolomond swung himself into the tunnel and slid down into the belly of the beast. Blasts of frigid air buffeted him as he slid, but despite the circulating gusts, the temperature within H'ranajaan's body was unbearably hot. Everything Tolomond touched scalded him, searing his flesh; he could smell himself cooking, crisping. But he would not stop. He crawled forward, toward the coconut-shaped crystal sphere that hung suspended, connected to dozens of fizzing wires.

Its heart, Tolomond thought. And he wrapped the chain of his hook-blade around the connecting electric wires. He said, "You make a mockery of life," and he called on all the strength left in him to tear at those cables.

In a shower of blue and yellow sparks, they were ripped from the components to which they'd been attached. The light within the core flared, causing Tolomond momentary blindness, and then it dimmed, leaking energy and black smoke.

In a shower of sparks and metal shards, the core exploded.

H'ranajaan roared, the noise causing its innards to rumble and jolt. Then it fell still. And, then, it simply fell.

Tolomond drifted weightlessly as the dragon hurtled downward, toward New El. His tunic and skin scorched by the still-scalding metal at his back, his eyes weeping fiery tears that evaporated to mingle with the smoke, for close to half a minute, he prayed and waited for the inevitable.

When the steel beast crashed onto the ground, Tolomond could not be certain if it was he who'd screamed.

42

FROM HER VANTAGE POINT, a mezzanine between the first and second floors, Alina surveyed the darkened lobby of City Hall.

Within these white-marbled, garishly colored chambers, directives that affected the entire Nation of El were issued by *twelve men*—twelve men nominated by their own families to represent the financial and political interests of the Elemental class. Twelve men just like Ordin. Or, worse, *Walazzin*.

City Hall also happened to be the largest bank in the world, holding loans over presidents, kings, and emperors. Supposedly, the gelders in its reserves numbered in the low trillions.

Looking at the vaulted ceilings, the forty-foot-long drapes of plush velvet, the fireplace as big as a barn, Alina began to believe all the rumors she'd heard about this place over the years. Half a dozen crystal chandeliers hung from long gilded chains. Covering the walls were frescoes of men and women with vacant expressions, who wore puffy maroon or midnight blue shirts and tricornered hats. Row after row of polished wooden desks occupied the open center of the chamber. Every chair, couch, table, ottoman, candlestick, and other ornament was no doubt a priceless antique.

Alina had trouble imagining how much it must have cost to build this place. You could probably have bought and sold a hundred—a thousand—

of her hometowns for the same price. It seemed the Twelve Families had more money than the gods themselves.

Jaw-droppingly luxurious as all this was, though, Alina had no time to take the tour. She turned left and headed for the stairs.

In a moment of clarity, she thought about what she was doing, and continuing suddenly felt impossibly stupid, suicidal even.

Her knees locked; she began to hyperventilate.

Then a voice—her voice—whispered to her from the edges of her mind that there was nothing for her down here; her future lay above, almost within reach, and what was she prepared to do about it?

She took a deep breath, focusing, the Fyrevein once more burning away all her fear.

Her doubt, however, remained.

Yes, her quarry—the solution to all her material problems—awaited at the top of this very tower. And yet, she had no idea what she'd do once she got up there.

She'd always stuck to the principle that killing *any* living being was morally wrong. But, remembering Sheriff Lowing's reaction, the disappointment and condescension he'd subjected her to… he had made it clear that he would only ever have been satisfied if she'd destroyed the demon. And that was just so awful. Okay, fine, so demons weren't the easiest Aelf to defend in terms of the value of their existence—especially ones like Osesoc-ex'calea. They were parasites who fed on human emotions, after all. Still! Not all Aelf were like that. Many of them were simple creatures (with magical abilities). Some were even fundamentally good, like Mezami. And, besides, the exact same categories applied to human beings: some were good, some crappy, and others just mediocre.

If Alina took even one step down the path of deciding who *deserved* to live or die, how far would she have to go before ending a life became so much easier than saving it?

The Elementals, of course, would refuse to see her side. Their opinion would be no different from Lowing's; if anything, they'd be even more bullheaded. She couldn't imagine The Authority shelling out the gelders for the Bane of New El's bounty if she didn't come back with its head in a gift-wrapped basket. After the events of this morning, they probably wouldn't pay any *Terrie* Raver—let alone someone who'd been arrested a few hours before, who'd forged her license, who'd stolen and lied, who'd protected a Pyct.

It felt like half of everyone would be happier if she'd just give up and shrink away, and the other half couldn't care less what she did one way or the other. Lowing, Baraam, the Ravers, they all urged her to surrender her ideals, become just like any one of them.

Did they ever doubt themselves like she did? Did they ever wonder if what they believed made any sense at all? Seemed unlikely.

And, there it was. She'd figured it out. Her *doubt* must be a good thing: it kept her questioning, curious, open-minded. It was her strength.

So, it shouldn't matter what Lowing, Baraam, or anyone else proclaimed. They weren't gods. They weren't any better than she was. And they had *no right* to command her to murder.

They had no power over her.

Faced with equally slim chances of successfully closing this Rave and receiving the reward, but more determined than ever before, she asked herself why she was pushing forward. The answer came quickly: "Because I always finish what I start."

It's what Tahtoh would have done, sure, but she wasn't doing it for him. She wasn't trying to prove anything to anyone else, living or dead. This was just a job she had to finish for herself. On her own terms.

There were two hundred Ravers just outside, each one itching for a chance at the prize. Anyone willing to fight through half-a-thousand Enforcers would stop at nothing short of victory. Damn the cost.

However, she wanted the win more than any of them. It wasn't just the money anymore. She had to know, firsthand, how this would all end. Some sliver of her consciousness was calling, from the back of her mind, telling her that this moment was history in the making, and she was part of it. She couldn't turn away, not now that the sounds of the battle were drawing nearer—bodies slamming against doors and walls, the rattle and tap of gunfire, echoing arcane shouts.

She had gotten into City Hall first. That might have been her only advantage, but it was an advantage all the same.

No turning back.

The mezzanine on which she stood was connected to the stairwell by a walkway. The stairs were white marble, open, and bordered with coin-shaped brass railings, and they were switchback—each staircase ascended only half a floor, requiring a 180-degree turn to reach the next flight.

Even though there were sixteen levels between her and the top of the tower, taking the elevator seemed like a bad idea (what with Baraam's stunt with the minute-hand having cracked the tower wall, and the colossal crow-beast perched on the roof).

She felt the time-crunch, the mere moments she had before reality—slicing, spell-slinging, murderous reality—would come crashing inside.

So, armed with only her determination and her doubt, she ran.

Legs and arms pumping, chugging air, she'd made it up three flights before the second-floor windows burst. A pair of Igniomancers tumble-rolled onto the mezzanine, hurling fireballs at each other, one deflecting with a roiling orange-flame shield, the other with a kick. The fireballs rebounded in opposite directions, exploding on the ground floor; a dozen desks and chairs erupted in flames.

Even as windows shattered and walls shook, Alina pushed herself onward. Running faster than she'd ever done before thanks to the Niima-infused liquid coursing through her body.

She heard the crack of a bullwhip, and her head twitched to find the source of the sound. A length of braided leather snapped against the brass railing, looping 'round and 'round. Then, attached to the whip, a blur of a person swung up from the lobby, under the arched base of the stairwell, flying upward like a loose pendulum. And this acrobat corkscrewed seven-hundred degrees through the air, landing—perfectly balanced—on the staircase in front of Alina.

It was a young woman with mostly inch-long purple hair, the longer strands near her ears clinging wetly to her cheeks. Her leather vest bore the image of a rearing, roaring bear.

Breathing hard, Alina said, "Vessa, wasn't it?"

"Vending Machine Girl?" Vessa crossed her arms, whip limp at her feet. A drop of blood slid from a cut on her scalp. "Small world."

Alina tapped her palms against her pant legs. "Pretty crazy out there, I bet."

"Yah."

Vessa held her breath. Alina swallowed.

Below, the front doors smashed open, and the two clashing armies poured into the hall—bullets and pulse blasts bouncing off shields; magical beams glancing off high-tech reflective body armor.

"Are we supposed to fight now?" said Alina.

Vessa shrugged. "Cherry might be my favorite flavor, but that doesn't mean I'm letting you beat me to the punch."

She turned on her heels and broke into a sprint, Alina—hesitating only for a second—right behind her.

They'd made it up three more half-floors when a violent tremor knocked Alina against the brass railing. She clung to the metal, her balance completely thrown. She turned; a grim-faced man dressed all in blues and greens rocketed upward in the narrow gap between the staircases, a stalk of indigo flames erupting behind him. Alina brought her arms up in an "X" to cover her vitals, and the intensity of the force threw her backwards, the sting of searing heat on her face and hands and knees as she braced against the railing.

Another crack of a whip made her open her eyes. From the staircase just opposite Alina's, the whip caught the blue-flame-spouting Raver in the forehead, knocking him out. He toppled and fell out of sight.

Vessa, free hand on her hip, winked at Alina.

Alina pointed behind her, shouting, "Watch it!"

Leaping from the nearest crystal chandelier, a long-limbed, muscular woman with short-cropped blonde hair, dark skin, and a mango-colored robe collided with Vessa, slamming her against the wall.

Cesthra Ci of Quartz-Ragvar dropped her greatclub and wrapped her fingers around Vessa's throat.

Alina ran up the steps, looping right, and right again. She'd nearly closed the distance when Vessa did something Alina couldn't see from her angle, but it was enough to shove Cesthra back a few feet. Smashing into Alina, the mango-robed Raver retrieved her greatclub from the floor and swung at an upward angle, aiming for Alina's teeth. Alina swooped under the club, her hair blasted back by the force of the blow. As she did so, she connected a jab—fingertips extended into a spear-hand—with Cesthra's lower back, right where the kidney would be.

The attack winded Cesthra, who grimaced, but, blaring her battle cry, she lashed out again, this time cracking the floor just short of where Alina had been. Vessa wheeled her whip overhead, lashing out at Cesthra's shin and chin. The first strike had been a feint; the second snapped Cesthra's head forward, and she, too, fell unconscious.

Kneeling, catching her breath, Alina looked up to find Vessa's hand extended.

"Thanks for the assist," said Vessa, helping Alina up.

Vessa's eyes went wide. Alina followed Vessa's gaze to her own arms. The indigo fire from a minute ago had partially burned away the sleeves of her jacket. Through the charred, flaking strips of material, her gray flesh and black feathers had been revealed.

Quirking an eyebrow, lip curling up, Vessa opened her mouth to say something, but her lips twisted in pain and confusion. She frowned at the red-fletched arrow that had pierced her shoulder, and she staggered back a step, flipping over the railing.

"No!" Alina reached out to catch her, but she'd been too late.

Clothes flapping, Vessa fell.

Thinking fast, Alina traced runes in the air and flung out her hands, palms facing the ceiling. A block of white marble wall folded towards her, a crimson cloth awning attached to it, and slammed into the side of the stairwell in an unnatural "L" shape.

Vessa's limp form slapped against the cloth, bouncing, rolling, sliding, and, finally, thudding against the wall three or four stories down. Nestled there, she lay still.

Hopefully, that had been enough to save her.

Alina faced left, ducking aside as the archer loosed another red arrow, which clacked harmlessly against the wall behind. Trying a crisp back-kick, the archer simultaneously tugged another arrow from his quiver, gripping it just beneath its steel head, stabbing at Alina. She backstepped, sidestepped, and then she found her back to the next flight of stairs.

Seven or eight more Ravers clashed just below, two or three fighting their way up to the archer. Alina caught only flashes of movement—sparks as a sword-tip scraped the floor or glanced off gleaming ethereal mage armor; the swish of an ice-javelin piercing its target—as she dodged the attacks of her own opponent.

As she weaved, she heard a pair of bodies thud. Then another. The fight was catching up to Alina and the archer, and his brief hesitation allowed her to sweep his legs. He landed on his stomach with an "Oof."

Alina found herself staring into the blue eyes of Hens Popjay, one of the scarier entries on Ordin's list of Ravers to watch: the Raver of Ravers—the serial killer.

From behind the greasy bangs of his drooping fauxhawk, Popjay grinned at her. "Thanks," he said, licking first his lips and then one of the shiny but scratched circular blades he clutched. He stooped to finish the archer off, slicing him in the back.

Were those chakrams he carried? Even in this desperate moment, Alina flashed back to the weapons manuals she'd pored over when she was younger. Tahtoh had ensured that she'd learned to counter strikes from most slashing, bludgeoning, and piercing weapons. He'd been relentless, running her through hundreds of drills, whacking her with the wooden dummy weapons over and over. She'd carry the bruises with her for days, and he'd look at the welts, say *tut-tut*, and demand she move faster. Or, next time, he'd hit her harder.

Often, she had dreams of dodging, weaving, slapping Tahtoh's wrist, getting smacked on the calf, poked in the ribs, cracked on the shoulder.

Tahtoh's training hadn't been limited to variations of swords, daggers, spears, bows, and guns, however. He'd been equally adamant about familiarizing her with more unusual killing tools. For example, the *chakram*—a blade in the shape of a circle, good for throwing and quick, up-close slashes.

At the time, Alina had pestered him with questions like, "When am I *ever* going to be fighting someone using a katar? Or tiger claws? Or chakrams?"

Well, now, staring into Popjay's manic eyes, she felt she owed her Tahtoh an apology. He must have reasoned that Alina might one day stand opposite a Raver who was intent on killing her. Whether he'd known or only guessed, he'd been—once again—infuriatingly right.

Popjay stepped on top of the archer.

Alina took a step back, raising her fists.

Glancing gleefully at her clawed monster-hands, Popjay said, "You li'l freak."

Alina made a quick sign, casting her earth-shifting spell. But Popjay stepped in, bending at the waist, swirling so fluidly that, for a moment, it seemed as if had no bones in his torso. His chakrams whizzed inches in front of Alina's chest and forearms, and her concentration broke. Her spell fizzled.

Popjay waggled a finger at her, leaping forward to deliver twin-chakram downward strikes. Alina didn't know what possessed her to do so—desperation, instinct, rage—but she caught the chakrams, one in each hand, and clenched.

His smirk vanished, Popjay tried to wrench his weapons free from her grasp, but she held onto them, gritting her teeth. She could feel the Fyrevein burning inside her, erasing her physical limits.

The battle in the lobby still raged, but more and more Ravers had managed to break away from the Enforcers by now. Some came up the way Alina had; others scaled the walls with grappling hooks, sprouted magical vines, launched themselves off rising stone pillars, or simply teleported up floor-by-floor in showers of lights or puffs of smoke.

"Oh, it's such a shame we don't have enough time to *really* get to know each other," said Popjay, and he kicked Alina in the chest. "But we'll have to make this quick. Papa's on the Rave."

Cackling, he advanced on Alina, sinewy, milky-skinned arms raising his chakrams above his head.

Wheezing, Alina stood up, ready for round two.

Then she felt a hand on her shoulder.

A man in a dark leather jacket put himself between her and Popjay, his lightning-shaped earrings gleaming as electricity sparked from his extended fingers.

"*Baraam bol-Talanai*?" Popjay laughed, shouting, "The gods saw fit to grant me a real twofer today, I see. If I take you out, I'll be a legend."

Baraam cracked his knuckles, raised his left hand, and said, "If."

A spear of lightning slammed into Popjay's abs, sparks forking into his head and hands and feet, frying his horrible hairdo; he was thrown backward, flying dozens of feet through the air. He bounced off a distant column, near the front windows far below.

Without facing her, Baraam said, "You'll do everything you can to make certain I fail to keep my promise to the Master. I see that now."

From behind, wielding a pair of pistols, a Raver hopped up the steps, over his dead or unconscious colleagues, and took two shots at Baraam. The bullets rebounded off an invisible bubble of force, and Baraam leapt forward and backhanded the gunman over the edge with a noise like the crackle before the hammer-drop of thunder. The *boom* came in the form of his gaze, which fell upon the next batch of Ravers. They caught sight of Baraam and backed away uncertainly.

After hesitating, one of them yelled, "He's just one guy, for gods' sakes," and lunged up the stairs, his rapier swishing in a complicated feint-feint-slash combo.

Before he could reach Baraam, however, a cloud of darkness fell upon him, also covering those behind. When it cleared, three seconds later, the Ravers, including the fencer, simply stood there. Slack-jawed, arms dangling, swaying gently.

A figure, clad in a midnight blue cloak, materialized in front of Baraam. The black pupil of a golden eye, set deep within her dark coyote mask, flicked toward Alina.

Around the figure swirled tufts of fog—blacker than black, absorbing the color around it—and the mask shifted shape even as it looked back to Baraam, waiting, saying nothing.

"You," Alina breathed.

43

ALINA STOOD BETWEEN THEM, the elusive Dream Queen and the world's top-ranked Aelfraver.

The Dream Queen's single gold eye fixed on Baraam. The voice should have been muffled by the mask; whispered as it was, it should have been impossible to hear above the battle raging just below. But the words were clear, as if they were being breathed directly into Alina's thoughts. "Baraam," she said.

Baraam shook his head. "*Morphea.*"

Morphea raised her shimmering, silver-gloved hands, her slender arms weaving a pattern of such speed and complexity that Alina couldn't follow it. An orb of bubbling darkness—boiling tar—spawned in mid-air, expanding, spreading. It phased through the floors and steps above and below, stretching in all directions, covering the way leading down, the open sides of the stairwell, everything.

All noise faded to a dull roar, then to nothingness. The sphere was semi-translucent; Alina could still make out the crimson, tangerine, and ivory streaks of magic missiles crashing into shields and the shield-less. But, muffling the sounds of murder and sapping it of color, the bubbling forcefield made all that chaotic racket feel like a distant dream.

Inside the newly created hollow sphere, hiding her arms behind her back, Alina watched Baraam and Morphea carefully.

They stared each other down.

Alina backed away as far she could, bumping against the railing, hearing the faintest hiss emanating from the black sphere.

Was she about to get caught up in a nightmare duel between these two?

Another tense moment crept by. She waited, unsure of what she could possibly try that wouldn't get her killed.

Finally, Morphea's eye swiveled to regard her. "Alina K'vich. You made it to the end." A statement delivered in monotone.

Baraam's hand shot out toward the Dream Queen. Alina flinched.

Morphea sighed. One of her silver-gloves disappeared inside the folds of her cloak. She pulled out a wad of gelders and slapped these onto Baraam's waiting palm.

He counted the bills, nodding. "This will help replenish what I recently 'lost.'" He flicked his head back towards Alina.

Alina exhaled. "Alright, I'm confused. What's *happening*?"

Pocketing the money, Baraam said, "We had a wager as to whether you would make it this far."

Tapping her forehead, claws pricking the skin just a little, Alina said, "But, this whole time, you've been doing *everything you can* to boot me back to Truct."

Face totally neutral, Baraam said, "I had a feeling it wouldn't work."

"Okay, time-out. Are you saying—wait. Did you—did you *reverse-psychology* me, Baraam?"

"Not at all. I was completely sincere in my efforts to discourage you. But I knew you'd stop at nothing."

Alina bit her lip. To Morphea: "And you. You tried to terrify me into going home. That night on the bus."

Her mask could not hide the slightest inflection of a smile in her voice. "Still, I had hoped you would rise to the challenge."

"Then why bet against me? I don't get it. Any of it."

"I admit, despite my hopes, I didn't have enough faith in you."

Clutching her skull, Alina shouted, "What? Who even *are* you?"

Morphea waved off her frantic question. "There will be time for that later. For now, there remains nothing and no one between the three of us and the top of this tower." To Baraam: "She's ready."

"I completely disagree." Baraam crossed his arms. "She could be killed. We don't know what awaits us up there."

Placing a hand on his shoulder, light as the touch of sleep, Morphea told him, "I do. And, more importantly, I know what *she* is." She laughed—a sound like sprinkles of fairy dust falling upon a wicked-minded wind. "Come now, Baraam, you can't think her standing here—with us—is an accident. If she is here, she's ready. There is no denying it any longer. Dimas would have agreed with me."

"How can you be so certain?"

"You know the answer to that."

Alina had never had the privilege of seeing Baraam appear embarrassed. His face flushed; his gaze dropped to the floor; he shifted his weight from foot to foot. Morphea had him on the ropes.

"Very well," he grumbled. "Not for you, though. For the Master."

Morphea nodded. "For Dimas."

"Baraam," said Alina, shaking her head. "Could you please start making sense? Who is this weird masked lady? How does she know my grandfather? How does she know you? What are you both *talking* about, damn it?"

Clearing his throat, Baraam gave several false starts before he managed to say, "The Master, he had me swear to keep you safe. This would have been a month or two before he left."

"Died," Alina corrected.

"Died." A tear or two had begun to pool in his eye. He cleared his throat again. "He told me that you were the most important thing in the world to him. That I should keep you from harm at any cost. I swore I would."

"He abandoned me. And so did you."

"I may not have always been physically present, but I had friends reporting on your progress."

Alina gritted her teeth. "You're trying to buy the literal roof from over my head!"

"I would never leave you without a place to stay, but you're not ready to manage The School. You are only a child," Baraam barked back.

"Today no longer," said Morphea quietly.

"The School should have been mine," said Baraam.

"Well, you know *that* isn't accurate," said Morphea. To Alina: "Dimas K'vich entreated me also. He asked of me that I test you."

Alina scoffed. "Now *that* sounds more like him."

"Neither Baraam nor I had any idea of when your heart would stir, nor when circumstances would drive you to pursue a goal beyond your means."

"Uh, not to sell myself short or anything, but I've been going out on Raves for a year now. On my own." She crossed her arms, cocking her hips. "I took out a demon."

"Yes, and that binding spell you wove was quite impressive." Morphea applauded. Three slow claps. "What was it you used in place of an exorcism circle? Your cellular phone, wasn't it?"

"You were there?" said Alina.

Morphea bowed her head, placing a hand over her heart. (Where Alina assumed her heart would be.) "I am less comfortable with leaving things to chance than Baraam, here."

"No, you had less *confidence* in her," he retorted. "There is a difference."

An explosion shook the entire stairwell, and a crack spread from its base to the floor on which they stood.

"It is only a matter of minutes before The Authority sends forth its death squads to quell this upstart. The conclusion to this discussion must wait." Even as Morphea spoke, the cracks spread, deepened, widened. The stairwell fell away from under Alina's feet, and she let out a scream, grasping for anything within arm's reach.

Several panicked, life-flashing-before-her-waking-eyes instants passed before she was able to consciously realize that Baraam and Morphea were simply floating there, unfazed. As was she.

The bubbling, hissing black sphere hung, suspended, hundreds of feet above ground-level, holding the three of them aloft at its center.

Morphea looked up, toward the remains of the stairwell which clung to the roof of the tower. And the sphere glided slowly upward, carrying with it the Dream Queen, the top-rated Raver in the nation, and Alina K'vich.

Their feet alighted on the uppermost remnants of the stairwell, and the magical bubble of boiling tar dissipated.

As Baraam brushed past her, Alina grabbed him by the elbow. "So, you were… rooting for me, from the start? Kinda?"

"Don't read too deeply into it."

"You *care* about me, don't you?"

"Alina. Would you just—*stop*."

She clapped a hand over her mouth. "You do." She spread her arms, giddy. It was all so surreal. "This is where we hug, right? I'm feeling it. It's hug o'clock."

He dragged his rough palm over his stubble. "Infantile," he grunted, not meeting her gaze. He clapped a hand onto her shoulder again, squeezed. Then he shoved his hands in the pockets of his scuffed-up leather jacket; a spark of electricity ran up his neck.

Morphea took the lead. The stairs carried them to the highest point in the Capital, and therefore all of El, the crown of the skies—where awaited the elusive Aelf.

"No choice any longer, I suppose. You're in it, now," said Baraam. "Whatever happens, stay close to me. I'll handle this."

Alina crossed her arms. "You do know what that thing is, don't you?"

"An Aelf I'm going to kill."

"Talaganbubăk."

The name caught him completely off-guard. Chuckling, he said, "Don't be ridiculous. The Master slew that creature long ago."

"I'm telling you, I'm right. Just *believe* me, for once."

"It's not possible."

"Fine. How about we bet on it? Shall we say a *million* gelders?"

Rolling his eyes, he turned his back on her. "Let's just go. Do as I do. Let the beast make the first move. Analyze its patterns, then counterattack. Remember your training."

"Any other basic instructions you'd like to give this rookie who *definitely* hasn't been taking care of herself for a very long time?"

"Yes," he said flatly. "For once, *try* not to do anything rash."

44

WHEN TOLOMOND CAME TO, the dragon's inner workings had cooled and gone dark.

He pushed himself up, leaning on his elbows, and dragged himself toward the only light source. Past the monster's silent machine organs and up its throat, he crawled. He wriggled his way between its sawblade teeth. Its mouth wasn't open wide enough for him to slide out, so he wedged himself against its palate and, with his feet, levered its jaws apart.

Tolomond fell out of H'ranajaan's maw, striking a metal manhole cover. The flesh of his arms and legs had bubbled and blistered all over. The steam wafting upward stung his pinkened skin.

He limped forward a few feet before turning to inspect where pieces of the dragon had met the earth. On the way down, it had struck several structures, warping its exoskeletal plates and exposing its wired guts; parts of it had snapped clean off.

There was something poking out from under the destroyed abomination's talons. A pale hand.

Tolomond approached the dragon's claw, squatted, wedged his fingers beneath the twisted metal frame. Pushing through his heels, he growled from the strain, eyes bulging, and he rolled H'ranajaan's monstrous arm off whatever it had crushed.

Slumping, Tolomond panted and inspected the owner of the hand. It had been an unholy marriage of man and machine, this thing; its components lay in fragments around its cracked false skin and warped titanium-reinforced skeleton. Atop what had once been a head, there remained a single tuft of undulating purple-blue hair.

Near the hair, a blue light switched on, and a small ridged metal box emitted the following tinny, whispered last words: "I'm sorry. Tell her I'm—" The voice cut off; the light faded. The semi-organic heap of ruined man lay perfectly still.

Tolomond rejoiced: Ordin Ivoir was dead.

Killed by the very servile beast he'd summoned. *Yea, for evil ever contains within itself the seeds of its own destruction.*

Just as he was set to sing the praises of The Author of Creation, however, he took pause. Feeling a sudden and inexplicable agony, above and beyond the burn-wounds and the cuts all over his body, he dropped to one knee.

He looked down, noting that on the front of his tunic blossomed a flower of blood—an ever-widening bloom of bright red seeping into the wool.

In a daze, he swiveled his head, searching the bags of garbage, the stacks of metal junk, but saw nothing.

From behind him, someone said, "Pyct'Tzi: avenged, I." A small creature—the head of a mouse, but with claws and the legs and hooves of a goat—hovered on fairy wings in front of his nose.

It was covered, head-to-hoof, in blood. Tolomond's blood.

"What—"

The Pyct tensed, its minuscule muscles bulging, veins in its neck and chest pulsating. A scarlet aura flowed from its form.

After so many battles fought over the course of the past twenty-four hours, and the lifetime before it, Tolomond was spent. He awaited the smiting blow.

The Pyct shot forward like a bullet—a raging, red-burning bullet—and it punched straight through Tolomond's breastbone, drilling through his body, until it burst out from between his shoulder blades.

Tolomond sucked in a jerking, bubbling gasp. As he struck the ground, his right knee dislocated.

He tried to cough but could no longer draw breath.

The Author calls me home. So begins a new chapter.

The Pyct hovered over him.

I am ready, Lord.

The last thing he saw was the glow of purple emergency lights—The Authority was coming.

Kill me, he silently urged the Pyct as his consciousness faded. *I'll not rot in a cell. Not again. Kill me. Free me!*

With his final moments of focus, he patted the ground beside him, his fingers closing around a shard of glass. Palm gushing blood, he lifted the shard, and he tried to gouge out his eyes, but he lacked the strength.

His unworthy eyes.

He closed them.

And never again would they open.

45

THE CLOCKTOWER BELFRY WAS a labyrinth of gears, levels, and chimes. As Alina, behind Morphea and Baraam, climbed the final steps, she was greeted by dim light filtered through heavy tattered curtains and layer upon layer of cobwebs. Piles of centipede husks littered the floor.

The clock struck six, the deafening, brassy booms resounding within Alina's chest. She covered her ears, but it was no use, given her proximity to the multitude of massive bells.

When the echoes and the ringing in her skull finally ceased, she followed her companions around corner after blind corner. She ducked under spiderwebs, hanging clappers, clicking gears and other components. With each careful step, her heartrate rose, beating a crescendo against her sternum.

She kept a watchful eye out for any ladder or other roof access.

A few paces ahead, Baraam hissed.

"What is it?" Alina whispered.

"Morphea?" he said. "Morphea!"

Alina looked around. The midnight-cloaked woman had disappeared.

"Just like her," said Baraam. He kept moving.

In this way, for several more minutes, he and Alina crept through the belfry. Until they felt they'd explored every inch of it.

They were so close to their goal, yet they'd somehow missed any means of getting to the roof. Alina turned this way and that, mentally retracing their steps, finding nothing.

Then Baraam gestured for her to come close. His voice quiet as the flutter of moth wings, he said, "It's here."

Alina's eyelids twitched as she resisted the urge to wildly spin around. The Fyrevein was acting up again, boiling her insides. It took all her willpower to keep still. Like trying to lasso and subdue a bucking horse with a shoestring.

"I can feel its gaze on us," Baraam added, closing his eyes. "It's coming." His eyes shot open. "Alina, don't let it—"

A pall of pure darkness swept over them. It was so thick that Alina could no longer see Baraam, even though there'd been less than a foot between them.

She reached out for him; her fingers grasped nothing but air. "Baraam," she cried, but no sound escaped her throat. The words lodged in her lungs, lingering there, choking her. She hacked, bending over, spitting, but nothing would come out. The black smoke and her unspeakable words mingled within her, weighing her down. Her vision went dim, and she fell onto her knees.

Her world shrunk to a pinprick of light beaming from an unknown source. Perhaps it was the gate to heaven, she thought, until she found herself back in the bathroom. White porcelain sink. Running hot water. Foggy mirror. All the familiar elements.

Except, this time, she was no child; this memory was much more recent.

Sixteen-year-old Alina had just returned from a trip to the gas station. She'd gone out for chips and soda. Tahtoh had been making dinner.

When she'd returned, she'd found The School empty.

At the stove, water had boiled over the lip of the pot, inside which rolled half-cooked pasta.

"Tahtoh?"

She'd checked every room. Twice. No sign of her grandfather anywhere.

Turning the stovetop burners off, she'd tried to think of a reasonable explanation. Had he wandered off? He'd sometimes leave without notice, true, but never like this. Not just before dinner. Not with a fire going. He wasn't so irresponsible. Or forgetful.

Alina had felt certain, then, that something was wrong.

Leaping downstairs, she'd pounded on Mrs. Qamasque's door until the older woman answered. Had she seen Tahtoh leave? Seated at the dinner table, her husband quietly explained that he hadn't, nor had Mrs. Qamasque.

Confused, Alina had returned upstairs, figuring Tahtoh would be back any minute. Then she'd heard the soft hiss of the running faucet. Hot water. Steam. The bathroom sink.

Twisting the knob to cut the flow, she'd noticed something floating in the pool of scalding water. Once the sink had completely drained, she recognized what it was.

A black feather.

She'd picked it up, examined it. With her sleeve, she'd wiped the condensation from the small oval mirror.

Something had moved—a shadow, flitting behind her. She'd turned to catch a glimpse of it, but it had gone. *If* there'd even been anything there in the first instance.

A black feather.

Refocusing, Alina clung to her reality—her current reality—within the belfry of City Hall. She told herself this was an illusion. That an Aelf with powerful psychic abilities was prying into her fears, using them to smother her. She wasn't really dying. It was all a trick, similar to the virtual-magical unreality into which Ordin had dragged her just a few hours prior. This, too, was fake. It only *seemed* real.

Her self-pep talk was working. The choking dark began to recede ever so slightly. With each passing moment, she felt more confident.

Once her racing mind had slowed from a gallop to a trot, she found that she could breathe again. And stand. And look at her arms—

Her arms ridged with *black feathers.*

The veil of darkness fell from her sight, and she stared into the golden, crimson-flecked eyes of the Talaganbubăk, the Bane of New El.

The crow-like monstrosity, up close, was naturally far more impressive than when viewed from half a mile away—as it withstood all the shells and light-nets and bombs The Authority could throw at it. Its eyes alone were half as big as Alina's entire body. The fact that it had wedged itself within this maze-like enclosed space, without destroying the roof or disturbing any of the machinery, seemed insane. Until you remembered that it could shift its shape at will.

The first time she had been faced with it, back at The Gildhall, Alina had seen the Talaganbubăk take the form of a roughly man-sized shadow. A walking black hole. That shape had obviously been an illusion, and, Alina intuited, so was this current one. This crow skin was probably about as real as the nightmare she'd just escaped.

"Alina, stay back," shouted Baraam. He hurled a lightning bolt at the creature's face, striking its beak.

A plume of smoke rose from the blackened spot, but the Aelf seemed otherwise unconcerned. It did, however, shift its attention—slowly—toward Baraam. One huge, bird-like talon at a time, it wobbled in place, moving to face its attacker.

During this maneuver, the Talaganbubăk's extremities were not obstructed or even hindered by the bells, chimes, gears, levers, or even the steep slope of the roof just above.

"It's an illusion, Baraam," she said, her suspicions confirmed. "Revomancy."

"Its claws feel real enough," he answered. He was bleeding from three crisscrossing gashes stretching from his shoulders to his hips.

He could hardly stand. *Baraam* could hardly stand. That seemed impossible.

This Aelf had grievously wounded *the* Baraam bol-Talanai, besting him in under two minutes.

"We tried it your way," she told Baraam. She ran towards him, hopping over a row of gears, ducking under a chime. Again face-to-face with the crow, she said, "What do you want?"

Baraam raised a blood-slick hand. "Alina, what are you doing?"

"This is the Talaganbubăk—Longcandles, Child-snatcher, Father Crow. It's a sentient being, and it's been alive for hundreds of years." She stared, unblinking, into the Aelf's eyes. "And I want to know why it came to New El."

"You can't *reason* with monsters." Baraam shoved her behind him, glowering up at the creature. "There is only one answer to such abominations." His fists crackled with white energy. "As Ravers, we swore an oath to exterminate the Aelf."

"Well," Alina said, cracking her neck, "everyone does keep reminding me I'm *not* an Aelfraver." Digging her claws into his muscled back, she pivoted, wrenching with all her might, and threw him aside.

He crashed into some long-unused wooden scaffolding, his foot landing in a bucket. A cloud of dust rose around him. Coughing, he opened his mouth to speak. But it was obvious by his surprised expression that he couldn't find the words.

Its list of targets reduced to one, the Talaganbubăk focused on Alina.

Gazing into its oval pupils—abyssal pits in which she might forever lose herself—she stared at her own unimpressed reflection. And she shrugged off the hypnotic effect before it could take hold again.

"Nice trick, but don't think it'll work twice," she said, standing firm. "Now, I asked you a question."

The Aelf let out a long, slow, rumbling noise—the stirrings of a volcano that has not awoken in ages. It was *laughing*.

"Something funny?" Alina said, praying to Buthmertha that she sounded a *lot* more confident than she felt.

When the Aelf's laughter subsided, the volcano asleep again, it spoke.

And it said, *"Well done, my little Cabbage. Well done."*

The crow—nothing more than an image, after all—wafted away like so much fog. What was left in its stead was a man—well, a man-like figure. It was slightly hunched, gray-skinned. Black feathers ran up its legs and arms, two wings folded on its back. Most of its body was covered by a long cloak, also black, and on its head it wore a wide-brimmed hat of the same color. Its eyes—glimmering gold—narrowed, and it smiled its fanged smile at her.

But, even with all these details overloading her brain, even with *all* the differences—and they were many—she recognized this creature. It was, in fact, someone she'd once known better than anyone else. Or, so she'd thought.

Choking up, Alina said, *"Tahtoh?"*

Though pockmarked, narrower, sharper, and *gray*, this was the face of Dimas K'vich.

"Tahtoh?" she repeated.

"Master?" said Baraam. Though Alina couldn't take her eyes off the creature—her grandfather—in front of her, she heard Baraam disentangling himself from the trash heap into which he'd been thrown.

"Yes, Cabbage. It's me," said the Aelf.

"Lies, Alina," Baraam shouted, limping forward, clutching his chest. With the electric heat springing from his fingers, he cauterized his wounds, wincing. "It's attempting to fool you again. Stand aside and let me finish it."

"Boy," said the Aelf, glaring at Baraam. "You've done well to escort her here. But now I wish to speak with my granddaughter."

"You *dare* wear his face?" A great well of energy burst forth from Baraam, filling the space with the smell of ozone and burning toast. He flung bolt after bolt at the creature. "Filth. Monster. Deceiver." After more than a dozen blasts, he was spent.

He slumped.

And the Aelf stood there. It tried to play Baraam's assault off as unimpressive. But the yawn seemed forced, and Alina noticed a twitch of pain as it lifted its hand. Baraam had hurt it, now that he was hitting the real creature and not the illusion. But would it be enough?

Tongue lolling, Baraam panted.

"Are you quite finished?" said the Aelf.

Baraam fell to the floor, unconscious.

"Good." The Aelf squared off with Alina.

"You're not really him," she said. "I won't believe it. You're not going to trick me again." Was she trying to convince it or herself? "I don't know if your beef is with the whole city, or just us Ravers, but you must want *something*. So, spit it out, already. Why are you here? Why do all this? Finally got tired of luring children into swamps?"

The Aelf rolled its eyes. "Slander. I offered the children freedom. They were lost and, in many cases, terrified and abused. I gave them a home. You of all should know better than to believe the propaganda of humans against us."

"'Us'?"

"The 'Aelf,' as the humans have narrow-mindedly named all of the thousands of species across numerous ecosystems. We are of many tribes, and we were here long before the humans came to be. And, if I have anything to say about it, our kind will endure long after they've gone."

"A threat? Makes sense. You're a mass murderer. Turns out, you wanna wipe out all humanity. Great. Really winning me over, here."

"I do not wish the death of humanity. They will bring it upon themselves—sooner, if left to make their own choices." The creature sighed. "They need us, as they always have."

Alina growled, "You should wear a different face if you want me to try to take *any* of this seriously. My grandfather was a good man, and now he's dead, and you're using him like a prop."

"Lina." The Aelf spread its razor-feathered arms. "It *is* me."

"No. Nope."

"Look at your arms. Now look at mine." It approached, holding up its hands. "How do you explain this?"

Alina backed away. "Nah, see, if you really were Tahtoh, you'd know he made me read *all* the books. Which is how I learned the Talaganbubăk famously haunted depressed and isolated children. Especially around Truct, where I'm from. For all I know, *you're* the one who cursed me. This weird stuff I'm going through doesn't prove anything. Now, I'll ask just once more. *What do you want?*"

Lowering its hands, the Aelf said, "For you to understand."

"Understand *what*?" Alina screamed.

"Your heritage. The legacy of your family—your Uncle Mateus. Zatalena, your mother."

"Don't you say their names."

"I will if I wish. She was my daughter. He is my son."

Alina's scream carried throughout the belfry, and she ran at the Aelf. It sidestepped. The wild punch she threw dented the twenty-foot-tall bell just behind the creature.

The warped echoes faded.

Breathing hard, Alina dropped to her shins and said, "If you're Dimas K'vich, tell me why you left."

It kept its distance, answering, "To finish what I and others began, long ago. War is coming."

"There's a war happening outside right now."

"A mere skirmish. The squabbles of single-minded apes. The war I speak of has been millennia in the making, and it will end only when the last dragon dies."

"Dragon?" Alina chuckled weakly. "There hasn't been a dragon in centuries. 'You' taught me that."

In a spurt of smoke, the Aelf was in front of her again. "Yet there's one alive, still, and she sleeps closer than you may think."

"And that's why you're here?"

"No, no. I came to this seat of human arrogance for a much simpler purpose—to make life more difficult for our enemy. And to settle a few scores in the process." It knelt, so that their eyes were level. "Cabbage, do you remember what I told you, that day I found you in the hedge maze?"

Alina looked up at the Aelf. "You said you'd make me an Aelfraver."

It smiled, almost warmly. "Ah, no, I promised to teach you how to *track and hunt* Aelf. Remember?" It reached out to caress her cheek.

She let it. Gently, with its clawed fingers, it lifted her chin and tapped her on the nose—three times—just as her grandfather used to do. When she'd been a small child, orphaned and in a strange new place.

"Tahtoh?" she said, this time—despite the evidence of her eyes—believing her heart.

It really was him. His rasping voice. His slightly off-kilter jawline. He even smelled the same—pine and sunflower seeds.

Dimas K'vich took her into his arms. "My child," he said softly.

Clutching his sharp feathers, she sobbed onto his neck.

She could hardly believe it. Her head was spinning. Had she let herself be hypnotized again?

But, no, this was real. All her senses acknowledged the truth of his presence. He was there, really there—the man who'd raised her—wrapped in the scarred gray skin of the Talaganbubăk.

At last, he said, "I want nothing more than for this moment to last. But there's something I need from you." He released her, standing again.

She got to her feet, wiping her eyes (taking care not to claw them out).

Dimas inhaled deeply. "I spent half your life teaching you compassion, the needlessness of all this killing. I wanted you to be more than the heedless, stamping, brutish Aelfravers who came before you. Most of all, I knew I would need an heir, one able to finish my work." He sighed again. "There's too much to explain. But I have faith: you will recognize the enemy of your bloodline when you see him. He will make himself known in due time. And you must be ready. From the very moment of your birth, you were marked for death—or worse. I am so very sorry. Please believe that I never wished for it all to fall to you. My will, however, is bound to a design older than even the Nation of El."

"What are you saying?"

"It began long ago, and there is no time now for the whole tale. But you know of my lie about the Talaganbubăk. As you have seen, I am he; he is me. I have spent untold lifetimes gathering strength and support. You will find friends in even the unlikeliest of places." His spoke quickly, even frantically now. "And, with your eyes opened to the truth, you must find a way to end the imprisonment of Ji'inaluud. It must be you. With his power threatened, our enemy will reveal himself. He has poisoned all creation, slowly, for ages. Our only chance is to lure him out. If you fail, it will all have been for nothing. It must be you who finishes this task and absolves us of our great burden."

Alina's shoulders sagged. "You were an Aelf." She couldn't believe what she was saying. "The whole time. My whole life. And I never knew."

"Four thousand years allow for much practice and study of the arcane. I am not without my secrets."

Alina held up her hands, wiggled her inhuman fingers. "I'm an Aelf."

"You are my granddaughter. My blood. Our very souls are inseparable. Nothing anyone tells you—not ever—can change that."

"We're *hybrids*." She punched a wooden beam, splintering it.

Tahtoh placed his hand on her head. "Listen to me. Our time has run out. I wish it were not so. But, at any moment, the horde of mindless animals below will storm this tower. Skilled though she is, Ruqastra's spell will hold them only so long. You must listen closely, and fulfill my final request."

"Final…?"

"Alina, my beautiful granddaughter, I waited for years to see how our blood would shape you. Some part of me knew, from the moment of your birth, what you would become. And the better part of me regrets it, but we must act, as we always have done, for the good of our family. Never forget what I tell you now: it was *he* who had your parents murdered, but *you* were the one he wanted. And I will not let him have you. It must therefore be you who carries on, who carries our hopes to their conclusion." A gray tear rolled down Tahtoh's gray cheek. "With my powers, you will be safe, hidden from his eyes. This will buy you some time."

"I don't under—"

"I brought you here for one purpose. You must kill me."

She shook her head, shouting something at him. She reeled, unable to understand the words of anger and confusion that poured from her own lips.

"Alina." His voice took on the harsh, sharp inflection he'd always used when correcting his students as they drilled. Suddenly, it was like she was back in class. And that familiarity—swirling in this haze of panic and doubt—was enough to focus her thoughts. "Tell me, what is Egogenesis?" he quizzed her.

Mind as foggy as that old bathroom mirror, she parroted what she'd read years ago: "'The process by which certain species of Aelf may grow stronger through the consumption of their sires. Examples of Egogenetic Aelf include the Varhund, the Pyct, the Dragon, and the Sevensin.'"

"Excellent," said Dimas, pride bursting from his words. "Now, understand the truth. Know your heritage, Alina—you are of the stock the humans call 'Demidivine.' A Sevensin. You are human and Noble, a child of two peoples. As such, you may succeed where I failed. You are the only one who can mend this broken world of ours. Not because you were marked by a god or heralded by prophets, but because of *who you yourself have chosen to become.*" His voice softening again, he concluded: "But my very existence limits your potential. And you must be in full possession of your Noble soul if you have any hope of defeating the one who would destroy you—and everyone you care for. Time has watered down what remains of our bloodline. What is left of us is spread too thinly. We have essence left for one final battle." He leaned in close, whispering, "Kill me Alina. Consume my heart."

"What? I—No. What kind of sick joke is this? You left me alone to run off and fight some kinda holy war, being all cryptic about it, and now you want me to kill you? Is this a test?"

"Yes, it is." Dimas sat down and crossed his legs. His arms he left open, exposing his chest. "And there is only one answer."

"'There's always another option. Killing is a last resort.' Isn't that what you used to say?"

"And look at how soulful you are! How kind! How courageous! Even in the face of death, even in the presence of a great and terrible Aelf more powerful than anything you've ever seen, you refuse to surrender your convictions. I am *so* proud of you."

From below, in the direction of the ruined stairwell, she could hear thudding. And voices.

"They're coming. They're coming, Lina, and they cannot find us like this. We will be exposed. End it. Now. Before they see and all is lost." He clasped his hands, pleading with her. "I have over-exerted myself. I grow weak. I will not be able to stop all of them. It must be now. And it must be you."

She jabbed her clawed finger at him. "No." She crossed her arms.

He growled. Then he got to his feet, ambling over to Baraam, his gait stiff-in-the-knees, just as it had been in his human form.

"What are you doing?" said Alina.

Dimas did not answer. Instead, he wrapped his fingers around Baraam's ankle and lifted his leg, dragging him past Alina and over to the obscured window.

With a lazy chop of his free hand, the curtain, the window, the walls, and the entire roof were torn apart. The stones and glass shards and shingles were swept aside, and Alina was suddenly engulfed in bright morning light.

After her eyes had adjusted to the sun, she noticed Tahtoh standing on a plank that jutted out from the now-exposed and ruined belfry. He dangled Baraam's unconscious form over the edge.

"Tahtoh, don't—what are you—"

"It's quite simple, Alina." His stare was unbreaking, iron. "I will drop him in thirty seconds. Unless you do something about it."

"Let him go."

"That is precisely what I will do. In twenty seconds."

The wind whipped at his long black cloak, snatching his wide-brimmed hat from his bald gray head.

Alina took a step forward, hands at her sides. "You're making a mistake. I don't even like him. And—and, if he dies, all my problems go away. I'll get to keep The School, and I'll never have to worry about him breathing down my neck ever again."

"If that is your choice," said Dimas. "Ten seconds."

Stealing another step, Alina said, "He was your best student, though."

"No, he wasn't. Ruqastra was. Obedient, loyal, wise Ruqastra—if only she'd been my granddaughter. She would have done as I asked."

"I know what you're trying to do."

"I don't care. Five seconds."

"You wouldn't hurt Baraam."

"Four."

"He's your student."

"Three."

"He loved you like a father!"

"Two."

Alina lunged for Baraam, attempting to grab his other leg, an arm—anything.

Tahtoh yanked the unconscious man away from her and bared his fangs, grimacing. And he let go.

Baraam began to fall.

Unthinking, acting on impulse fueled by her exhausted anger and the dregs of the Fyrevein, Alina channeled all her remaining Niima into the most powerful Geomantic spell she'd ever cast. She extended the floor, borrowing stone and wood from the surrounding walls, even siphoning a portion of the large bell she'd dented. The result: where, milliseconds before, there'd been only air, an L-shaped, patchwork platform spontaneously burst forth and caught Baraam's limp body.

Her relief was short-lived.

Tahtoh grabbed a fistful of her hair, tearing at her scalp, and, before she could think or feel anything, she thrust her clawed hand out like a spear and pierced his torso.

Tahtoh's look of anger gave way to relief. He smiled, stumbling backward, falling to his knees.

Alina clutched in her fist a pear-shaped, see-through, gelatinous… light. That was the only word for it: a light, given tangible form. Even as she stared at the thing, it seeped into her hand, like water into sand, until it was gone. Or, rather, until it was entirely *inside of her.*

She looked to Tahtoh, who smiled and mouthed, "I love you." And, like the golden essence that had been his heart, he, too, disappeared. His body disintegrated into pinpricks of light, melting away, melding with the air.

On her hands and knees, she scrabbled over to where he'd knelt, but she was too late. There was nothing left of him; Dimas K'vich had been returned to the sky.

Lead-limbed, she dragged Baraam's body away from the edge and checked for a pulse. He'd live.

Falling onto her back, she was too exhausted to think, scream, cry out, or do any of those things she felt she really ought to have done. Her face was water-soaked putty. Moist cheeks, and drooping lips and eyelids.

Gazing down upon Pluto Plaza—its blackened craters, the bodies that littered it—Alina experienced an overwhelming urge to return to the earth. The Terrie surface world. Home.

The Elementals could keep the glitz and shine of their plastic planet. After today, she was done. Out.

A thud and the sounds of rapid footfalls. Alina turned around to see several Ravers spilling onto the belfry (what was left of it). They all just, sort of, milled about. Scratching their heads, no doubt wondering where their prey had gone off to.

Minutes later, The Authority arrived. Enforcers erupted from the stairwell like agitated ants, surrounding the bells, the Ravers, and Alina.

Alina didn't have the energy to protest, even as she was manhandled into a pair of Niima-nullifying cuffs.

The other Ravers were treated the same. Even Baraam.

Except, Baraam had something to say about all this, once he'd regained consciousness. He demanded that he—and Alina—be let go. His demands were refused. So, he lifted his shaking hand, snapped his fingers, and blinded everyone with a flash like an exploding star.

Alina felt him scoop her up, and she said nothing. She did nothing. She felt nothing.

Maybe she *was* nothing.

On some level, she was aware of the fact that she and Baraam were flying, transported inside a bolt of lightning. But she was on the ground before it really hit her how strange this was. The lightning bolt, sure, but also that Baraam had just gotten her off that roof. Gotten her out of being arrested.

And, before she knew it, she was on solid ground again, where she'd been standing only an hour or two ago. Waiting for the Talaganbubăk to show up. Waiting with—

"Cho," Alina called, snapping out of her dreamlike state of shock. "Cho!"

Snaking her way between several people gawking at the flaming, crumbling heap that was City Hall, the little bald girl appeared.

Alina took Cho in her arms. Tears flowed and mingled. Alina couldn't speak or think; she was entirely consumed by a singular grief, a grief of too many facets to name. It spilled from her in great heaving eruptions, rocking her from her core outward. She cried until her abs burned, until the muscles in her face stung. Images of Ordin, her half-remembered parents, and her grandfather grappled one another in the bloodied arena of her mind. And it was all she could do to growl incoherent snippets of fury and remorse.

Baraam separated the two of them with a firm hand. "The Authority are coming. They'll be rounding up all Ravers. It will go badly for those who are apprehended." He grabbed Alina's elbow. "We have to get you to the train station."

"Her too," said Alina, wrapping her arm around Cho. "Her too."

He hesitated.

Then, "Fine. To Mercy's Approach. *Now.*"

46

TOLOMOND AWOKE BUT FOUND he could not open his eyes, nor could he move his arms. He lay on his back. Strapped down. Or chained. Neck wouldn't turn. Mouth wouldn't open.

A voice like spoiled butter said, "Wakey-wakey, Tolly, m'boy. Hierophant's not done with you yet." The man who was speaking, his breath smelled of burning pine needles. "Your body, at least." He placed his wet lips on the prone Tolomond's cheek and gave it a sloppy kiss.

Tolomond tried to scream, but only the feeblest moan slipped out from between the cracks in his chapped lips.

"Are you afraid, Tolly? Don't be, don't be. You've been chosen, after all. We brought you *back*, see. And now, while we rebuild you—making a few key modifications, naturally—you and I, we get to spend a lot more time together. Just like the old days, Tolly. Remember? Like when you were a kid, just an innocent little lump of clay for me to sculpt. It'll be just like back then." The speaker nuzzled his nose against the prisoner's, inhaling, long and deep and contentedly. "When I'm through with you, you'll be *perfect.* And good thing, too. The Author's not done with you yet."

The doctor left then, and, in the darkness, Tolomond had only his own whimpering for company.

So it went on for hours or days or months—silence so pronounced and oppressive that it sat on Tolomond's chest, pressing the air from his lungs.

When the doctor returned, Tolomond yearned for those moments of suffocating silence, yearned for the absence of saws and hammers and needle and thread—and the constant drip-water chuckle of his torturer.

47

IN DIRECT CONTRAST WITH the pall over Alina's heart, and the festering after-panic that had torn through New El, the sun shined as brightly as it had in weeks, perhaps months. Spring was just around the corner, and with it would come the blooming of buds, the foaling of young—all that new life, ripening. But Alina could see only death—garbage in the streets, smog in the air, and men and women and children scuttling away from her as she passed. Like she was carrying a bouquet of plague-ridden rats.

She looked down at her arms and found they'd reverted to their regular old human shape and hue. How this was possible, she couldn't say, and she didn't much care. She'd been emptied. All emotions drained from her like water from the bottom of a cracked glass.

Cho kept pace with her but said nothing. There wasn't anything to say. And who knew where Mezami had gone.

Just ahead, Baraam was shouting at his phone. "You knew. You knew everything. About the Master. About *her*. You kept me in the dark—no, you listen to me for once. You never—" He paused, a spark crackling along his shoulder and neck as he clenched his jaw, waiting for the person on the other end of the line to finish speaking. "And you've left me with the job of cleaning up, as usual. Later, then. But you are not dodging the question next time.

I am owed answers." Another pause. "Mercy's Approach, yes. Platform 3. 8:33 a.m. to Gladjaw? I have it covered. Already handled." He hung up, and he fidgeted with his phone for a few more moments, thumbs ablur.

Then he turned so abruptly that Alina and Cho nearly collided with him.

Baraam said, "I will be escorting you to your transport to Gladjaw Junction. Once you've arrived there, you'll be on your own." He asked Cho, "Do you still have any of the cash you stole from me?"

"Uh," said Cho, fingers interlaced behind her back. "Yeah?"

He nodded. "Then that should get you both a bus ticket back to Truct." He turned around to continue walking.

"Baraam," said Alina, causing him to stop. "I don't have a home in Truct anymore. Remember?"

He slowed, looking up, stiff-shouldered. "I have… retracted my offer on The School."

Alina's jaw dropped. "You called Qamasque?"

"Sent her a digimail. My lawyers will draw up any documents related to severance of contract. I will make the Qamasques understand. Anyway, their irritation doesn't concern me. What does is the storm brewing in the wake of this morning's riots."

"I don't know what to say." Alina intently stared at a litter-collector drone as its vacuum tube sucked up a discarded soda can.

The larger significance of Baraam's words and the morning's events finally struck her: The Authority and the Aelfravers had fought one another. They were enemies. Would it be enough for The Gild to disown the Ravers who'd triggered the incident? Would the Twelve Families demand the Grandmaster's resignation? Or, would all those Ravers be executed as traitors?

"They're going to come after me," said Alina. "The Enforcers."

Baraam cocked his head, sniffing. "Why would they? You weren't at City Hall. You have an airtight alibi."

"What's that now?"

"I spoke to Mr. Amming of *Amming & Sons* in Truct not fifteen minutes ago. He confirmed that you are currently seated at his dining table, enjoying a stack of blueberry pancakes and tolerating his son's poor attempts at humor."

Alina gave a shuddering sigh. She didn't know what to say. She settled on, "What are you gonna do, though?"

He thought for a moment. "Make the best of it. I have… some decisions to make. In light of what… happened back there." He set off again.

Following, stumbling a little, Alina said, "Hey, we've still got a lot to sort out, you and me. About Ordin and—and Dimas. But, Baraam? Thank you."

He made no reply.

A few minutes later, a squad of half a dozen Enforcers blocked their path, training their rifles on Baraam and Alina. One of them shouted a challenge, "That's far enough, Ravers. Back up, bellies down, and—"

Baraam gave a dismissive wave of his hand, and a lightning bolt struck the middle officer, tendrils of electricity zapping from shoulder to shoulder and head to head. After twitching for a second or two, all six fell, all at once, their suits smoking faintly. And Baraam's hand spasmed as another arc of static spurted from it before he dampened his Niima.

"I am nearly tapped," he admitted.

"I'm beyond tapped," said Alina.

"Don't worry," Cho piped up. "I'll beat up anyone else who bothers us."

For the rest of their journey to the train station, no one else did try to stop them. The streets were nearly vacant, the Elementals likely still hiding in their homes, waiting for the official "All Clear." And The Authority must have been out in force, but with so much ground to cover—and so many high-priority and dangerous fugitives to apprehend—they were spread thin. Not all the Aelfravers who'd fought in the Battle of City Hall had been captured, and a few of them were nearly as dangerous as Baraam bol-Talanai.

The whole walk to the train station was eerily quiet. During this state of emergency, absent were the hum of hovercraft and the cacophony of human voices mingling on the streets; even the holographic advertisements had been disabled. Only the occasional stirring of a rodent in a garbage can or the bark of a nervous dog could be heard, always out of sight.

It wasn't until they reached the entrance to Mercy's Approach Station, shadowed by the towering statues of the long-dead Aelfravers who'd built this city, that Baraam slowed his pace.

Alina didn't know *how* she knew, but she sensed what must have been bothering him. "They're waiting for us behind the next set of statues," she said.

"Ten dudes. With guns." Cho's expression briefly went blank, her eyes flashing scarlet, darting rapidly left and right. "What do we do?"

Shaking the tension from her wrists, Alina stepped forward. "We've already performed several acts of terrorism today. Might as well add vandalism and destruction of property to the list." Niima surging from the soles of her feet to the tips of her fingers, she thrust out her arms, and asphalt stalagmites speared from the ground, rocking the statues. The heroic effigies wobbled before toppling.

The metallic screech of moorings snapping was followed by the domino booming of the rapid-fire crashes that cracked the pavement and destroyed a large swath of wrought-iron fence, tearing up the grass, demolishing flowerbeds and hedgerows. As the statues fell, ten men and women in red vests rolled out of their path, revealing themselves as they narrowly escaped being mulched.

Amid the shattered memorials to these legendary heroes and heroines, stood the would-be ambushers.

The dust settled.

The gold and red of their uniforms declared them to be Enforcers in Walazzin's pocket, but they didn't look fancy enough to be his household Chimaera Guard. No over-the-top eagle helmets or lion-paw pauldrons.

One by one, the mercenaries got up, patting their shoulders and their legs. Handguns snapped up, drawing red beads on Alina, Baraam, and Cho.

"That was not the best opening move," said Baraam, holding his hands up.

Alina imitated his gesture, and muttered from the corner of her mouth, "I was banking on that maybe scaring them off."

One of the Enforcers stepped forward, peering down the sights of her handgun. "We don't want problems with you, Ravers. We're only after the girl."

"Care to explain?" asked Baraam.

"Long story, but—" Alina took a deep breath "—Cho was taken in by the Walazzin patriarch after her family died, probably at the hands of said Walazzin patriarch, and he had her locked away in his villa or whatever, where he'd have his servants dress her up like a doll, and he'd put this weird wig on her, like she was this porcelain little fragile trophy-thing and not, like, a living, breathing person, so, when I found out about all that, I went to grab her, and I may have had to lie just a little bit to get in, but once I was in, the butler and his cronies gave me the run-around, so I went snooping, and that's when I found Cho, looking like I just described, and I couldn't leave her there—not like that—and then we had to get the stuff they took off Cho, some of it being *my* very important stuff, but Walazzin cornered us with his uptight Chimaera goons, so I, uh, well, I kinda wrecked the guy's study, and then we escaped. Barely. It was rough."

Baraam sighed. "Lina, have you just made me an accessory to kidnapping?"

"Technically, yeah. But is it *really* an abduction if the victim is willing?"

"An interesting hill to die on. I wonder what a judge will think."

"Rather not find out."

"Give us the girl," the Enforcer yelled. "No one needs to get hurt."

"What does Walazzin want with her?" Baraam asked, loudly enough for them all to hear.

"None of your concern, sir," said the Enforcer. "That girl is the ward of my employer, and that's all you need to know. We've been far too patient with you both already, but I'm willing to give you to the count of five."

"Or what?" said Alina, scooting in front of Cho. "You're not going to shoot us. You might hit her."

"That's it." The Enforcer holstered her firearm, drawing a steel-studded baton in its stead. Her colleagues behind her did the same. "Negotiation's over."

With effort, Baraam pushed himself to his full height. The air around him smelled like ozone. The hairs on Alina's neck stood on end. Baraam said, "You are not going to let her go, are you?"

Alina stepped forward. "I'm willing to eat a bullet over this."

"And I cannot let that happen. So…" Baraam's fingers twitched, and he slung a bolt at their ambushers. The spell arced past the ear of their leader but slammed into one of the other officers, who cartwheeled through the air, thudding onto the ground.

Walazzin's red-clad stormtroopers hefted their batons, charging, their forewoman commanding, "The girl mustn't be harmed."

Side by side, Alina and Baraam braced themselves. Then there came a wail, high-pitched and far-off. Or, possibly, its source was close but very small.

Something larger than a bullet, and only slightly slower, shot between Alina and Baraam, and one of the red officers soared into the air to be deposited on the fingers of the nearest statue that was still standing. Hanging by his scarf, legs flailing, the Enforcer shouted for help.

Baraam took advantage of the confusion to lob another pair of bolts, each one striking true. Two bodies slumped, unconscious before they hit the ground.

A mousey, blue, goat-hooved form buzzed in front of Alina's nose.

"Mezami?" said Cho.

The Pyct flexed his biceps, and, though his face wasn't capable of a wide range of expressions, the twinkle in his eyes was almost mischievous.

Winding his arm, Baraam prepared to lash out at Mezami, but Alina got between them, saying, "Woah, woah, he's with us."

Baraam grunted, "The company you keep," and, with a boom of thunder, drove his fist into the body armor of the nearest officer, who crumpled.

"Take left: I," said Mezami. "Take right: you."

Drawing on what little energy she had left, Alina raised a wall of stone and asphalt, blocking the path of the four Enforcers on the right. The Pyct slammed into the two on the left, who rebounded off the wall and did not get up again. With one final surge of Niima, Alina stretched the block into a dome, trapping the remaining Enforcers.

Sweat poured from her scalp down the length of her nose. She bent double, panting.

At her back, Baraam said, "That was… not bad."

Dabbing at the sweat with her sleeve, she said, "You did alright, yourself."

"You shouldn't have pushed yourself so hard." Baraam offered her an arm for support. "Niima Deficit Sickness is nothing to take lightly."

"I'm not gonna get the Nids, Baraam. I'm fine." She accepted his help, straightening, and she noted how hard he fought to not pull back, to hide the revulsion in his eyes as he avoided looking at her arms.

Patting her on the back as awkwardly as was possible, he ignored the muffled shouts of the contained Enforcers and marched off, leading the way. "We're nearly there."

Cho looked to the dome of rock. "Won't they choke to death in there?"

Alina shook her head. "That right there's all I had left. It'll collapse in, like, a minute. We gotta get out of here. So, come on."

"There won't be any trains running, though, will there?" said Cho.

"Of course not," said Baraam without turning around. "Which is why I chartered a private shuttle."

Ultimately, they hadn't even needed to enter Mercy's Approach Station. They'd cut across the parking lot, where a white oval-shaped transport hovered just above the asphalt.

"Auto-piloted," Baraam explained as they walked up to the vehicle. "That way, only we will know. Are you sure you want the Aelf with you?" He nodded toward Mezami, visibly squirming at the thought.

Alina said, "Non-negotiable. You were there: he saved all our buns. Mine more than once."

Baraam had no witty reply, so he popped open the shuttle's large trunk. He pointed toward the bags within. "Toiletries, a change of clothes, etc. Should be everything you need."

"Wow. Well, thanks."

"You can thank 'Morphea.'"

"Yeah, and when will I ever be seeing her again?"

He shrugged. "Probably sooner than you think." He pulled the bags out of the trunk before slamming it shut. "Or never. That's part of the 'fun' with her."

Wrapping the bags' straps around her wrists, Alina paused.

He shot her a look that said, "Something wrong?"

"Baraam. Do you see me differently now?"

Releasing a long, steady breath through his nose, he answered, "What do you want me to say? How could I not? You're…"

"Not human," she finished.

"Well." He cleared his throat. "You'll always be a little sharp thorn in my side. And you're still as impossibly stubborn as ever. You are only… It's a matter of…" He gesticulated vaguely, unable to find the words.

"You're always saying all Aelf should be eradicated."

"I do believe that."

"Well, what about me?"

"You're not an Aelf, Alina!" But it was clear by his tone that he didn't really believe that. There was no conviction to his statement. He'd said what he'd said because he wanted confirmation from her.

But she didn't have the energy or the desire to make him feel better about what was happening to her. "Is that so? Then what am I?"

"I don't know," he said, running his fingers through his curly hair. "I don't know." He placed his hands on her shoulders. "But I would never let you come to harm."

He let her go, hands finding his pockets.

It was clear that he was lost—adrift in a storm of conflicting loyalties. She couldn't think of how to break through the barrier he'd raised. Their dynamic felt different, and yet the same: whether she'd admit it or not, she'd always wanted him to acknowledge her worth, and he still refused to. At least, he seemed to still think of her as a helpless child. Though that fact had always irked her, for once she was able to take comfort in it. If he thought of her as a silly little kid, he couldn't wholly see her as a monster.

Even though she might just be one.

At any rate, there remained that familiar wall between them, a wall built up of words unspoken and unspeakable. And, with everything that had happened in the past week, perhaps time was the only hammer that could hope to knock it down.

She got on the shuttle.

Digging a bag of cheesy crackers out of the carry-ons Baraam had provided them, Cho said, "Hey, Lightning Guy," giving him a thumbs-up. "You're alright."

For the first time in a long, long while, Baraam grinned. Still hunched, the nasty gashes on his chest bleeding a little, he lifted his hand, holding it still. A motionless wave.

Alina and Cho hopped aboard the small shuttle. The tan interior was roomier than expected. There were six seats with built-in Watchboxes, each by a window. The seventh seat was facing the windshield, set over a console with a stick and a whole lot of dials and knobs.

The engines whirred, and a speaker above the compartment doors dinged. Alina and Cho stepped backward, finding their seats as the hatch automatically closed.

The shuttle shot forward, quickly picking up speed. Baraam's face blurred, and he and Mercy's Approach were quickly gone from sight, lost over the horizon of New El. That horizon was aglow, just as it had been when Alina had caught her first up-close glimpse of The Capital while sitting next to Ugarda Pankrish.

Gild Master Pankrish, who had been murdered the day before yesterday.

Thinking of him made her remember Ordin, and she wondered what he was doing, right now, and whether he regretted betraying her.

After she let the intertwining snakes of anger and helplessness slither through her gut for a moment, she decided to instead focus on the shrinking high-rises of New El, set ablaze by the early morning light.

Then there was only the empty blue of the open sky.

When the shuttle landed, Alina's eyes lingered on the sun-stricken majesty of The Capital and all its glistering towers, once more as far-off as they'd always been. As much as it was a city of cutting-edge technology, it was also a city of old magic; a city of unparalleled wealth and the depths of poverty; secrets and bold-faced lies; Aelfravers and Aelf.

New El held its mysteries still, but Alina, for one, had had her fill of them. She couldn't imagine ever going back. Even had she wanted to.

She was wrong, of course: she would return one day, when a war between nations and ideologies would spill into the heart of the homefront. When one king would be unseated, and another crowned. When the very Chains of New El—Consortio, Libra, and Concordia—would be severed and The Capital would plunge earthward to its final destruction.

But, between her and those days of dust and ashes, there remained some distance yet.

Breaking her gaze from The Capital, she unloaded the goodie bags Baraam had gifted to her and Cho, and she felt grateful that—despite everything having exploded in her face at every turn—she was left with the chance to hang onto The School. If only for another month. Another week. Maybe she could still figure something out, scrape the money together. There had to be some way.

As her daze wore off, she remembered that The School was no longer the last piece of her grandfather she had left.

When she thought of him, she felt her heartbeat in her palm as fiercely as in her chest, and she held her hand up to the sun, flexing her fingers. The warmth of the golden light within, the essence or soul or whatever it was—the *real* last piece of her grandfather—lived within her. As long as she kept going, he survived in some way. That's what she thought he'd tell her, if he could.

Sevensin. Demidivines. Eaters of their own kind, they survived by consuming their parents and siblings. That's why, according to legend, there were only ever a handful of them. If Egogenesis was really, well, *real*, and not some imagining of Gild scholars, was it true that Dimas had slain his parents, brothers, sisters? Did they all live inside Alina, now? And, how weird and *terrifying* to think of all that—of what it meant.

There must be more to this story, she thought.

No matter what, though, one fact was beyond argument: Dimas K'vich had lied to his granddaughter her entire life. Every anecdote, every conversation, moral, and every promise—every *breath*—a lie.

He could—*should* have prepared her for this. Taught her to accept what she was, not hide it from her.

Her thoughts drifted again to the purely mundane but most urgent. She'd lost her phone in the struggle against Tolomond Stayd. Good luck getting that replaced, broke as she was.

In the plus column, though, there were Cho and Mezami. Misfits, just like Alina. They might all starve together, but, at least, maybe, they could be happy for a while.

Maybe Cho could teach Alina how to be a thief.

Alina sighed.

At Gladjaw Junction, using a little more of the cash Cho had lifted from Baraam, Alina bought tickets for the bus back to Truct, politely nodding and smiling as the clerk grilled her about what had happened on The Capital—had she seen anything? She hadn't, she said, suggesting he tune in to the six o'clock news.

The news would indeed cover it, but the Twelve Families—the Plutocrats—would make certain that this story would be spun as all others had been before. Another fluke, mistake, or—better yet—a secret double-bluff triumph of The Authority. A plot to capture treacherous Terrie Aelfravers before they could commit further acts of terror.

Alina was glad to leave that noise behind.

On the bus, Cho nodded off almost immediately, drooling against the finger-print-smudged window. Mezami remained hidden within Alina's torn-up hood, snoring.

Bored, Alina finally unzipped her carry-on to rummage through its contents. Then she unzipped the interior pocket and found an envelope.

She gasped, and then let slip something between a guffaw and a sob.

Inside the envelope was more cash than she'd ever seen before. More than she'd even thought she'd ever hold.

Six-hundred thousand gelders. Enough to buy The School. Three or four times over. Picturing Baraam's stoic face as they'd parted, Alina breathed, "Merciful Buthmertha." And she burst into tears.

She stowed the gelders back in the envelope and set the bag on the overhead metal shelf. Every fifteen minutes, she checked to make sure the money hadn't disappeared.

It was still there. Every time.

48

WHEN THE DELIVERY GUYS dropped off the new queen-sized mattress, they scuffed the paint near the front door. Mrs. Qamasque had squawked at them, complaining about the mud they were dragging in, during their entire journey up the stairs.

Alina directed them to her bedroom, just off the kitchen. Maneuvering through the narrow space between the fridge and stove was a bit tricky; most of The School had been setup as a training area, with all the "living spaces" crammed into one little corner.

As more nicks and scratches were left behind, she made a mental note to buy some paint. Spruce the place up a bit. Sunset orange, maybe. Or tropical yellow.

She tipped the men, and they left. Then night came and, even though spring was officially in full swing, it got cold. She tossed a log or two in the fireplace and snapped her fingers. Warm flames licked the wood, releasing the calming scent of hickory.

For the next hour, she vegged out, idly flipping through newsfeeds and cat videos on her new phone.

The old lock on the front door clicked and squeaked (Alina added its replacement to her expanding to-do list). Cho entered, carrying a few full plastic bags.

She dropped the goods off on the linoleum kitchen counter, pulling the items out one by one, cataloguing them, "One loaf of bread, multigrain. One gallon of goat's milk. One dozen free-range eggs, brown." This went on for a minute or two. "And, for the *peas duh resistance*—one oversized box of double-stuffed sandwich cookies for the music video marathon tonight."

Alina set to putting away all the perishables in the icebox and the canned goods in the pantry. "How was work?"

"Looong," Cho said emphatically. "But I learned how to take apart a v8 engine today. So many shiny little gears."

Cho's employment at Mr. Ovaris's auto parts shop had earned Alina quite a lot of goodwill with the old coot and his family. Ovaris had immediately been impressed with the nimbleness of Cho's fingers and her knack for picking up new skills. Alina prudently hadn't told him about the implants in Cho's brain that tripled its processing power. Instead, she'd spun a yarn about Cho being Alina's second (or was it third?) cousin and how she was looking for a trade and had always loved machinery. Most of that had been a lie. The part about having an aptitude for fixing things, though, turned out to be true after the fact. Being twelve, and a lowly apprentice, she wasn't paid a whole lot. But it gave her something to do, helped keep her mind occupied, and she'd insisted. So.

After all the groceries had been put away, Alina sat down in front of her new personal computer. Sleek, black, shiny, and powerful as all hell.

Sliding onto the new couch, Cho searched for the Watchbox remote. "For real, though, you gotta stop buying stuff, Li."

Alina, staring at the monitor, snapped out of her reverie. "Huh?"

"It's like, I'm our only source of income right now, but you keep shopping online like foot massagers and electric toothbrushes and video games are going outta style. The money'll run out eventually. Just sayin'."

"Yeah, in like five years."

"*Eventually*."

Swiveling around, crossing her arms, Alina said, "*Okay*, so I've bought some stuff. A fair amount of stuff. But I have it under control. It's all things I've needed for a long time but couldn't afford."

In reply, Cho pointed at the nearby brand-new 3D printer, then to the big pile of clothes beside her on the couch. "Ya haven't even taken the tags off these yet."

"You're giving me flak over *clothes*? People need clothes, Cho. And, for the record, everything else I spent was to help me fix up the place. Maintenance and repairs that were a long time coming, what with this apartment having been rundown for so long. Dimas wasn't exactly big into upkeep, so…" Seeing Cho's unimpressed expression, Alina added, "Once you're a homeowner, you'll understand."

"Oh. *Oh*. Will I, now?"

"Didn't hear any complaints when I bought you that VR game a week ago."

"That's educational. I've learned so much about resource management, and, and hand-eye coordination. And, like, other things I could mention if I wanted to."

"Yeah, yeah, yeah."

"Anyway, you're gonna have to get a job at *some* point. Or you'll go crazy in here. Hanging out with just Mezami, listening to him say stuff like, 'Buy toilet paper: you. Clean toilet bowl: I.' You're gonna have a meltdown. Ya need to start being productive."

Alina threw her hands up. "I've only ever been good at one thing, and no one will hire me to do it."

Cho sighed, shaking her head. "Been through this, Li. There's more uses for magic than Raving."

"Such as?"

"Uh. Well, I can't just on-the-fly come up with careers for you. But there's a computer right there. Why doncha plug into the wide world beyond and figure it out." She got up, dug around in the pantry for a bag of microwaveable popcorn. "But hurry up. It's almost time for 'Say No to the Bro.'"

Alina smiled, swiveling to face the computer monitor. "You're a bad influence."

The microwave dinged. Cho said, "Where's Mezami?"

Without taking her eyes off the search engine page, Alina typed with one hand, and, with the other, indicated the attic.

"How many'd he kill today?"

"Fewer. Maybe they've finally had enough."

"Eesh. You'd think the first batch would have told their friends to stay away."

Alina shrugged.

The attic access trapdoor opened, and the fluttering of wings caught Alina's attention. She heard Cho say, "Mezami! How many times I gotta tell ya—while we appreciate your work—*no rats in the living room*."

They squabbled for a few minutes, Mezami getting quite irate when Cho tossed his trophy kill in the garbage and took the container out to the curb. When she came back, she offered him half her bowl of kettle corn, and he was appeased.

"Oh my gods, it's starting," Cho squealed.

Alina powered down the desktop, giving it a little pat of appreciation. And the three of them sat down as the music cued the recap of last week's drama-filled group date and tear-jerker of a Selection Ceremony.

The piano-heavy theme song of "Say No to the Bro" kicked in.

"So cheesy," said Cho, stuffing popcorn into her mouth, her eyes glued to the screen.

"I know," said Alina, smiling. "I love it."

In the intervening three months since the events at City Hall, there'd been a handful of related stories whose developments Alina followed every night, staying up long after the others had gone to bed.

To cover her digital tracks, she always used a proxy server. You never knew who might be monitoring her search history, and there was no need to make it *easy* on them.

First on her list was the search for the missing heiress of the Torvir fortune and estates. By rights, Choraelia Rodanthemaru Dreintruadan Torvir owned a little *over* one twelfth of the industry and land of El. Naturally, her retrieval was a top priority, the national security task force in charge of the case spearheaded by one of Plutocrat Wodjaego Walazzin's personal lieutenants. The reports compiled by Alina's news digest app all indicated that Choraelia Torvir had last been seen in the company of two unidentified Aelfraver dissidents headed to Mercy's Approach. No doubt, they'd absconded with her to one of the provinces. "Inquiries" were being made, the usual suspects rounded up for questioning. In summary, plenty of arrests, but no real leads. Of course, that's not what the journalists had written, not exactly, but Alina knew how to read between the lines.

Maybe one day, Walazzin would track Cho down. But it wouldn't be tonight.

Each time she read the words "unidentified dissidents" or "insurrectionists of unknown identity," Alina breathed a little more easily. Whatever favors Baraam had called in, they clearly had done the trick. For now, his and Alina's names remained unconnected to the Battle of City Hall.

The confusion and chaos certainly had helped. Even the nightly news couldn't completely whitewash the unrest caused by the destruction of the Elemental Bank and New El's century-old defender, H'ranajaan. The mechadragon had been smashed to bits—with no witnesses present to report the culprit. It was argued by various talking heads that, given the level of damage done, H'ranajaan had to have been battered by military-grade weaponry. The perpetrator or perpetrators remained at large.

The second narrative of particular interest to Alina had recently come to a close. Baraam had been hounded by the paparazzi for weeks concerning his response to the incident at City Hall, a fiasco that had since been cutely coined "the Pluto Panic." Ever at his side, his lawyers had always answered for him, grunting into the microphone, "Our client feels no need to comment on his position concerning said event. He has only ever served and protected our nation. That's a matter of public record and clear to all. No questions." Baraam's dour expression had been another consistent factor; every photograph in the tabloids, every news spot, showed him sporting the same sour scowl behind his gold-rimmed sunglasses.

To the tabloids, the lack of evidence tying him to the fateful battle between the Ravers and The Authority only made him seem *more* suspicious. The media was relentless in seeking to get a rise out of him: as the days stretched into weeks, they camped in front of his home in Ralis, chased after his car as he was driven to and from Gild HQ, photographed him the very *second* he showed his face anywhere. Wherever he went, they stalked him, until, finally, he called a press conference in Pluto Plaza. Behind him had been several construction crews hard at work, day and night, repairing the city infrastructure damaged during the battle. (By the way, all the Ravers who had taken part? Licenses revoked, and fifteen-to-life in prison. All the ones who'd been caught, anyway). The first part of Baraam's Q&A session had been centered on the Aelf and what had happened that day. He'd declared that, yes, he'd been present at the battle—in the interest of keeping order—but, no, he had had no prior knowledge of the incident or its causes.

Asking follow-up questions, the reporters had been a bit more respectful than previously because, this time, Baraam was speaking for himself (his lawyers sweating buckets in the background).

All in all, the first stretch of the conference was boring. The last bit, though? Much different story. Alina must have watched the video clip of those final couple minutes at least a dozen times.

Baraam had said, "Time and time again, I have declined to speak about the rebellious acts of my lesser colleagues several weeks ago. Today, I will be clear: I categorically condemn their decisions to attack The Authority and the center of government of our Capital. However, despite my lack of specific knowledge on this topic, its effects have rippled throughout our city and have touched me on a personal level. I come here today to speak not of the past but the future. After much deliberation, I am announcing my retirement from The Gild, effective immediately. As we speak, Registrar Karabura is striking my name from the rolls. I am no longer an Aelfraver."

The assembled reporters had instantly begun firing off questions. Even the construction workers had leaned on their power drills, idly set down their drone controllers, and listened in.

As Baraam fielded questions, the cymbal and drums of lightning and thunder had sounded, the storm mounting in intensity. Then there'd come a flash so bright and a bang so close that many of the reporters had gasped and ducked low.

Smiling, Baraam had removed his sunglasses and tossed them aside, saying, "That will be all. Thank you."

And, because he'd always had a flair for the dramatic, he'd exited the stage via a bolt of lightning, carried off into the sky.

That was three weeks ago.

Every few days, someone would post a blurry snapshot taken on their phone, or there'd be a dubious comment about spotting *the* Baraam bol-Talanai. Alina checked the alerts she'd set up for his name, but these supposed sightings never amounted to more than rumor.

The paparazzi soon lost interest, finding a new object of their love-hate affections—the new Number One Raver, Rancisca Cuenzi, a tattooed, foul-mouthed, and *ripped* former sailor from Xaveyr Province.

Alina had to admit, it was really fun to watch Rancisca's first meeting with the Plutocrats and Gild Grandmaster. All those old men didn't know what to make of Baraam's replacement: she was short, but her presence filled the room; she swore, well, like a sailor, but was also extremely polite; and her handshake injured one of the Masters in attendance. You could tell because he was *visibly* in pain.

Each day there was a new video of her being awesome, and people were eating it up. And that was probably the point. Whether she knew it or not, she was part of the show now. Part of what kept both the Elementals and Terries from thinking too carefully about what had happened to City Hall, H'ranajaan, the Consul's son, and the other dead nobles…

Anyway, Baraam had left *Thunderbolt*—his chain of martial arts schools (and/or gyms)—in the care of The Gild's civilian wing, a board of directors who would certainly find ways to profit off this deliciously mysterious turn of events.

And, well, that was it. Where he was, or what he was doing—Alina was in the dark just as much as everyone else. She knew, though, that she'd see him again. He always turned up; the spotlight had a bad habit of finding him.

The third and final story Alina followed with feverish intensity was the long, slow, grinding court case to decide the fate of Ordin Ivoir's property. The Ivoirs, apparently, were not exactly united in their intentions and priorities. A faction of Ordin's uncles and cousins had staked a claim on the assets he'd hidden within the Darkthreads, citing their wing of the family's ties to criminal forensics. A flimsy argument, Alina thought, amounting to, "*Oh, let us look after all the money because we work with people who sometimes look after money.*"

The news cycle took especial care not to explore too deeply the issue of *why* criminal forensics might be involved in tracking down Ordin's stashed loot. He had been, after all, the son of a Plutocrat.

Meanwhile, his parents appeared in court each day—via teleconference. They were still tied down, in the process of acquiring the rights to mineral resources in the colonies. Teleportation spells across such long distances were expensive and nausea-inducing. From afar, they watched the state prosecutors air their son's dirty laundry. (The word online was that the prosecution had been bought and paid for by the Walazzins.)

Once rumors of *how* Ordin had died started circulating, he became somewhat of a folk hero in certain circles. Some of the less scrupulous blogs Alina occasionally perused (to get a wide range of opinions) claimed Ordin had been working against The Sanctum—which was part of the "worldwide shadow government, a cabal made up of the elite of the elite, who would stop at nothing to enslave the minds of all freethinking human beings." People were holding Ordin up like he'd been a selfless champion of social justice or something.

Alina could only shake her head and angrily prevent herself from submitting replies to all these ignorant comments. You could call Ordin a lot of things, but "selfless" most definitely wasn't one. Nor had he been entirely selfish. He'd at least always talked a good game; there'd been a reason behind everything he'd done. And the more she thought about his self-described end-goal—ascending to the Plutocracy in order to *change* it—the more she found there existed within her heart one small corner reserved for respecting him.

She'd mentally play back the conversations they'd had, remembering how easily and consistently they'd knocked each other off-balance.

She couldn't understand why he hadn't been honest with her. Why he'd worked for Baraam. She'd hated him *so much* for that.

Except, it turned out that Baraam's motivations had been more complex than she'd originally thought. He'd been working against her, trying to discourage her at every turn. But she'd since found out that was just his way of showing he cared. A moronic, macho way to go about it, but still. And he'd believed in her, despite it all, despite his fears and doubts—he'd believed she'd make it to the top of City Hall in the end. He'd known she'd prove him wrong.

So, what did that say about Ordin, then? If Baraam wasn't heartless, then was Ordin really such a scumbag for acting the way he'd done?

From his perspective, as he'd said, he'd only been trying to waste her time. And, to his credit, he'd even done so quite charmingly on occasion. She had to admit that she'd liked their dallying. Some of it.

But now he was dead.

When she'd first read the news, the day after the bus ride back to Truct, she hadn't known how to feel. There'd been only numbness, a lack of reaction. It wasn't until four days later, when she'd read an article about an ice sculptor coming to Puurissei that she'd broken down. She'd spent the day in her room, journaling.

That night, she'd burnt the journal.

Afterward, on impulse, she'd ordered a VR headset (a G4L4-XY mk IV, to be exact). Close enough to the ones he'd had in his weird, disorganized office. The package had taken such a long time to arrive that she'd forgotten about it until it did. Her stomach knotted every time she'd thought about ripping off the cellophane and installing the headset. Eventually she did. And every night afterward, she returned to the Sea of Deleted Comments, where she ambled beside the hissing waves of forgotten private messages, the syllables like foam between her toes, the unrequited emotions gritty like sand.

She brought a digital net she'd designed—a sieve of sorts. With it, she trawled the waves, wave after wave, searching for something. She held out no hope; after all, *everyone's comments* ended up here, to be sorted through, repurposed, siphoned for banking info, or what have you. The likelihood of finding something of Ordin's was slim to none.

Yet, tonight, just as she was ready to call it quits and get her four hours of sleep, she scooped something up in her net—a digimail, displayed as a message in a bottle. When she wiped the grime off it, she saw it was addressed to her.

She uncorked the bottle; it vibrated, its neck fizzing, and then he was standing there, two feet in front of her.

She gasped, "Ordin?" and backed away reflexively.

When he didn't reply, she noticed he wasn't even looking at her. His gaze focused just above her left shoulder. He was probably staring into a camera, she realized.

A recording.

It was so realistic. All the details were there and crystal clear—from his overpriced high-necked autumn sweater to his signature hair. His face was redder than usual; he'd been crying—or was about to.

Part of her—a very small and wretched part—felt the slightest satisfaction, but the rest of her lashed out in anger for even briefly taking comfort in his pain. And, of course, she felt worse still when the reality of his death hit her once again.

A ripple of static passed over the nearly still image of Ordin. Then it began to speak.

This is what it said:

Alina,

I do not expect you to understand why I acted the way I have. I want you to know, though, the truth—my side, so that you may judge for yourself whether you could ever consider speaking to me again.

What I have done is unforgivable. I used you. That much is fact. I was hired by bol-Talanai to obstruct you at every turn, and I accepted the task. I can only guess at why he would want to keep you from the Rave. Regardless, you trusted me, and I deceived you. I am so sorry.

I thought it would be easier. All of it. When we negotiated our deal, he described you as a naïve little girl, out of her element, wide-eyed and idiotic. Nothing could have been further from reality. You are awesome, and I never use that word lightly: I am in awe of you.

Yet, I find myself conflicted. I promised bol-Talanai I would do him this favor. In exchange, he would bring me one step closer to the prize I have been searching for half my life. But now—I can hardly believe it myself—I don't really want it anymore. Something in me has changed.

I can't explain it, nor can I put into words what's come over me. I have behaved so stupidly. I am ashamed. However, I can say with unshakable certainty that much of what I did, I did to protect you. Admittedly, sometimes that which you needed protection from was my own doing.

There has been only one other decision that I have regretted as much as taking advantage of your trust in me.

Even as I record this message, my nerve is failing me. I hope I have within me the strength of character to tell you how I feel about all this.

About—well, about you.

The truth is, I don't want to lose myself in the Darkthreads anymore. That desire has left me entirely. Instead, I only want—

There the recording ended. Ordin's image sparked and disappeared. The bottle and its message drifted away, lost in the waves of the Sea of Deleted Comments.

In that moment, she wanted, more than anything, to bring him back. Even for an hour. Were that possible, she didn't know whether she'd strike or hug him, but she would have loved to have the option.

He was gone, though, and he wasn't coming back, and she hadn't had the chance to say goodbye, or I hate you, or any of the million things she might have told him.

The hard lesson staring her in the face tonight was that real life didn't present challenges, opportunities, and everything in between in gift-wrapped packages. There were no bows to be tied, no greeting cards with cheery or wise jokes and proverbs on them.

Sometimes you cared about someone and they stabbed you in the back and you hated them and they just died on you before you even had a chance to come to terms with any of it.

Other times, you hunted your own grandfather down like an animal, and he gave you cryptic messages about the future and you were saved from being thrown in big-girl prison by the very same guy you assumed hated your guts and thought you were a speck of dirt and you just wanted your grandfather back but there was no way that was going to happen so you just had to live with the knowledge that you're a freak and alone.

She remembered Ordin's face when he'd noticed her arms and her new-found strength: his habitual easy confidence had leaked out his ears; he'd seen her for the monster she was.

Inside the Darkthreads, time did not behave the way it did out in the real world. Had Ordin recorded his message before or after discovering her true nature? Did it even matter?

The waves of the forgotten lapped at Alina's feet, and her silent laments passed equally unheard.

She pulled the VR headset from her eyes and took a few deep breaths.

Lumbering into the kitchen, she downed a full glass of room-temperature water and fell into bed.

Mezami woke her with a series of taps on the tip of her nose.

"Door: man."

She stirred, frying her eyes with a full blast of sunlight charging in through the blinds. "Uhh." Squeaking as she stretched, she flopped out of bed, made sure she was dressed—still wearing what she had on last night, which was just typical Alina—and made for the front door.

It must have been well past nine in the morning; Cho had already left for work, leaving her bowl of cereal half-finished, spoon resting directly on the table. Wads of napkins bunched up near a pile of mandarin rinds. Alina rolled her eyes at the mess.

Without thinking, she opened the door.

Halfway through a yawn, she blurted, "Calthin."

"Alina."

After the… episode on top of the clocktower, her arms had briefly reverted to their human shape, size, and color. However, over the next several weeks, she'd frequently experienced what she called "flare-ups," when her gray-scaled skin would poke through, or a claw would jut out unexpectedly. The source of these "flare-ups" was hard to pin down. They'd happen after she'd slept too little, slept too much, eaten too much, eaten too little, yelled, cried, laughed too hard. Whatever the exact reasons, she felt confident in her conclusion that the Sevensin arms came back whenever she was feeling *a lot* of something.

This morning, her arms had apparently taken on their full-blown claw-and-spike gray, up to her bare shoulders.

She panicked.

Though she'd quickly put them behind her back, she knew she'd been a blink too slow in doing so: Calthin had caught a glimpse of her wrists and hands.

He scratched the back of his neck. "It's really good to see you."

Sliding over to the couch, she grabbed the extra-long-sleeved sweater draped over its back and threw it on. Having just rolled out of bed, her voice raspy, she had to try a couple of times to ask, "What are you doing here?"

"Got tired of waiting for you to come by the shop. For the apology."

"Apology?" her cheeks burned, all embarrassment concerning her condition gone. "You think *I'm* gonna apologize after what you—"

He held up his hands. "No, no. *I'm* here to apologize. The stuff I said to you—first of all, I didn't mean any of it. More importantly, though, it wasn't my business and you needed a friend and, well, I screwed up. And I'm sorry, Alina, really. I should have been there for you, but I wasn't."

Crossing her now-covered arms, leaning back at the waist, she squinted at him. "Yeah, you goofed pretty hard that night, didn't you?"

"I'm hoping it's not too late to un-goof?" Lines formed around his green eyes as he assumed a sheepish grin.

"I dunno. It's gonna take a *lot* of work. You might quit halfway through, so why bother?"

"Got news for ya: Ammings don't quit."

"And you think K'viches do?" Her smirk came naturally.

His expression turned grave. "I heard some of what happened up there. Do you want to talk about any of it?"

She tapped her chin. "Nope."

"Oh, okay." He nodded, snapping his fingers awkwardly. He caught sight of something. His eyes widening, he let out a yelp and rushed inside.

"Come in, why don't you," she muttered, closing the door.

He had found the jacket, the one he'd given her just before she'd left for The Capital. He put his fingers through three bullet holes, and then traced with his palm various scratches, tears, and scorch marks.

She watched him break down, silently, stoically. He wouldn't dare show it, but he was dying inside. This beautiful thing he'd made, to see it so thoroughly abused… She almost went over to him, but she wasn't done being angry with him yet. Not quite.

"Buthmertha give me strength." Releasing a long, ragged sigh, he held up the savaged jacket and asked, "Would you, um, want a new one of these, or…?"

She thought about it. "Nah, I like this one. Especially now that it's broken-in."

"Broken-in? It's hanging by a *thread*."

"Was that a pun? At a time like this?"

"Unintentional. Point is, this thing's *had it*. I'm amazed what's left of it hasn't been blown away by the apartment's air conditioning." With the reverence and care of a monk handling a holy relic, he folded and hung the jacket over the back of a nearby chair. Rapping his fingers on the counter, he said, "So, clearly, they kept you busy up there. Are you sure you're alright?"

"I'll be *fine.*"

"You know, I really could replace it for you. If you wanted. I owe it"

"I don't want a replacement. Could you mend it instead? Patchwork is more my style anyway." She shifted her weight to her back leg. "Maybe add some extra padding to the sleeves? Something, um, tear-resistant?"

Calthin inadvertently glanced at her hands. He cleared his throat. "I'll figure something out. It's the least I could do. Can I borrow a trash bag?"

She gestured toward the kitchen sink. "Be my guest."

He stooped, opening the cabinet under the sink, and pulled out a thirteen-gallon black plastic bag, stowing the jacket inside it. "Let's hope it survives the walk back to the shop."

With a nod, he exited The School.

She called after him, "I'm still pissed at you."

His head popped back into view. "Eh?"

"I said, I'm still pissed at you. But thanks for stopping by."

Chuckling quietly, he waited in the doorway for a moment. He stared off into space, lost in thought. Then he said, "Not today, by any means, and I know I haven't earned it yet, but at some point in the near- to distant-ish-future, perchance, would you, maybe, at some point, wish to enjoy an ice cream or something? With me? By way of my continuing to apologize for having been so crappy to you?"

"Calthin. You're doing it again. That thing you do."

"Right. Well, your friends are invited, too. Of course."

"Oh, cool. I'll let them know. And then I'll let you know."

"Yeah."

Alina hesitated. "You've heard about Mezami, then? What he is?"

"I could tell you nothing about you surprises me anymore, but it's more so the case that—when it comes to you—one has to get used to insane surprises."

With a shrug, she said, "Turns out having a Pyct around is huge help. Haven't had to slap down one gelder for pest control so far. And all he needs food-wise is a daily slurp from Tahtoh's old Niima generator." (Which she'd retrieved from Rooster as soon as she'd returned to Truct, paying him in cash while shrugging off all his awkward advances.)

"I once ate butter with a spoon, straight out of the container. Who am I to judge?" Calthin lifted the trash bag and waved.

She watched him walk down the cramped staircase and out the Qamasques' front door. Then she ran to the window overlooking the street and followed his progress a few moments longer.

Out of sight.

Late that night, half-asleep, in the dark, Alina blindly slapped around her bed. When her palm thwapped her phone, she grumbled and, through bleary, half-lidded eyes, banged out a message to Calthin:

tell your lil bro to come by the school sometime

got a few martial arts forms i can show him

and Calthin

thx for stopping by

its good to be back

She tossed her phone into the corner, where it bounced on the carpet.

Exhaling a long, warm, sleepy sigh, she wrapped her body around her fluffy new body pillow and slept a sleep free of troubles. Jaw unclenched, neck relaxed, spine supported by a cloud-like comforter.

And she thought of absolutely nothing, all the dread melting away from her for the first time since she could remember. The first time since her parents had died and she'd come to live at The School.

Tomorrow she'd continue to shape the place into a home. Yes, she'd continue the work of restoring this old house, tearing out the rot and rebuilding, spit-shining the memories.

Tomorrow, Dimas's School would be nudged one inch closer to rebecoming the sanctuary it once had been to her, when her grandfather had taken her in.

She would, eventually, have to contemplate and decide on what Dimas truly was—had always been—and what that meant for her. But that could wait till tomorrow.

Tonight, she would sleep. And, as the suffering and panic and night-terrors of all her years melted from her body—a sensation so powerful and liberating that there trickled from her eyes a steady, unbreakable stream of tears—she dreamed.

Around noon she stretched, squeaking as her joints popped, and she got up for a glass of milk and a sandwich. On her way to the kitchen counter she passed by the bathroom.

A glint of light from the mirror. The rush of water in the sink.

It took her half a second too long to realize the water was off, and she'd completely covered the mirror in crisscrossing strips of solid blue duct tape.

No one was in that bathroom. Not even Mezami, who'd switched on the Niima generator in the attic and had begun siphoning some of its stored energies; she heard him burp contentedly.

Quiet fell over The School, a blanket of noiselessness, like when you only realized how loud your place usually was during a power outage, when the fridge, the air filter, and the cat's water fountain all suddenly stopped running, and you were left alone with nothing but the gentle humming of your own hyperactive mind.

This moment was filled with *that* kind of almost-silence.

Alina turned toward the couch and, when she saw the dark figure sitting there, her skin crawled.

A mop of tangled black hair, black wolfs-head mask, midnight blue robe, silver gloves.

Clenching her fists, Alina channeled her Niima, ready to rumble.

"I did not come here to fight you, Alina K'vich," said Morphea. The form of her mask shifted to a widely grinning face.

Far from appeased, Alina absentmindedly scratched the thick leather bracer covering her wrist. "What *are* you doing on my sofa?"

The mop of stringy dark hair undulated as if underwater. "I thought we might have a chat, you and I." The strands drifted subtly in Alina's direction.

"About…?" Alina circled around the furniture to face her unexpected guest.

"The future." Morphea's one, uncovered, golden eye fixed on her. "Yours. Mine. Ours."

Perching on the edge of the cabinet that held her Watchbox, Alina fiddled with her thumbtack earrings and waited for clarification.

"I shall be direct." Morphea folded her silver-gloved hands in her lap. "I would take you as my apprentice. There is much I can teach you. Much more still that we might learn from one another."

"Hah! Sorry, but I don't know you, lady. And, as a rule, I don't do business with people whose faces I've never seen. That goes double for Revomancers who've been stalking me month after month."

The pause that followed was ravenous; it bit at the time and space between resident and visitor, champed and chewed, its jaws tearing away the seconds and the inches, swallowing everything, until there was nothing left to the room but the two women and their staring contest.

Her eye unblinking, Morphea said, "Very well, then." Her silver-gloved hands drifted up to her mask and, with considerable care, removed it.

Underneath that dark-as-pitch and twisted theatrical visage was the ochre complexion of a human woman. She had winter-pine-black, curly hair, which formed a halo about her head. Brown flecks freckled her cheeks and nose. But for her gold eyes, she looked an awful lot like Baraam.

That's when it hit Alina. "I know you. You're Ruqastra bol-Talanai."

Ruqastra, Queen of Dreams, nodded.

Fingers interlaced, tapping her thumbs together, Alina perched herself on the back of the couch. "Tahtoh told me someone would come. I just didn't know it'd be—well—*you.*" She scratched her cheek. "So, you knew my grandfather?"

"As well as anyone he trained."

Alina gasped. "He trained you? You? Just who *are* you, anyway? To him, I mean."

Neutral of expression and flat in tone, she explained, "I was his star pupil. Years ago, he informed me that, if any ill fate were ever to befall him, he would leave The School in my care. But he was wrong to choose me."

"Oh?"

Ruqastra whispered, perhaps to herself, "He trusted me to gauge your capabilities. He left me with that charge, and he told no one else about—" She paused. Then, at a regular volume, "Alina, you're ready."

"For what?"

"This." Morphea held a sliver of green, glowing rock in her palm.

Alina sucked in a breath. "The missing piece…?"

Morphea nodded. "From the Lorestone you found that night, in the Crystallarium."

"Where'd you get this?"

"Your grandfather."

"I knew it! I knew he must have been the one to mess with the thing. He never could resist meddling." Alina shook her head, nibbling her lip, thinking hard. "What's—what'll I find in it?"

"Answers."

"To?"

"Who Dimas was. Who your parents were. Who you are." Ruqastra's smile blindsided Alina. Regardless of its intended effect, it was profoundly unsettling. "Where your uncle is."

Mateus K'vich. The only family Alina had left.

Well, no. That wasn't wholly true.

There were, after all, two types of family: the one you were born with, for better or worse, and the one you got to choose—your best friends, your tribe, your whatever-you-might-call-thems.

Alina's biological family contained more than the average number of dysfunctional members. Dear old mom and dad had dragged their five-year-old daughter into an unstable tunnel aimed directly at a fortress-like bank, and she'd nearly been smothered. And how could she ever forget her last meeting with her grandfather? On that clocktower. With Baraam…

Even though her blood relatives had caused her so much misery, and done their best to get her killed, they were still tugging at her heartstrings—which was pretty impressive, really, because they were all dead now.

Except for Mateus.

Yes, there were two types of family, and, ultimately, there came a time in every young person's life when they had to choose who to stick with, cling to, and rely on.

"So, Alina, what'll it be?" she muttered to herself.

Her uncle was indeed the only surviving member of the family she'd been *born into*, but, she realized, she had since *chosen* a new family.

She now had Cho and Mezami. And, long before them, there'd been Calthin; the Ammings had always been kind to her. They'd always been *there* for her. When she'd felt depressed, alone, frightened. When Tahtoh had left on one of his many mysterious trips that Alina now *really* didn't know how to feel about. While he'd been off plotting a shadow-war or whatever, the Ammings had taken care of her like one of their own.

She finally understood who'd really been looking out for her all along.

Glaring at Ruqastra, Alina couldn't think of one good reason to listen to this liar in her living room.

There was still so much to do at The School. By Buthmertha, it'd only been a *month* since her cluster of near-death experiences in The Capital.

Maybe she didn't *want* to go charging after her deadbeat uncle.

Maybe she felt she deserved to make her own decisions for once, without the pressures of mentors, peers, bills, and all manner of other obligations weighing her down.

Maybe she could at last afford to live her own life.

Mateus, some guy she'd met once when she was three or four, or the friends who'd *bled* with her?

"Tempting offer," she told Ruqastra. "Hard pass."

"Excuse me?"

"I don't think I do wanna see Mateus, as a matter of fact. He never gave a squawk about me. *He* never made the effort. Why should I?" She paced as she spoke. "Besides, who gave you the right to barge in here and start listing your demands? I haven't forgotten who it was that pushed me into the fight against Dimas."

The heavy-duty gloves she wore to cover up her gray, scaly hands during her flare-ups had already started to fray at the fingertips and knuckles (so much for that "lifetime guarantee").

She flashed back to the tower, to that final split-second in which she'd been made to break the most fundamental tenet of her personal code.

Sometimes she could still feel the heat of his blood on her clawed fingers.

Her voice the rumble and hum of a small earthquake, Alina said, "You walked me right into a trap."

Ruqastra cleared her throat. "*You* did that. I tried to discourage you, recall. On the bus, before all this began"

"Stop! You egged me on. Made the mystery irresistible." Alina scowled. "Don't try to gaslight me."

"Think what you wish. Everything that happened was the will of Dimas, your grandfather, the man whose legacy you now shirk."

"I'm not 'shirking' anything. I wouldn't even know where to begin. I'm just saying—" Alina tossed the sliver of Chrononite back at Morphea, who, without moving, caught it in midair with a look, and it hovered there, between them—"it's hard, just trying to get by. And, right now, I really don't think I can deal with a bunch of dead people demanding that I live *their* version of my own life. I'm just not gonna do it." She sighed. "I've been thinking a lot about my grandfather, about what a sick man he must have been. In the end. He must have changed over the last year because *my* Tahtoh never would have put me through what I—never would have forced me to—" She looked Ruqastra in the eye. "I've got a lot to process. And, maybe, when I'm done healing, the seed that was planted that day will be able to grow. But, for now, I think I—yes, I need you to leave."

Ruqastra blinked. "But it is your charge to seek out the shards of the sundered, to balance the scales, to hunt the earth and sky for our great enemy and lay waste to him. These trials were millennia in the making!"

"Eh."

Eyes narrowed, Ruqastra said, "To be clear… You are turning down my offers of tutelage and answers concerning the fate of your family?"

"It's looking that way, yeah."

Ruqastra rose to her feet. "Understood."

She put her mask back on, walked up to the Watchbox, touched her palm to it, and shrank down, stepping into the blackness of the screen.

Just like that, without a word of protest or comfort or condolence, the Dream Queen had gone.

Alina searched the whole house for Ruqastra or anything she might have left behind—any magical or non-magical spying device or boobytrap or anything else seemingly out of place. She found nothing.

When she turned on the Watchbox, she half expected Morphea/Ruqastra to jump out at her. But that didn't happen either. All Alina saw was the expected grainy black and white and grayscale chaos of static.

Lost in a daydream, she idly flexed her fingers. A sharp tearing sound summoned her back to reality: her razor-sharp claws had shredded her third pair of new gloves; the black spines had punctured her leather bracers.

Shaking her head, she jogged over to the fridge and wrote on the dry-erase board, *EVEN STRONGER HAND GEAR* and then *DAMN THE COST.*

The spines would someday sprout again into full-blown feathers, she figured. Unless she plucked them. She'd tried it once, and the pain had been so intense she'd almost passed out. It was as if the quill points had grown so deep they'd fused with her bones.

One day, maybe not too long from now, she might no longer be able to cover up her… differentness… with accessories. One day, the change might become permanent—might cover her whole body. With what she was, with how Dimas had looked in his *natural* state…

She sighed a heady, shuddering sigh, and felt a little better.

There would be plenty of opportunities to worry about all that later. She didn't have to bother with these problems *today.*

She was only seventeen. There was time.

There was time.

She caught a glimpse of a shape in the static of the Watchbox—a shape that resembled the Dream Queen's silhouette, reaching out to Alina, offering her a shadowed hand.

Alina switched the set off.

She went to grab a can of *Cherry Punch!* from the fridge.

Next to the ice tray in the freezer, she found the lump of Chrononite humming faintly.

"Huh," she said.

And she reached for it.

Then a loud bang made her jump and turn.

Cho had kicked the door open. Clutching a fluffy pillow, grinning like a maniac, she was standing inside a huge plastic bag with holes cut out for her arms and legs. It had been stuffed with dozens of rolls of toilet paper.

"You may have won the last round, K'vich," Cho shouted, "but my new hyper-advanced suit of power-armor means I will *dee-stroy* you in tonight's 'Surprise After-Midnight Pillow Battle Royale.'"

"Cho, honey. Please, be reasonable." Alina set her can of soda down as the freezer door glided shut. "You're being ridiculous. Everyone knows I am *invincible.*" She sprinted for her bedroom, lunging for her own pillows.

Cho intercepted her, bonking her on the head two or three times, but Alina rallied, giving as good as she got.

After several minutes of squealing and stomping and laughing, there came a loud knock on their door. "Children! Stop this right now. No more."

Only after Alina managed to wrestle a flailing Cho to the ground did she shout, "Sorry, Mrs. Qamasque. It won't happen again."

But she and Cho giggled even as she said it. That was one promise they simply couldn't keep.

ELEMENTAL GLOSSARY

For more lore of the world of El, visit *blankbooklibrary.com.*

Aelf (also, "the Others") – A blanket term denoting all those creatures that are neither human nor animal. Each species is endowed with a magical attribute. Over millennia, human scholars and hunters have organized the Aelf into nine distinct categories: Liliskur, Raccitan, Uardini, Mythidim, Legionari, Collosi, Ushum, Demidivines, and Uult.

Aelfraver (a/k/a "Raver"; archaic: "Reaper of Elves" or "Reaver") – Those whose profession it is to hunt the Aelf. The term "Aelfraver" is an adaptation of the poetic "Reaper of Elves." Originally, it was believed that all Aelf were the magical creations of the Elves, an assumption proven false centuries ago. The name "Aelf," however, has survived scholarly correction.

There are a wide variety of private training programs designed to transform a young mage into an Aelfraver. However, anyone seeking to become a full-fledged member of the profession must take the grueling final exam at The Gildhall in New El. Only then may one (legally) hunt Aelf for pay.

Aetherthreads – The state-run and state-monitored information network that facilitates all manner of digital communication, from sharing images with friends via digimail to tracking the real-time location of every single Asset of El. It is common knowledge that The Authority keeps a close eye on the everyday activities of everyday people using this medium. For this reason, some have turned to the Darkthreads as a means of avoiding unwanted attention (see Darkthreads).

Auggie (a/k/a "Licksy" a/k/a "Ability Augmentation Elixir") – Alchemical concoctions created through a blending of the medical and arcane arts. Only a mage can brew an Augmentation Elixir. The severity of the effect (and side-effects) depends on the strength of the brew and the ingredients used. Generations of trial and error resulted in many failed attempts and deaths—often by disintegration of the skeletal system, liquification of the muscles, or spontaneous human combustion. The most common Auggie categories are: *Corpraega* (enhances the drinker's physical capabilities); *Synethesial* (allows the drinker to taste or smell colors or see/hear smells); *Chronolastic* (stretches time from the perspective of the drinker, elongating one second into ten, or a minute into two, depending on the strength of the brew); and *Chronomora* (alters the drinker for corporeal movement through time).

Author of Creation, The – The One True God according to the doctrines of The Sanctum, a rapidly growing religion whose principal place of worship is the etched stone mountain in downtown New El. Overseen by the Hierophant Pontifex Ridect, the zealous adherents of The Author (called Sanctumites) have done their utmost to spread their beliefs—both in New El and in the Twelve Provinces. In three short centuries, their work has grown the organization from a marginal cult, worshipping an esoteric and long forgotten deity, to an officially recognized religion with ties to many major political families (within the Nation of El and abroad).

Authority, The – Organized in 1630 in the wake of the political unrest in Cantus (just seven years after it was conquered by El), The Authority was created in order to suppress riots and maintain control of the Nation of El's contemporary acquisitions of territory and resources. Growing in influence over the centuries, The Authority presently boasts headquarters in every major city within El (and many outside it). A special division of The Authority, the Jaandarmes (also called "Dragoons") serves the Consul personally as a private security and police force.

Buthmertha – "Holy Buthmertha," goddess of the hearth and the family, patron of the lost and downtrodden, protector of orphans. (See "Gods.")

Chains of El – The magic keeping New El aloft—woven by the Twin Dragon Kings—is so immensely powerful that the planetoid would drift into the cold reaches of space were it not for the three great chains tethering it to the earth: *Consortio* ("Fellowship"), *Libra* ("Balance"), and *Concordia* ("Harmony").

Chronology, Elemental – In El, time is counted from the slaying of the Twin Dragon Kings—that day beginning the year 0. The year as of this tale is 3502 "After El" (A.E.). Prehistory is reckoned in years "Before El" (B.E.).

As El goes, so the world follows: the Elemental Calendar is the standard international time measurement system.

Chrononite – An element of unknown origin discovered as early as 300 B.E. by explorers of The Elder Isle. If the hieroglyphics of long-dead civilizations are to be believed, the use of Chrononite grants dominion over time, space, life, and death. Although, this has yet to be confirmed.

Colonies of El – As the world's undisputed superpower, El commands dozens of client kingdoms, puppet monarchies, "neutral" territories, and colonies. The largest of this last category are Agadur, Glasku, Oronor, Sicacor, Tinoch, and Zinokla.

Consul – The head of the government of El and the tie-breaking vote on the Council of Plutocrats (see also "Plutocrats"). Every ten years, the Plutocrats of the Twelve Families elect from among themselves the next Consul, whose men enjoy special social and financial privileges.

Darkthreads – A magically enhanced series of digital networks that feed into sub-universes maintained by a shadowy collective known only as Gnosis. The identities and motivations of Gnosis remain a mystery, but many Assets of El have turned to the Darkthreads for transactions of all sorts, some more nefarious than others. Not *all* users of this service are career criminals, but the simple act of logging on represents a criminal offense in the eyes of The Authority. Users of the Darkthreads are often called "ThreddHedds" or "Thredders."

El, Nation of – El is divided into twelve nearly equal-in-size Provinces, each named after its governing Family. Beginning in the north, and proceeding clockwise: Xaveyr, Ivoir, D'Hydromel, Kracht, Malach, Walazzin, Torviri, Denadon, Hruvic, Reautz, Udutetta, and Caelus.

ELCORP – The corporate-political mega conglomerate that owns, operates, and profits from almost all the doings of the Nation of El. In many ways, ELCORP and El are indistinguishable from one another, as the masters of one are the masters of both: the Twelve Families own ninety-nine percent of the company's shares, and the Plutocrats (selected by each of the Families) also serve as board members of ELCORP.

Elemental(s) – The name for the inhabitants of New El, a reminder of their privileged status as dwellers of the sky.

Elemental Bank, the – The biggest bank in the world and seat of government of the Nation of El, located on Pluto Plaza, Divitia District, New El. It is commonly called "City Hall" because, from the twelfth floor of its clocktower, the selected Consuls serving on the Council of Plutocrats weigh, measure, and control the business of their country. The Elemental Bank is the political and economic heart of ELCORP.

Gild, The – The premier, government-sanctioned school for the study of magic and the Aelf, founded in 1507 A.E. It is also the international organization responsible for licensing and policing all Aelfravers, all over the world. Its first Grandmaster was Uzimsar Kwurdla.

Gildhall, The – The headquarters of the foremost school wherein aspiring Aelfravers are taught the theoretical and practical aspects of their trade. Located in the Perium District of New El, The Gildhall is the only institution legally permitted to administer the Aelfraver licensing test and is comprised of six distinct structures set within two layers of isosceles-triangle-shaped walls: the Azurite Alchamer, the Iron Wheel, the Stone Keep, the Adamantine Manor, the Labradorite Dome, and the Crystallarium.

Gods – Of the seventy-seven sanctioned deities, twelve chief gods and goddesses make up the most widely worshipped pantheon in El: Plutonia, Buthmertha, Caï-ana-eïa, Daïshr-og, Ononsareth, Ka-Yehrost, Yarilo, Sulla Mazdahur, Nninithin, Rinakvi, Skrymga, and Zo. Official Elemental Doctrine dictates that Plutonia, the Goddess of Fortune, is the head of the pantheon.

Only a handful of divinities are specifically outlawed, including Éëtion (primarily worshipped by the seminomadic Kadician desert-dwellers) and Mydras'shymm (ancestor-god of the Ozari).

H'ranajaan – Perhaps the most awe-inspiring reminder of The Authority is H'ranajaan—the Machinamantically powered artificial dragon. It has watched over The Capital for a century.

Iingrid – Short for "Integrated Intelligence National Grid," Iingrid is the built-in organizational assistant in most civilian-use personal mobile devices.

Independent Raver Schools – Aelfraver training facilities officially recognized by the government but not directly affiliated with The Gild.

Magic – Studied throughout the world by every human culture, magic is divided into eight principal disciplines (and sixteen sub-disciplines): Terramancy (Geomancy, Phytomancy); Aquamancy (Lacomancy, Tempetamancy); Machinamancy (Engeniomancy, Partumancy); Revomancy (Somniomancy, Somnexiomancy); Deïmancy (Divinumancy, Daemoniomancy); Ignimancy (Caloramancy, Conflagramancy); Caelomancy (Luxomancy, Umbramancy); Corpromancy (Necromancy, Zoiimancy).

New El (see also "The Capital") – A city built upon a sphere of earth suspended ten thousand feet above sea level, the seat of power of the Twelve Families and the Capital of the Nation of El. According to legend, the planetoid and the temple atop it were constructed by legions of human slaves some four thousand years ago. It was lifted into the sky by the combined powers of the Twin Dragon Kings, the tyrant rulers of the world. Following the rebellion of the enslaved, the Dragon Kings were overthrown by twelve champions, who claimed the sky-city as their dominion, naming it "New El." The city is divided into twelve districts: Decus, Divitia, Dyrex, Esperant, Eleru, Fidae, Iuscat, Lexat, Negotopus, Perium, Tilitatem, and Triditio.

Niima (See also "Magic") – When first discovered, Niima was believed to be an internally generated essence that powers the casting of magical spells. This is partially true. Niima, in some ways, is similar to physical stamina; for example, overexertion quickly leads to exhaustion, and rest will replenish one's Niima reserves. Also, one's Niima pool can be expanded through stress training of the body and mind. There is at least one crucial difference between Niima and stamina, however: while everyone has some amount of physical stamina (and the capability to increase that amount), Niima is a resource possessed only by mages. And, this energy—while created inside the body—is also present *outside* the body. Niima is radioactive, and, although the body of the mage regenerates cells destroyed by spell-casting, the older the individual in question, the likelier one of two results will occur: slower and less effective cell regeneration, leading to organ failure; or, accelerated cell reproduction, causing certain cancers. In extreme cases, enough Niima channeled through the body can result in instant death.

Pinkojack – A derogatory term for anyone in the employ of the government, either local or national. The word refers to the standard pink sheets of paper on which the bureaucracy's physical written records are kept and "jack," which is roughly synonymous with "lapdog." Essentially, to call someone a "pinkojack" is to accuse that person of utterly thoughtless servitude to the government—at the cost of their honor.

Rave – An officially sanctioned bounty on a specific Aelf or group thereof. The bounty may be lawfully cashed in only by a Gild-licensed Aelfraver ("Raver" for short)—a professional hunter of Aelf.

Raver License – Students of The Gild, usually at fifteen years old, are issued a provisional Raver-T License. Following graduation, the completion of a two-year probationary period, and the successful closing of a Gild-assigned bounty, this Raver-T License is replaced by a Raver-X, which designates the owner as a full-fledged Aelfraver. The third type of License, and by far the most difficult to acquire, is the Raver-S. Only through extraordinary service to The Gild, or by becoming a high-ranking member thereof, may a Raver-S License be granted. Even then, the matter is put to a vote by the Council of Masters. The top *quarter* of one percent of Aelfravers are the proud owners of Raver-S Licenses, and as such they enjoy untold benefits throughout the nation—merchant discounts, free meals in many restaurants, corporate sponsorships, and more.

Terrie – A pejorative abbreviation of "Terrestrial." Used by Elementals to reinforce the social divide between themselves and those born and raised on the earth below New El.

Twelve Families – The descendants of the Twelve Champions who led humanity to victory against the Aelf and the Twin Dragon Kings more than 3,500 years ago. Ever since, El has been led by the representatives chosen from each of the favored Twelve Families.

BESTIARY

For a more complete Aelf Bestiary, visit *blankbooklibrary.com.*

The nine types of Aelf, ranked by threat-level, lowest to highest:

Liliskur – Sometimes called "Worms" due to this category including only non-sentient and (relatively) harmless species.

- *Chernoboggle* – Barely even a nuisance, chernoboggles are miniscule parasitic creatures that feed on the dreams of humans and, sometimes, animals. Long believed to be a myth, the existence of chernoboggles was proven in 1778 in what has been called the first-ever sleep study.
- *Ka'a'tee* – Commonly known as "Katy Tears" because of their distinctive mewls (*"Kay-tee, kay-tee"*), the *ka'a'tee* evolved over the centuries to appear nearly indistinguishable from feral cats. Their harmless appearance provides them a significant advantage when hunting their preferred prey—cats and dogs. The fur of a *ka'a'tee* is most often black or orange, leading to a great deal of superstition concerning breeds of actual cats bearing the same coloration. The most notable feature of the *ka'a'tee*, however, is its ability to teleport across short distances—between one and thirty feet—allowing it to quickly climb or escape even the most treacherous areas with ease.
- *Marlok* – Known for their strong herd instincts, when spotted in the wild, the *marlok* can frequently be seen migrating in a wedge formation—safety in numbers.

Raccitan – This category belongs to the small-to-medium-sized pack-hunters and other dangerous Aelf-fauna—be they clawed or spiked, flying or land-bound.

- *Einharthrak* – A white-furred dire wolf native to icy mountaintops. Fire is its principal weapon against its rivals, its prey, and its frigid environment. With its lightweight skeletal system and flying-squirrel-like skin flaps, the *einharthrak* can also glide from rock to rock. Because of the relative flimsiness of its bones, this beast hunts in large numbers for safety and prefers to run its prey to exhaustion before closing in for the kill.

- *Hrilliuk* – A dog-sized rotund herbivore. The spines on its back are heat-seeking. The paralytic venom in which these are coated is non-lethal in small doses. However, anyone foolish enough to hold their ground after being pierced by a *hrilliuk's* spines will receive a second—fatal—volley.
- *Hyndun* – A legless lizard native to deserts and steppes. A small dose of its venom could kill an elephant in less than a minute.

Uardini – Spirits of forests, mountains, lakes, and rivers, the Uardini are as varied as nature itself. They are non-sentient, though some do assume humanoid forms.

- *Vlindra* – A giant moth-like creature native to the deciduous forests along the Ozar-El border. It sheds once per year, the husks being sought after for their powerful neurotoxin used in most pest control. Touching the husk with one's bare hands can lead to hallucinations, followed, usually within minutes, by a messy death. A *vlindra* that has freshly shed emits spores that cause blindness when inhaled in even trace amounts.
- *Paoph* – Toad-like creatures with flat backs, the *paoph* stack themselves upon one another for warmth and safety. Native to swamplands, they are fiercely territorial.
- *Raea* – A race of creatures made extinct during the Extermination War. The only hints at the appearance and characteristics of the Raea survive in song and ancient temples. Some stories claimed that this was a race of formless air spirits; other less flattering tellers spoke of lumpy, sightless, squawking chickens missing their feathers—clumsy, oafish things that reeked of fish and blood.
- *J'kugn* – The Cantusians say that a great warrior may bind the souls of those he has slain in stone totems—which must be carved from living rock—and set these to guard his home and family. If ever either are threatened, the spirits of the dead will awaken inside the totems, becoming indigo tigers with red eyes, and they will fight to protect their sworn home and family until every piece of them is destroyed.

Mythidim – Sentient. Terrible. Cruel. Cunning. These are a few of the politest descriptors given by Aelfravers to the Mythidim.

- *Elves* – From the Elves, humankind derived the term "Aelf," which eventually came to be associated will all non-human, non-animal denizens of the world. This was most likely due to the Elves being the most visible and cleverest foes of early humanity in the wake of the claiming of New El. The Elves are divided into two subspecies: *Iorian* ("Children of the Stars") and *Rioan* ("Children of the Deep")

- *Lords and Ladies* – Animated by an ethereal inner glow, these spirits are "born" in places that have endured a high concentration of suffering and death—battlefields, for example. Also called Widows-grief, the Lords and Ladies may appear as a beautiful human wearing nightclothes or the attire of a noble man or woman, but they are nothing more than hungry sprites feeding upon the echoes of human pain. With their mind-altering magics, these beings are able to naturally confuse and lead astray the careless battlefield historian or graveyard walker out on a fatal field trip.

- *Pycts* – The Pycts are a species of sentient Aelf ranging in height from seven to eleven inches. Their features are distinct: they have dragonfly-like wings, mouse-like faces, badger-like claws, and goat-like hooves. The males' fur is most often a shade cobalt or navy blue, while the females' is silver or gold. The Pycts' social structure is tribal, each tribe aware of others but entirely self-sufficient. The tribe is typically comprised of between twenty and one hundred individuals. Possessed of a hive-mind, these sentient Aelf have developed a most peculiar trait: if not eliminated all at once (within the hour), any who survive the deaths of their fellows will absorb the psychic and physical energy of the fallen, making them much harder to kill. This variation of the peculiar (and extremely rare) ability known as Egogenesis is the subject of vigorous study and debate.

- *Thaal* – A subset of Iorians that evolved to survive through parasitic Corpromancy, feeding off the blood or psychic energies of their victims (hence the terms *Sangothaal* and *Psychothaal*). Many biologists contend that the *Thaal* would better be classified as *Legionari*.

Legionari – Dangerous parasites and miscellaneous abominations make up this category.

- *Demons* – There are as many varieties of demons as there are human sins—Greed, Apathy, Wrath, Vanity, Sloth, etc. Their own name for their kind is "**Rel'ia'tuakr**" whose nearest translation in human tongues is "Undermoon and Overstar."

- *Hybrids* – The offspring of tabooed unions of human and Aelf; in academic circles, they are called "Homonculi."

- *Jallintope* – Sentient frog people with ape-like, hairless arms. Supposedly the result of a careless experiment by a deranged and power-mad hermit mage. Not to be confused with the *paophs.*

- *Umbrites* – Shadow-born shapeshifting parasites, Umbrites are formless while unattached to a host; when feeding, they meld with its shadow. Umbrites survive off the fear of their hosts, and the former stoke this fear through the careful trickling of anxiety directly into the consciousnesses of the latter.

Colossi – All those Aelf that are larger than the average city bus but *non-sentient* belong to this category.

- *Dan'yn'daup* – Train-sized worms that burrow huge tunnels in the earth. They use the saw-like bony protrusions on their backs to grip onto rock when navigating the magma-laced chasms miles below the surface.

- *Góra'cień* – With a 30-foot wingspan, the scaly, long-necked *góra'cień* is a carnivorous predator predominantly found in the westernmost regions of El. Early settlers of these territories, pressing ever deeper into the untamed wildernesses of the continent, needed to contend with flocks of these beasts.

- *Lemlar* – Also called "cave ape" because its facial features are vaguely reminiscent of a silverback gorilla's. There, however, the similarities end. The hairless, fleshy lemlar has no arms nor legs but boasts ten muscular tentacles which it uses to navigate its preferred environment—forgotten lakes, deep underground.

- *Schildkrabe* – A mountain-sized turtle, an active volcano having grown upon its back. Only one has ever been confirmed to exist—on an island in the Suur-al-Swalpan, the Sea of Dreams. It was accidently killed in 2122 by a fracking operation that shattered its shell, infecting its flesh.

Ushum – Included in this category are all those Aelf that are massive, brutal, and *sentient.*

- *Dragons* – By far, the most infamous example of this subcategory are the Twin Dragon Kings, H'ranajaan and Ji'inaluud. Together, they ruled over armies of sentient Aelf foot-soldiers and millions of human slaves. From an academic standpoint, their partnership was noteworthy because Dragons were, in every other case, solitary and preferred to keep well away from human beings. After the deaths of the Twin Dragon Kings, the Aelfravers spent centuries ruthlessly hunting down and destroying every last Dragon they could locate.

Demidivines – Ancient, patient, their true natures are often obscured by the erosions of millennia.

- *Sevensin* – Almost nothing is known of the Sevensin. The sole surviving account is an old (and dubious) Monraïc legend claiming they were born of the seven-sourced magic that brought the Aelf into the world in the first place. There were said to be seven gates opened by the Iorians, the sorcerers whose aim it was to exterminate all humanity with one final spell. From these seven gates poured the Aelf, led by the newly spawned Sevensin—each of which bore the face of a man but the hideously deformed and monstrous body of a squid, a hawk, a spider. The last of the Sevensin faded from history in the earliest years after the slaying of the Twin Dragon Kings.

Uult – Believed by most to be mere superstition, the only evidence for the Uult's existence lies in scraps of a myth and epic songs of the ancient world.

About the Author

J.R. Traas is an author, editor, and tutor who has published over twenty books, as well as various short stories and poems.

With well over a decade of teaching experience, it has been his privilege to instruct dozens upon dozens of young people in a plethora of subjects. Some of his students have won awards and scholarships for their writing. One of them calls him "Gandalf"—the highest compliment he has ever received.

Gandalf lives near Atlanta with his wife and their animal friends.

Heading over to *Blankbooklibrary.com* is the simplest way to reach him and, if desired, join the conversation. If you liked this story, please leave a review and spread the word. Cat food, after all, doesn't grow on trees.

MORE BY J.R. TRAAS

Thirsting Gulch, Part One:
a dark fantasy apocalypse horror saga

No one remembers how or why the world ended. The fog stole who they were, where they came from. Ærin stares into the fire, until waiting becomes too hard. She grabs a torch, walks into the darkness.

(fantasy horror, gore, death, some adult language)

***on the landslide catwalk*:**
there are no sure footings

A by turns humorous and gushy collection of 200+ short to medium-ish poems about honesty, love, and trying to laugh along with life.

(some adult language)

WITH SILAS JACKSON

The *Bag Men* series (18+)

A post-apocalyptic action thriller with an evolved zombie twist, beginning in the year 2069—43 years after the end of our world. (Follow us on facebook.com/SACBPH)

(explicit sex and violence, gore, death, torture, racism, bigotry, adult language)

Bag Men: 2069 (Episodes 1 & 2)
Bag Men: Waste (Episodes 3 & 4)
Bag Men: Trinity (Episodes 5 & 6)
Bag Men: Volume I (Episodes 1-6, and "Santos: A Bag Men Story")
Bag Men: Vanguard (Episodes 7 & 8)

Bag Men: Radioactive (Episodes 9, 10 & 11)
Bag Men: Origin (Episodes 12 & 13)
Bag Men: Hydra (Episodes 14-19)
Bag Men: Siege (Episodes 20, 21 & 22)
Bag Men: Cleave (Episodes 23 & 24)
Bag Men: Mutation (Episodes 25 & 26)
The Sisterdale Six: A Bag Men Story

Birds Are Not For The Cat

(adult language, violence)

Arbitrary rules, convoluted instructions, invisible management, horrific *accidental* deaths: all part of the deal in the workplace for Pete and Sam, two factory floor stooges who become pretty sure someone—if not everyone—is trying to kill them.

Birds Are Still Not For The Cat

Birds Will Never Be For The Cat

Ligeia/Bryndt

(fantasy violence)

An epic fantasy-mythology with elves and wild men; a tale fueled by dueling perspectives

---

WITH JONES HOWELL

The Safest December

The debut collection of Georgia poet Jones Howell. Focusing on the silent killers—emotional abuse, faltering relationships, and the bitter cold of winter—*The Safest December* contains twelve poems that may light the way through the toughest season of the year.